K-9 CORPS
THE LAST RESORT

KENNETH VON GUNDEN

ACE BOOKS, NEW YORK

If you purchased this book without a cover you should be aware that this book is stolen property. It was reported as "unsold and destroyed" to the publisher and neither the author nor the publisher has received any payment for this "stripped book."

This book is an Ace original edition,
and has never been previously published.

THE LAST RESORT

An Ace Book / published by arrangement with
the author

PRINTING HISTORY
Ace edition / January 1993

All rights reserved.
Copyright © 1993 by Kenneth Von Gunden.
Cover art by Cliff Miller.
This book may not be reproduced in whole or in part,
by mimeograph or any other means, without permission.
For information address: The Berkley Publishing Group,
200 Madison Avenue, New York, NY 10016.

ISBN: 0-441-42496-1

Ace Books are published by The Berkley Publishing Group,
200 Madison Avenue, New York, New York 10016.
The name "ACE" and the "A" logo
are trademarks belonging to Charter Communications, Inc.

PRINTED IN THE UNITED STATES OF AMERICA

10 9 8 7 6 5 4 3 2 1

WISH WE WEREN'T HERE

Freeman-Mawalzi said, "I vote that we continue on our current course, get the hell out of Battlefield, and then come back for your friend."

Ray looked at Beowulf, Robin, Mama-san, and Gawain. "Who votes for that option?" Silence. "Okay, that's one vote for your proposal, Mr. President."

Ray looked into the serious dog faces. "Now then, who votes for going after Ake?" Beowulf, Robin, Gawain, and Mama-san spoke up as one. "There you have it," Ray said. "The electorate have cast their votes. We're heading west, after the floater and the biplane."

"Why did I even bother?" Freeman-Mawalzi wondered out loud.

"Shall we start?" Ray said.

"Wait a minute." Freeman-Mawalzi pulled out a map cube and studied it. "Unless this map is inaccurate, what lies in that direction is . . ."

"Yeah?"

"What lies that way is a forty-meter-high wall buttressed by a powerful force field."

"What's on the other side of the wall?" asked Ray, afraid that he knew the answer.

"Dinoland."

Ace Books by Kenneth Von Gunden

STARSPAWN

The K-9 Corps Series

K-9 CORPS
UNDER FIRE
CRY WOLF
THE LAST RESORT

1

The prison ship *Purgatory* had moved outside the local system and was preparing to make the five-light-year jump that would take it to within a few million kilometers of the penal colony, located on a human-habitable satellite circling a massive planet in the Van Hooreen system.

"Do they know we're here?" Ray Larkin asked *The Spirit of St. Louis*'s computer.

"No," the computer's female voice replied. "Between the usual traffic—even out this far—and the new cloaking device you purchased on Santiaguito, we are virtually undetectable at this distance."

"What if we gets closer?" Beowulf asked.

"That will be the real test," the computer admitted.

"But you will know when they are going to jump, right?" Ray asked nervously.

"Within a picosecond," the computer replied, its voice all business.

"Good," Ray said, rubbing his chin as he stared at the readouts projected in front of him. "All we have to do, then, is time this maneuver perfectly and we're home free."

"Humans are remarkably optimistic in the face of data which suggests—"

"Shelve it, bubble brain," Ray ordered. "If this works, it works. If it doesn't . . ."

Ray made sure all the dogs were secured in their acceleration couches and then readied himself for the insanely dangerous maneuver he had plotted out with the computer's assistance. *Yeah, right*, he thought. *I dreamed it up but the computer crunched the numbers.* He sighed. When he outlined his one-in-a-million hare-brained scheme, the computer presented every single reason it could come up with why it wouldn't—couldn't—work. Then, reluctantly, it allowed that while Ray's plan was improbable, to say the least, it was not indisputably impossible.

So here they were.

"Energy levels in the prison ship's singularity engines are beginning to climb," the computer reported to Ray. "I calculate the jump will occur within twenty seconds."

"Good. You know what to do."

At five seconds to jump time, the computer maneuvered *The Spirit of St. Louis* to within seven hundred meters of the prison jumper. "We are in position," the computer announced in that infuriatingly business-as-usual voice that drove Ray bonkers.

The prison ship jumped.

The larger ship transported *The Spirit of St. Louis* with it, inside the sphere of influence generated by its mass.

"Whoa!" Ray said as his insides protested being yanked from normal space and thrust into the nothingness of hyperspace.

"It worked," the computer said without inflection.

"Of course it worked," Ray said indignantly. He gestured at himself with his thumb and said, "Wile E. Coyote, Super Genius."

"If the theory of multiple universes is correct," the computer told him, "then the probability is high that this is the only one in which you have remained alive for as long as you have."

Ray snorted. "Always with the odds. You're so damned predictable."

"Something I must admit that you are not—unless it can be argued that you unfailingly seek situations that risk failure and death."

"Hey, you gonna release us now or what, Ray?" Beowulf asked, his gravelly voice relayed from the ship's lounge.

"Sorry. In a minute."

"Now what?" the computer asked.

"I don't know," Ray said. "I never expected to survive that little maneuver we just pulled."

"But you said . . . I mean—"

"Relax, will you? I was just kidding. Sheesh."

★ ★ ★

Ray looked around the drab interior of the visitation room and sighed. He'd been so pleased when Ake had sought out female companionship. Ake was close-mouthed about an early, sour marriage, so it made Ray happy to see him enjoying the company of women again. *Who could have foreseen that Ake's coming out of his shell could have led to this?* he asked himself.

"Listen," Ake Ringgren said earnestly to Ray. "I didn't know Mora was married."

"Uh-huh," Ray replied dubiously.

"Anyway, there we were—*flagrante delicto*—when her husband walked in. I guess she'd done this sort of thing before, because he seemed prepared for what he found."

"Prepared? How so?"

"He had a gun. A nice big nasty slug-throwing pistol."

"Ouch!"

"I'm getting to that part," Ake said. "So he pointed the gun at me—or so I thought—and pulled the trigger. It was the loudest noise I ever heard in my life. I felt the blood splatter all over me, but I didn't feel any pain. I figured it was because I was in shock . . . then I realized he'd shot Mora, not me."

"And that's when you killed him?" Ray asked.

Ake frowned. "No. That's when he called the authorities and they came and put me under arrest."

Now it was Ray's turn to frown. "I thought you said you'd been arrested for murder. If he killed his wife and you *didn't* kill him, what in the holy heck are you doing in this cell charged with murder?"

Ake sighed. "This is Cromwell, Mr. Potato Head. It's one of the more puritanical and bass-ackwards planets in this quadrant of the galaxy."

Ray knew that, but he hadn't considered the implications, or what it really meant. "Yeah, but—"

"But nothing. I was committing adultery with a married woman and when her husband killed her, his was a legally permissible and socially acceptable act. Since I was a party to his wife's infidelity and 'encouraged' her to violate one of this culture's strictures, it is *I* who am considered to be the one responsible for her death."

Ray's jaw dropped. "That's crazy."

"You'll get no argument from me. Nonetheless, it is the way the legal system operates on Cromwell."

"Well, we'll get the best defense attorney money can buy and at the trial . . ." Ray's voice trailed away. "I'm afraid to ask, but why are you shaking your head?"

"I have already been found guilty and sentenced to the punishment satellite for life."

"Without a trial?" Ray gasped. "Even on Cromwell you're supposed to get a trial."

Ake shook his head. "I told you that I suspected Mora had done this before. So did her husband, apparently, since he had hidden a holochip recorder in the room. It got everything—including the murder. Once the Soldiers of God—a rather impressive name for the police, don't you think?—tested the recording and verified that it was intact and untampered with, a trial was deemed unnecessary."

"Unnecessary, my ass!"

"That's the way it is, Ray," Ake said grimly.

"When are you being shipped out?"

"Tonight."

"Tonight! Jesus!"

At Ray's exclamation, the guard standing watch stepped closer and admonished, "You watch your language or you'll be joining your friend. It is against the law to take the name of our Lord in vain."

"Yeah, right, Torquemada," Ray muttered.

Ake ignored this last exchange. "Yes, tonight—unless I volunteer for electrochemical rehabilitation and accept a brand-new personality." Ake reconsidered that. "Or should I say 'bland new'?"

"Tonight," Ray mused. "That doesn't give me much time."

"Forget about it. Forget me," Ake pleaded.

Ray laughed. "Afraid I'll get you into *real* trouble?"

"Seriously, Ray, there's nothing to be done."

"I'll be the judge of that."

★ ★ ★

"The prison ship with Ake in it is just ahead of us?" asked Ozma.

"That's right," Ray replied.

"Although Ray is probably correct, I cannot verify the other ship's location," the computer volunteered. "Many of my instruments are inoperative in hyperspace."

"Only a little more so than in normal space," jabbed Ray.

"Hahahaha," chortled Sinbad. Like all the dogs, he felt the computer was altogether too cheeky with their leader and was pleased to see Ray put "her" down whenever possible.

"Yes, more bioplasmic humor—most amusing," the computer commented. "But forgive me for pointing out that we will not be in hyperspace for very long; it seems only prudent to begin the rescue operation as quickly as possible."

"The machine-woman is right," Beowulf growled, shaking his big shaggy head in irritation. "We gots to save Ake now; jokes can come later."

"Let's get moving, then," Ray said. He opened a locker and pulled out five blast- and bullet-resistant moly-weave protective wraps made especially for scout dogs. Bending to his task, he quickly got the dogs into them. That done, he got out his battle suit. Once Ake had told him how an "Ivanhoe" had saved his life on Hephaestus, Ray had insisted on buying three of the suits, one for a backup unit.

"You *can't* buy them," Ake had told his partner. "They're for sale only to recognized military and paramilitary forces."

Ray had laughed at that and pulled out a wad of bills large enough to choke a cholo. "Oh, I think I can find someone who'll 'recognize' us when I show them this."

Ray was right, of course. Ever since the fall of the Federation, money and might were the two universally recognized constants. That was somehow reassuring.

"Boy, ya looks funny in that suit!" guffawed Gawain as Ray closed the fasteners and sealed himself in.

"Yah," agreed Mama-san. "Ray looks like a big black rubber guy." She thought about that for a moment and her eyes widened. "Hey—Ray looks like the gorilla guy in that old sigh-fi sinny!"

With that image now burned indelibly into their minds, the dogs howled with laughter after Ray put the helmet on. The helmet clinched it. He *did* look remarkably like the "Ro-man" of bad sinny fame.

"Thanks, Mama-san. It's too bad Ake doesn't know that 'Robot Monster' is on his way to save him; he'd rest a lot easier." Because of the Ivanhoe's small speakers, Ray's voice had a slightly unreal quality.

"Why only five dogs?" asked Tajil. "Ya got nine wraps, 'nuff for everyone."

"Because that's all of us who'll fit into the pod. Like I explained, it's me, Beowulf, Grendel, Robin, Sinbad, and Mama-san."

"Hows come ya takin' Mama-san and Grendel instead of more of us guys?" asked Frodo. The dogs weren't sexist in human terms, but they were male-dominant.

While Grendel bared her teeth at Frodo, Ray explained, "If I limited it to males only, I could take only Beowulf, Robin, Sinbad, and one other dog—maybe even you, Frodo. But because of their smaller size, I can take both Grendel *and* Mama-san." Ray made a gesture which announced that all discussion was over.

"Ahem," said the computer politely. "The shuttle pod is ready and waiting."

"Here we go, guys," Ray said, suddenly serious.

Ray waddled into the shuttle pod, and his five-dog team followed. "Close," Ray said, and the computer sealed the hatch. "Everything okay?"

"All is nominal," the computer reassured him.

Ray sighed and placed his glove-encumbered hands into the waldoes—which conveniently fit themselves to his fingers. "Then open the outer doors and release the bolts."

"Done."

"Here goes nothing." Ray maneuvered the pod out of the snug plasteel cocoon that enveloped it and they were suddenly in the eerie emptiness of hyperspace. "I should have said here we go *into* nothing," Ray muttered.

The forward holo revealed the massive shape of the prison jumper, just a few hundred meters away. There was no source of illumination in hyperspace, but the nearby craft glowed with its own external lights. Ray knew that no ESPer, no 'scraper, would have walked the ship's skin otherwise.

This might be a first, Ray thought. *I don't recall ever seeing anything about small craft travel* within *hyperspace. Maybe no one has ever been stupid enough to do anything like this before.*

"Say, you know something," Ray said to the dogs as they closed the distance between them and the looming mass of the prison jumper. "I bet no one's ever been ballsy enough to do something like this before."

"You mean stupid 'nuff?" asked Beowulf.

Ray laughed. Beowulf knew him too well.

"How we gonna get in?" Mama-san wondered as they slowly approached one of the big jumper's airlocks.

"I purchased the override codes from a cashiered ship's crewman," Ray said, his eyes never leaving the display readouts.

"What if he sold you phony codes, or alerted the authorities?" the computer asked.

"He was pretty pissed at being cast loose on Cromwell," Ray responded. "I think he sold us the real thing."

"We gonna find out real soon," Beowulf said.

When they were less than a meter from the prison ship's slightly pitted hull, Ray stilled the shuttle's forward motion with blasts from the front maneuvering jets and keyed in the numerals and letters that would cause the airlock to open up. As it obligingly did so, Ray allowed himself to breathe again. Then he eased the small shuttle into the opening like a shell being loaded into a gun barrel.

Ray took a breath. "If we're lucky there won't be any guards or crew members in the area, but the ship's computer will probably be more than a little curious why and how an airlock just cycled open and then shut."

"Gotcha," Beowulf said.

"Yah," agreed Grendel. "We be ready for anythin'."

"Good," Ray said, nodding. "Because 'anything' is what we can expect."

II

The display readout showed that the air pressure inside the shuttle bay had stabilized. Ray took a deep breath and said, "Open." The shuttle pod's hatch irised open as ordered and before them the prison ship's interior beckoned invitingly.

"Let's go, gyrenes!" Ray said as he ducked his head and wedged his way through the too-small hatch and out into the bay, his energy rifle in one hand and a small duffel bag in the other. Beowulf, not pleased that Ray had violated team protocol by exiting first, led the other dogs out of their small craft.

"Nobody here. That good," Beowulf said gruffly.

"Yah—for them," Sinbad said.

"Tough guy, hah?" Mama-san said sarcastically.

"Knock it off and check out the area, willya?" Ray muttered, clutching his energy rifle.

"Ray right," Beowulf said, embarrassed that Ray had to tell them their job.

A sudden noise froze everyone in his tracks. It was the sound of a hatchway opening. Ray motioned for the dogs to hide themselves. He stepped behind one of the *Purgatory*'s shuttles, put down the bag he carried, and checked his rifle's setting.

"If you ask me," a low-pitched voice rasped, "the damn computer needs a visit from the repair division. I mean, sensing that the airlock opened and shut—by itself—in hyperspace? That's about as likely as—"

"As a prison ship being boarded by a scout dog team," Ray finished for the startled speaker—a muscular, if somewhat overweight, crewman. His companion, the man he'd been bestowing his wisdom upon, was taller and thinner . . . and quicker to act. He reached for his sidearm, a small energy pistol clipped to his belt.

Ray pressed the firing stud on his energy rifle and the man folded up silently. "He's just sleeping," Ray said to the man's shocked compatriot. "Now it's your turn." Ray washed the stun beam over the slack-jawed man and he dropped to the floor.

"You dint kill 'em," Robin said in a voice that made clear he didn't know what to make of Ray's actions. "Why?"

Ray shot a sharp look at the big, reddish dog. Born on Terra and brought up as a brute, Robin still retained a touch of his former self. *That may not be all that bad*, Ray thought. *I've civilized and "muzzled" the other guys so much that Robin might occasionally remind them—and me—just how fearsome a scout dog can be.*

Ray shrugged. "No need to. I expect I'll have to use the lethal setting sooner or later, but until then I'd rather not mow people down indiscriminately like a pop-holo hero."

"You gonna tie 'em up?" asked Grendel.

"It'd be a waste of time. After that electroneural hosing down, they'll sleep for a long, long time. If we're still here when they wake up, we'll be here forever."

"What we do now?" asked Beowulf.

Ray bent over—a difficult maneuver in his Ivanhoe—and picked up the small canvas bag he'd brought along. "All I have to do is find a control panel somewhere in here and plug the Iron Maiden into it. She should be able to analyze the hostile system and tell us where we can find Ake."

"The other machine will let our machine-woman do that?" asked Sinbad dubiously.

"Not really," Ray replied, pulling a jumble of wires and plasmetal from the bag. "But, if we're lucky, in the fraction of a second she'll get to look around before her presence is discovered and she's frozen out, our 'machine-woman' will learn everything she needs to for us to successfully complete our mission. That's if she can still function successfully across the brief stretch of hyperspace that separates us from *The Spirit of St. Louis*."

"Too many ifs," growled Beowulf.

"Well, *I* believe in fairies—and I'll clap my hands to prove it," Ray replied.

"Fairies . . . ?" said Robin, confused.

"That's jes' Ray pullin' more stuff outa his twenny-eff century brain," Mama-san told the puzzled dog.

"Well?" Ray asked the computer via the Ivanhoe's communicator.

"I maintained contact for a full microsecond instead of the less satisfactory nanosecond I feared. The extra time not only allowed me to determine how many police and crewpersons are on board but also to plant some potentially crippling counterprogramming."

Ray didn't seem to hear or understand the importance of what the computer had said. "Did you pinpoint where Ake is?"

"Yes."

"Do I have to guess?"

"Let me show you."

A rapid-fire series of images flashed through Ray's brain via the small communications device he had implanted in his skull: flat schematics of his current position and where Ake was being held; a holographic representation, also from above, that then rotated to show the multiple levels of the ship and how they could get there from here, and a startlingly realistic representation of the targeted cell block.

"Great stuff!" Ray enthused.

"I have also sent as powerful a disruptive signal through the enemy computer's network as I was able. It may do nothing at all," the computer reiterated. "However, if any of my counterpart's programming, whether routine or defensive, was not adequately protected during that instant, it may have been affected."

"How can we tell if it *has* been affected?" Ray asked.

"If we are successful."

"Sounds like Russian roulette: if I put the gun barrel to my head and pull the trigger and nothing happens, then there's not a shell in the chamber."

"There is something else," the computer said.

"Yeah?"

"The *Purgatory*'s computer has alerted the crew and the paramilitary police who guard the prisoners to our presence."

"How many bad guys are we up against?"

"There are approximately forty-eight security personnel capable of defensive activity, and sixteen crew members to operate the ship."

Ray's brow wrinkled in puzzlement. "That's all? I mean, in terms of a firefight, that's too damn many—but it seems too few to guard the prisoners and run the ship."

"I cannot speak about the ratio of guards to prisoners, but my opposite number runs the prison ship, much as I run *The Spirit of St. Louis*. There is little need for human intervention in routine functions."

"Yeah, but repairs and—"

"There are maintenance robots for such dirty and dangerous jobs."

Ray grudgingly accepted the computer's arguments and then added, "Too bad there are no robots to do *this* job."

"Hey, *no*," protested Beowulf.

Ray laughed and rubbed the big lionlike dog's ears as best he could with his gloves on. "That's right—humans and dogs should get to do the fun things."

"Then the 'fun' is about to begin," said the computer.

"They're coming?"

"Right through that door . . . and in less than sixty seconds, I would estimate."

Ray didn't waste time undoing the hookup that had made the invasion into the enemy computer's neural pathways possible. He simply dropped the gear and pushed the selector on his rifle from a stun setting to a lethal one.

"They's comin'?" asked Beowulf hopefully.

"To quote the machine-woman, 'Right through that door.'"

"Good," said Robin, eager for action.

"Yah," agreed Sinbad and the others.

"Let's meet them on our terms, then," Ray suggested.

"In the corridor?" asked Beowulf.

"In the corridor," confirmed Ray. "You and me, at least."

Ray waited until all eight of the defenders had passed where he and Beowulf had hidden themselves in a small service room off the corridor that led to the airlock before he said, "Take 'em,

Beowulf!'' and leapt out. The startled guards turned just as Ray opened fire.

A coherent beam from his energy rifle burned a hole through one man's chest and sliced the top off the head of the woman behind him.

After a return beam struck him full in the chest and its energy was effortlessly absorbed by the battle suit, Ray pumped several far more devastating bolts into his attacker. One of the guards aimed an energy pistol at Beowulf but never got a chance to press the firing stud as Grendel's charge landed her smack in the center of his back and sent him flying. She quickly tore out his throat.

Robin, Mama-san, Sinbad, Grendel—and now Beowulf—made short work of the remaining guards. Ray grinned at the successful execution of his plan to split their forces, leaving the other dogs behind to close the trap.

"Good," said Beowulf. "We got all eight."

"Yeah," Ray mused. "Only forty more to go."

III

At the computer's urging, Ray and his team moved as quickly as they could, rushing down corridors, piling onto lift/drop platforms and changing levels—anything they could to maintain a headlong, furious pace intended to avoid unnecessary contact with the ship's defenders while getting them closer to their goal.

"This is great exercise," huffed Ray, bound up in his heavy Ivanhoe, "but—"

"Yah," agreed Robin. "Good exercise."

"But we can't keep it up all day," Ray finished as they hurried past several cleaning robots. One of the 'bots looked after them in apparent disinterest. "We're going to be coming out of hyperspace soon and the *Purgatory* can call for a warship to blast *The Spirit of St. Louis* into a million pieces."

"Your point is well taken," the computer acknowledged.

A crew person, a woman, poked her head out of a hatchway as the unlikely sextet rushed down the corridor toward her. *Where the hell did she come from?* Ray wondered. *Doesn't she know what's going on?* Ray had slung his rifle across the back of the Ivanhoe and now carried an energy pistol in each hand. As her mouth opened in surprise, Ray shot her once with the energy pistol he held in his left hand. It was set to stun. The one in his right hand delivered a lethal charge. The woman toppled silently back into the room.

Although no one had asked, Ray explained, "Like I said before, the crew are basically innocent bystanders. I don't want to kill any of them unless it is absolutely necessary."

A clamorous clanging now resounded throughout the ship.

"Oh, shit!" Ray exclaimed. "We're coming out of hyperspace."

2

Secure in his Ivanhoe, Ray turned his attention to the dogs. "Get down on the floor," he told them. He pointed. "There, against the bulkhead."

The dogs obeyed and Ray dropped to his knees and then onto his chest. "This should be a warning to me not to get fat," he said as he snuggled up against the dogs, hoping to wedge them all securely against the bulkhead. A klaxon blared one last warning.

The prison ship jumped.

Ray felt—or imagined that he felt—his insides respond to a powerful if evanescent tidal pull. He wondered if he was still the same person, or if the transition from hyperspace to normal space had resulted in his body being broken down into individual atoms and then instantly reassembled. Ray knew that it was rumored that people who jumped a lot, like starship crews and 'scrapers, aged more slowly than groundhogs. They also got a little "funny."

"Wow!" exclaimed Robin, his blue eyes bright with excitement. "I loves jumpin'—it's keen!"

"Yeah, keen," said Ray, getting to his feet about as gracefully as a pregnant hippopotamus. Ever since *The Spirit of St. Louis* had "lost" twelve years in a jump, Ray and the rest of the dogs were less thrilled with the whole business of jumping. As a "new" dog, Robin had no such baggage to sour the experience for him.

Watching Ray's struggle to stand up in the Ivanhoe, Sinbad asked, "Why you wearin' that thing anyway?"

Before Ray could answer, Beowulf, his ears pinpointing sounds coming from around a bend in the corridor, announced in a low voice, "Someone comin'!"

To the big dog's consternation, Ray stepped in front of him and the rest of the dogs. Given the protection the Ivanhoe afforded him, Ray's action made sense; it didn't, however, go down well with Beowulf. The way Beowulf saw it, dogs were supposed to protect their human leader—not the other way around.

It didn't take long for the source of the sound to become apparent when five guards turned the corner. Packing a plethora of weapons, they opened fire with their energy rifles the moment they came to bear on Ray. Ray was struck by at least six bolts in quick succession—*snap-crackle-pop*, *snap-crackle-pop*. The Ivanhoe's low-res Kierkian field, encasing the battle suit like a one-molecule deep plastic wrap, sparked and glowed as it absorbed the multiple hits.

"Ha!" cried Ray. "Poor fools. Mere bullets cannot harm the ferocious, rubber-suited Godzilla!" He returned the guards' fire with powerful focused-energy bolts of his own as he continued to be the recipient of numerous hits which had no obvious effect on him. Two unprotected guards went down immediately. Fortunately for the other three, they sported chest deflectors which were not unlike the dogs' wraps.

"They gots their own protection," said Beowulf, peering around Ray.

"Yes," agreed Ray, holstering his energy pistols and unslinging the rifle on his back. "But it's limited."

"Limited?"

Ray fired and pencil-thin bolts burned through the remaining three guards' heads, causing gouts of blood and brain to explode messily out the back. "Yuck," said Ray. Then, as the guards tumbled to the floor, he added, "Yeah, their protection is limited to their torsos." With his suit still sparking and hissing, Ray turned to Sinbad. "That answer your question about what good my suit is, furball?"

Before Sinbad could respond, the computer announced, "The enemy computer is transmitting a message to the nearby prison satellite."

"How long do we have?"

"Ten minutes; fifteen at the most."

"Fifteen minutes? Shoot, there's time for a coffee break, then."

"Larkin!" said the computer sternly, using his last name as it always did when it rebuked him.

"Oh, all right," he sighed.

Ray made a hand signal and Beowulf took the point. They moved out smartly, painfully aware of the time constraint they were laboring under.

"Left," the computer told him. "Good, now go straight for about a hundred me-e-e-e—" the computer's voice disappeared in a burst of static.

"The computer's gone, guys," Ray announced. "We're probably too far inside the belly of the beast for the signal to get through."

"We on our own?" asked Grendel.

"Yepper."

"Good," said Beowulf.

"It's just us now," Ray agreed. "Let's show these tight sphincters what a Man-Dog team can do."

There's nothing like life-and-death situations to sharpen your senses, Ray told himself. He felt more alert and alive than he had in ages. As if to prove his point, this flashed through his mind at the same time he was aware of everything surrounding him: the wailing of the "intruder" sirens, the breathing of the dogs, his own breath rasping in and out of his slightly open mouth as he lumbered under the weight of the Ivanhoe, the strobing of the corridor lights overhead, the stenciled numbers on the bulkheads. He could even feel the small pouch of rubies rubbing against his breastbone as he ran.

It's probably the rubies, he admitted to himself. The three good-sized rubies in the pouch were more than sufficient to augment his modest psychic abilities.

When Mama-san said of the sirens, "Them things hurts your ears," Ray silenced each one they passed by pointing the rifle at it and blasting it.

"Thanks," Mama-san said appreciatively.

"Any time," huffed Ray.

When they came upon a series of drop/lift tubes, Ray skidded to a halt.

"I gots a bad feeling 'bout this," moaned Sinbad.

Although Ray shrugged sympathetically, very little of his action was transmitted through the Ivanhoe. "Yeah, I know you guys hate drop tubes, but we can't risk any of the personnel or freight elevators. It's the tubes or nothing."

"We doin' this for Ake," Beowulf reminded the team.

The other four dogs exchanged glances and realized there was no other option open to them—not if they wanted to save Ake.

"Okay," said Grendel. "We do it."

Beowulf grinned a crooked canine grin that faded as he realized what their resolve meant: They had to suffer a drop. But maybe it would be a short one . . .

"How many levels we gots to fall, Ray?" the big dog leader asked.

"If the computer was right about the cell block, it's seven levels beneath us."

"Seven?" Beowulf whined.

"Don't worry about the drop," Ray told him as a small amount of blood trickled out of one nostril and down to his lips. A flick of his tongue carried the salty taste to his mouth. "I can sense a squad of defenders on the fourth level down."

"Defenders?"

"Yeah. They're armed and watching the tubes, ready to blast anyone who passes through." While Beowulf gulped, Ray continued: "I'm gonna go first, say 'Hi,' and then I want the rest of you to follow me using the other tubes. But don't start until you hear a grenade explode. Got that?"

Beowulf stood there for a long second, looking serious, then he nodded. "Gotcha, Ray."

"Yah," said Robin.

Ray glanced around at his team. "Hey, you guys are always telling me how much you want to have some dangerous fun, aren't you? Well, you got it."

"Yeah . . . fun," said Sinbad sourly.

Ray set the controls on the dogs' tubes for their seven-level drop, and his own for his initial four-level drop and then the secondary three-level drop that would deposit him on the cell block deck. That done, he readied a grenade and filled his hands with his energy pistols.

He frowned. What was it Wild Bill Hickok was quoted about a similar situation? *Oh, yeah: "When I draw and pull I must be sure!"*

As he approached the tube, his resolve wavered. Then he thought of the Cowardly Lion on the way to help save Dorothy and smiled. "Uh, guys, there's just one thing I want you to do for me."

"Yah?" they chorused.

"Talk me out of this!"

II

Feeling a bit like Santa Claus stepping into a chimney on Christmas Eve, Ray stepped into the drop tube and fell like the proverbial rock. The tube's anti-grav field kicked in as he approached his destination level and he gently, if rapidly, decelerated and then bounced in midair, held in place by invisible forces that always seemed like magic to him.

"Jesus!" someone shouted when they saw him bobbing there.

Although they'd been waiting for him (well, waiting for someone), it nevertheless took the guards a fraction of a second to open fire. Energy bolts erupted. Plasteel-jacketed bullets stuttered into Ray's Ivanhoe like the first fat drops in a summer's thunderstorm. His answering laser beams rent the air like yellow-white strokes of lightning. Ray gave as good as he got, his two-fisted firing making him look like an old-time sinny cowboy—maybe Wild Bill himself—blasting away with a six-shooter in each hand.

The match was as uneven as it was fast-paced: Safely cocooned inside his Ivanhoe, Ray was as impervious to the firepower directed at him as a diver in a wetsuit would be to the water from "squirt" guns. The same could not be said for his adversaries, however. Ray efficiently blew them away.

As he decimated his foes, Ray realized that using a grenade would be overkill. But since he had told the dogs that a grenade was their signal to use the drop tubes, he had no choice but to hurl one at the few remaining guards. They gave up and ran, and the grenade's explosion damaged only nonliving materials.

Ray then dropped the remaining three levels and scanned his surroundings for hostile players. No one; the area was uninhabited. He was almost immediately joined by the dogs, who arrived breathless but no worse for wear.

"There, that wasn't so bad, was it?" Ray said.

"Can we do it again?" asked Robin.

"Later, if we're still alive," Ray told him.

"Doan say that," moaned Sinbad. "You takin' 'way our 'centive to go on."

"Which way?" asked Beowulf, all business.

"That way." Ray pointed. Beowulf nodded as Ray unslung his energy rifle, ejected a power pack, and slapped a new one in. He did the same for his pistols.

"Someone comin'!" shouted Mama-san.

Ray whirled, extended his right arm, and fired the energy pistol at the shape coming down the corridor. His aim was true and the little 'bot he burned a hole through began to spin uncontrollably, sparks flying from its "wound."

"Oops," said Ray, glancing at the pistol in his right hand as if to accuse it of wrongdoing.

"You killed a 'bot," said Grendel helpfully.

"No shit, Sherlock," Ray said disgustedly. He looked at the unmoving 'bot, foul blue-black smoke pouring from it, and said, "Come on, let's keep moving."

With the computer's purloined map of the *Purgatory* in his Ivanhoe's memory, Ray was able to lead his team to the cell block area with little difficulty. When it was just a few turns, twists, and hatches away, Beowulf asked, "There be many guards there?"

"I dunno," Ray admitted, unable to sense anyone yet. "Whatever they've got left, I guess. Can't be too many."

"Yeah," agreed Beowulf. "Some gots to guard the captain and the crew."

Ray shot Beowulf a look of frank admiration. Beowulf was not only big and tough, loyal and brave, he was pretty damned intelligent as well. It was a measure of Ray's appreciation for his dogs' abilities that he didn't add, not even unconsciously: "For a dog . . ."

Ray slowed to a jog, then to a walk, and finally came to a complete halt. "Why we stoppin'?" Beowulf queried.

"The cell block entrance is just ahead, around the next turn and at the end of the corridor."

"Good," Robin beamed.

"Yeah, but I'm not getting anything from there," Ray said, thumping his chest where the rubies were to make his point clear. "There's no one there, and that doesn't make sense. Why should they leave it unguarded? They've resisted the hell out of us every step of the way so far. Why leave the cell block entrance naked?"

"Lemme take a look," suggested Sinbad.

Ray gestured toward his chest with a thumb. "Nah-uh. I'm the one in the walking tank. *I'll* be the one to stick my head around the corner and see if it attracts hostile fire."

Beowulf's eyes glinted at Ray's perfect setup. "There some good jokes I could be makin' now, but I too nice for that."

"And don't think I don't appreciate it, Beowulf," Ray said, his grin hidden by his helmet. Then his smile faded and he moved along the wall until he was prepared to take a quick look. "Here goes nothing," he said, peeking around the corner and down the corridor.

"Jesus!" Ray pulled his head back as a fusillade of energy bolts struck the wall.

"What's that?" Beowulf growled.

"I don't believe it," Ray said, more to himself than in answer to Beowulf's question. "'Bots."

"'Bots?" repeated Robin questioningly. "How can them little 'bots be shootin' at ya? Isn't that 'gainst their brains?"

"Well, against their programming, Robin." Ray thought for a second. "You said 'little,' Robin. There wasn't anything little about these guys. If anything, they look like the holos I've seen of battle androids from before and during the so-called 'robot wars' of years ago."

He reached his arm around the corner of the wall and fired several bursts down the corridor and then stole another look. "Yep, they're heavily armored anti-personnel models, all right."

Ray recalled that the multiarmed android war machines contained pseudo-quantum-gravity brains, the only AI mind matrixes to even approach the capabilities of the creatively superior human brain. This semiautonomy was what made them coldly effective fighting machines—and was the basis for their eventual suppression by the humans who'd made them.

Beowulf frowned a dog frown. "But you said them things is outlawed. Bin outlawed since those 'bot wars."

Ray nodded. "Until now, not even the dying Federation was ballsy enough to break the covenant against robotic warriors. It says something about the people who've imprisoned Ake, doesn't it?"

"They 'sposed to be good guys, but they's really bad, hah?" said Grendel.

"You got it."

"What you do?" asked Mama-san.

Ray blinked a certain number of blinks and his visor changed from opaque to clear so Mama-san and the others could see his baleful expression.

"Oh . . . sorry," Mama-san said.

★ ★ ★

It took Ray several minutes to fully activate and then modify the Ivanhoe's defensive capabilities. The million-credit suit was capable of many things. What he wanted from it was within its parameters, but took a certain amount of rethinking and reassigning of the suit's basic mission. He wanted the Ivanhoe's controls adjusted to switch instantaneously from a semidefensive, semioffensive mode to a totally defensive one.

"Well, here I go," Ray told the dogs. "Get away quickly and wait for the agreed-upon signal before you return."

"Okay, Ray," said Beowulf. "Good luck. We luvs ya." The others seconded Beowulf's sentiment.

"I love you guys, too."

After ordering the suit's elementary AI circuits to play "The Ride of the Valkyries" through the external speaker patches at preposterously high levels, Ray waddled around the corner and into a maelstrom of laserbeam energy. All but a fraction of the Ivanhoe's internal power was going into maintaining the suit's Kierkian field. One of the more ingenious features of the heavily armored battle suit was its ability to first absorb and then turn at least some of the energy impacting the field into a portion of its own supply.

Paradoxically, then, the intensive firing from the warrior fighting machines actually strengthened the Ivanhoe's Kierkian field effects.

If Ray seemed invincible, and he was as long as his field generator didn't fail, the robotic soldiers seemed equally oblivious of the short, powerful bursts of coherent energy he directed at them. *It's a standoff*, Ray thought as he walked down the corridor amid a manmade electrical storm of incredible ferocity. *Of course, my musical selection is probably causing severe psychological damage to their logic circuits.* He thought about that for a moment. *Yeah—right*!

No unprotected living thing could have survived for more than a few seconds in the long corridor. The plasteel bulkheads at both ends of the corridor warped and glowed, their polycarbon molecules agitated by the streams of highly disruptive energy impacting them.

Ray tried to mentally prepare himself for the ordeal he was about to undergo. *The best thing to do is not to think about it at all*, he cautioned himself.

Only meters from the two robots, he killed the music and announced, "Hi, honey, I'm home."

"You are illogical, human," one of the killer 'bots replied.

"At the very least," Ray agreed, nodding his helmeted head.

"It seems that our weapons are useless against your suit's defenses," the second robot pronounced. "We must resort to a cruder but more effective method of discontinuing your life maintenance functioning."

"Yeah? And what's that, pray tell?" Ray asked, not really wanting to know but unable to prevent himself from posing the question.

"We must seize you and tear open your suit through our superior strength."

"Feelin' your Wheaties, eh?"

The first robot cocked its triangular-shaped head quizzically at Ray, the gesture suggesting a metallic praying mantis somberly regarding its intended quarry. "You continue to make inappropriate and illogical statements." It considered that for a moment. "Ah, yes: It must be that odd human trait known as 'humor.'"

"Hey, you're not as dumb as you look," Ray allowed, his knees shaking.

"We will analyze your recorded statements later and attempt to discern the humorous content," the second robot said. "But now it is time to destroy you." The two robots approached.

Scared silly, Ray nonetheless managed to shout, "Danger, Will Robinson!" Giggling at his own insane jocularity, he turned his back to the robots—who were so puzzled by his inexplicable behavior that they momentarily halted their advance. Then, in a more controlled voice, he whispered, "Begin Altair-Four Morbius sequencing."

Enunciating the word "sequencing" caused Ray to immediately fall into a protective trancelike state. Two seconds later, the small atomic device he had strapped to the back of his Ivanhoe exploded and everything within a hemisphere of roughly four meters was enveloped in a nuclear holocaust.

★ ★ ★

The blast sent a shiver through the ship's molecular-steel skeleton.

"Jeez!" exclaimed Robin.

"Hope Ray's okay," Grendel said.

"Take more'n that to hurt Ray," Beowulf said to the concerned dogs who had turned to him for reassurance.

Ray might have agreed with Beowulf, had he been conscious. The limited, if powerful, explosion did its job, blowing the robotic war machines to bits before they could tear open Ray's Ivanhoe and pluck him out like armored crustaceans hungrily pulling a hapless mollusk from its protective shell.

The Ivanhoe had both absorbed and redirected the fury of the explosion, transmuting some of the energy into subatomic gracco particles that stretched into light-year-long multidimensional strings. With the correct instrumentalities, a creature a billion light-years distant could have detected the picosecond-lasting display.

Ray, however, saw and heard nothing.

His self-induced state of suspended animation ended after five seconds and he regained full consciousness.

I'm alive, he told himself, amazed by that simple fact. *I'm alive and in possession of all my faculties.*

<*Such as they are, short stuff,*> a voice said in his head.

<*Ake! Where the hell are you?*> Ray smiled. The psi-enhancing power of his rubies were aiding him one more time.

<*That's a fair question, but a more useful one might be where the hell are* vous*?*>

As the dust and debris that swirled around him subsided, Ray surmised that he was one deck below where he had been prior to the explosion. That wasn't just a guess—he could see the smooth-edged hole in the floor he'd fallen through; a hole caused by the explosion.

<*I . . . ah . . . think the explosion knocked me down to the next level, Ake.*>

<*The explosion? So that's what that loud noise was. Look, Ray, stop kidding around and get me out of here.*>

"Gee, don't thank me too much for coming to your rescue, Ake," Ray muttered under his breath even as he realized Ake's words were not only a show of bravado but also a conscious attempt to reassure them both.

<*You might let me know how many guards are in the cell block with you,*> Ray directed at Ake.

Ray caught several flashes of thought—from Ake and from unknown others—and then Ake told him, <*There are four in here, keed, but . . .*> Ake fell silent.

<*But what?*>

<*You aren't going to believe this, partner, but they very much want to surrender to you.*>

<*You're right . . . I don't believe you!*>

III

Ray swiveled his head to take in the hundreds of freed prisoners milling around the central cell block area. "I had no idea there were so many prisoners on one of these things," he confided to Ake.

"I admit I'm prejudiced," Ake began, "but it's clear that the government of Cromwell, the New Puritan Parliament, is repeating the errors of its namesake."

"I think all totalitarian governments make the same stupid mistakes," Ray mused. "They want conformity of belief, of thought, of expression. They fail to see the paradox: They want people to accept the status quo and be part of the herd at the same time that they expect to have a complex society function with nothing but followers."

Ake nodded. "Yeah. No original thoughts, no new ideas, no challenging the established norms—it all adds up to stagnation. A lack of vision, a ban on seeking out new ideas or new ways of connecting the old, means your society slowly falls apart since all the dreamers and risk-takers are imprisoned or dead. Take them away and the only ones left are the drones."

"No drones here," said a middle-aged man who'd been eavesdropping on Ray and Ake's conversation. He was stocky and muscular—Cromwell was a heavy-gravity planet—and sported a shock of black hair that constantly risked falling into his glittering jade eyes.

Ray shook his head. "No, I wouldn't take you for a drone. Who are you?"

"I'm Peter Gabriel, a former pilot. I captained a commercial freighter in our local system," the man said, extending his hand. Ray took it and, even though his own was encased in one of the Ivanhoe's gloves, immediately felt like he'd stuck his hand into a hydraulic vise. "The better question is—who are you?"

"I'm Judge Crater. Have I been gone long? I—"

Ake bumped Ray with his hip. Off balance, Ray took several involuntary sideways steps. "Pay no attention to him. He can't help himself," Ake said. Sticking out his own hand, and enduring the same finger-crushing grip that almost paralyzed Ray, Ake continued, "We're the leaders of a free-lance scout dog team that for reasons I can't even remember thought it might be a good idea to spend a little time on Cromwell. In my ignorance, I ran afoul of your, ah . . . shall we say somewhat 'restrictive' . . . legal system."

"Poked the wrong lady," Ray added helpfully.

"Anyway, when the Masked Madman here learned I was being given a free one-way passage on the *Purgatory*, he and the rest of our team decided to intervene."

"You're just a goddamn dog team?" Gabriel blurted out. He instantly glanced around, fearful that his blasphemy might have been overheard. Then, realizing his changed circumstances, he grinned wickedly and said, "Goddamn." He laughed in delight. "Shit-fuck-piss!"

"Sounds to me like this little angel has realized that Sunday school is out," Ray said, nudging Beowulf.

"Heh, heh, heh," rumbled the big dog.

3

Unlike Ray and Beowulf, Ake was somewhat disconcerted by Gabriel's profanity. Good-hearted and earnest, he had assumed the first thing a person would want to do when freed of mental and intellectual shackles would be to think great, liberating thoughts. It had never occurred to him that the freedom to think and speak whatever you wanted to included the freedom to curse like a Space Marine.

The rest of Gabriel's comment sank in and Ray protested, "Hey, we're not 'just a dog team'!"

"I'm sorry," Gabriel said, coloring slightly.

"No need to apologize," Ray told him. "We're all guys here."

"Oh, no we not!" protested Mama-san.

The former prisoner stared openly at Mama-san. "Ai-i-i . . . they *do* talk," he said.

That's right, Ray remembered. *The Soldiers of God made the dogs remain inside clearly delineated areas—so they wouldn't mix with the population.* He shrugged mentally. *It would have been better for us all if Ake had stayed inside the "ghetto," too.*

"'Course we talk," said Robin. "We's scout dogs."

"I've seen everything today," Gabriel asserted. "First, a walking man-tank, and now talking dogs."

"The elephants and camels will be coming later, along with the dog-faced boy," Ray said, his voice issuing from his suit's speakers. "Oops, sorry, Beowulf."

"Are you *all* named for angels, by the way?" Ake asked Gabriel.

"Yes," the man nodded. "Well, almost all of us. Our hereditary leader's name is Oliver Cromwell, and he is the twenty-third Lord Protector of the planet that bears his forbears' name."

"This is all most interesting," Ray said, his expression belying his words, "but I think we need to think about what happens next." He nodded his helmeted head at the newly freed prisoners. "Think you can find enough men and women in that bunch to fly this crate once the dogs and I have secured the control room?"

"Sure," said Gabriel. "But don't you mean 'if' you and the dogs can secure the control room?"

"Nah—he means when," rumbled Robin. He showed his teeth.

"Oh."

"Hey, you're free," Ray said, putting a gloved hand on the Cromwellian's shoulder. "Think of how many times you can say 'poopy ca-ca' now."

Ake burst out laughing, more from nervous tension than anything else. Actually, Ray's words seemed hilariously incongruous to him—not because they were typical "Ray-speak," but because they seemed at odds with the intimidating Ivanhoe that encased Ray and made him appear so formidable to an observer. *I guess intimidation* is *the goal*, Ake thought, wiping tears of laughter from his eyes.

"Sure, Kemo Sabe, laugh at the fat boy," Ray's voice boomed from the Ivanhoe.

"C'mon, who are you people?" Gabriel asked, looking from Ake to Ray and back to Ake again.

"Ever hear of Allison's Rangers?" Ray asked, his voice still strangely modulated by the Ivanhoe's circuits.

"Yeah," said the stocky freighter captain slowly. "Hey—you part of that outfit?" he asked, his voice full of wonder.

Ray's helmeted head moved from side to side. "Nope," he said, walking away.

"But you said . . ." The black-haired man's voice trailed away. He turned to Ake. "Really now, I mean it. Who are you guys? Who *was* that guy?"

Ake couldn't resist. "Son, that was the Lone Ranger." Then he doubled over, laughing hysterically.

Gabriel looked at Beowulf and said, "The Lone Ranger? Who the hell's the Lone Ranger?"

★ ★ ★

"Please move expeditiously, there are only minutes until the three fighter craft from the prison planet arrive," *The Spirit of St. Louis*'s computer told Ake and the five dogs, its voice coming from the open hatch of the shuttle. The computer's information was old news to Ray, who'd already reestablished a communications link with the computer via his suit. The seven of them complied and soon crammed themselves into the small shuttle craft.

"Now I know where that cliche about sardines in a can came from," said Ray as the dogs piled on top of him.

"Me and the dogs are the sardines," Ake told him. "You're more like Prince Albert in a can."

"Ah, the rich smell of Old-Earth tobacco," Ray said theatrically, putting a gloved hand on his chest and pretending to inhale.

"Speaking of rich smells," said Ake, "I wish you dogs would bathe more often." His voice was muffled because his face was shoved against Robin's flank.

"Hah! You doan smell like no spring mornin' neither, Ake," said Grendel.

"Yah," agreed Beowulf. "Smell like a bad place—a prison. Fear-hate smell on Ake."

"I told him sponge baths in the sink weren't sufficient," Ray tut-tutted.

"I simply will never understand humans," said the computer.

"Too bad you weren't around to meet the two killer 'bots from Hell," Ray told the computer. "You three would have gotten along famously. You could have swapped stupid human stories."

"I am a loyal member of our crew," the computer said sharply in response. Then, more softly, "Now my feelings are hurt."

Ake maneuvered his right leg, freeing it, and then kicked Ray solidly. <*Yes, dear,*> Ray told Ake via their internal comlink. "I'm sorry. I apologize," Ray said to the computer—even though he didn't believe for a moment that the computer's "feelings" were hurt.

"Apology accepted," sniffed the computer.

"That was awfully fast," Ray said.

"I took into account that you are a human and don't know any better."

The crowded pod gently bumped against the side of *The Spirit of St. Louis*. "Careful, watch the paint job," Ray cautioned.

After the bay doors had cycled shut and the airlock had filled and stabilized, the shuttle's hatch opened and Ake and the dogs scrambled out. As for Ray, the word "scramble" was not currently in his vocabulary.

"Hey, don't forget about me," the Ivanhoe-encumbered Ray said, having more than a little difficulty pulling himself through the circular pod opening. "This brings back my very first memory—Mom always said I was a difficult birth."

"We're finally home," Ake said, ignoring Ray's ongoing blather. "So why don't you slip out of that rubber suit now and . . ." He turned back to see Ray pop out of the hatchway like a cork from a bottle and fall on his face on the floor with a loud *whomp*. "I spoke too soon—the Ivanhoe saved your life again."

"Nah, Ake, Ray landed on his head," Beowulf pointed out as he returned from greeting the rest of the team. "His skull so hard he doan need the suit to protect him."

Ray rolled over, sat up, and cracked the seal on the helmet and lifted it off his shoulders. "Hot damn, it feels great to get that thing off!"

That was all the waiting and wiggling-with-barely-contained-pleasure the team needed. They had already loudly and urgently welcomed back Beowulf and the others—now it was Ray's turn. Ray was immediately surrounded by happy, whimpering dogs. "Ray, we missed you!" Frodo said.

"Yah!" chorused the other dogs.

"It's great to see you, too," Ray said as his face was thoroughly licked by four big pink tongues.

"Dog slobber," said Ake, shaking his head. Hearing his voice caused the dogs to redirect their attention and affection to him. "Oops," he said when he saw their heads swivel toward him. They "attacked" and Ake went down in a mass of fur.

"Warning!" the computer announced. "I am initiating defense procedures and moving us closer to the prison ship. They are about to raise their force field and we must be as close to them as possible to receive the maximum benefit of their defenses."

"We get any closer and we're going to be *inside* the damn ship," Ake pointed out. "I've been there and I'm not anxious to go back."

"All the more reason for you to go get everybody strapped in, Ake," Ray said from the floor. "It's going to take me a few minutes to completely extract myself from this contraption—especially after I was so rudely interrupted by the mutts."

Not having human lips, Tajil made the closest approximation of a raspberry that he could.

Nodding at Ray's words, Ake said, "Right. It's strapping-in time." He flashed a hand signal to the dogs. All business now, they dashed past Ake, down the corridor to the lounge, and jumped up onto their specially made acceleration couches. Ake secured their restraints, his practiced doctor's hands moving quickly.

Meanwhile, like a snake shedding his skin, a flushed Ray emerged from the suit that had so effectively shielded him from danger. He was glad the dogs weren't around to tell him how much he, too, smelled of fear, hate, and the sour residue of adrenaline.

"I will assist you, sir," said Chips II, their shipboard domestic 'bot, rolling up to Ray's side just as he'd finished extracting himself from the Ivanhoe. Since the 'bot's form followed function, Chips looked like a cross between a garbage can and an octopus.

"How do you manage to do that?" Ray asked, irritated.

"I beg your pardon, sir?"

"How do you manage to time it so that you arrive moments after your services are no longer needed?"

"I'm sure I don't know, sir," the little 'bot said. His well-modulated, English-accented voice was a simulation of one of hol-vee's most popular characters of a few years past, the butler-detective Hollingsworth.

"Go clean the head or something," Ray told the 'bot. *Who ever heard of a lazy domestic 'bot?* he mused. Then, looking at the Ivanhoe lying in a heap on the floor, he said, "Actually, fumigate this damn thing and return it to its locker."

"As you wish, sir."

"They're coming," Ake's voice announced from a nearby speaker patch.

Ray turned on his heel and sprinted into the cockpit area. "I saved you a seat," Ake said, indicating the co-pilot's chair.

While Ray plopped down and secured himself, Ake sighed and ordered up the full panoply of holographic displays available to him.

"What's the sigh for?" Ray asked, turning to stare at his friend and partner.

"Nothing," Ake said. "Nothing."

Ray just shrugged. He'd try again later. For now, he asked, "What's the plan?"

In response, Ake said, "Tell the man, computer."

"There are six fighter craft approaching from the satellite's surface and—"

"Six? I thought you said three," interrupted Ray.

"Three more have been dispatched and will join the original three in two minutes and fifty-seven seconds. The others are commencing their attack now." A series of explosive flashes from the area of one of the *Purgatory*'s anti-spacecraft batteries confirmed that hostilities had indeed commenced.

"Why are they attacking?" Ray asked. "How do they know that we seized control of the ship and installed the former prisoners as the new crew of the *Purgatory*?"

When Ake directed a look at him that implied that Ray would need a brain boost to reach moron level, Ray colored and said, "Ah, yeah. I guess there *are* things like communications and recognition signals these days, huh?"

"You got it, Einstein."

"If you two will stop hectoring each other long enough to pay attention to what's important," said the computer, speaking as if to a room full of rebellious kindergarten-age kids, "then we can assist the *Purgatory*."

"I'm sorry if I seem not to be paying attention, computer," Ake said, "but I really don't see that anything is required of us carbon-based units at this time. Your direction of the defenses, whether programmed or spontaneous, seems to be more than adequate for now."

"That is certainly true," the computer agreed, its female voice sounding pleased.

"What defensive measures *are* you taking, however?" Ray asked.

The computer beamed a holo projection similar to Ake's in front of Ray. "As you can see, the three fighters . . . ah, here come the other three. The six fighters are attempting to attack so close in and at such high speeds that the *Purgatory*'s batteries cannot adequately target them as they flash by directing their limited firepower at the ship's weaker points."

"Are the 'weaker points,' as you call them, really all that vulnerable?" Ake queried.

"Not really," the computer responded.

"Then why are the fighters even bothering to make the effort?"

Ray wondered. "Is it orders? Are they supposed to make a futile flyby or two for the record and then break off or what?"

"They probably hope to occupy the attention of the *Purgatory* until *God's Truth* arrives."

"I know I'm going to hate myself for asking this question, but what's *God's Truth*?" Ake asked.

"Be nice to each other and exercise three times a week," Ray joked.

Ignoring him, the computer said, "*God's Truth* is a star cruiser that jumped minutes after the *Purgatory* reentered normal space."

"Jesus Christ!" exclaimed Ake.

"No," Ray said, constitutionally unable to prevent himself from cracking wise. "The *Jesus Christ* is in another part of the galaxy." When Ake shot him a give-me-a-break look, Ray held up his right hand and intoned, "God's truth."

II

With a communications link established between the *Purgatory* and *The Spirit of St. Louis*, Ake and Gabriel were able to put their heads together. Ake and Ray learned that one of Gabriel's first orders had been to rechristen the *Purgatory*; the former prison ship's new name was the *Exodus*.

"Do you have any ideas, Captain Gabriel?" Ake asked over a tight-beam transmission so focused and short-range that there was no danger of it being picked up by someone else.

"As a matter of face, I do," Gabriel responded, his image hovering in the air between Ake and Ray. His hair neatly combed, wearing his mantle of authority as captain, Gabriel seemed a new man.

"What does it require of us?"

"Very little."

"Uh-oh," moaned Ray. "I'm not sure I like the sound of that."

"And why is that, Larkin?" Gabriel asked, his holographic image turning to look directly at Ray.

"I like to be in charge of my own fate."

"Well, this time you'll have to trust me."

"You been a jumper jockey a long time?"

"Six years."

"Six years!" Ray sputtered, then realized a Cromwellian year was approximately two and a half times as long as a Terra-standard year.

Gabriel saw that Ray had made the necessary conversion in his head. "Yes, more like fifteen years by your calendar."

"This plan of yours, what does it involve," Ake asked.

"First, we head for deep space."

"Oh, shit!" swore Ray. "That means—"

"Yes. That means it involves jumping."

"Make that a double shit!" Ray said. He undid his restraints and got up. "I'm going back to the dogs," he told Ake. Pointing a finger at Gabriel's sometimes solid, sometimes transparent image, he said, "Don't make me sorry I saved your ass."

"If my plan works, I will be repaying the favor," Gabriel said.

"And if it doesn't?" asked Ake.

"Then we will this day wade across the river Jordan and dwell in the house of our Father from this time forward."

Ray paused and turned back toward Gabriel's inconstant image. "If you get there first, ask him to put out extra towels."

The star cruiser *God's Truth*, trailing its six fighter escorts like a great white shark trailing scavenger fish in its wake, followed the *Exodus* at a distance of several thousand kilometers, waiting for the prison ship to jump.

"Look at that thing," Ake said, indicating the massive warship. "It's gonna make mincemeat out of us the first chance it gets."

Tajil's voice came through the intercom system. "Hey, doan talk 'bout food like that."

"Mincemeat," Ray mused. "Anybody ever actually *eat* any mincemeat? I wonder what it tastes like."

"I can't believe you're contemplating what mincemeat might taste like at a time like this!" said Ake, busy making minor—and essentially pointless—instrumentation adjustments.

"I think I likes it better if'n Ray talks 'bout food instead of what it be like to be blown up by battleship," Beowulf said pointedly.

"I guess you're right, Beowulf," Ake conceded.

"We are jumping," the computer said.

"Shit!!" everyone chorused.

After the momentary wave of nausea and generalized feeling of displacement had passed, Ake asked, "Computer, based on the information available to you concerning Captain Gabriel's jump, can you make an educated guess where our exit point might be?"

There was a moment of silence, then the computer responded. "Yes, I can estimate the possible normal space reentry targets."

"You sound a bit hesitant to do so, computer," Ray said.

"While we know more about hyperspace than we ever have before, there is still much we do *not* know." That emphasis on "not" impressed Ray: the computer rarely inflected its words.

Ake traced the sides of his mouth with a finger. "But that is not why you are loath to speculate, is it?"

"No," the computer admitted. Without further prodding, the computer volunteered, "Three of the top eight reentry trajectories are dangerously close to stellar bodies."

"You mean—"

"Yeah." Ray spoke before the computer did. "Gabriel's going to bring us out within pissing distance of a sun."

★ ★ ★

As it turned out, the shortest jump required to bring the *Exodus* dangerously close to a star was a mere six minutes. In light of that, and desiring a flawless communications hookup between the two ships, Ake insisted that the computer order an actual physical connection between *The Spirit of St. Louis* and the *Exodus*.

The computer tried to nit-pick. "It seems to me that a vocal connection is adequate since—"

"Just do it," Ake ordered, impressing Ray with his resolve.

"Why the linkup?" Ray asked.

"When someone takes me by the hand and asks me to jump into a furnace with him, saying, 'Trust me,' I want to make sure he knows what he's doing."

"I wonder if he knows if he knows what he's doing?" Ray pondered.

"Me, too," said the image that was coalescing in the cockpit.

"Hello, Captain Gabriel," Ray said. The holographic projection was seated in a command chair and Ray could see parts of the *Exodus*'s control room.

"Yeah, hello," said Ake, waving his hand distractedly. "Now then," he continued, "since you overheard our misgivings, *do* you know what you're doing?"

"I hope so," said Gabriel's image brightly. When that failed to change Ake's worried expression, he continued, "Because we are coming out of hyperspace in less than four minutes." He stared off to the right as if looking over Ake's shoulder. "Ah, three minutes and thirty-two seconds to be exact—our pursuers have little time to evaluate their options and to make the appropriate preparations. They must decide to follow us out when we emerge in the local cluster, or to remain in hyperspace until they can plot a less problematic exit."

"And if they do that they will lose us," Ray said.

"Exactly."

"Sounds good," said Ake, grudgingly. "But what if they decide to follow us out?"

Gabriel's figure shrugged. "Yes, they may do that. If they do and if neither of us is destroyed by the nearby sun, then I will jump again and plot an egress that brings us closer to a sun." He smiled grimly. "I will do this until they either stop following us or one or both of us are destroyed."

"Oh," said Ake tonelessly as Gabriel swiveled in response to one of his lieutenants' voices and accidentally or deliberately broke the connection.

Ray undid his restraints and got up. He shook Ake's hand. "It's been great knowing you, partner."

"Where do you think you're going? We're jumping in a few minutes."

"I'm off to the dispensary to get some sun block," Ray said. "Think a rating of 2,000,000 will be enough?"

It took Ake only a moment to realize that Ray was going back to be with the dogs. As close as the two of them were, Ray's lifelong bond with his team was unassailable. No one, not even his friend and partner, meant as much to Ray as did his dogs.

"Hi, guys and gals," Ray said as he walked into the lounge where the dogs were strapped into their couches. "Howya doing?"

As he rubbed Beowulf's broad head, the big dog looked up at him and said, "You not back here for nuthin'. You think this might be it, donja?"

"Yah," agreed Mama-san. "We mebbe not gonna make it."

"Release us, Ray," Beowulf pleaded.

Ray drew in a deep breath, held it, then breathed out. "Sure," he said, and began to undo their restraints, starting with Beowulf. Then he undid Mama-san, Ozma, Grendel, Frodo, Sinbad, Tajil, Gawain, and Robin.

"We *gonna* die?" Gawain asked.

"I don't know," Ray admitted. "It's certainly possible."

"Then we dies together," Sinbad said, licking Ray's face. Ray hugged the reddish-brown and white dog as the others followed Sinbad's example. Ray pulled ears and thumped sides.

"Guess I haven't always been the perfect leader, have I, guys?"

Beowulf was shocked by Ray's words. "Ray . . . you the bestest leader a team could have! Why you talkin' nonsense?"

Ray knuckled Robin's head, then met Beowulf's eyes. "Maybe Anson, Pandora, and Littlejohn would disagree," he said softly.

"No!" the dogs protested.

Gawain looked around as if making up his mind about something. Then a look of resolve crossed his canine face. "Everybody thinks I a goofus," he began. When the others protested feebly, he shook his shaggy head and said, "No, it true." Then he focused his brown eyes on Ray's baleful face. "But now you the one bein' a goofus, Ray, if'n ya thinks we doan know that doin' what we was born to do is real dangerous besides bein' fun. We know we kin die any time."

"Thank you, Gawain," Ray said, humbled.

The others were awed; never had they heard Gawain put so many words together at once.

"Wow—that was swell, Gawain," an impressed Tajil said, nudging his brother affectionately.

"My puppy!" sniffed Mama-san.

Without warning, the ship jumped.

"My God!" Ray said.

III

"The force field is at full power," the computer's emotionless voice reported.

"Hang on back there!" Ake's voice boomed.

Ray and the dogs needed no prodding to grab onto whatever they could. Ray, at least, had hands; the dogs were forced to clamp down on any available hold with their powerful jaws.

"What in the sam hill is—" Ray managed to get out before *The Spirit of St. Louis* bucked and rolled so violently that he was first tossed into the air, then bounced off the floor, and finally flung against one of the empty acceleration couches. Ray looked up, his eyes widening, and got out of the way of the similarly flying Tajil just in time.

"Whoof," said Tajil, his landing knocking the air out of him.

Ray tried again. "Hey, I . . . argh!" This time he was sandwiched between Ozma and Robin, and all three of them slid across the floor and partway up the wall.

The fierce forces that had buffeted the ship subsided slowly and Ray was able to catch his breath.

"Rinse cycle?" Ray wondered.

"Oh, I doan feel so good," moaned Frodo. He got to his feet and tried to walk, but swayed uncertainly like a drunken sailor.

Ray, staring at the markings on the big black-and-white dog's side, said, "Stand still, Frodo, you're making me seasick." He clapped his hand over his mouth and closed his eyes.

"I *am* standing still." Lurching to one side, the dog added, "Well, tryin' to, anyhow."

"Everyone all right back there?" Ake's voice asked, his concern apparent.

"I think so," Ray said, giving the motley assembly a quick visual once-over. "Lots of bumps and bruises, but nothing serious."

"What happened?" asked Beowulf.

"Beowulf, you took the words right out of my mouth," Ray said.

"The *God's Truth* followed us out of hyperspace," Ake explained.

"Yeah?"

"With four times the mass of the *Exodus,* they got caught in the nearby sun's gravity tides and were pulled too close. The heat overwhelmed their fields and the ship blew up like an illegal fireworks factory."

"The fighters?"

"No sign of them."

"We're home free, then?" Ray asked.

"Looks that way, partner."

"Great," Ray said. Then: "Ah, Ake?"

"Yeah?"

"Could you send Chips down this way? We need a little janitorial work out of the lazy slacker. It seems someone threw up in here."

"Can do." Then: "Who threw up?"

"I did," Ray said, turning on his side and . . .

4

"Where are we going, if I might inquire?" Ray asked Ake.

"That's a good question."

"Thanks," Ray said, dropping his eyes modestly before looking up and persisting, "How about a good answer?"

"How about a punch in the kisser?"

The dogs present stirred restlessly; Robin, younger and newer than the others, looked from Ake's face to Ray's and back again to Ake's. He was unused to hearing his two masters exchange cross words.

Acting like nothing had passed between them, Ray ignored Ake and pressed the glowing square pinned to his shirt. Then he stared into the holo display of the quadrant before them.

No one spoke. After what seemed an eternity, Chips appeared.

"You rang, sir?"

"Chips, ole buddy, fetch me a nice tall gin and tonic on the rocks with a twist. Make it Beefeaters, please." He frowned. "Do we have any more Kolln Vineyards?"

"Yes, sir."

"Good. Bring Ake a white wine then. Something cheeky but not snotty," Ray said, still not looking his partner's way.

"As you wish, sir." The little 'bot whirled and rolled away slowly.

"You'd think Chips was getting paid by the hour, wouldn't you?" Ray asked of no one in particular. Then he added, "That was a rhetorical question, but that doesn't mean someone can't respond to it."

"Well," began Frodo. "I think—"

"Someone whose initials are Ake Ringgren, that is," Ray said pointedly.

Now embarrassed by his uncharacteristic outburst at Ray, Ake murmured, "Since you decided that we both need a drink, may I wait until Chips returns before I say anything?"

Ray sighed. "Chips is on his way . . . but so's Santa Claus. I swear you can time that lazy bucket of bolts with a sundial."

Ake rolled his eyes to indicate to whatever higher power might be watching over them the futility of trying to have a normal conversation with Ray. "You win, you little wiseacre."

"Hey! I resemble that remark!"

Ake smiled, but the strain of the last few days showed in his face. Usually, Ake appeared to be about seventeen, his flaming red hair topping an innocent and unlined face. Now he looked closer to his nominal age (he and Ray didn't count the twelve years they "lost" in hyperspace). On the verge of speaking, he reconsidered, and simply sighed wordlessly.

"That's it!" Ray blurted out as he snapped his fingers.

"What's it?"

"That damn sigh. You've been doing a lot of that lately. A lot of 'woe is me' sighing."

"I have? Really?"

"Really." Ray turned to Beowulf, who'd just plopped down in the cockpit to eavesdrop on his humans' conversation. "Is Ake sighing a lot, Beowulf?"

"Yah," Beowulf agreed, rubbing his big head against a projecting piece of plasteel.

Unconsciously mimicking Beowulf's action, Ake scratched his head. "Hmmm . . . I hadn't noticed."

Chips rolled up with the drinks. "Your drink, sir," he said, proffering Ray a glass. When Ray took his drink from the 'bot, Chips served Ake a perfectly chilled sauvignon blanc.

"What is this?" asked Ray, looking at the glass in his hand.

"Your gin and tonic, sir."

"I know that. I mean, what is this—a child's portion?"

"I have been instructed to bring you smaller portions, sir," Chips said blandly.

"Uh-oh," said Beowulf. He knew that getting between Ray and a drink was like trying to take Robin's temperature with a rectal thermometer.

Before Ray could point a finger of accusation at Ake, the computer spoke up, admitting, "I ordered Chips to serve you smaller drinks, Ray. My recent full-body analysis of you indicated a need for you to cut down on your alcoholic intake."

"Oh, you ordered my drinks watered, did you?" Ray said hotly. "I oughta get a pair of pliers and—"

"Ray?"

"Yeah, Ake?"

"Your drinking, my sighing—and our mutual temper tantrums—I think I know what's the matter."

"Good. Let me in on it, then."

"We need a vacation."

★ ★ ★

How in the name of Mohammed's mother-in-law did I get myself in this situation again? Ray asked himself rhetorically as he walked *The Spirit of St. Louis*'s skin like a little bird hopping about a hippopotamus's back picking parasites out of the cracks and folds of the huge creature's flesh.

When ships jumped, hypermatter—invisible to all but those with psi abilities—accumulated on their hulls. After a dozen or so jumps, fewer if the jumps were long ones, the hypermatter began to exert a drag on the ship. If allowed to accrue, the hypermatter would eventually prevent the ship from exiting hyperspace. Since that was a fate too horrible to contemplate, someone—usually, but not always, a 'scraper—had to sense it and exorcise it by passing his or her living flesh over and through it. That done, the will-o'-the-wisp substance would drift away, whisked into oblivion by unimaginable currents.

Because of her recent adventures, *The Spirit of St. Louis* had accumulated eight jumps without being scraped. Theoretically, Ray knew, the ship could make as many as four or five more jumps without incident.

That made Ray snort. *Yeah. Theoretically, I could put a slug-thrower to my head and pull the trigger and my atoms would get out of the way long enough for the hunk of metal to pass harmlessly through my skull and brain. Theoretically, that is.*

Ray's skepticism was based on more than the inadvisability of twitting Lady Luck. Once, forced to act the role of a 'scraper, he had foolishly looked deep into the featureless void and been forced to confront horrific reminders of his less-than-innocent past. In response, his senses had been overwhelmed by a sanity-protecting blackout that resulted in *The Spirit of St. Louis* languishing in hyperspace for over an hour. After Ake retrieved the unconscious Ray and made the jump back to normal space-time, a full twelve years had somehow passed in the "real" world.

Ray would rather swallow razor blades than repeat that experience.

Quickly and efficiently, his abilities amplified by the rubies he wore, he found and dispatched the ribbons of hypermatter that clung to the ship's skin. Refusing to look into the foggy mist that swirled around him, he did his job and nothing more.

Sometimes I forget what makes them priceless, he thought. *Without the rubies an ESPer would have a helluva time locating the hypermatter on his or her own.*

Finished with his hazardous chore, Ray glanced at the elapsed-time readout displayed in one corner of his helmet. It read 5:12 . . . 5:13 . . . 5:14. *Pretty damn good*, he told himself.

Now to hie myself back inside, put on my jacket with the leather patches on the elbows, trick Chips into giving me a man-sized drink, fill a bowl with Ake's best leaf, start a roaring fire in the fireplace, and sit watching the flames with a loyal courser at my feet—Beowulf will do.

He paused at the airlock, chanced a quick look out into the nothingness of hyperspace, laughed, and said, "Kiss my butt!"

II

"What are you looking at?" Ray asked Ake. Ake was nursing a soft drink and staring intently at a holo.

"Ake hearin' how wonderful we is," Grendel said.

"Yeah . . . well, sort of," Ake said, grudgingly agreeing with Grendel's assessment. "When Captain Gabriel explained to the other recipients of Cromwell's hospitality who was responsible for their freedom, many of them requested an opportunity to make a recording thanking us."

"Sounds wonderful," Ray agreed. "It also sounds like it could lead to someone getting a swelled head if he took such gratitude too much to heart."

"You just gonna have to chance it, Ray," Robin jabbed.

"*Touché*, D'Artagnan," Ray said, appreciating the dog's sarcasm. Then, to Ake, "Have you watched many of these so far?"

"About half of the eighty-five or so Gabriel tight-beamed over to us before the *Exodus* went its merry way."

Ray whistled. "Can you stand that much adoration?"

Ake pretended to fight back tears. "Since I don't get any thanks around here from you guys, it's music to my ears."

"Uh-huh. I suppose you didn't tell them who *really* saved their bacon, did you?"

"I tried, believe me, I tried, but they laid their appreciation at *my* feet like a wreath while I vainly protested that you were the hero. They took my protestations as further evidence of a very becoming modesty."

"I think I'm gonna throw up!"

"*Please*, sir," said Chips. "Not again."

Ray cupped his hand around one side of his mouth and leaned conspiratorially toward Ake. "It wasn't cleaning it up that bothered Artoo Detour so much as having to watch every one of the dogs come over and sniff it."

"Thanks for sharing that," Ake said, wrinkling his nose in disgust.

"So," Ray said, "Any of these nimrods have anything more interesting to say than 'God bless you and keep you'?"

"Actually, yes." He fumbled at the controls, gave up, and simply said, "Play message number seventeen, please."

A head-and-chest holographic image of a middle-aged, double-chinned, bald man appeared. "Hello, Dr. Ringgren and Mr. . . ." He glanced at something held in his hand, out of the image. "Ah, Mr. Larkin and dogs. My name is Harris Webster. Like you, Dr. Ringgren, I am an outsider who ran afoul of the law while on Cromwell. My crime was an entirely inadvertent one—as I've been told yours was." He grinned sheepishly and scratched his bald pate. "That's the truth, but I suppose everyone on the *Exodus* makes that claim.

"I wish to thank you for saving my life—and I mean that literally. I wouldn't have lasted three months on that blasted prison satellite." He shook his head at the thought of such a fate and stared off camera, as if glimpsing his own dead body lying nearby in a bier.

"How much of this do we have to watch?" Ray implored Ake.

"Just button your lip and pay attention."

"The reason I went to Cromwell in the first place was to drum up business for Neverland—"

"At least he didn't say 'Never-Never Land,'" Ray said.

"Sh-h-h!"

"—the resort I own in the Yurigamo cluster. I thought wealthy Cromwellians would be dying to get offplanet and away from the Soldiers of God, the secret police, for a while—and I may still be correct in that assessment—but I quickly ran into difficulties with their arcane legal system when I attempted to pursue business as usual." Webster laughed a mirthless laugh. "That is, business as usual anywhere in the galaxy but Cromwell. Can you imagine a man of my wealth and influence—forgive me for not bothering with a show of false modesty—being treated in such a manner anywhere else except a theocracy like Cromwell? It boggles the mind."

"Gosh, this is interesting," Ray deadpanned. Ake simply made a fist and shook it warningly at him.

"The point is," the heavyset man continued, "I am the owner of a number of resort planets, the finest of which is Neverland. I'm inviting you to come and enjoy what my pleasure world has to offer for as long as you wish to stay. Absolutely free of charge, of course."

Ray sat up.

Ake turned to Beowulf and said, "He got Ray's attention finally by saying the magic word: 'free.'"

"If you decide to accept my offer, I will meet you there when you arrive. It'll be a vacation of sorts for me, as well. My other business interests—"

Ake froze the image, nudged Ray, and said, "He isn't kidding about his 'other business interests.' I looked him up in *Who's Who* and he owns outright or has shares in half the businesses between here and the core."

"He's richer than us, huh?"

"Ray, Harris Webster is one of the richest men in the galaxy, if not *the* richest."

"I wonder if he plays poker?" Ray mused.

When Beowulf hooted at that, Ake laughed and said, "I agree, Beowulf. To paraphrase an old joke: If you want to end up with a million credits, stake Ray to *two* million in a poker game."

"Ah, just roll the damned message," said Ray, chagrined.

Ake said, "Computer, pick up from the beginning of that sentence again, please."

"My other business interests have kept me away from Neverland for far too long. I myself have not been back for nearly three years." Again Webster looked down at his unseen hand. "The coordinates for Neverland are . . ." He squinted. "I can't read this; it's too small. Captain Gabriel will append the coordinates to the end of my message. Thank you."

"Stop here, please," Ake ordered the computer. "Well, what do you think of that?"

Ray got up.

"Hey, where are you going?"

"To dig out my bathing suit, my fishing rod, and my tennis racket," Ray threw back over his shoulder as he left.

★ ★ ★

The way to Neverland wasn't a matter of taking the "second star to the right and on till morning." It was much more complicated than that. Much more. The computer showed them exactly how far away the Yurigamo system really was.

Ray and Ake stared at the holographic image of the Milky Way as it floated before them in the lounge, slowly but perceptibly turning on its axis.

"Here's the home system—Sol and its planets," the computer said as a red dot glowed and blinked in one of the spiral arms far out from the center.

Thinking of all the "you are here" signs he'd seen in his life, Ray asked, "And where are the rest rooms?"

Tajil, whose ears he was forcefully rubbing, snorted. The others, the computer included, simply ignored Ray's comment.

"And here is the Yurigamo system." An amber dot glowed to reveal its location.

"Jee-zusssss!" Ray exclaimed, sounding like he was speaking the sibilant K'a-niian language.

Ake gasped and picked up Ray's glass of bourbon and water and gulped down what remained, briefly choking as a little of the liquor got into his windpipe when he unconsciously subvocalized his dismay.

Tajil looked puzzled by their reaction. "What's the big deal?" he asked, ambling over to the floating projection and moving his nose the six centimeters between the two dots. "It doan seem all that far to me."

The Yurigamo cluster was in the truncated, twenty-three-thousand-light-years-long spur that projected out from the spiral arm about fifteen to eighteen thousand light-years ahead of the location of the solar system. Both Ray and Ake were aware that one-thousand-light-year jumps were considered to be pushing the envelope of acceptable risk. They were also aware that a voyage to the spur would entail perhaps ten separate jumps of that magnitude—more if they tossed in a few shorter-duration jumps for safety's sake.

"It's far, Taddy," Ray said softly. "Believe me, it's damned far."

"Why would anyone build a resort at the end of the universe?" Ake wondered and then looked at Ray expectantly.

"I have absolutely no idea," Ray said, consciously confounding Ake's expectations of a smartass reply.

"So the sales 'bots doan come knockin' on your door!" said Gawain suddenly, proud of himself for thinking that up.

Ray and Ake stared at each other for a moment, then burst out laughing.

★ ★ ★

While Ray and Ake slept the sleep of the dead—they had pondered the significance of the number of jumps required to reach their destination over a plethora of drinks—the dogs gathered in the lounge to discuss the recent turn of events.

Underlining his position as leader, the "alpha wolf" of the pack, Beowulf formally greeted each of the other eight dogs in his team.

"'Lo, Frodo," the big lionlike dog rasped to Frodo.

"'Lo, Beowulf." Frodo licked Beowulf's neck and face, showing obeisance. With the death of Littlejohn on Terra, Frodo had assumed the mantle of second-in-command. Beowulf was not entirely comfortable with Frodo in such an important position in the team, but his primacy within the pack made it impossible for Beowulf to assign that all-important role to the more steady Sinbad. Not that the black-and-white Frodo wasn't brave enough or intelligent enough, rather he bordered on being too headstrong and independent for such a disciplined position.

"'Lo, Sinbad," Beowulf greeted Sinbad. A handsome reddish-brown and white dog, Sinbad's only fault was his occasional obnoxiousness. Actually, when Beowulf considered it more carefully, he had to admit obnoxiousness was a trait that Sinbad had very nearly outgrown. It made him wish more than ever that Sinbad could be his number two.

"'Lo, Beowulf." Sinbad also signaled his subservient position relative to Beowulf by puppylike behavior: crouching low and licking the big dog's face.

"'Lo, Mama-san," Beowulf intoned.

"'Lo, Beowulf," Mama-san replied, dutifully performing the ritual submissive routine. As the mother of the puppies, fathered by Anson, another member of the original nine-dog team, she had a special place in Beowulf's affections.

"'Lo, Ozma."

"'Lo, Beowulf." Beowulf took special note of Ozma's moods and feelings. She and Littlejohn had long had an especially close bond, and when he'd been killed Ozma had been deeply wounded emotionally. Although she seemed much better of late, Beowulf guessed that much of that was an act: She would never forget Littlejohn and might never be fully whole again without him.

"'Lo, Grendel."

"'Lo, Beowulf." The third female on the team, Grendel was quiet and careful. But as soon as he had characterized her as such, Beowulf reconsidered. With Ozma's emotional devastation, Grendel had become more talkative, had emerged a little more from her shell of silence. She would never rival Gawain or himself for loquaciousness, but she was speaking up more, trying to tease, coax, and cajole Ozma back into being her old self.

After both Tajil and Gawain, the only two "puppies" from Mama-san's Chiron-born litter to remain with the team, paid their respects to him, Beowulf could not help but make note of their differences. Where Tajil, a red dog second in size only to Beowulf himself, was intelligent, his brother Gawain was a bit dense. Both, however, were fiercely loyal; they would not hesitate to give up their lives for Ray, Beowulf, or the rest of the team.

"'Lo, Robin."

"'Lo, Beowulf."

Robin, another red dog, was the team's latest addition—having joined up on Terra following Littlejohn's death. After Ozma, he was Beowulf's most pressing concern. Ill-trained and taught to be a brute while on Terra, Robin had made enormous strides at being integrated into the tightly woven team. But he was still capable of showing flashes of his old self, and Beowulf feared his reverting to savagery if the right—that is to say, *wrong*—conditions presented themselves.

"So, what we gonna talk about?" Frodo asked.

"Doan know, 'xactly," Beowulf said. "Little bit of everythin'—

what's bin happenin', what this bay-kayshun may mean—but nuthin' special, either."

"Where we goin'?" Gawain asked.

"Place called Neverland," Tajil told his brother.

"Nebberland? What's that?"

"Nev-ver land," repeated Tajil, better at saying his V's than the other dogs.

"Yah, yah. So what is it?"

"Beowulf tole ya already," grumbled Ozma. "It's a bay-kayshun place . . . you know, where ya has fun."

"Oh," said Gawain. "We takin' a job there?"

"No," explained Tajil. "A vacation is when you *doan* gots a job."

Gawain was puzzled—admittedly not a new occurrence. "How can that be fun, then? We has fun when we has a job."

"Beoples gets tired of their jobs, Gawain," Grendel said. "Ray and Ake is *real* tired right now."

"I think they bin tired since we was on Terra," Beowulf said. "They thought they would feel better, but they dint."

"Yah," agreed Robin. "And fightin' them bad beoples and 'bots to get Ake back dint help none."

"So what should *we* do?" wondered Mama-san.

"What Ray wants us to do," opined Beowulf.

"Doan we always do that?" said Frodo.

"Yah, but we lets him an' Ake know how we feels 'bout things," Robin said. "I think Beowulf means we should jes' say yah to anythin' they suggest."

"Yah," said Beowulf, nodding his big shaggy head.

They continued like this, talking for a long time, until finally, Beowulf said, "Let us say the Law."

"What is the Law?" intoned Beowulf.

"*To place duty above self, honor above life.*"

"What is the Law?"

"*To allow harm to come to no Man, to protect Man and his possessions.*"

"What is the Law?"

"*To stand beside Man's side—as dogs will always stand. Together, Man and dog.*"

"Good," said Beowulf.

III

Yeltsin was a refreshing contrast to Cromwell. Where the latter was a tightly controlled and regulated one-government planet, the former was a loose confederation of city-states devoted to the accumulation of capital, where order was maintained by a *laissez faire* legal system that assumed that anything that was not specifically outlawed was permitted if not actively encouraged.

Things were so lax and informal that they were able to satisfy ninety-five percent of Yeltsin's customs rules and regulations while in orbit around the planet. Then, once the computer had given over control of the ship to the spaceport's pseudo-quantum-gravity computer, they had landed and endured a cursory onboard inspection. Having grown cynical in his old age, Ray was pleasantly surprised to learn that it was unnecessary to slip the customs agents a few hundred Fed-creds in return for a clean bill of health.

As he put his wad of bills back into his pocket, Ray reflected that they represented two things that had so far resisted change: The first was that despite centuries of attempts to produce cashless societies, money—real bills or coins—had never disappeared because there would always be a need for "off the record" financial transactions. And the second was that the now defunct Federation, no longer the center of authority in the galaxy, had bequeathed its currency to the marketplace. Fed-creds were not only accepted almost everywhere, they were actually preferable to the local issue. Like the rubles of Old Earth, before the Second Russian Revolution, many "official" forms of cash were essentially worthless and unexchangeable.

"This is my kind of planet," Ray said, breathing in the crisp, fresh air as he walked down *The Spirit of St. Louis*'s ramp and onto the plascrete spaceport landing field.

With the dogs streaming around the two men to take up their defensive positions, Ake agreed. "After Cromwell, I think it'll be a long time before I'm comfortable with a place where you can be arrested for practicing normal human behavior."

"Or simply for acting the way you do," Ray said, making sure to smile; they were both taking extra pains to make sure their usual good-natured, we've-been-partners-and-friends-for-years-so-we-can-say-anything banter was not mistaken for real insults.

What a pisser! Ray thought to himself. *To have to add "just kidding" after everything we say, after all we've been through together, makes it abundantly clear exactly how ground down to the nub the two of us really are.*

Defusing the situation through his obliviousness, as he was

wont to do more and more these days, Gawain said, "I jes' loves new planets—there's so much to see and to smell."

"Aye, that there is, matey," Ray agreed, squinting one eye almost shut and pretending to chomp down on an imaginary pipe.

"Oh, wait—I know who that is," Ake said, his forehead wrinkling as he concentrated. Suddenly, a look of recognition crossed his face. "Potpie!" he blurted out.

"You're absolutely right," Ray said, not having the heart to correct him. He did, however, shoot Beowulf a knowing wink.

"Potpie!" moaned Gawain. "Doan mention food!"

"Yah, I's hungry, too," Tajil agreed.

"I guess we could get something to eat if there's a place that caters to your kind," Ray said pointedly.

"Our kind? You means handsome, strong, and smart?" asked Frodo.

"Of course," Ray affirmed.

5

Ake watched the dogs wolfing down their food, fascinated by how quickly they made it disappear. Ake liked food for more than its ability to satiate his hunger. He also liked food for its aroma, for its flavors, for its appearance, for its manner of presentation, for the associations it aroused—memorable past meals that had included whatever it was he was currently enjoying.

Had he not become first a physician, then a spy, and then an adventurer, Ake could easily have become a chef. He enjoyed everything about food, including its preparation. With Ray and the dogs, he had few opportunities to indulge his passion for preparing and cooking first-class meals.

The dogs, more gourmands—a marvelously polite word for gluttons—than gourmets, were bad enough, but Ray wasn't much better. For someone who had lived in alien cultures and eaten whatever was put in front of him, he was remarkably cautious and hesitant about food; "Will I like that?" was one of his frequent queries when confronted with something new. To Ake's chagrin, Ray's great culinary love was pasta—in all its forms and shapes. He jokingly confided to Ake one day that it was his favorite "because it has no bones."

As the dogs made their meals vanish as if by magic, Ake was amused by a thought that suddenly occurred to him. He realized that he could make a steak disappear by throwing a cloth over it and Beowulf and then pulling back the cloth to reveal . . . that the steak had vanished into thin air. *Yeah, into not-so-thin Beowulf would be more like it!*

"What are you thinking about, Ake?" Ray asked, observing the look on Ake's face.

"Huh? Food. I'm thinking about food."

"Our meals will be out any minute," Ray told him, misinterpreting his response.

"I can wait," Ake said truthfully.

Since the dogs had been so peckish, the team had stopped at the first greasy spoon they came to. Instead of complete dinners, the establishment served only sandwiches and bar food.

"Boy, I could eat anythin'!" Gawain said.

"Be careful, I think you may get your wish," Ake told him.

"A table for eleven," Ray said to the robot hostess who glided up silently.

"I am afraid that is impossible."

"No, traveling faster than light is impossible," Ray corrected "her." "Seating us at a table is relatively easy."

"I mean it is against our policy."

"We doan wanna make no trouble," offered Beowulf helpfully.

"I will get the owner," the 'bot said, rolling off immediately.

"Dogs, eh?" the chef/owner said when he saw them. He pointed to a sign which said that the establishment excluded all animals from the premises.

"Robin, this gentleman says they don't serve dogs," Ray said.

Robin assumed an aggressive stance, and bared his teeth. Ray meant it as a harmless show, but for Robin it was no act.

The man looked at Ray, then at Robin, then back at Ray. He spread his hands. "I'm sorry, I forgot: Scout team dogs are exempt from that prohibition."

"What exempt mean?" Gawain asked as they were shown to their own private dining area.

"It means the guy wants to live a while more," joked Frodo.

Ray sipped his drink slowly, aware he could become lightheaded if he guzzled it on an empty stomach. Finally, their sandwiches arrived, delivered by a servibot that had seen better days. Ray dug into his BLT eagerly, but Ake found his own meal to be singularly unappetizing.

"Eat," commanded Ray. "You gotta keep your strength up."

"Yeah, yeah." Ake took a few halfhearted bites, then put his sandwich down. "Sorry. I guess I'm just not in the mood for it."

When Ake saw Tajil eying his ham and cheese sandwich, he asked, "Do you want my sandwich, Taddy?"

"Yah!"

Ake put his plate down in front of the big red dog and, like magic, the sandwich disappeared. "For my next trick . . ." Ake said *sotto voce*.

"What did you say?" Ray asked, his mouth half full.

"I said, 'Mind if I go to the bar'?"

"The bar? Why?" Ray queried.

"Might be a good place to pick up a 'scraper."

"Yeah," admitted Ray. Then he asked, "What, you don't trust your old partner to do the job right?"

"Does my old partner really *want* to do the job?"

"You got me there."

"Also," Ake pointed out, "people tend to lose their heads when you visit the bar."

Ray cringed at the memory. "You're two for two."

"I can go then?"

Ray cocked his head and shot Ake a look. "I ain't your Mommer or Dadder, Captain Trimble."

"That's true." Ake got up to leave.

"Just one thing."

Ake stopped. "Yes?"

"Take Beowulf with you."

Ake looked at Beowulf, who grinned back. "Okay."

"Are you wearing your needle gun?"

Wordlessly, Ake rolled up his sleeve and showed Ray the small weapon strapped to his wrist and forearm.

"Be gone with you, then."

After they left, Grendel said, "You know . . . they's only two things wrong with the food here."

"What's that?" asked Sinbad.

"It doan taste all that good *and* you doan gets very much of it."

"Hee, hee," giggled Ozma.

Pleased that she had made Ozma laugh, Grendel looked at Ray and winked. Ray winked back and sipped his drink.

II

Ake found an unoccupied table and ordered a gin and tonic and a liter bottle of water. Checking the seal carefully to make sure it hadn't been tampered with, Ake opened the water while he sipped his drink; then he carefully replaced the liquor he'd consumed with water from the bottle. *I have to keep a clear head*, he reasoned.

His eyes sweeping the bar area, Ake decided he'd rarely seen a nastier-looking bunch of squarenuts in his life. Had he said this to Ray, Ray would have pointed out to him that he made that same observation in every bar he ventured into.

Looks like a penal colony reunion, he observed. Then he decided that wasn't fair—to penal colonies. After all, he himself had almost ended up a permanent guest at one. Checking out some of the physiognomies looming out of the smoky air, he was glad he was armed to the teeth. *Wonder why the owner doesn't want to admit animals? Could it be he thinks the patrons would frighten them?*

Ake had queried the bulky 'bot that had brought his drink and it now returned to his table with a small replica of an Aladdin's lamp and placed it in the center of the table. Touching the wick with the tip of one of its utility fingers, the 'bot lit the lamp and moved away.

The lamp burned with a yellow-green flame. Ake sighed. This all seemed awfully contrived to him; it was as bad as any of the moronically complicated message sending or receiving procedures he'd had to perform when he was an undercover agent for the Programmers too many years ago and too many klicks distant to bear thinking about.

If Sidney Greenstreet shows up in a fez, I'll know I'm really in one of Ray's old sinnys, he told himself. That made him sit up: He had actually remembered the actor's name. *Ray would be proud of me.*

<*I am, partner, I am.*>

<*Hey! No unauthorized mind-reading, please!*>

<*Sorry.*>

<*Sometimes I wish you'd never gotten your communications implant,*> Ake said crossly.

<*I said I was sorry,*> Ray reiterated. <*I'm going now. Bye. Write if you get work.*>

<*Oh, hell, wait a minute. You don't have to leave if . . .*> Too late. Ake no longer sensed Ray's presence.

"You and Ray talkin' in your heads again, aintcha?" said Beowulf.

Before Ake could reply, a soft, yet full-bodied, voice said, "Hello. Do you mind if I join you?"

Startled, Ake looked up to find himself staring into the eyes of a painfully thin young woman who was either totally oblivious of her appearance, or an ESPer. Or both. *Don't be dense,* Ake chided himself. *She's obviously an ESPer.*

"No, of course not. Please have a seat." Ake guessed she was in her late twenties or early thirties. Her skin—on her face and neck and wherever else it showed—was mottled by ugly red and purple blotches. And here and there small yellow-crowned pustules had erupted from crusty patches on her skin. Ake recognized it for what it was: 'scraper skin.

'Scraper skin, Ake shuddered, fighting back pitiful images. *What a sorry disease.* Then he admitted to himself that what so provoked his distaste was merely—if one got down to facts—a psychosomatic condition. By no means hypochondriacs, ESPers generated enormous inner stresses when forced to confront the horrors of hyperspace almost daily; that was the basis for their psychosomatic symptoms.

"I always like to make sure first," the young woman said. "Sometimes people light the lamp without realizing that it is meant to send a signal." She pulled out the table's second cuddle chair and plopped down into it as if she hadn't sat down in a week. Cheaply constructed, the chair wobbled beneath her modest weight and strained to conform to her body.

"May I smoke?"

Remembering the smartass answer Ray gave a man who asked the same question, Ake said, "Just till you smolder and burst into flame."

If he was looking for a reaction, he didn't get it. The ESPer simply smiled and said, "As you can see, I have all the bad habits."

"All?"

She smiled enigmatically. Ake stared at her.

After she had tolerated Ake's stare for long enough, she asked mildly, "I'm the example that proves the stereotype, eh?"

"No, not at all," Ake replied hastily. "That is . . . ah . . ."

The ESPer threw back her head and laughed a hearty laugh, smoke dribbling from her mouth and nostrils. "I hope you have a better poker face than that."

"Heh, heh, heh," Beowulf rumbled.

"Ah, yes . . . your faithful furry companion. A scout dog, if

I'm not mistaken." The woman shrugged, indicating she was aware that guessing that Beowulf was a scout dog was no huge accomplishment—no more than Ake guessing she was an ESPer and a 'scraper.

"Yah," agreed Beowulf.

"So why did you laugh, scout dog?"

"You 'minded me of somthin' Ray said onct: 'He has a real poker face . . . someone hit him in the face with a poker!'" Beowulf laughed again, but neither the young ESPer nor Ake joined in his merriment.

"Sheesh," the big dog said. He would have blushed if he could. "I guess ya hadda be there."

"I guess," agreed the young woman. Then she looked at Ake with piercing eyes. "And you, I take it, are Ray?"

Ake shook his head. "No, my name is Ake Ringgren. Ray Larkin is my partner."

That got the young ESPer's attention. "Ray Larkin and Ake Ringgren," she said slowly. "Not *the* Ray Larkin and Ake Ringgren?"

Second billing again! Ake told himself, chagrined. "Oh, no, of course not. We're two completely 'other' people who happen to have exactly the same names," Ake said, a tad more sarcastically than he intended. "Yes, of course—we're the *the*'s themselves."

"Who'd say they was them if'n they wasn't?" added Beowulf rhetorically, trying to be helpful.

The woman nodded. "Yes. And who'd say he or she was a 'scraper if he or she wasn't?"

You bet! Ake thought. To be an ESPer was bad enough; to be a 'scraper as well was compounding the problem. Still, given the low-level hostility and resentment directed at ESPers, it wasn't much of a step down to go all the way and become a 'scraper as well.

The young woman looked at him and nodded, and Ake suddenly felt embarrassed. "You can read my thoughts, then?"

"A little," she admitted. "Usually I just get a sense of a person's emotions, but I can pick up thoughts and images if they're projected strongly enough."

"How 'bout me?" asked Beowulf.

"You're hungry and you want another bowl of beer."

"Ah, too easy!" said Beowulf.

"So you think I just made a good guess . . . Beowulf?"

"Hey, that pretty good."

K-9 CORPS: THE LAST RESORT

"*I'm* not psychic," Ake told her, "so why don't you let us know your name?"

"I am Katerina Golnikov." She paused and added, "But most people call me Kate."

"Pleased to meet you, Kate." Ake proffered his hand. She put her smaller hand in his and Ake observed how warm and moist it was.

"Pleased to you meet you, Ake." She smiled down at Beowulf—although he was so big even lying on his side that "down" probably was the wrong word to use since his head almost came up to hers. "Pleased to meet you, Beowulf." Then she sighed and seemed ready to say something more.

"Hey," Ake said. "That's for me to do," meaning her soulful sigh.

"Heh, heh," chuckled Beowulf, understanding perfectly what Ake meant.

But Katerina Golnikov frowned in puzzlement. "I'm sorry. What is for you to do?"

"Sighing," Ake said, winking at Beowulf.

"I do not understand."

"Private joke," explained Beowulf, winking back at Ake. It came out as "Brivate," of course.

"Rutters!" she sighed.

Both Ake and Beowulf laughed. Not knowing why, exactly, Golnikov found herself joining in.

★ ★ ★

"Five thousand Fed-creds a jump!" Ray roared. "I thought you knew how to bargain better than that, buddy."

"Neat!" said Tajil, enjoying Ray's accidental alliteration. "Can ya say 'Sasha sells seashells by the seashore'?"

Ray gaped at the big red dog, then buried his face in his hands.

"Hey, doan cry, Ray," said Mama-san.

His shoulders heaving from laughter, Ray lifted his head from his hands, a huge grin plastered across his face. "You guys." He giggled. "One of these days . . ."

"And although we dropped a nice hunk of change in buying the planet Anson as a rehabilitation and training center for scout dogs," Ake reminded Ray, "our investments have a way of spewing out geysers of cash with next to no effort on our part. We're still so rich we stink."

"I thought I was the spendthrift and you were the miser," Ray told him.

"Five thousand credits a jump?" said Ake, tilting his head and tucking his chin into his chest like a kindly parish priest cajoling a contribution from a reluctant philanthropist. "You spend more than that a month seeking out and buying old copies of *Famous Monsters of Filmland, Uncle Scrooge*, and the rest of that twentieth-century ephemera you collect."

"Oh, all right," said Ray, knowing when he was beaten and throwing in the towel. Still, he gave it one last shot. "I suppose you comparison-shopped for the best rate?"

Ake thumped Frodo on the back, pointed at Ray, and said, "Frodo—go bite his nuts off."

After the dogs stopped hooting, Ake continued. "There are exactly four 'scrapers available for hire on Yeltsin, and only two of them right here in Randville, the spaceport. When the first and only 'scraper I spoke to agreed to do the job for a reasonable sum of money, I said yes. She seems like a good person. If we shopped around, we might do as well, but I don't think we'd do better—and we could easily do worse. The money isn't really important, so I hired her on the spot."

Ake's eyes narrowed. "Any other questions?"

Ray had pulled back slightly at Ake's outburst. "Ah . . . no."

"Good."

III

It was strange having a third person on board *The Spirit of St. Louis*, Ray thought. With just Ake and the dogs on the ship, he found himself going through the motions of a number of reassuring routines—reassuring because of their predictability. The dogs were much the same way: They had their morning and evening rituals, and they liked getting fed the same time every day, no matter how arbitrary the concept of "time" became when one was aboard a spacecraft flitting in and out of the corporeal universe and the normal space-time continuum.

During their fourth jump, however, Ray came to a conclusion that swept aside his annoyance at having to share the ship with an outsider. "You know," he said to Ake, "I sure am glad someone else is out there, walking the hull, instead of me."

"Even someone as overpaid as Kate Golnikov?" Ake asked slyly.

"Yes," Ray admitted. "Even someone as overpaid as her."

Ray left unsaid another reason he was glad to leave the task of facing the horrors of hyperspace to someone else. It was something that had come up when Ray first showed some of their remaining rubies to Golnikov.

"But why do I have to keep my eyes closed?" Golnikov asked.

"Ray likes to surprise beople," Grendel told the 'scraper.

Ray carefully deposited a half-dozen Rostoff rubies on the countertop. Without opening her eyes, Golnikov gasped in pleasure. That impressed Ray: The rubies' purity and power were such that the 'scraper could see them through the raw energy they emitted, and the amplification they provided her already impressive natural psi abilities.

Golnikov opened her eyes. "So many! And all so beautiful! My God, where did you get them?"

Ray smiled and shrugged noncommittally, turning his hands palms out in the universally recognized gesture: "So, whatta you expect me to say?"

Golnikov understood perfectly. "I guess I wouldn't answer that question, either." Then she reached out tentatively with her left hand and caressed them gingerly, one by one. "They are marvelous specimens; they speak to me in a clear, crystalline voice. With stones like these to help me, I can guide us across the universe."

"Uh, just to Neverland will do nicely."

Kate Golnikov picked up the rubies, one by one, and set them back down again. Then she repeated the process. Finally, she placed the tip of her index finger on one particular stone. "This is it; this is the ruby I shall wear when I walk the ship."

She held the ruby in the palm of her hand and curled her fingers into a fist. Ray reached over and cupped her hand in both of his, staring into her eyes.

"You feel it, too, don't you?" she asked, her eyes shining. "You have the power, too."

"I have a little," Ray admitted. "Maria Valdez told me that much."

"The cat woman?"

"Yes."

<Yes. I see her.>

<You do?>

<Yes, I do. I also see that you two . . . oh . . .>

Ray nodded. Then, feeling a trickle of blood emerge from his right nostril, he took his hands away from hers.

"They make you bleed," she said, wonder in her voice.

"Yes."

"But you are not an ESPer?"

"Not without the rubies, no," Ray replied.

"That is odd," Golnikov told him, the ruby still radiating powerfully in her closed hand.

"It is? Why?"

Golnikov looked away, as if she could not bear to endure his steady gaze when she told him. "They say that those who bleed in the presence of the rubies possess the gift."

"What gift?"

"To go to the center."

Ray was getting impatient. "The center? The center of what?"

Golnikov looked up, meeting his eyes finally. "The center of existence."

Ray got up. "I'm going," he announced.

Golnikov gasped. "You're going?"

"Yes . . . to the bathroom."

Ray grinned a dopey grin and walked away nonchalantly—Mr. Smartass leaving the room. But underneath his facade, he was cold and afraid.

He sensed there were at least two doors to this "center of everything."

One of the two, Ray intuited, was in hyperspace.

★ ★ ★

Ray, Beowulf, and the rest of the dogs looked up as Kate Golnikov trudged slowly into the lounge to strap herself in for their final jump back into hyperspace.

"Everything okay up top?" Ray asked, aware that she would have said something by now if there was something wrong.

"No problemo." Golnikov's voice dripped fatigue.

"We will be jumping back into normal space in exactly two minutes," the ship's computer informed them. "I see everyone is secured."

"We's like bees in a bod," said Sinbad.

"Good," the computer said, all but clucking like a watchful mother hen. The computer knew that if all was well, they'd come out of hyperspace within a few million kilometers of Neverland's binary-star system.

"Ever been to Neverland before, Kate?" Ray asked, hoping to strike up a conversation that would take his mind off jumping.

"Neverland? No, never." She laughed wearily at her own weak pun.

"Well," Ray said. "It's supposed to be the cat's pajamas, the bee's knees, and the way to San Jose."

"Huh?"

"It's supposed to be random," Ray explained, forced to revert to a slang word she *would* understand.

"Oh. Yeah, that's what I've heard from other 'scrapers who have been there."

"Is it true what they say about 'scrapers who arrive there?"

"What do they say?"

"That they have to work the next flight out. That they're about as welcome as itching powder on a nudist planet."

Golnikov laughed, then said, "I heard those rumors, too, and at first I didn't put much credence in them. It's always been my belief—and one that's been borne out over the years—that 'scrapers are as welcome as anyone else just about anywhere as long as they have what it takes." She rubbed her fingers together in a universal gesture and said, "Money talks."

Ray nodded and she continued. "I figured that staying on Neverland probably took a freighter full of money and since most 'scrapers don't have that kind of money, that's why we shipped out as soon as possible." She paused and continued strapping herself in.

Ray sensed that she wasn't finished. "Yeah, so get to the 'but.'"

"Okay. But then I found out that it was true—that 'scrapers were being turned away at the door, so to speak. That we *couldn't* stay on the planet, even if we had the credits to do so." She frowned. "No, that's not right, either. At one time, 'scrapers were free to spend their hard-earned credits there just like anyone else. It's only been in the last three years or so that the more restrictive policy has been in effect."

"Three years?" Ray asked.

"Yeah. That figure have some significance for you?"

Ray was about to reply when a chime sounded and the ship jumped.

"Whoa!!" Ray and the dogs exclaimed. Any thoughts he might have had about the possible importance of the "three years" remark evaporated.

Used to feeling turned inside out, Kate Golnikov closed her

eyes and rested; it took more than a hyperspace-to-normal space jump to get her attention.

"Well, that's our destination," Golnikov said, pointing to the big blue marble floating in the air in front of them.

"That's it?" Ray asked, scratching Beowulf's erect ears.

"That's Neverland in the flesh, so to speak," Ake said. "We're among the relative minority of people who have enough chips to afford this place," he added. "But we're getting in free. I love it!"

"Ake's carrying the first credit he ever earned in his pocket," Ray explained to Golnikov.

"That's not true," Ake said. "It's back in my cabin."

6

"We're being particle-scanned," the computer informed Ake.

"I'd be surprised if we weren't," Ake replied, lounging comfortably in his control chair and nibbling on a piece of fruit.

"I must confess I am impressed by the intensity of the scan and by its thoroughness. Clearly, the system defenses are superb."

Standing behind Ake's chair with Kate Golnikov and Beowulf just to his rear, Ray cleared his throat and said, "Take it from people who know—kilos of money can buy anything. I expected Neverland to have a state-of-the-art defensive system in orbit."

"In orbit, yes," agreed Ake, preparing to push the last of his snack into his mouth. "But we're more than a hop, skip, and a jump away from the planet itself. That they have early warning systems out this far is really impressive."

"We is still a jump away?" asked Beowulf nervously.

"Huh?" said Ake.

Ray thumped Beowulf's sides, whacking the big dog so loudly that Golnikov, still unused to their rough play, flinched. "Ake was only using an old expression, Beowulf," Ray told the normally stoic and undemonstrative leader of his team. "It's not that kind of jump."

"Oh." Beowulf said, clearly relieved.

Golnikov laughed. "Big tough doggies! Scared of jumping!"

Beowulf bared his teeth and growled, "It not smart to pick on a scout dog."

Ray knew that Beowulf was simply playing tit for tat, but he also realized that Golnikov didn't know that, not for sure. "Now, Beowulf," he told his leader. "We've saved up the credits to pay this ESPer—you and Robin don't have to rip her throat out like you did to all the others we owed money to."

Ake swiveled around, saw the numbed expression on Golnikov's face, and laughed. Unsure what response would be appropriate, Golnikov laughed, too. Halfheartedly.

"You rutters!" the computer scolded. "You shouldn't be allowed in polite company."

"Rutters . . . ?" repeated Ray, shooting Ake a look.

Ake shrugged and said, "I've been tinkering with her programming since we have a guest on board. I thought the Iron Maiden needed a little more personality."

"I'd say you succeeded."

"You can worry about me later," the computer told them. "Right now Kate needs to be reassured that Ray and Beowulf were just playing adolescent games. Adolescent *male* games," it added.

Ray immediately went into a "Huck Finn" mode, shoving his hands into his pockets and digging at the carpet with the toe of his boot. "Ah, shucks, Aunt Polly, I shore is sorry I done said sumpthin' wrong. I rilly dint mean nuthin' by it. An' ole dog Shep here is mighty sorry, too."

Golnikov tried to maintain a straight face but couldn't. She made a half-strangled sound and said, "Apology accepted." Then, with a twinkle in her eye, she added, "By the way, Aunt Polly was Tom Sawyer's aunt, not Huck's."

Ray's face lit up. "You read Twain?"

Golnikov nodded. "Despite my rather full social calendar, I do manage to get through a couple of books a week."

That impressed Ray on two levels: first, that she read books instead of falling back on the hol-vee or pissing her life away in realistic but ultimately pointless *VR* escapades, and secondly that she was comfortable enough with herself to allude to her lack of a normal social life.

"Kate reads quality literature, too," confirmed the computer, in whose memory cores the library resided.

"Dickens?" Ray queried. Golnikov nodded. "Borges?" Another nod. "Heinlein?" Another nod. "Ling Tang?"

"Yes, even the poems of Ling Tang."

Ray whistled and Beowulf shot him an annoyed look; the dogs disliked "random" whistling. "Damn, the conversations we could have had!" Ray exclaimed. "I thought you were . . ." A guilty look crossed his face and his voice trailed away.

"You thought I was 'just a 'scraper.'" A smile remained on her face, but it was fixed.

"No. Well . . . I . . . ah, I mean . . ."

"Let me know when we're ready to land," Golnikov said, leaving.

Ray looked at the floor. "Shit," he said softly.

Ake wasn't sure if they were approaching Neverland or falling down the rabbit hole; a heavily guarded rabbit hole. "I wonder why this place is so well protected? I mean, since this location is on the edge of nowhere, someone would have to make a concentrated effort to reach a system this isolated. It doesn't make sense." Ake shook his head.

"What doesn't make sense?" asked Ray, entering the control room with a soft drink in his hand.

"The chains and bolts on the front door of this place."

"Oh." Then Ray sipped his drink and said, "Well, aren't there a lot of incredibly rich or powerful people sitting on the river banks with their toes in the water? A terrorist or kidnapper could bag his or her limit in one day."

Ake threw a startled look in Ray's direction. "Hey, that's a good point. You aren't as dumb as you look, Cisco."

"Who could be?" added the computer dryly.

"What is this, Insult Ray Larkin Day?"

"Every day's a holiday on Neverland," said Ake.

Ray looked at the ceiling as if to say, "Why me, Lord?" Then he suggested, "Maybe I'll just leave and come back in and we'll start over again."

"I have a better idea," said the computer. "Why don't you just leave and *not* come back in?"

Scratching his head and muttering something about losing control, Ray turned and shuffled out of the control room.

"Huckleberries!" exclaimed Ake gleefully. "Were we nasty to him or what?" He tapped the control console as if the computer were literally inside and said, "Maybe I should tweak the reprogramming job I did on you, computer. When you're the equal of Ray in the insult department, something's changed."

"Not yet, please," implored the computer. "This is amusing. It is fun."

"Yeah, fun." Ake looked at the holographic projection of Neverland in the center of the display area; it was growing larger and larger by the minute. "I wonder if we're going to have as much 'fun' down there?"

II

Sighing and pretending to feel unwanted, Ray headed back to be with the dogs. They were eager to see their destination, so Ray called up a holo projection. Although the cockpit was truly the control room, the computer was capable of projecting navigational or other images anywhere on board *The Spirit of St. Louis*.

"Jeez," said Beowulf. "That's a funny planet, hah?"

Ray saw what Beowulf meant. A water world, even more so than Terra, Neverland possessed four modest-sized continents, a few dozen smallish archipelagos, and little else. "You know," he said, "now that I think of it, I've never seen a brochure or atlas or anything that actually showed what Neverland looked like."

"Big secret, hah?" asked Tajil.

"I guess so, Taddy," agreed Ray. He rubbed his chin. "Ah, computer, could you tell us—that is, if you're speaking to me—what sort of landing instructions they're beaming up?"

"Yes, I can."

After a long pause, Ray sighed and said, "Go ahead then, please."

"Do you see this island here, essentially equidistant from the four main land masses?" A speck in the ocean briefly glowed.

"Yeah."

The computer enlarged the small island and anyone but Ray would have said that the speck was barbell-shaped. Undisputed holder of the title "Mr. 20th Century trivia champ," Ray decided that the land mass resembled the hourglass that the Wicked Witch of the West used to show Dorothy how much time remained until her execution.

"This is Midway Island," the computer explained. "The landing field is located here"—one end of the hourglass briefly pulsed—"and the hotel/casino complex is situated here"—the other end of the hourglass now glowed.

"Can you show us any or all of the big islands?"

"No."

"Why not?"

"The port authority computer will not authorize the release of that information."

"What if we took a brief detour and passed over one of the main islands?"

"We would be shot down."

"Golly!" said Frodo.

"I agree," said Ray, staring at the holo and rubbing his chin thoughtfully.

"Well, here we go," Ray said to Ake, Kate Golnikov, and his team. They walked down *The Spirit of St. Louis*'s ramp and into the brilliant midday sunlight. "Yumpin' Yiminy!" Ray said, shielding his eyes against the glare. Since he wasn't wearing so much as a moly-weave vest, he couldn't escape the nagging sensation that he was stark naked.

"Smile, darn ya, smile," Ake chided him as the dogs ran down the ramp ahead of them to take up protective positions.

"I guess I should, shouldn't I?" said Ray, trying out one of the weakest and most insincere smiles Ake had ever seen.

"Yah," agreed Gawain. "We's on a fun planet now. You should be happy."

"See?" said Ake, nudging Ray. "You should be happy."

"Oh, I am. I'm delirious with joy."

"What are you two blathering about?" asked Golnikov as a small floater containing a woman and two men approached the ship. One of the men had flaming red hair and pale skin, much like Ake's.

"Ray's become so used to blasting his way into places that simply walking in unarmed unnerves him," Ake explained to the ESPer. Ray pointed to his needle gun strapped to his wrist and gestured at his right boot, where his bush knife was hidden. "*Almost* unarmed, that is," Ake added with a grin.

The floater carrying the welcoming trio slowed and settled gently to the ground. The three got out and approached the group warily, eying the dogs with a certain amount of apprehension.

"Scout dogs," the flame-haired man said. Ray now saw that while the young man shared Ake's hair color he was neither as thin nor as tall as Ake. "I thought they were all but extinct." Ray didn't like his tone of voice.

"We *look* like we's eggs-stink to you?" challenged Robin.

"Remember your place," Beowulf rumbled.

"Sorry."

"Please excuse Dilon," the woman said, exchanging a look with the young man that could have bored a hole through moly-steel. She slowly extended her left hand and allowed Beowulf to sniff it. Ray approved her good sense. "Dilon is not only my assistant-in-training but also very young. He is still learning the importance of manners."

Dilon made a token effort to appear properly abashed. "I meant to give no offense."

Sure, Ray thought. *And fish don't piss in the water.*

"None taken," said Ake smoothly. *Not on my part, kid. Ray'll probably want to toast your tongue on a fork.*

"Thank you," the woman said. She had brown hair interlaced with gray and tiny lattices of wrinkles under and around her eyes which became apparent when she smiled. There was a living adornment piercing one of her nostrils, an emerald jewel bug. The jewel bug was a tasteful if blatant proclamation to the world concerning her status and wealth. "I am Leandra Boosra, Neverland's manager. This is Aron Ku'brol, our head of security"—the other man with her, a compact, sturdily built individual with piercing black eyes, nodded slightly—"and you have, of course, already met Dilon Lanskgaard."

"Pleased to meet you," replied Ake. He indicated Kate and said, "This is Katerina Golnikov." Shifting from one foot to another, he added unnecessarily, "Our 'scraper." Golnikov nodded but said nothing. "And this gentleman is Ray Larkin, my partner."

"How do," Ray said, tapping his forehead with two fingers—like a Star Scout giving his superior a salute.

"And I am Ake Ringgren." Ake inclined his head slightly, as if bowing to royalty.

<*Don't overdo the humility bit,*> Ray told Ake. <*She ain't the Queen of Sheba.*>

"Are you two—" began Dilon Lanskgaard.

"Yes, we are," said Ray.

"But you don't know—"

"Yes, I do," Ray finished again.

"From all I've heard from my old friend, Natasha Bukovsky," said Boosra, "these gentlemen cannot be anyone *but* whom they say they are—the infamous Ringgren-Larkin scout team."

"See," Ray told Ake. "You got first billing this time." Privately, he transmitted <*Why's she acting like she just now found out who we are? Surely Webster told her who his guests would be.>*

<*One would think so,*> Ake beamed back.

"What 'bout us?" queried Frodo.

"And their famous dogs," Boosra added.

Ray looked at Beowulf and silently mouthed, *Famous?* Beowulf grinned crookedly.

"Jeez," said Gawain, beaming proudly.

"Watch it," chided Frodo, "Gawain is gettin' a swell head."

"Swelled," corrected Ray absently. *She knows Bukovsky,* he told himself.

"Where is our host," asked Ake. "Where is the esteemed Harris Webster?"

"Mr. Webster is waiting for us at the hotel. Since his return to Neverland, he has not left the main complex." She paused and glanced at her two companions. Then she said, "The incident—his near incarceration on Cromwell's prison satellite—appears to have strongly affected him. Harris is not himself these days; he seems a less voluble and optimistic man since his awful experience."

Ake looked at Ray, who shrugged noncommittally but said privately <*Yeah, he was forced to use his salad fork for the main course. Who could experience an outrage like that and not be affected?*>

<*Behave yourself. He's a nice man.*>

"I'm sorry to hear that," Ake told Boosra. "But why are you telling us all this? Heroes of the universe though we might be, we're still strangers."

"I . . . I don't know," Boosra confessed. She looked confused. "I thought since you two—"

"Ahem," said Beowulf.

Boosra smiled. "I thought since your team came to his rescue once, you might do it again. Perhaps you can help us to find some way to get him to come out of his shell, to become the man he once was."

"Hey, we're Spanky and Our Gang," Ray told her. "If we can't jolly him up, no one can."

Boosra seemed not to know what to say to that, so she simply said, "May I introduce you to the wonders of Neverland?"

"Yes, you may," Ake beamed.

"Ah, are you folks armed?" asked security chief Ku'brol. He

spoke Fed-stan English with a thick but not immediately recognizable accent.

"That depends," Ray said after thinking the question over for a moment. "Do needle guns count?"

Before Ku'brol could reply, Boosra made a tiny, almost imperceptible gesture. Ray thought that Ku'brol's charcoal eyes flashed in annoyance but he couldn't be sure. Ray glanced at the restive Robin and guessed that the security chief and the red dog had certain traits in common—the foremost being a desire to kill every suspicious stranger up front and sort the innocent from the guilty later.

"Yes and no," answered Ku'brol, looking first at Boosra and then at Ray and Ake. "While we frown upon weapons in the main areas, we are realistic about their presence. Many of our clients understandably wish to retain the means to defend themselves should the need arise."

Ake said, "Even though you believe that your off- and onplanet defenses are more than adequate to any threat?"

"Precisely," agreed Ku'brol, pleased that someone recognized the challenge to his competence in the implication that guests might need their own weapons.

"To answer your question directly, then," Ray said to Ku'brol. "Yes, we both wear needle guns and I also have been known to carry a bush knife or a quiver blade in my boot."

"You are afraid of attack, even with your dogs to protect you?" Lanskgaard said, not quite sneering.

Ray smiled disarmingly. It was so broad and warm a smile that it made Beowulf nervous—he'd seen that smile before and knew that behind it Ray could be preparing to do anything. In this case, however, all Ray did was say, "My body weapons have saved my life on more than one occasion. If you had done your homework and were as knowledgeable about my professional history as I think your superiors are, you would not need to inquire into the matter."

Aware that Robin was edging closer and closer to Lanskgaard, Ray turned his head slightly and brushed a finger across his cheek. Robin nodded and slowly backed off. Ray observed that while Lanskgaard was oblivious of all this, neither Boosra nor Ku'brol was.

"You must be wondering if you're going to be spending your entire stay standing here on the landing grid," said Boosra finally, clapping her hands together.

"I *had* heard there was more to the planet," said Ray amiably.

"Come, then," Boosra said. "We must begin again in order to make you feel welcome on Neverland."

As if waiting on Boosra's words, a large floater appeared from nowhere and settled to the ground in front of them. Ray's and Kate Golnikov's jaws dropped, and even Ake was impressed by the luxurious-looking floater. Giving the fifteen-by-five-meter platform an appreciative glance, Ake guessed that Daae-Fujiwara negative-gravity motors alone must have cost a fortune.

Boosra had anticipated their reactions and explained, "We call this particular people-mover *Cleopatra's Barge*."

"An apt name," Golnikov said.

In addition to a wide variety of chairs and sofas, the floater carried a complement of domestic 'bots and what appeared to be three or four human attendants. Seeing their physical perfection, even at a distance, Ake wondered if they were humans or android pleasure units.

"Please climb aboard our welcome wagon and make yourselves comfortable," Boosra told them.

"Even us big hairy dogs?" asked Beowulf.

"Even you big hairy dogs," laughed Boosra.

The dogs sniffed the floater cautiously, and Beowulf was the first to climb aboard. He quickly trotted from one end to the other, smelling and inspecting until he was sure things were as innocuous as they seemed to be.

After both Frodo and Grendel joined him and agreed that all appeared well, Beowulf said, "Okay. C'mon up, everyone."

While Ku'brol's sour expression was evidence that he disliked having his security arrangements second-guessed by dogs, no matter how intelligent they might be, he said nothing and simply followed the others aboard the floater.

When a long-legged young blonde woman handed Ake a glass of white wine as he boarded, he accepted it gratefully and turned to Ray and said, "I could get to like this kind of treatment."

Ray nodded as he accepted a tall, frosted gin and tonic from the same beautiful woman. "Beats a sharp stick in the eye any day."

Gawain sniffed indelicately at the blonde woman and then asked with absolutely no hesitation, "Hey, is you a robot?"

Ray immediately had two reactions: One was *Ouch!* But the second one was *Thanks for asking the question I wanted to ask, Gawain—if I had the nerve to be so rude.*

"Yes and no. I'm an android," the blonde said, smiling broadly and warmly at Gawain. "I can see that you're a scout dog. Are *you* real?"

Gawain drew back in amazement. "Jeez, yah! Doan I look real?"

"You look perfectly real," the android replied. "Don't *I* look real, too?"

"Yah," Gawain had to admit. "But you doan *smell* like a real person."

"That may be," the android replied, turning her megawatt smile on Ake, "but I can do almost everything a human woman can." She paused for effect. "I can even do some things no 'real' woman can do—not unless she's a contortionist."

Ake gulped and colored to match his hair.

"Damn plastic prosties," Kate Golnikov muttered under her breath. Feeling a light, yet firm touch on her arm, she turned.

"Are you with anyone special, or are you presently unattached?" asked the most handsome man Golnikov had ever seen—and she'd seen plenty of them.

He's an android, an artificial being, Kate Golnikov thought. Then, even though she knew this handsome hunk who looked searchingly into her eyes while he awaited her response wasn't really a human being, Kate Golnikov suddenly decided it didn't matter all that much after all. "I . . . I'm unattached," she finally got out, dropping her gaze demurely.

"I would be delighted to show you around when we get to the hotel," the handsome android said. Golnikov decided he had the squarest jaw she'd ever seen on anyone outside a romance hol-vee.

"Thank you. I'd like that very much."

Sensing someone coming up behind him, Ray slowly turned to see what "she" looked like. *I'm not going to get all excited by a goddamned machine*, he promised himself. *I'm not. I . . .* Then he saw it/her. *Arnold H. Christ! Take me now, Jesus, take me now!*

III

The pleasure barge's journey was not a long one, but it seemed to take forever to Beowulf and the other dogs. Beowulf had rarely seen Ray drop his guard so quickly. The big dog guessed that there were several explanations for this uncharacteristic lapse. First, Ray had been at so high a level of awareness for such a long time that to expect him to keep it up indefinitely was unrealistic. Second, or so it seemed to Beowulf, Ray *wanted* to believe that he had found a safe haven, a place where he could let his hair and his guard down. Until Ray reverted to his old, suspicious self, Beowulf reminded himself that *I will hafta be 'specially alert.*

While Ray, Ake, and Kate Golnikov focused most of their attentions on their hosts—and Beowulf fretted—the other dogs marveled at the impressive scenery.

"Jeez, lookit that!" exclaimed Sinbad as the barge floated serenely down the middle of a roadway surrounded on both sides by huge, sculpted flora. "Is them things trees or what?"

"I think so," said Mama-san.

"How comes they looks like monsters and witches and other weird things?" asked Gawain, staring at the branches, bent and twisted into bizarre shapes.

"I dunno, Gawain," replied Mama-san. "I think that one there is 'sposed to be a whale, and that one beside it looks like a ship."

"A ship? Ya mean a spaceship?"

"Nah, a pirate ship."

"Oh."

"Stop rubber-nekkin' and pay attention to what might be *under* or *behind* them trees," Beowulf admonished the team. "Since Ray and Ake's too busy makin' gooney eyes at fake beoples to see trouble comin', we gots to be extra careful."

"Yah," agreed Robin. "Jes' cause this place looks peaceful, that doan mean it is."

"Beowulf and Robin is right," agreed Tajil. "We should act like scout dogs."

"Jes' one thing," Gawain asked Grendel in a low voice. "What kinda guy is *that* plant 'sposed to be?"

Grendel looked. "I'm not sure," she whispered back, "but I think it's a knight."

"A knight?"

"You know—King Archer and the Knights of the Roun' Table."

"Oh."

7

"Please," said Ray as the android, who had said to call "her" Marla, pressed firmly against him and attempted to nuzzle his cheek. "You must stop this." He gulped. "Right now," he added unconvincingly.

"Why?" she whispered, not stopping.

Maybe the dogs could tell the androids weren't human, but Marla sure as hell smelled like a woman to him. Nonetheless, Ray gently pushed her away. "You're very persuasive, I must admit, but you're just wires and cables and plasteel covered by a petroplastic exodermis. As your—friend—confessed to Gawain, you're not real."

The android woman looked into his eyes and said, "While I am not human, I am as real as you are . . . simply different. You are tendons and blood vessels and bone covered by a fragile outer wrapping of skin. We are both intelligent beings whose mental processes are the result of complex electrochemical reactions."

"Stop that," Ray said, removing the android's roving hand.

"Why do you resist?" the android asked.

"I never liked shooting fish in a barrel."

"Shooting fish in a barrel?" The beautiful android's brow wrinkled—perfectly, Ray had to admit.

"It's just an expression, honey."

"I see."

Ray smiled. "There's another giveaway. You didn't slap my face or at least complain when I called you 'honey.'" *Actually, Ray thought, That's not necessarily true in this instance; "escorts," human or not, are rarely insulted when you call them things like "honey."*

"But don't you find me attractive?" the android asked, pursing "her" lips and pressing her perfectly proportioned body even more firmly against his. Ray could feel her erect nipples against his chest. A part of him with a mind of its own began to press back.

"Ah, as you can probably . . . ah, sense, I find you very attractive," Ray said, staring into her turquoise eyes. "At least, the 'caped crusader' does."

"Well, then . . . ?"

"Darlin', read my lips—you're not real. Nobody as drop-dead gorgeous as you would find this little Pennsylvania Dutch boy to be her dream hunk. Not before you even know who I am."

"So who are you?" the android asked in a breathy, husky voice that made Ray want to bite her neck.

"Rudolph Valentino—but that's not important." Ray carefully disengaged himself from the android's embrace. "What's important is that there might be someone here—a real woman—who will find me attractive for myself and not because she's been programmed to stroke my . . . ah, ego."

The stunning android pouted. "So you don't wish to play with me."

"Oh, I do, I do!"

"But you said—"

"I *want* to, sure, but I'm not going to."

Meanwhile, Frodo was edging closer and closer to the couple, trying to be inconspicuous. The black-and-white dog had several questions he wished to ask Ray. Awaiting an opportune time to interrupt, Frodo could not help overhearing Ray's conversation with Marla.

"Why not?" the android pouted.

"If you want the truth, I'm in a long-term relationship," Ray said in a confidential tone. Frodo's ears went on full alert.

"With whom?" she asked.

Ray held up his right hand and flexed his fingers. "The two of us have been an item since I was a teenager. Even if Betty Jo or

Mary Lou said no I always had a date." Seeing Frodo gawking at him, Ray gave the dog a big wink.

Frodo looked at Ray, then at Ray's hand, then at the android woman . . . and burst out laughing so hard everyone on the barge turned to look.

Ray's android companion reluctantly acquiesced to his wishes and ceased directing at least some of her unwanted attentions at him. He decided to look at the passing scenery. Only now did he take note of the spectacularly shaped trees that had so amazed the dogs. But the trees weren't the half of it. The floater was progressing at a stately pace down a ribbon of plascrete that snaked through an ever-changing landscape, a landscape of the imagination.

While they ascended and descended gentle hills, objects at the side of the road came to life. That wasn't quite true, Ray decided. The roadside attractions were clearly animated just before they came into view, thereby giving the illusion that they were perpetually in motion. Having figured that out, Ray then guessed that they ceased putting on their show as soon as the floater had passed by.

"What is all them things, Ray?" Beowulf asked, relieved that Ray had finally decided to pay attention to the surroundings.

"Previews," Ray replied. "Coming attractions."

"Ya mean they is what's on them bigger islands?"

"I think so."

"They's not real."

"No, they aren't."

Beowulf and the other dogs stared as a green-clad teenaged boy, followed by several children in nightclothes, flew up beside the floater and paralleled it for a few minutes, waving and smiling.

"Is that . . . ?" began Grendel.

"Yah, Beter Ban," said Ozma.

Ray glanced in Ozma's direction, pleased that this unexpected show had made her forget about Littlejohn for a while.

A tiny dot of light that seemed to be trailing golden specks of fire like a Fall of the Federation Day sparkler joined the children and the impish-looking boy and they waved one last time, pulled up in midair, and watched the floater leave them behind.

"Yikes!" exclaimed Robin. "Lookit that!"

Just coming into view were several massive reptilian forms.

K-9 CORPS: THE LAST RESORT 75

"Wow," said Ray appreciatively. "Those are damned impressive holos, aren't they?"

"Yah," agreed Gawain, unconsciously assuming a semisubmissive stance. In contrast, Robin assumed a fighting stance, even though he was aware that the giant reptiles weren't real. Acting as instinctively as Gawain, his upper lip began to curl back to reveal his teeth. Several of the other dogs followed his lead and bared their fangs.

Even Ake disentangled himself from his newfound friend to stare at the awesome primordial creatures that now flanked the floater. "Hey, what's going on?" he asked Ray.

"Just a little advance look-see of what's available in the theme parks," Ray told him. "Nothing important. You can go back to sucking face with your living doll."

Ake colored and Ray felt a twinge of regret for twitting him. "My acceptance of our hosts', ah, hospitality may seem a little out of character for me," he admitted. "But remember what happened to me on Cromwell. At least 'Marilyn' doesn't have a husband with a slug-thrower."

"There is that," Ray conceded.

Just as the holos of Peter, Wendy, and the lost boys had flown within a few meters of the floater, several pterodactyls now swooped in to eye them suspiciously.

"Is them birds or what?" queried Sinbad.

"They're the ancestors of birds," Ray explained. "They're flying dinosaurs—pterodactyls."

"Terry-dack-tills?" repeated Sinbad, rolling the word around in his mouth. "Terry-dack-tills." He liked the sound of it.

A mother triceratops, a holo programmed to be "protective" of five smaller versions of herself, made several bluff charges at the floater, each time stopping short and retreating before again lowering her head and faking another rush.

"Gets the adrenaline going, doesn't it?" Ray said to Beowulf. "I know none of this is real, but seeing one of those babies heading in your direction sure loosens you up."

"I dint see the babies charge," said Gawain.

"Well, no, they didn't, Gawain," began Ray. "When I said babies, I meant . . . oh, never mind."

"Okay."

"Boy, they's more than jes' holos, ain't they?" said Mama-san, wrinkling her nose at the rank reptilian odor.

"Yeah, they go all out to be realistic," Ray agreed. "Maybe too realistic."

Before long, the dinosaurs, including a Tyrannosaurus and several awkwardly graceful Barosauri, gave way to yet another display.

"Wow!" said Sinbad as a propeller-driven airplane with a red circle on its fuselage flashed overhead, pursued closely by another flying machine, each of its wings bearing a single white star. They could hear the telltale stutter of machine guns.

"Hey, what are those?" asked Kate Golnikov, coming up for air.

"Fighter planes," Ray said, his head following their airborne dance. "They're aircraft from World War Two."

"World War Two?"

"That's what Terra's second major multinational conflict of the twentieth century was called," Ray explained.

"So what are they doing here?" Golnikov asked, frowning.

"You honestly have no idea?"

"Honestly."

"I think they're representative of a 'war' park."

"A war park!" Golnikov rolled her eyes. "I don't believe it. Rutters!" she snorted.

Ray shrugged. *Hey, I'm just explaining it, not endorsing it*, he thought. As far as he was concerned, coming to Neverland to spend your time playing anachronistic war games was an odd choice. But then, he considered, not everyone led a scout dog team and found himself in more than enough life-and-death situations without having to seek out phony ones.

"The war park," said Ray to no one in particular, "if that's what it is, is probably a prime destination for regimen-bound money accumulators who lust after action and adventure the same way I'm looking forward to a nice uneventful rest."

"Not *too much* rest," begged Sinbad.

"That hasn't been a problem for me yet," Ray responded.

"Hey, lookit that!" shouted Tajil.

Ray looked and saw that the floater was being followed by a woman on a bicycle—only she was bicycling a few meters above the road.

"Hot damn!" exclaimed Ray. "It's Miss Gulch!"

"Who?" asked Tajil.

"'Nother Ozzy character," explained Beowulf.

"Yeah," Ray agreed. As they watched, she pulled up alongside of them. Her image shimmered and suddenly she was a green-skinned witch riding a broomstick instead of a prim spinster sitting atop her bicycle.

"Golly!" said Gawain.

The witch unleashed a loud, crackling laugh and pointed a long finger in Ray's direction. "I'll get you, you interfering pest, just you wait and see." She glanced around the floater. "And your little dogs, too!" With a final cackle, she vanished in a cloud of black smoke.

Ray laughed uneasily and said to Marla, "I know it's only a holo, kinda like a haunted house at Halloween, but I must admit the witch gave me a cheap thrill."

The android nodded. "It was strange, though."

Ray made a face. "Strange? How was it strange?"

"The witch always appears at this point in the journey, it's part of the show, but I don't believe I ever heard her say anything before. How odd."

"Hehhehheh," Ray laughed uneasily.

II

They passed through the neck of the hourglass, a high pass that allowed the passengers to see the vast ocean on either side of the narrow strip of land.

After the road snaked through vast fields of red, violet, yellow, and white poppies, the plasglas towers of the hotel/casino finally came into view. Ray was impressed. Reaching high into the sky, the hotel complex vaguely resembled Emerald City gleaming in the distance.

"I take it that's our destination?" Ray asked the android temptress who had not completely given up trying to seduce him.

When she stuck her tongue—and it felt as warm and moist as a real tongue—into his ear, he pulled away in surprise and asked, irritated, "Why do you do that sort of thing without prior arrangement? Don't you ever run into folks from Cromwell or Cristos? I should think they would find such behavior unseemly, to say the least."

"Oh, they're the most receptive," Marla cooed.

"I guess I shoulda figured that," Ray said sourly.

"What a grumpus."

"Knock it off or I'll buy you and pull all your wires out."

"I haven't any wires, I'm—"

"A pain in the butt," finished Ray.

Marla looked exasperated. "I *am* a very sophisticated model, Ray."

"Can you play a mean game of chess?"

"Clothed or unclothed?"

Ray shook his head. "You never give up, do you?"

"No," she mouthed more than spoke.

"Well, I never give in, either."

"The irresistible force meeting the immovable object?"

"Yeah, I guess so."

"Round one goes to you," the android woman conceded.

"Oh, what's my prize?"

"Me."

Ray's exasperated bellow made the dogs look his way in concern.

III

Their android companions reluctantly bid them farewell, at least for the time being. Ray would have expected to see them again even if Marla hadn't promised to look him up once he was settled into the hotel. "Here's looking at you, kid," Ray said to Marla as they parted.

"Goodbye, dearest Ray."

"Forget me, find someone else—you're still young," Ray told the gorgeous android. "Remember, we'll always have Paris."

"Forget you, Ray? Never."

"That's what I'm afraid of."

The hotel. Although they had spent years of their lives flitting around the galaxy, from one far-flung and underpopulated planet to another, Ray and Ake had been inside their share of luxury establishments. Even so, nothing they'd seen had prepared them for the Neverland hotel and casino. Later, Ray was to reflect that it had reminded him of nothing so much as a vulgar Terran desert resort town called Las Vegas.

They were met at the door by two giants in Queen's Guards' uniforms, their height made even more imposing by their tall headpieces.

"Algarrans?" Ake asked Ku'brol, assuming the two had to be from a planet which routinely produced such specimens.

"That's correct, Dr. Ringgren," Ku'brol replied. Suddenly

voluble, the security chief continued, "At first we considered that the job would prove to be too tedious for humans, but after an abortive assassination attempt almost succeeded when our robotic doormen could not respond appropriately because of the injunction against robotic violence, we were forced to alter our staffing. Since then we have relied exclusively on humans."

The guards' eyes followed them like the eyes in a holoportrait, and Ray felt a tinge of discomfort. Then he looked at the dogs and was reassured by the knowledge that the pack could tear the giant Algarrans limb from limb in seconds.

"I'll take my leave now," Ku'brol said, backing away as the massive, ten-meters-high front doors ponderously swung open.

"Yeah, catch ya later," Ray said absently.

Inside, things became even more impressive. For one thing, there was a lot of empty space. Actually, Ray reconsidered, the reception area was empty of people but otherwise boasted exquisitely designed and finished furniture.

The nearest wall emitted a faint, warm glow. "Photogenic bacteria?" Ray asked. Ake nodded. "I thought so," Ray said.

The bacteria's carefully considered colors contributed to the interior's welcoming atmosphere. It was almost *too* welcoming in Ake's mind. It made him want nothing so much as to plop gratefully into one of the inviting chairs or sofas, sip a white wine, and closely examine the insides of his eyelids.

Hearing Ake sigh, Ray nudged him and said, "Stay awake, Sniffles, or you won't get to see Santa come down the chimney with the gifts."

Seeing Beowulf's and the other dogs' noses wrinkle as they sniffed the air, Ray guessed that the climate control was probably pumping soothing and tension-dissipating pheromones into the air. The dogs could sense them, but the pheromones had no effect on canine moods since they were human-targeted.

"Wow," said Kate Golnikov. "Where's the people-mover to take us to the reservations desk?"

"The lobby and reception area *is* quite large," Boosra said. "Since the identities of our guests are known and confirmed before their arrival here, however, there is no need for a reservations desk."

"And you have no 'drop-ins,' I guess," Ray said. "No one saying, 'Me and my life companion were just passing by when we seen your sign and thought we might stop in and see if you could fix us up with a double for the night.'"

Ignoring Ray, Ake asked, "You confirm via retinal scans?"

"Yes . . . on the barge," Boosra replied. Then, turning to face Lanskgaard, she said, "You may leave us now, Dilon." The surly youth turned on his heel and strode away, clearly as pleased to be leaving them as they were to see him go.

<*If they knew all along that we were coming, why the feigned surprise at our identities when we arrived?*> Ray queried Ake.

<*It's probably just an act. You know, to be social, to make conversation with the guests when they arrive.*>

<*Uh-huh.*>

Boosra now set out across the wide expanse of carpet. As Ray felt himself sinking into its luxurious pile, he wondered whether it was a synthetic or a natural fiber.

"This carpet is wonderful," said Golnikov. "What is it?" she asked, conveniently saving Ray the effort of posing the question himself.

"Bascane," Boosra replied.

That impressed Ray. The sheeplike bascane were renowned for their superior wool . . . *and* for their sweet and tender flesh. Bascane wool was extremely pricey because the highest grade came only from free-range animals—and it seemed that nothing aroused the hunting instincts of predators more than the scent of a herd of timid, slow-moving, and altogether stupid bascane. Since scout dog teams—not robots—made the best shepherds, the wool and meat cost those with a desire for it dearly.

"There must be hundreds of square meters of carpet in this one area alone," Golnikov marveled.

"That's correct," Boosra replied. "And each guest suite is similarly appointed."

They approached some large, treelike plants growing out of a small oasis of soil. Just beyond the plants, a robotic quartet was playing soothing nineteenth- and twenty-first-century chamber music for an audience of two: a man and a woman sitting in individual cuddle chairs. The man was a mountainous mass of fish belly–white flesh poured into a tuxedo whose seams apparently had the strength of polysteel. He had one of those strange single-tuft-of-hair beards that Ray found particularly unattractive. The woman, garbed in a simple evening gown that shrieked expense, was smoking a long black cigarette, and looked like the guest of honor at a wake—shocking red lipstick painted onto a heavily rouged face that might have seen Apollo 9 lift off.

"Hello," Boosra said as they walked past.

The couple smiled faintly and continued nodding their heads to the music.

When they were out of earshot, Ray asked Boosra, "I take it there's a convention of the undead at the hotel?" This was followed by a mild "Woof" as Ake's elbow to his side momentarily knocked the air out of his lungs. Boosra apparently made up her mind that no response was the best response.

The small group turned a corner and was confronted by an undersea vista that left them momentarily flabbergasted.

"A holoscenic?" Ray asked, rubbing his side where Ake's too-sharp elbow had poked him.

"Actually, no," Boosra replied. "It's a plasglas tank that holds several million liters of water."

Inside, great fishes glided effortlessly through the crystalline water, propelling themselves with almost imperceptible flicks of their fins and tails. Schools of fish as brightly hued as the kitschy neon signs that had recently become popular again stuttered right and left, up and down, moving like a score of bodies sharing one sensibility among them. Ancient-looking sea turtles, as gracefully mobile in the water as they were awkward and stiff on land, languidly stroked their way through the translucent water, staring out at the visitors with wise and world-weary expressions. They gave the impression of seeing all with their large, knowing eyes.

There were other sea creatures in the tank, as well.

"Hey, is them beoples?" asked Gawain, his voice full of wonder.

Ray saw what prompted the big dog's question: long-haired sirens with fish tails. Mermaids.

"No, not really," answered Boosra. "They are actually genetically manipulated fish. They look deceptively human, but the resemblance is only skin deep."

"Does one need a license to go fishing?" Ray asked Boosra.

In addition to causing Ozma to snuffle loudly, Ray's question seemed to baffle Boosra. "Ah . . . fishing?"

"Never mind," Ray said, waving a hand. "I wouldn't know which end to—"

"Yeah, right," Ake interrupted. "Let's finish the grand tour later. I could do with a hot shower and something to put in my stomach after the wine I had on the floater."

"I guess that's a request for no further ado," Ray said, watching Golnikov nod her head in agreement. "As for myself,

I'm always up for further ado. However, I yield to the wishes of my delegation in this matter."

Beowulf hooted at that, guessing that Ray was being contrary. The big dog assumed that Ray was just as bone-weary as himself, Ake, and the rest of the team.

"Good," said Frodo. "I's hungry as a cholo."

"Lead on, McDuff," Ray said to the thoroughly flummoxed Boosra.

8

After a striking-looking woman appeared out of nowhere and led Kate Golnikov down a corridor to her own suite, Ray, Ake, and the dogs were shown to theirs by Boosra.

The suite was dazzling, the sort of accommodations for which the word "luxurious" had been invented. An entryway led into a spacious reception area with chairs, sofas, more bascane carpeting, stunning original artworks both on the walls and placed around the room, a fully stocked bar, scads of state-of-the-art communications and copying machines, and a three-meter-high fireplace—"I guess that's for when we want to roast a pig," Ake observed.

After sticking his head through double doors into the main living area just beyond, Ray turned to their host and joked, "I suppose these sparse quarters will have to do us until our real rooms are ready."

More used to Ray's constant banter by now, Boosra replied, "That's right. This suite is part of our animal companion accommodations and is intended for your team. Your rooms aren't made up yet." The dogs grinned; this new lady was quickly learning how to talk to Ray.

After making a "tsk, tsk," sound, Ray said, "Nah, you can't fool me. If this is for the dogs, where's the dead varmint carcass for these fuzzbutts to roll around on?"

"I'm afraid you have me there," conceded Boosra.

There was a knock at the door, and Boosra admitted several tall and muscular hotel staffers bearing some of their belongings from the ship.

Watching them manhandle the luggage and trunks with ease, Ake had a sudden suspicion. "Say, are these guys androids, too?"

<Good one, Ake,> Ray told him privately. <I always loved it when I was a kid and grownups talked about me as if I was in a coma or not standing there in the same room with them.>

<You're right,> Ake conceded. <Of course, if they are androids, they won't care.>

Although the young men ignored Ake's question and continued with their efforts, Boosra answered him. "No, they are not androids," she said. "They're as human as you or I."

"Wow," said Beowulf. "That makes 'em twicet as human as Ray!"

"Remind me to murderize you later," Ray said, but his mind was on other things. He was beginning to see why and how the costs added up to make this place perhaps the most expensive destination in the galaxy. In an age of cheap robotic labor, it was both inefficient and costly to use humans in "demeaning" roles usually reserved for machines. He guessed that these men—*what's the old term for them? Yeah, now I remember: "bellhops"*—were well paid to perform their menial tasks.

"Do we tip?" Ray asked Boosra. Before she could answer, he turned to the bellhops and said, "We know you're here and you have ears. Honest." A faint smile lifted the corners of one man's mouth.

"There is no tipping permitted until you leave."

Ray looked at Boosra and tugged at his earlobe. "What if I want to ensure good service for my whole stay?"

"On Neverland, it is not necessary to bribe the employees to do their jobs correctly," she answered stiffly.

"I guess there's a first time for everything," shrugged Ray. Then, leaning over to whisper conspiratorially—but still loud enough for the others to hear—into the ear of the bellhop who'd almost smiled, he said, "I'm going to check for peepholes in the shower; I don't want anyone getting his or her jollies by eyeballing my naughty bits."

The bellhop looked puzzled.

"I beg your pardon, sir?"

"You do? Well, you're forgiven, just don't let it happen again."

Sensing that Ray was becoming even more hyper than usual, Ake said to Boosra, "Unless there's anything else you have to tell us, I think we need to be alone now and unwind, if you don't mind."

"Certainly," Boosra said. She had an odd, slightly stunned look on her face. "You need to know where things are, of course, and to become acquainted with the hotel and the parks, but that can wait." She glanced at Ray as if she was afraid he might say or do something else.

"Thank you," Ake said. He followed behind Boosra and the two bellhops as they walked to the door. He saw them out and then turned back and faced Ray with a cat-and-canary look on his face.

"Yeah?" asked Ray, puzzled. "What is it?"

"Your naughty bits!" said Ake, collapsing in helpless laughter.

"Well, for heaven's sake," said Ray, drawing himself up like an affronted society matron. Which made Ake laugh all the harder.

Robin looked at Beowulf. "It too late to join 'nother team?"

★ ★ ★

They soon discovered that the suite really was enormous, each room opening into one or two others of impressive size. For security's sake, the place of windows were taken by magnificent floor-to-ceiling holoscenics. There were a total of eight rooms— counting the three bedrooms but not the bathrooms or dressing rooms. Each bedroom was connected to its own bathroom and its own dressing room. Ake had glanced at the rows of hangers and cubicles for shoes in his dressing room and laughed.

"What's tickling your funny bone now?" Ray wondered, ambling in and peering around.

"Look at the size of this dressing room," Ake said. "If you and I put in all the clothes we have with us, got married and had seven kids each, and put our wives' and children's clothes in here, we'd still have room enough left over to hangar *The Spirit of St. Louis*."

"Pretty impressive," Ray agreed.

"Hey, what's that in your hand?" Ake queried.

"My dowsing rod," Ray replied, holding the Y-shaped piece of wood up for Ake's inspection.

"Your dowsing rod?"

Ray stuck a thumb in the middle of his own chest and jabbed.

"Remember, *I* have the power. Especially when I'm packin' my rubies."

"*Are* you packing your rubies?"

Ray inserted the tip of his left index finger just inside his left nostril, withdrew it, and held it out for Ake to see.

"Blood?"

"Yeah. The rubies are charging my 'power' cells, all right."

"And what are you going to do with that power . . . Carrie?"

Ray was impressed even though he'd been on a DePalma kick lately and Ake had seen him watching some of the old sinnys.

"Very good, Professor Backwards, very good indeed."

"Well?"

"I'm going hunting."

"Hunting? For what?"

"Allegories along the Nile."

"C'mon, be serious for once."

"Oh, awright. For bugs."

"Bugs?"

"Try here," Ray said when the stick moved in his hands and the tip pointed at a lighting fixture. It was the oddest sensation, Ray decided. It was like holding a small but muscular animal that squirmed and wiggled in an effort to pull from your grasp. The stick became a living thing when confronted with what its holder was searching for.

"Yassir, boss," Ake said. He got down on his hands and knees and felt around in the thick carpeting. "Ah, hah!" he said triumphantly. A one-centimeter-square patch of carpeting lifted up. Underneath was a small electronic device the size of a pinhead. "We found your missing brain," Ake informed Ray.

"How many zat?" Beowulf wondered.

Putting this most recent prize with the others, Ake silently counted them up. "Eleven so far."

"Leven!" exclaimed Tajil.

"Want to bet we're not done yet?" Ake asked. Since Ake's offer was a sucker bet, there were no takers.

"They sure doan wanna miss a word you'uns two say, huh?" Beowulf said, shaking his big shaggy head.

"We're such sparkling conversationalists, who would?" intoned Ray, feigning sincerity. That made Beowulf shake his head even more vigorously.

"C'mon," Ake implored his partner. "On to the next one."

Ray sighed, held the dowsing rod out in front of him, concentrated, and followed the stick's authoritative pull. "Looks like we got another one," he said as the dowsing rod led him to the toiletries cabinet in Ake's bathroom.

As Ake moved soap, depilatory cream, and other sundries around, Ray waved him off. Puzzled, Ake stepped back and allowed Ray to take his place in front of the cabinet.

"Ah, Mr. Ku'brol, this is Ray Larkin. When we're done doing this, we'd like not to have to go through it again. You can help by not trying to rebug our suite, okay? Thanks. We'll see there's something extra in your envelope come payday."

Looking tired, Ake asked, "Are you done?"

"Yepper. Let's hurry up and pinpoint this one so we can move on."

"How many ya think there are?" asked Tajil.

"Bill-yons and bill-yons, Taddy," Ray said wearily.

"Really?"

"A slight exaggeration. And I sure as hell hope there aren't too many more or someone's gonna be picking some of these out of his butt if I have to spend another ten minutes playing this asinine game."

After they had swept the suite clean of recording devices, they finally relaxed. In a perverse way, Ray had to admire the ingenuity of whoever had concealed all thirteen bugs so cleverly.

"What now?" asked Grendel.

"Sleep. Sleep to knit together our unraveled psyches."

"Oh."

II

Acceding to Ku'brol's request to bring no more than three of the dogs with him for their first face-to-face meeting with Harris Webster, Ray selected Beowulf, Mama-san, and Tajil.

"Why ya not takin' me?" asked Sinbad.

"There's no special reason except for the fact that I've agreed to take only three of you. That means six of you have to stay behind in the suite. And that's not such a bad idea for one very obvious reason."

"Oh," said Sinbad. Then he added, "Uh, what very obvious reason?"

"I think Ray wants ya to guard our rooms," Tajil said.

"That's right, Taddy," Ray said. Tajil's observation confirmed the wisdom of Ray's decision to take the big red dog along for his sharp canine intelligence. Beowulf was Ray's other self, both knew how the other thought and acted; Tajil, on the other hand, was just plain smart, one of the brightest dogs Ray had ever known.

As Ku'brol led them into an enormous elevator, Ake caught Ray's eye and said, "I wonder why Kate hasn't called us?"

"I do not mean to eavesdrop—" Ku'brol began before being interrupted by an incompletely muffled guffaw from Ray. Coloring slightly, Ku'brol continued. "I . . . ah, simply mean to inform you that Ms. Golnikov is quite likely departing Neverland at this very moment."

"What!" exclaimed Ake.

"Would you mind repeating what you just said?" Ray asked.

"Ms. Golnikov is a 'scraper and not a guest like yourselves. It is Neverland's policy to place 'scrapers on outgoing vessels as soon as possible. As it happens, the owners of a yacht were looking for a 'scraper so that it might depart today."

Since Ku'brol looked a bit unhappy as he said all this, Ray wondered if it was because he was cognizant of how phony it sounded. Glancing at Ake, Ray could see that his partner was clearly fuming, containing inside himself a level of anger that he rarely reached under normal circumstances.

<Want to tell me why you look like you're ready to bite the head off a wolverine?>

<Later!>

<Uh, I have no problem with that.>

"I think we would like to go directly to Mr. Webster now, with no further ado," Ray said to Ku'brol.

"Certainly," Ku'brol said. "The Midas suite, please," he voiced for the elevator's sake.

It seemed to Ake and the dogs that the elevator hadn't budged when, just before the doors opened, a softly authoritative feminine voice announced, "The Midas suite."

"We there already?" asked Tajil. "I dint feel nuthin'."

"This is the Neverland Hotel," Ku'brol said, assuming that reminding the guests of that fact was more than sufficient explanation for whatever they might encounter.

Ray noted that the elevator's voice was not entirely accurate in what it said. They were outside the Midas suite; they still had to pass the suite's security measures. Ku'brol spoke into a small communications patch on his lapel, and he also pressed his palm against a sensor on the door.

"Finally," Ake stage-whispered as the door opened, revealing an interior worthy of the Midas of legend himself.

By now somewhat numbed by the luxurious trappings that were the norm for the Neverland Hotel, Ray paid scant attention to the dazzling furnishings and the cornucopia of exquisitely rendered art pieces and readied himself to focus on his initial encounter with the great and powerful Harrison Webster.

Ray caught Ake's eye and the taller man leaned over expectantly. "Yes?"

"If Webster turns out to be a giant floating head surrounded by balls of fire, I'm outa here."

Ake smiled, thought a second, then replied, "Before you get your courage?"

"Courage I got—some common sense might be nice."

After leading them through several enormous rooms whose functions seemed indeterminate, Ku'brol finally came to a bedroom dominated by a massive, canopied bed. "King-sized" was not adequate to describe it, Ray thought. Perhaps "continent-sized" would be more like it.

At the head of the bed, directly in the center, propped up by a plethora of pillows, sat a wan-looking Harrison Webster. Standing by the side of his bed, attending to him, was Boosra.

"Good morning, gentlemen . . . and dogs," Webster said, somehow diminished by the enormity of the bed. "I am pleased that you accepted my invitation."

"A chance to visit Neverland is hard to refuse," Ake said.

"Yes. I wish I myself got here more often," Webster said, glancing at Boosra.

"You said something like that on the original message you sent us from the *Exodus*."

Squirming a bit, Ray spoke up. "Ah, this is a sort of embarrassing question to have to ask," he began, "but it would be even more embarrassing, I suppose, were we to overstay our welcome. So, just how long a stay are we talking about here?"

Webster lifted and dropped his shoulders. "Since a month has become the standard vacation length, that seems a logical period of time for you to immerse yourself in Neverland's pleasures."

"A month!" exclaimed Beowulf. "Sorry," he said immediately, looking ruefully at Ray.

"Is there a problem with that?" Webster asked.

Looking at Beowulf and then at Ake, Ray said, "No, I don't think so. However, Beowulf is a working dog and I don't think he likes the idea of lying around for a full month with nothing to do."

"Who said there is nothing to do?" Webster queried. "Besides, if you should happen to enjoy your stay so much that you'd like to extend it, I am prepared to offer you a permanent position as part of our overall security team."

So profound was the effect of Webster's unexpected offer upon Boosra that neither Ake and Ray could help but see her shoot a glance heavy with significance in Ku'brol's direction. For his part, Ku'brol revealed his feelings with a sharp intake of breath.

<Seems like "Poppa" is making decisions the kids don't appreciate,> Ray transmitted to Ake.

<I agree.>

Aloud, Ray said, "That's a wonderful offer, Mr. Webster. We will certainly consider it seriously."

"That's all I ask."

"Tell me," Ake said. "Why is it that you get back to Neverland so infrequently?"

Webster weakly waved a hand. "I am hideously rich. Like the mythical Midas for whom this suite of rooms is named, everything I touch turns to gold—figuratively speaking, of course, gold no longer being the precious commodity it once was. And since I do my best to be a conscientious businessman, I endeavor to manage my holdings sensibly. I take my position seriously because I am aware that my many companies provide jobs and security for thousands and thousands of families."

"An entrepreneur with a heart," smiled Ake.

Again, Harris Webster waved a hand. "Forgive me if I seem immodest or attempting to paint myself as a philanthropist. I can be as hard-headed as the next man. Ask anyone I've bested in a hotly contested negotiation. I'm no plaster saint."

"It's just that the natural byproduct of doing good for yourself is that you do good for many others as well, eh?" asked Ray.

"Exactly. That is the classic rationale for capitalism, both historical and modern."

Ray flashed him a thumbs-up gesture. "Here's to greed with a heart."

"Tell me," Ake said, giving the pasty-looking businessman an evaluative look, "what seems to be the matter with you?"

"Do you think that because I have chosen to greet you from my bed that there is necessarily something wrong with me?"

"In this instance, yes."

"Once a doctor . . . ?"

"Always a doctor," Ake finished.

Webster sighed. "The medical staff here tells me it is simply my Moore's World malaria acting up. They say it's nothing some rest and precisely targeted medication can't control."

"You wuz on Moore's World?" Beowulf asked.

"Yes," Webster told the big team leader. "I take it you have been there as well?"

"Yah."

"Vomitous place, is it not?"

Beowulf hooted at that. "Yah, my sed-a-ments 'xactly."

Ignoring this exchange, Ake asked, "Would you like me to take a look at you, Mr. Webster?"

Before Webster could speak, Boosra said, "That will be unnecessary, Dr. Ringgren. Mr. Webster's personal physician and our medical staff here are quite capable of seeing to his welfare."

"I'm sorry. I didn't mean to imply that they're not," Ake said, not sounding sorry at all. "It's just that another medical opinion never hurt anyone."

"Thanks anyway, Doc," Webster told him. "But if Ms. Boosra here thinks it's unnecessary, then I must go along with her."

<*Yeah, right,*> Ray told Ake. <*If Boosra jumped off a cliff, would he?*>

"As you wish."

"Now then," Webster said, rubbing his hands together. "Let me tell you about Neverland and what you can expect."

"We's all ears," said Mama-san.

As Webster told them the story of Neverland—its concept, development, and realization over twenty-five years—an android or a human assistant approached Ku'brol as unobtrusively as possible—thereby, paradoxically, catching everyone's full attention—and whispered something in his ear. Ku'brol's face expressed surprise and then frustration and, possibly, anger. He spoke into the messenger's ear and the latter nodded and exited.

"Wish I knew what that was all about," Ray muttered softly to no one in particular.

His keen ears picking up Ray's words, Beowulf ambled over to Tajil, who was standing closest to Ku'brol. After a few seconds of conversation, Beowulf came back to Ray and said, "That guy tole his boss that Kate Golnikov dint leave; somethin' went wrong with the ship she was 'sposed to fly away on."

III

"This is terrific, Kate!" Ake was saying to the 'scraper as she relaxed and chatted with them in their sitting room. "I never expected to see you again."

"That makes two of us," Kate said.

Mama-san made a deep-throated *whuffle* sound to indicate her pleasure and said, "It nice to have 'nother female 'round onct in a while."

"Yah," seconded Grendel. "We's still outnumbered, but ya gives us one more on our side."

"For Pete's sake," Ray said. "I'll get married and have four daughters if that'll help."

"Yeah?" asked Gawain. "Who ya gonna marry?"

"Not gonna be that Boosrabitch," opined Tajil.

Not wanting to, Ray nonetheless laughed. "Now cut that out! She's been civil to us."

Ake raised his eyebrows. "I don't know. I might have to agree with Taddy. Boosra and Ku'brol have both gotten a tad frostier since they found out Kate wasn't leaving."

"Yeah, they have," Ray admitted. He looked at Kate, gave her a warm smile of appreciation, and said, "So they gave you a bye on catching the next flight out, eh?"

She returned his smile. "Yes, five of the crew of eight came down with Mako's Disease. A bit surprising in this day and age, but they turned out to be Rejectors who, obviously, hadn't had all the required inoculations."

"What is Mako's Disease?" asked Ozma.

"It's something terrible," Ray replied. "You look like this"—he made a fish face, puffing out his cheeks and putting his hands on either side of his neck and moving them to mimic gills—"and you can't take a leak unless you're in the water."

While Ozma and several of the dogs guffawed, Gawain asked, "How kin ya leak if'n ya is already in water?" When Tajil whispered in his ear, he said, "Oh."

"What is Re-jectors?" asked Mama-san. "*You* tell us, Kate," she added, throwing Ray a meaningful look.

"We have all," she began, indicating Mama-san, Ray, Ake, and the rest of the dogs, "been pumped full of the required serums so many times, we take it for granted that everyone else is immunized as well." She shrugged. "Most are—except for Rejectors. Like the good folks on Cromwell, Rejectors are religious extremists who don't believe in things like preventive inoculations against disease. They dismiss much of modern medicine."

"Cromwell . . . ?" said Ray wonderingly.

"How did they get this far, I wonder?" asked Ake. "You're questioned all the time concerning whether or not you've had the required series of inoculations."

Kate shrugged again. "The answer is simple: They lied. That, and they had false papers claiming they were properly protected."

"So you're stuck here?"

Kate's smile got wider. "Yeah. For at least two weeks and maybe longer."

Ray recalled the reactions to the delivery of that news in Webster's suite. "For some reason, that's pissed all over Ku-'brol's and Boosra's potato patch. Any idea why?"

"None whatsoever."

"I doan like it," intoned Beowulf.

"Me neither," added Frodo.

Ake was paying scant attention to these exchanges. Instead, a look of furious concentration on his face, he rubbed the side of his nose with his long index finger and mused out loud: "You know, isn't it rather strange that a ship full of Rejectors came to be on Neverland in the first place? They're well known for their anhedonia, after all."

"Anhedonia?" said Kate.

"Yeah. It's a psychological term. Anhedonics are people who lack the ability to derive pleasure from life."

"Gee," said Beowulf. "It not make any sense for them kinda beoples to come to a bay-kayshun world."

"Bingo."

9

"Can I ask a stupid question?" Ray inquired of Boosra as she and Ku'brol led the three humans and three dogs on a tour of the Neverland Hotel.

"Certainly." She smiled and nodded at a passing man wearing a safari jacket. He had the boiled-lobster look of a sedentary type who suddenly has a chance to go out into the sun and forgets to come in before he's fricasseed.

"Just how many people stay here at any one time? I mean on average, not the exact figure."

"Leandra cannot answer that!" Aron Ku'brol said sharply, his dark eyes blacker than thunderclouds. He balled and unclenched his fists as mindlessly as a newborn babe. His seething anger and top-heavy build made Ray think of Bluto, Popeye's constant foe and rival for Olive Oyl.

"That information is of the sort we are extremely loath to make public," Boosra said, less forcefully than Ku'brol. Nonetheless, the colors of the living jewel in her nostril rippled to show her emotional unease.

Ray glanced around the immense elevator that had easily accommodated all eight of them. "I don't see any spies or assassins lurking about, and presumably the only bugs in here are your own, so what's the problem?"

Shrugging, Boosra replied, "I suppose you have a point. While the hotel can comfortably accommodate as many as four hundred guests, it rarely is host to more than two hundred and fifty—which is the approximate number currently in attendance."

"All this for two hundred ad fifty people," said Kate Golnikov. She whistled softly. "That's amazing."

"It is Neverland," said Boosra, as if that simple statement of fact explained it.

The elevator's doors opened when it reached the mezzanine level of the hotel. Beowulf, Frodo, and Grendel trotted out and quickly looked right and left. "Okay," Beowulf said, clearly irritating Ku'brol by his actions.

As causally as he could, Ray glanced behind them, down the corridor, and noticed three men following them at a discreet distance. While they were all well dressed, they certainly didn't look like guests of the hotel.

The last time they were in the public areas of the hotel, it didn't take much of a leap of imagination on Ray's part to pretend that they had been checking into King's and Kubrick's Overlook in the dead of winter. Today, the premises were more alive with people coming, going, or simply standing around talking. With a few exceptions, everyone was dressed in vacation clothes; the sort of clothing that proclaimed the wearer's willingness to go along with making a fool out of him- or herself. The clothes shrieked, "In real life I'm a substantial and important person but on vacation I become a class-A dork quicker than you can say tourist."

Nearly everyone did a double take upon seeing the three huge scout dogs. "Guess you don't get many dogs here," Ray said.

"No," Ku'brol said icily. "We do not."

"Your loss."

"Two of the hotel's three restaurants are on this level," Boosra said matter-of-factly, hoping to move on before something nasty developed. "Maxim's is the most notable; the chef is the famous André de Tothea."

"He make a decent cheeseburger?" Ray asked. Boosra seemed at a loss for words.

Ake glanced about him. "The concert hall, the swimming pool, a couple of lounges, and the game rooms are also on this level, right?" he asked.

"That's correct, Dr. Ringgren," replied Boosra, relieved to be speaking to someone she knew how to respond to.

"Hm-m-m," said Ray, poking Ake in the ribs with an elbow.

"Someone's been studying the hotel's layout in the guest information cube we found in our suite."

Boosra continued. "The game area includes a bowling alley and a—"

"A bowling alley!" exclaimed Kate Golnikov.

"Yes. Bowling is an archaic game played with a ball and numbered pieces of wood. Well, they aren't really wood, of course. It has become quite the rage here the last year or so." She sniffed as if to make clear she disapproved of such a plebeian pastime.

"The next thing you know, golf will make a comeback, too," Ray said.

"There *is* a course behind the hotel, as a matter of fact. It's quite near the maze," Boosra told him. "I find golf to be another puzzling form of recreation. Try as I might, I cannot see the attraction in hitting a little ball around expanses of grass."

"Wow!" Ray said. "It's Twentieth-century Land. I've read so much about bowling and now I can actually do it." He grinned slyly and said, "Don't tell me you still have Jarts, too."

"Ah, no, I don't believe that we do," replied Boosra, having no idea at all what "Jarts" was. "There *are* any number of more contemporary leisure pursuits available in addition to our nostalgic ones. We have Banno jumping, of course, and one of the best null-gee gymnasiums to be found anywhere."

"Of course," said Ake.

A handsome couple, looking to be in their mid-sixties and well preserved, approached. They maneuvered ever so slightly toward the other side of the corridor. "Good day, Ms. Boosra; Mr. Ku'brol," the man said. The woman, who wore enough star sapphires to ransom a king, simply smiled.

"Good day, senator and Mr. Rami," Boosra and Ku'brol replied as the senator and her husband swept past.

Dilon Lanskgaard showed up and immediately whispered something into Ku'brol's ear. "You'll excuse me, please," said Ku'brol. He walked briskly away without bothering to wait for a response.

<*I won't miss laughing boy,*> Ray transmitted to Ake.

<*Me either. But I'm not sure we got the better of the tradeoff.*>

<*You got a point,*> Ake conceded. <*Lanskgaard is a minor pain in the ass in training to become a major pain in the ass.*>

<*Is this a private conversation, or can anyone join in?*>

"Jeezzus!" Ray blurted out loud, startled as hell.

K-9 CORPS: THE LAST RESORT

"I beg your pardon?" said Boosra, cocking her head quizzically.

"Ah, sorry," Ray said. "For a minute there I convinced myself that I left the hot plate in my room turned on."

"Oh," said Boosra.

<She's probably thinking to herself, "I should have known better than to expect any other response from this strange little rutter.">

<Kate—is that you?> Ake transmitted.

<Yeah, it's me. Sorry. I didn't mean to give you guys such a start. I can stay out if it's a problem.>

<It's just that this is our private chat line,> Ray told her. <We had no idea anyone could break in our exchanges like this—I mean, this is a complex, coded, radio transmission.>

<Relax, Marconi,> Kate replied. <Not just anyone can. I'm an ESPer, remember—a damn good one. Don't worry, your line isn't that easily tapped.>

"The concert hall," Ake said to Boosra. "What kind of performances are scheduled?"

"Come, let's go there and I can tell you on the way."

"Lead on."

II

By the time they had left the concert hall and found themselves in the casino on the first level, the dogs were growing tired of the tour. "We gonna get to go back and get the others and go outside soon?" asked Frodo.

"Soon, Frodo," Ray told him.

"If you ask me, dogs belong outside anyway," sniffed Dilon Lanskgaard.

"Does your family have money invested in Neverland?" Ake asked the pale youth.

The question took Lanskgaard by surprise. "Why do you ask?"

Boosra looked as if she'd just been forced to smell something disgusting. "Dr. Ringgren understandably finds it difficult to comprehend how you can be an employee here when you act as rudely to guests as you do," she said. "He is correct—you are being most tiresome. Please leave us."

"But—" Lanskgaard sputtered.

"I said leave us." The pale-faced young man, now red with anger and shame, stalked stiffly away.

"Bye," said Grendel.

"I must apologize for Dilon . . . again."

"I'm sorry for my inference," Ake said. "But as you said, it's hard not to think he must know where the skeletons are buried."

Boosra smiled faintly but said nothing.

Ray thumped the dogs. "C'mon. I want to check out the casino for a little while. After that, after I play a few games, we can go for a walk." He looked at Boosra. "Ah, that is, if it's okay with you."

"Of course. This is a resort, not a prison."

Coulda fooled me, Ray told himself, glancing back at their three "shadows." "Yeah, right. Silly of me to put it that way."

"Can I help you gamble?" asked Beowulf as they entered the casino.

"You bet," said Ray.

Ake found a medium-stakes poker game that had an opening for another player, so he introduced himself and sat down. Frodo sighed and settled at his feet. He wondered what Ray and Beowulf were doing.

"Oh, there you are!" exclaimed a too-familiar voice.

"Lookit," said Beowulf. "It's the an-droid woman who likes ya so much."

"Hello, Beowulf. Hello, Ray," said Marla, tossing her shock of long blonde hair over her shoulder in a manner she knew men liked. Ray liked it, too, despite himself. He found himself contemplating her lush figure. *Plastic and wires,* he told himself. *Plastic and wires.*

"Hello, Marla," Ray replied warily. "How nice to see you again."

"Really?" she gushed.

"No," Ray told her. "But it's almost automatic to say so, and I couldn't stop myself."

Pouting fetchingly, she said, "You're mean."

"There, there." Ray chucked her under her chin—not unlike the way he chucked the dogs under their jaws. Because she wasn't human—or even canine—he found it difficult to treat her like a real person. Had he thought more about it, he would have been disturbed at how she brought out a side of himself he didn't especially care for. He wanted her so bad that his rejection of her was darker and more forceful than it would normally have been.

"Since your programming has you locked in on me tighter than the guidance beam from a smart torpedo, you might as well join me while I lose some money."

"Oh, goody," she squeaked with delight. "But you're going to win, not lose."

"That would be a refreshing turnabout."

"You leave it to me—I'm going to bring you good luck."

"You do that, kiddo, and you can have your way with me." Ray glanced around the casino, jingling the chips in his trouser pockets. "Now then—what to play . . . ?"

"How about baccarat?" Marla suggested.

"Baccarat," Ray said, wrinkling his brow questioningly. "Why baccarat?"

"Because that's what agent double-oh seven always used to play."

Ray's eyes widened in astonishment. "How did you know that?"

"My programming has been adjusted to better meet your needs, Ray," she responded seriously.

"Well, paint me blue and call me a turnip!"

She squeezed his arm. "That sounds like fun. Maybe after you take the bank at baccarat." He felt her warm breath on his cheek and entertained impure thoughts.

Ray looked at the ten thousand-credit chips in the center of the baccarat table and then at the banker sitting opposite him. He could also feel evaluative stares boring holes through him. *I guess they want to look the new boy over,* he thought. *They don't know what to make of me yet.*

The others were also staring because the decision to challenge the bank was now up to Ray. The player before him had declined to take up the bet after losing to the bank three times in a row. A fortyish man named Hudspeth who sported a pencil-thin mustache, he appeared a greasy-looking character who would not have been out of place in an old twentieth-century "smoker": an amateurishly filmed porno flick where the males never bothered to remove their dark socks.

"Since Mr. Hudspeth has decided against accepting the bet, the choice is now yours, Mr. . . . ?"

Ray lit the incredibly costly cigar he'd purchased from an android dressed and coiffed to appear like a "cigarette girl" of old and blew out a long plume of foul-smelling smoke. *Good cigar,* he thought.

"Bond. James Bond." He was rewarded by hearing Marla, who was massaging his arm, laugh.

He quickly corrected his statement. "A little joke for my faithful Indian companion and myself." Ray's broad smile faded as the puzzled looks on the faces of those around the table were proof that no one had the slightest idea what he was talking about; Ian Fleming's suave hero was ancient history.

Now feeling more than a little stupid, he said, "Actually, my name is Larkin. Ray Larkin." He shifted the fat cigar from one side of his mouth to the other.

"Bond, Larkin . . . whatever you call yourself, the bet is yours to accept or decline," said the banker, a slightly moist-looking man who clearly used a depilatory to keep his skull hairless.

"Banco," Ray said, taking a handful of thousand-credit chips from his right jacket pocket and tossing them nonchalantly on the table. He didn't bother to count them, aware that he had more than enough to cover the bet. "The cards, please, Mr. MacGuffin."

The bald man pulled four cards from the karkka wood shoe, and the croupier pushed Ray's two across to him.

After taking a deep draw on his cigar—*I better be careful or I'm going to make myself dizzy*—Ray glanced at his two cards. He had a queen and a five. The queen counted for nothing, so his hand totaled five. If he asked for another card and the new total came to nine or less, he would win. If the new card pushed him over nine, he would lose. *The hard part,* Ray thought, *is that the odds are almost exactly fifty-fifty that I'll either get a four or under OR a card that will put me over the top.*

MacGuffin impatiently tapped the shoe containing what was left of the initial six decks of thoroughly shuffled cards originally loaded into it at the start of play.

Ray had no choice, really. He had to go for it. "Card," he said.

MacGuffin pulled a card from the shoe and the croupier lifted it with his little flat stick and deposited it in front of Ray like a mother placing a pancake in front of her child. Ray turned the card over without looking at it.

MacGuffin's cat-with-a-canary expression told Ray he'd lost. He glanced down and saw that the card was a seven. He was automatically over. MacGuffin was not required to show his cards and he didn't.

"Oh," said Marla, disappointed.

Ray shrugged.

The croupier singled out ten chips and moved them from in front of Ray, adding them to the bank in front of MacGuffin. Ray puffed away and looked thoughtfully at the bank; it was now twenty thousand credits. The croupier gathered up the five discards and removed them from the playing surface.

MacGuffin raised an eyebrow and Ray nodded, taking two five-thousand-credit chips from his left jacket pocket. He put them down disdainfully, as if losing the money they represented would be a matter of no importance. The banker again slipped four cards from the shoe—two for himself and two for Ray. He waited for Ray to evaluate his hand. Ray glanced at the cards and a faint smile played across his lips.

Ray turned his two cards face up. A six and a three—a natural. MacGuffin now had to have a natural as well or the baccarat went to Ray. The banker turned over an ace—a one—and a king. He'd lost. MacGuffin suddenly looked a lot more moist.

Marla squeezed his arm and shoulder tighter when he took the bank. The others at the table gaped at Ray's good fortune, and a man who looked as if he had been mummified in the time of King Tut said, "Good show."

For Ray, it was just the first of many victories. He took the next bank and the next and the next, beginning a very profitable run.

★ ★ ★

Grendel watched Kate put a two-credit coin into one of the slot machines and pull the lever. Pictures of mismatched fruit appeared and Golnikov just sighed and repeated the process, the pulling of the lever becoming an automatic action.

"How come ya playin' that thing?" Grendel asked. "It fun?"

"I suppose so," Kate Golnikov replied.

"Ya 'spose so? Don't ya know?"

"Yeah, okay—it's fun in a kind of weird way. Every time you pull the arm you have a chance of winning. That's the thrill."

"Doan you like them card games and games with them little cubes?"

"I'm an ESPer," Kate explained. "No casino in the galaxy will permit an ESPer to play games where she might use her psychic powers to gain an unfair advantage."

"What 'bout Ray, then?"

Kate put a finger to her lips. "Sh-h-h. Don't let anyone else know that Ray has rudimentary psi powers. That's a secret."

Grendel frowned a dog frown. "Yah. I 'sposed to know better'n that. I goofin' up."

"Don't worry about it, Grendel. Besides," Kate continued, "Ray doesn't wear the evidence of his abilities on the outside of his body like a scarlet letter." She pointed to her blotchy complexion. "Most ESPers and 'scrapers do. *I* do."

"Oh," said Grendel. Then she asked, "That itchy? It *looks* itchy."

Kate put in another two-credit piece and pulled. After the displays stopped spinning she inserted another piece and repeated the action. Finally, she said, "No, it doesn't itch. Well, not usually. I have a cream I put on it when it flares up."

"Oh."

Kate Golnikov had nearly exhausted the basket of two-credit coins she'd been using to feed the one-armed bandits when she sensed an extremely delicate mental touch. Without otherwise indicating she was aware of anything out of the ordinary, she casually asked Grendel, "Do you feel anything funny, Grendel?"

Grendel looked around the casino warily, the fur on the back of her neck rising ever so slightly. "Yah. Like someone starin' at me behind my back."

Kate nodded. Effortlessly, without having to go through any elaborate preparations, she placed a low-level shield around her mind. The next step required more conscious effort: She carefully prepared a trap of sorts. Whoever was gingerly probing her would leave his or her mental fingerprints behind, even though he was denied access to her mind. *Walk up and peer through the windows,* she thought to herself gleefully. *When you do, I'll take a snapshot that will tell me who you are.*

"Who's doin' this, Kate?"

"I don't know." She stopped feeding the slot machine long enough to reach out and scratch Grendel's ears. "But I believe I'm about to find out."

III

As they left the casino together, but without either Boosra or Lanskgaard chaperoning them, Ray casually let slip that he was ahead more than a quarter of a million credits. While the others gasped, Beowulf said proudly, "Ray was a demon at back-a-rat."

"That's wonderful, Ray," Kate said. "What are you going to do with all that money?" She smiled slyly. "Are you going to spend it on Marla?"

Ray flushed. "She's—the android's—not a 'bar girl' trying to separate guests from their money . . ." He paused and a curious expression passed over his face. "At least, I don't think that's the case. I *did* have a helluva time getting her/it not to follow me back to our rooms."

"He really did," avowed Beowulf solemnly.

Ray looked slyly at Kate. "I cashed in the chips and told Boosra to open an account against which you can draw to pay for your room and other amenities while you're stuck here."

Now it was Kate's turn to become beet red. "You didn't have to do that."

"My poor old sainted grandma used to have an expression: 'The only thing I *have* to do is pay taxes and die.' I agree. I did what I did because money doesn't have a whole lot of meaning for Ake and me anymore, and using it to help you stay here seemed like a pretty good way to spend it."

"Ray's right," Ake joined in. "Besides, if Boosra and Ku'brol are so eager to get you offplanet, then we're not only prepared to resist them but also stubborn enough to want to find out why they're so insistent."

"Ah, let's continue this conversation in your suite," Kate told them, glancing around the hallway apprehensively. "The walls have ears."

When Beowulf sighed loudly, Ray said, "Let's make that outside. I promised the dogs they'd have a chance to get a little fresh air after the casino."

"Fine," Kate agreed.

Ray watched the dogs playing hound and hare, chasing each other maniacally across the otherwise deserted golf course. Turning back to Kate Golnikov, he said, "Lanskgaard! I don't effing believe it."

She put her hands on her hips. "Look, whether or not you choose to believe me, it was Lanskgaard all right."

"You're sure?" Ray persisted.

"Positive."

"He doesn't seem bright enough," Ray said.

"It has nothing to do with intelligence," Kate insisted. "It has to do with psi ability."

"And he has psi ability?" Ake asked.

"Out the yin-yang."

"I take it that means yes," Ray said dryly.

"But why are they so eager to see you leave Neverland?" Ake persisted.

"Isn't it obvious?"

Ray guessed where she was going but said, "Maybe, but pretend we're stupid."

"And the answer is . . . ?" Ake gently prompted Kate Golnikov when she didn't immediately respond.

"The answer is that I'm a 'scraper. And being a 'scraper means I'm also an ESPer."

"And . . . ?"

"And what!" she exploded. "Jesus jumping Christ, it should be obvious that there's something going on here that certain people don't want discovered!"

"People like Leandra Boosra, Aron Ku'brol, and . . ." Ake left hanging what he was going to say.

". . . And Harrison Webster?" Ray finished for him.

"That possibility has to be taken seriously," Kate Golnikov said. "But I'm not sure." She shook her head. "No, I don't think so."

"Me either," Ray agreed.

"Neverland *is* his resort," Ake pointed out. "One would think he would know if anything funny is going on."

"One would think."

"But you don't?"

"No, although I agree with Kate," Ray told his partner. "It has to be seriously considered. We can't rule it out without a thorough investigation."

"Why so eager to rush to Webster's defense?" Ake persisted.

"He hasn't been here in a couple of years," Ray said. "He's been an absentee landlord, leaving things in the hands of his 'trusted' employees."

"He still could be involved," Ake pressed.

"Yes, he could," Kate agreed readily.

"What we do now?" asked Mama-san.

Ray regarded her gravely. "Why, we're on vacation. We go over to one of the island continents and have fun."

"Is that a good idea?" Kate asked dubiously.

"If something funny *is* going on," Ray told her, "then the best way to find out is to act as if we suspect nothing. That way, we have access to every place everyone else has access to."

"We're just out to relax and have fun, remember?" Ake reminded her.

Kate made a face. "Fun."

Robin made an entirely different face. "Yah . . . fun."

10

Ray came fully awake in an instant. Someone had entered his room.

Forget about the door, he thought as he reached for a weapon. *How the hell did he get past the dogs?*

As his fingers closed on his quiver blade, he sensed a presence beside the bed.

"Don't," a familiar voice said. "It's only me."

He turned on a light. The tableau revealed by the lamp's soft glow was reassuring—on several counts. Not only did it illuminate Marla, fetchingly dressed in the sheerest lingerie imaginable, it also revealed Beowulf standing a meter behind the beautiful android, fur erect and jaws open.

"I think it's all right, Beowulf," Ray told the big dog, who was poised to attack at the slightest sign of aggression on the android's part.

Confused, Marla turned and saw Ray's defender for the first time. "Guess I wasn't as unobtrusive as I thought," she said.

"You did pretty damn good," Ray replied. "How'd you get in here, anyway?"

"Trade secret," Marla said, showing Beowulf that her hands were empty. Moving slowly and carefully, she lifted back the edge of the sheet and asked, "May I?"

"What if I say no?"

"You promised me if I brought you good luck that I could have my way with you."

"Maybe I did," Ray responded. "But what if I tell you that I'm not interested in what you're proposing?"

"I'd say that you're not a good sport." She lifted the sheet higher, looked down, and ran her tongue around her lips. "Then I'd also say that one of you isn't telling me the truth."

"Um, Beowulf, you can wait outside."

"But what if she wants to 'tack you?"

"I don't think that's what she has in mind," Ray told Beowulf as Marla turned off the light and slipped under the sheet to snuggle up against him.

"That's better," she said. She mussed his hair and added, "As for Beowulf's fears—yes, I am planning a 'tack—a tender 'tack."

Ray gulped. "Plastic and wires," he said. Then his mouth was too busy to talk.

Beowulf settled down outside the bedroom door, his head on his paws. He sighed and allowed himself to think about the handsome little bitch he'd met on Yeltsin. Then his stomach rumbled and his thoughts turned to food.

★ ★ ★

"I understand you're going to be paying a visit to one of the big parks," Harris Webster said, his voice sounding weaker to Ake than it had the last time they had seen him.

"That's right," Ray told him. "The three of us couldn't decide which one to visit first, so we left it up to the dogs."

"And what did they decide?"

"We dee-cided we wants to see some o' them dye-no-sores," Gawain volunteered. Webster laughed, weakly.

<He doesn't look good at all,> Ake told Ray and Kate.

<No, he doesn't,> agreed Kate.

<Maybe he'll allow you to examine him now,> Ray told Ake.

<Don't bet on it—he's a stubborn cuss.>

While this internal dialogue was going on, Sinbad, unnoticed by Ray or Ake, moved close enough to Webster for the bedridden man to reach out and pat the dog feebly on the head. Sinbad enjoyed Webster's touch, but it was the man's discarded breakfast tray on the floor that had caught his attention and drawn him to the bedside.

"Well, ah . . ." Webster paused, looking at Gawain. "I forgot your name," he said sheepishly.

"Gawain."

"Well, Gawain, they may look like dinosaurs, but they really aren't, you know."

"What are they, then?" asked a puzzled Kate Golnikov.

"They're genetically altered xenomorphs," Webster told her. "That is to say, they began some years ago as alien creatures which just happened to resemble Terran dinosaurs—superficially, of course. Our genetic engineers have been responsible for turning them into acceptable substitutes for the real things—which, being extinct for millions of years, are obviously not available."

"From the holos I've seen, they certainly look like real dinosaurs."

"Exactly," nodded Webster. "That was the whole point of our genetic manipulation and engineering. Under their skins, however, you would find far fewer similarities to their long-deceased models."

Ray had a puzzled look on his face. "You're talking about living creatures, Mr. Webster. That's all fine, but why do I seem to recall something about holos and mechanical reproductions?"

"That's because we have two totally different dinosaur parks," Webster explained. "Junior Dinoland is a family theme park, not unlike the popular Old Terran attraction of Spielbergland."

"Speelber *gland*?" asked Tajil, cocking his head quizzically.

"No, 'Spielberg*land*,' " enunciated Webster. Then he laughed, saying, "Spielberg gland!"

"Wasn't much of that destroyed by fire?" Kate asked.

"Yes, a malfunction in the giant mechanical shark started a blaze that consumed the whole facility in a matter of hours," Webster confirmed. "But to return to Mr. Larkin's question, Junior Dinoland is our family attraction, one that is completely safe for children of all ages. It is populated by holos and gentle, slow-moving mechanical simulations. All state of the art. We've had only a handful of very minor injuries in the almost two decades that the park has been open.

"The regular Dinoland, however, is the province of our biologically manipulated creations. There, they roam free and wild, completely independent of any outside control or manipulation."

"I take it you've had more than a few 'very minor injuries' in that Dinoland?" Ray asked.

Webster smiled. "That is correct. It is both a hunting preserve and a place where those who seek ultimate challenges can find one."

"Are you telling us it's 'nature red in tooth and nail' for real?" asked Kate.

"It doesn't get any more real," Webster confirmed.

Ray glanced at the dogs and saw that every one of them had a big canine smile plastered across his or her face.

"Lord help us," he muttered softly.

Webster looked puzzled. "You don't mean you want to visit Dinoland, do you?"

"That's 'xactly what we mean," Robin told him.

"I'd better see that your weapons are returned to you." His face registered another thought. "Oh, and you'll have to sign waivers of responsibility."

II

"I dunno, but I think Sinbad gonna be sick," Ozma said, watching the copper-colored dog's sides heaving.

"That's great," Ray said. "Nothing like being in a floater with a dog about to hurl his cookies."

Ake put his hand to his mouth. "Stop talking about it!" he blurted out. "You're gonna make me—"

"Uh-oh," said Gawain. "There he goes."

Sinbad's shoulders shook and, standing splaylegged, he expelled a nauseatingly liquescent mass. The other dogs were torn between concern for his well-being and an almost irresistible desire to comment on the contents of the expelled matter.

Ray didn't have time to ask Sinbad if he was okay before Ake doubled over and blasted his breakfast all over the floor of the floater.

"Ah, jeez, Ake," Ray said, putting down his sandwich and contemplating the mess his partner had made. He keyed the intercom and said, "Hey, can we get a 'bot back here to clean up?"

"To clean up what?" the co-pilot's voice queried.

"You don't want to know," Ray told him. "Just activate a 'bot and send it back, please."

"You're the boss."

Kate returned from the head with both hands full of paper towels, some moistened with water and some dry. She sat beside a white-as-a-sheet Ake and daubed at his mouth with one of the moist towels.

"Oh, please," he said, attempting to pull away. "You don't have to do that; I'm a disgusting mess."

"You're a disgusting mess? Look at me," she said, pointing to a fresh eruption of white and red pustules on her face. "I have to walk around like this all the time; you I can clean up in a minute. Now lean forward again."

"Thank you," Ake said gratefully.

"Is that water?" Ray asked rhetorically. He shook his head. "Mom taught me that saliva and facial tissues work best."

"Your mom teach you how to remove a boot from your butt?" Ake asked pointedly.

"No, she didn't," admitted Ray. He turned his attention to Sinbad. "Are you feeling better now that you've gotten that out of you?" he asked as a little maintenance 'bot appeared to mop up the offending mess.

"Yah," Sinbad managed to say. His sides heaved once or twice more, but that ceased and it appeared that he was safely past vomiting again.

Ray forced himself to look at the rapidly disappearing semiliquid, semisolid mass on the floor of the floater. "What *was* that? Did you eat something you weren't supposed to? Like a dead varmint . . . a kilo of bacon grease . . . a blowfish?"

"No, nuthin'."

"Okay," he said. "But it's not like you to get a queasy stomach like that."

"Hey, everything okay back there?" asked the co-pilot's voice.

"Yeah, why?" Ray answered.

"Well, we're landing in about a minute. Just thought you'd want to know."

"Oh. Thanks," Ray said.

The floater lurched, dropping ten meters or so, and Ake clapped both hands to his head and moaned. "Oh, jeez—I'm gonna be sick!"

"Not again!" everyone chorused.

★ ★ ★

Ake gulped. "I feel like we've been plopped down into Conan Doyle's *The Lost World*."

"I know what you mean, partner," Ray agreed.

"I didn't realize they were going to drop us off like that and then just disappear," Kate said, looking around the clearing in the rain forest nervously.

Just then three small creatures darted out, eyeballed them for an instant, and then hightailed it off into the intermittently lush vegetation. Although they looked like lime green-colored crosses between Terran chickens and Terran walking lizards, they were something else altogether.

They were dinosaurs.

"They some o' them dye-no-sores?" asked Ozma.

"Yes," replied Ake.

"Hey, lookit!" Frodo shouted, his voice full of excitement. "There's some more o' them dye-no-sores right over there."

Ray looked and saw that Frodo was correct. A small family group of modest-sized reptiles had entered the far edge of the clearing. Vividly colored and adorned with long hornlike appendages on their snouts, they moved gracefully into a patch of bright sunlight and then paused, their long noses curling as they sniffed the air.

"Jeez, see the noses on them guys," said Gawain. "I wonder if they smell good."

"They probably smell a whole lot better than you," Ray said almost automatically.

"Ray had a pair of lizardskin boots onct, I think," said Mama-san seriously. "They dint smell at all."

"Not on the outside, that is," corrected Ake.

"I thought they'd be clumsier—more awkward and slow," Kate murmured, staring at the three adults and four youngsters that comprised the wary group of *faux* dinosaurs.

"Not animals that size," considered Ake. "Maybe bigger ones, but the adults look to be about four or five meters long."

"They not dangerous, right?" asked Beowulf, suddenly apprehensive.

"Well, Mr. Expert, are they?" Ray asked Ake. Ake put his hand to his head in the way that showed that he was concentrating.

"According to the external I loaded up with info from the park rangers, these folks are vegetarians. They're also timid and nonaggressive—something which can't be said for all of the vegetarians we might encounter."

"That's true," said Kate. "I'm a vegetarian and I'm hardly a shrinking wallflower."

"You don't eat meat?" exclaimed Sinbad.

"No, I don't."

"I thought everyone eated meat," said an awed Gawain.

"Guess again," said Kate, awkwardly shifting the energy rifle slung over her shoulder from one place to another—so it could begin rubbing raw a whole new patch of skin.

Ray scratched his chin thoughtfully. "You can *shoot* meat if you have to, can't you?"

Kate just smiled enigmatically.

"They look like they waitin' for us to do somethin'," said Ozma, indicating the small family unit now regarding them as gravely as they were being regarded.

"Let's not disappoint them," Ake said. "We should begin moving toward the pickup point the floater's pilot told us about."

"Ah-h-h, we not leavin' already, are we?" asked Grendel. "We jes' got here."

"No, Grendel," Ray told the disappointed dog. "But it's ten klicks to the pickup area. Since we're going to be sightseeing the whole way, it'll take us a good while to get there."

"Oh, goody," Frodo said, his tail wagging.

"Ten klicks?" said Kate Golnikov, dismayed. "I walk the skins of starships," she reminded them. "I'm not used to hacking my way through vegetation like this."

"It will be good for you, then," Ake told her. "And it won't hurt any of us to get in a little exercise."

Ray made a raspberry and the dogs hooted before taking up their defensive positions around the three humans.

The human-engineered dinosaurs were not the only animals in the park, Ray noticed. Here and there small mammals scurried about, tiny surface-dwellers which had to be content with living under the domination of the terrible lizards who reigned in this world.

"You know," Ake said, "all this reminds me of Hephaestus."

"This be jes' like ole times there," seconded Beowulf, beaming a huge canine grin as he scanned their surroundings.

Ray had to agree. "Yeah, it *is* almost like being back on Hephaestus."

The rain forest made Ray feel at home—as did the distant volcanoes. *I wonder if those are real volcanoes,* he pondered. The sun-seeking trees and muggy heat further reminded him of Hephaestus. There were more than a few major differences, of course. This was supposed to be an epoch before the coming of the birds, so there were no macaws, or songbirds, or long-tailed woodpeckers to add color and noise to their surroundings.

The dogs ranged back and forth, circling around the three humans protectively. Even so, they got to experience a lot of the new environment. At one point, Mama-san stopped to sniff something on the ground.

"What's up, Mama-san?" Ray called to her. "What is that?"

"Somethin' big that eats meat stopped to shit here."

Ray started over, followed by Ake, Kate, and the other dogs. They surrounded the huge pile of droppings and stared in wonder at the sight.

"Wow, lookit all that," said Frodo.

Ray snorted loudly, causing Ake to point a finger at him and say, "Come on, out with it, damned spot."

"It's just—ha, ha—that we're—ha, ha—standing around staring reverently at a pile of dinosaur shit!" Ray wiped a tear from one eye. "You'd think we were gazing at Plymouth Rock or the Bellerophon Stone."

"Lizard boop," said Tajil and the rest of them joined Ray in laughing at their malodorous discovery.

A low, rumbling, yet piercing roar rent the air and they stopped laughing immediately.

"I'm going to hate myself for asking, but what in the wide world of sports was that?" Ray gulped.

Ake just pointed to the dinosaur droppings and said, "It could be our very large friend who produced this pile of instant fertilizer."

"Sounded angry, dint it?" said Robin.

"Yeah—that or hungry," Ray said.

They looked at each other. The dogs' fur rose and the humans clutched their energy rifles. "Ah, I think it's time we hit the road again," Ake said.

"You'll get no argument from me," said Kate.

"Ditto," piped in Ray. He turned to Beowulf. "Beowulf, round 'em up, head 'em out, yah mule train!"

Robin nudged Sinbad. "Ain't this great!"

III

"We certainly are getting to see a lot of variety," Kate observed.

"Yes, there are many types of animal life here," Ake agreed.

"That's true, but that's not what I meant."

"What did you mean?"

"I meant the flora, not the fauna. We've gone from a sort of veldt to this semi-rain forest."

"Like I said about terraforming—" Ray began.

"Listen," said Beowulf, stopping and cocking his head.

"Yeah, I hears it, too," Tajil said.

"Me, too," piped in Grendel.

"What is it?" Ray asked.

"It doan sound good for somebody," Beowulf explained. "Somebody is fightin' for his life."

Then the humans' ears finally picked it up: high-pitched bellows and shrieks. "Let's go see what's happening," Ray said, moving out already.

"I wuz hopin' he'd say that," rumbled Robin.

"I was afraid he'd say that," moaned Kate.

When the others caught up to Ray and Beowulf, they saw that man and dog had stopped at the edge of a ravine. The sides fell away so quickly and were so steep that the ravine quickly became a full-fledged valley, albeit a small one. Ray turned toward Ake and Kate when he heard them approaching and motioned for everyone to get down.

Flinching at the nerve-wracking screams which were almost continuous, Kate asked, "What is it?" She clutched her energy rifle to her chest like a good-luck piece.

"Look." Ray gestured with his head toward the origin of the sound.

At a distance of a hundred meters or so down the ravine, a horned herbivore was being attacked by a pack of ostrich-sized carnivores. Although the intended victim, apparently of the ceratopsian family, was a good seven meters long and armed with three large horns, it seemed a foregone conclusion that the battle would end in the death of the larger beast.

"My god!" exclaimed Kate.

"I'll say!" agreed Ake. Each of the four smaller dinosaurs took turns darting in to slash at the flanks of the ceratopsian.

"What are they?" asked Kate.

"They look like Deinos to me," Ake told her.

"We *knows* they's dinos," said Ozma crossly.

"No, no," Ake said. "Not *dye*-nose but *day*-nose. Deino is short for Deinonychus."

"Day-nose," repeated Ozma, rolling the word around in her mouth.

"Deinos are supposed to be pretty nasty brutes, aren't they?" asked Ray.

"*Supposed* to be . . . ?" said Ake.

Ray made a face. "Your point is well taken, Ake—they seem to be making short work of that poor grass-eater."

"Change yer mind yet, Kate?" Tajil asked with a canine smirk on his face.

"Huh? Changed my mind about what?"

"'Bout bein' a grass-eater."

"No, although I will take it under advisement." She shivered in the heat. "I assume then that those little monsters are what we should be especially watchful for."

"Yes," replied Ake.

"I thought you'uns said that the mostest terrible dye-no-sores was that real big tee-rex fellow," said Frodo. "Them day-nose don't look all that huge to me."

"Well, yes and no," Ake replied. "Tyrannosaurus *is* the biggest and nastiest of the carnivores, but he's a solitary kind of guy. These fellows might be only a few meters long, but they hunt in packs of four or five. They're as fast as Terran cheetahs or Andusian racers and when their speed allows them to overtake their prey, they have sickle-shaped claws to finish it off."

"Like these four are doing," Ray said, indicating the ongoing life-and-death struggle.

"Yeah."

Circling constantly, its massive horned head lowered in defense, the herbivore fought on valiantly against impossible odds. Distracted by a mock frontal charge by two of the Deinos, the doomed plant-eater was set upon from both sides by the other two. Leaping in and out rapidly, slashing with their murderous claws, they quickly ripped enough flesh from their victim's flanks to cause it to collapse from loss of blood. As it toppled over, its shrieks and bellows much weaker, all four seemed to go berserk, attacking it in a swiping, kicking frenzy.

"I'll never think of dinosaurs as being slow-moving or turtle-like again," said a stunned Kate Golnikov.

"Lookit them things go to town!" marveled Sinbad.

"Yeah, just look at them," said Ake. He caught Ray's eye and nodded.

"Okay, guys, gals, and Kate," Ray said, pushing himself back and away from the lip of the ravine. "I think it's time we move on."

"Yep," said Beowulf.

"You'll get no argument from me," said Kate, scrabbling backwards on her hands and knees. "Who knows what other monstrosities might be attracted to the area as a result of hearing what's going on down there?"

Ray stood, brushing dirt from his trousers, and said to Ake, "Well, Chingachgook, please lead us forward before you really are the last of the Mohicans."

"Ugh," said Ake.

11

It slowly dawned on Kate that the sort of rain forest that they had been tromping through was gradually giving way to a sort of swamp. "Gosh, isn't this odd?" Kate said, pointing out the change in the vegetation to Ake and Ray.

"Yes," agreed Ake. "And all in the space of a few klicks."

Noticing how quickly the ground was becoming spongy and moist, Ray said, "You know, I was a terraformer once, but I never encountered anything like this. It must have cost a lot of Fed-creds to put together the weather and climate control for this planet."

"I hates swamps," Beowulf said.

"Oh, I dunno," said Ray. "They aren't too bad—if you're an alligator, a muskrat, a frog, or a mosquito."

"Speaking of mosquitoes . . ." Kate said.

"Hey, they ain't none!" Sinbad exclaimed. Then he added, "Hey—is that what you meant, Kate?"

She thought of several smart-aleck responses, but decided to leave that area to Ray. One such wiseacre was more than enough. "Yes, that's what I meant."

"Just one more piece of proof that this place is well thought out," Ake said.

"You're right," Ray agreed. "Squadrons of blood-suckers would up the *vérité* level, but also the discomfort level."

"And who wants to pay to be uncomfortable?" Ake said.

"Who wants to pay to take a chance on getting killed?" Kate shot back.

"Oh, lots of people."

"Not 'people,'" Kate argued. "Men. Guys with too much money for their own good—and a testosterone level to match."

"Kate got ya there," Ozma told Ray.

"I do, don't I?" said Kate rhetorically. Striding backwards, she turned toward Ray and said, "Load that in your macho pipe and smoke it, Hemingway!"

Observing her as she walked backwards, Ray waited until the last millisecond to say, "Watch out for the—"

Kate stepped right into the middle of a mudhole. She gasped as brackish water slipped up and over the tops of her hiking shoes, completely soaking her feet.

"Goddamnit!" she cursed.

"I told her to watch out," Ray said to Mama-san.

"Too bad," said Ake sympathetically. "Wet feet are a bitch."

"Could be worse," said Gawain, trying to be helpful. "Could be rainin'."

As if triggered by Gawain's words, a distant peal of thunder erupted and rolled their way.

Ray laughed and said, "At least Gawain didn't say 'Could be worse—could be a shitstorm'!"

"Very fucking funny," muttered Kate as the first big fat drops of rain began to fall.

Ake looked up at the roiling sky and a heavy drop of water landed right in one eye. "Are we having fun yet?" he muttered under his breath.

Ray quickly produced a plastic tarp from the bag Tajil carried on his back, unrolled it, and told Ake and Kate to help hold it above their heads.

Since they were now all under the same protective covering, Ray said, "Peace? I turned my testosterone level all the way down."

"Peace," Kate said stonily, then, acknowledging his getting out the tarp, added, "Thank you."

"You're welcome."

"This ain't gonna last," Sinbad said, turning his face up into the rain.

Sinbad was prescient. Although the rain came down torrentially for two or three minutes, it then slowed dramatically, and finally petered out in a few last defiant drops.

While Ray rolled up and restowed the tarp, several of the male dogs took this opportunity to find a convenient bush and relieve themselves. Suddenly self-conscious with Kate nearby, they made sure they were out of her sight before doing their thing.

"Now that the vegetation is well and truly watered," Ray said, "we can continue our trek. Our five-kilometer mission: to seek out new horizons and interesting lifeforms, to boldly go where no scout team has gone before!"

"I 'member that," said Tajil. "That was *Wagon Train*."

Ray winked at Kate. She muttered something under her breath.

At one point, they stopped at the edge of a small body of water and watched as several fat and rubbery amphibians wallowed in the shallows, plunging their broad heads beneath the surface to pull up water plants growing on the bottom. The size and shape of a Terran hippo, except for a neck that was too long, each of the roly-poly creatures radiated a certain zest for life that was infectious.

"My old grandma—" began Ray.

"Here we go again," said Ake, rolling his eyes.

"—had a saying: 'Happy as a hog in a mudhole.' I'd say that fits these chubby chompers to a tee."

Hearing several of the dogs laughing, Ray turned in time to see a number of small web-footed lizards running upright across the face of the water, their legs a blur as they propelled themselves across the surface like mad windup toys.

"Lookit them goofy things go!" marveled Tajil.

Not everything in the water was as benign as the massive bottom-feeders or the water-skimming lizards, however. A snake swimming across the surface suddenly disappeared in a swirl of water. After a moment a long, loglike thing—only its snout, eyes and ears visible above the waterline—rose to the surface where the snake had vanished.

"Let's keep moving," Ake suggested.

"Good idea," said Kate. "I'd hate to be eaten by a log."

"I'd hate to be eaten by anything," Ray said, "but then I'm funny that way."

They walked for another ten minutes, each meter of the landscape filled with wondrous sights. "This is wonderful, isn't it?" Ray said.

Kate grudgingly agreed that it was indeed wonderful. "But

what happens to you if you run into trouble?'' she wondered. "I know we signed a waiver, but the resort doesn't just write you off, does it?"

Ake shook his head, then nodded toward the northwest. "There is a force-field-protected refuge about two meters in that direction, according to the map I committed to my external. It's one of dozens scattered about Dinoland."

"A refuge?"

"An underground shelter containing food, water, medicine, and a communications linkup with Neverland security and the park rangers' station just outside Dinoland."

"How do they keep the dinosaurs out?" Kate wondered. "I hear some of them are supposed to be pretty intelligent."

"There's no lock to pick, if that's what you mean," Ake answered. "You simply place your palm on the entry patch, and the hatch cycles open to admit you and only you."

"Oh," Kate said, brightening. "That's a good idea—a place to head for if you find yourself in over your head."

Looking down at her mud-encrusted feet, she said, "Why don't we head over there and take a load off our feet for a while?"

"There is a fifty-thousand-credit surcharge for using a refuge," Ake stressed.

"What?!"

Ake smiled. "I guess they don't want people chickening out and using the refuge for anything less than a real emergency."

"Do they still charge you if it is a *real* emergency?"

"Yep."

"Guess there's no point in shooting Ray in the foot, then, is there?"

"Hey!" said Beowulf.

"What's up, dog breath?" Ray asked Frodo when the black and white–marked dog trotted back from his position on the point.

"'Member when you tried out the quicksand on the bolcano planet, checkin' to see if ya could float?"

Ray winced. "Don't remind me."

"Well, I think they's some more o' that stuff up ahead," the big dog said.

"You sure, Frodo?" Beowulf asked.

Annoyed at being second-guessed, even by Beowulf, Frodo said crossly, "I thinks so, but y'can try walkin' 'cross it if ya wants."

"Quicksand?" said Ake, his face wrinkled in puzzlement. "On Hephaestus? I don't recall any quicksand incident."

"Yeah, quicksand," Ray told him. "The reason it doesn't ring a bell is because that was when Maria and the cats and the dogs and I were on the trail of Waldo Lynch and his Lost Boys. You were with the K'a-nii, off somewhere over the rainbow."

"Oh," Ake said.

Ray looked at Frodo and then Beowulf. "I have no problem with taking Frodo's word for it, Beowulf," he told his leader. "Let's detour around it."

"Yah," said Tajil. "Quicksand sucks."

II

"Can we stop for a few minutes?" Kate asked. "I'm bushed."

"Bushed?" repeated Ray evaluatively, glancing at the heavy vegetation that pulled at their legs. "Bushed? I wonder if the term originated in a similar situation."

"Stopping for a brief rest might not be a bad idea," Ake agreed. "I think we could kill two birds with one stone if we had something to eat and drink as well."

"Okay," said Ray dubiously. "However, I was hoping we could wait until we got out of these swampy lowlands before stopping."

"There's a nice open, dry spot over there," Kate said forcefully, unslinging her rifle and massaging her shoulder. She walked over to the grassy knoll she'd indicated and sat down.

"Um . . . I guess this is the place," Ake said.

"I guess so," Ray agreed reluctantly.

The dogs circled around a half-dozen times before plopping down with massive canine sighs. Ray removed the packs from Tajil's and Sinbad's backs and pulled out several packets of food and water. After getting the dogs started, he handed Kate and Ake their provisions. Kate eagerly popped up the built-in straw on the water pouch and sucked on it long and hard.

"Plain old water can taste pretty damn good," she said.

"What is this, roast beef?" Ake asked, eyeing the sandwich Ray had tossed him.

"What's the label say?"

"Roast beef. But it doesn't look like roast beef."

"So what? It all tastes like chicken anyway," Ray asserted.

"Food philistine," Ake admonished him.

Ray shrugged, watching the dogs inhale their victuals. "I eat to live, not the other way around. I'm concerned more with the spiritual side of things, not the mundane, physical aspects of ordinary life. I am one with the universe."

Kate sputtered and then said, "Look what you almost made me do! I almost shot water out my nose!"

Ray smiled. "That would have been worth two points for me. 'Course, if I can get Ake to blow his sandwich through his nostrils, that's worth much more—twenty points at least." He dug into his own sandwich. He didn't know what it was, but it tasted like chicken.

Without warning, a sleek-furred rodentlike thing the size of a raccoon but with the speed of a rabbit dashed through the middle of their small encampment, seized the food satchel in its teeth, and made off with it.

"Hey" shouted Robin.

Ray's jaw dropped in astonishment as Robin took off in pursuit of the bodacious thief.

"No!" shouted Beowulf as the others got up to chase after Robin. "The rest stays here. Gawain, you, me, and Tajil gonna follow Robin."

Ray leapt to his feet and grabbed his energy rifle. "Wait here," he said to Kate and Ake.

"Where do you think you're going?" demanded Ake.

"I've got to go after them."

"Be careful, shrimpkin," Ake told him.

"Aren't I always?"

Ray caught up to the dogs after a routine that included jogging for a hundred meters, then walking rapidly for the next hundred meters, and then jogging again. They were sniffing at the food satchel, lying abandoned on a small spit of sand jutting out into a murky expanse of water.

"Where's the culprit who stole our food?" Ray asked, glancing around nervously.

"Doan know, Ray," Beowulf replied. "We losed sight of him for a minute and then found the bag here jes' like this."

"But," Robin said. "I seen something disappearin' into the water."

Ray looked more carefully at the water; there were several streams of small bubbles rising to the surface. Beowulf and the others saw them, too.

"Be careful, Beowulf!" Ray warned.

"Yah, yah, I be careful," the big dog replied offhandedly.

Beowulf was concentrating too intently on the edge of the small body of water to pay much attention to Ray's words of caution.

"Are you sure that you saw something go into the water?" Ray asked Robin.

"If Robin say he saw it, he saw it," Gawain defended.

"I'm not questioning his honesty," Ray said to Gawain, "just his accuracy."

"Yah, I saw it here," Robin repeated. "Well, mebbe not the little fuzzy that stole our food—but somethin' slid into the water."

Ray scanned the water anxiously. If there *was* something just under the surface there, he didn't want any of the dogs getting too close to the edge. On land, especially with Ray's weapons, they were a fair match for any predator, but if something amphibious managed to get any of them into the water, its more natural environment, it would be goodnight Irene.

"There!" Tajil said. "There, did you see it?"

"See what?"

"Somethin' . . . somethin' under the top."

They stood peering intently into the water, so intently that they failed to appreciate that by standing at the edge of the little peninsula, they had left themselves vulnerable from a less obvious direction.

Suddenly, Ray looked at Beowulf with a strange half-grin on his face. Beowulf stared back, his fur rising raggedly. As they started to turn to confront whatever it was that had subtly aroused their senses, something large and powerful launched itself from the water onto the narrow spit of land behind them—blocking their escape.

"Oh, shit!" shouted Ray as the monster raised up on its half-fins/half-limbs and clumsily but vigorously crawled toward them, its jaws gaped open to display its impressive set of teeth.

The dogs immediately assumed a defensive posture in front of Ray, but even four of them would likely be no challenge for this prehistoric monster. It looked to be about eight meters long, weighing in between one and two metric tons. Its predator's instincts excited by the sight of so much meat, the creature lunged forward while making a peculiar grunting sound—"HHunnh, HHunnh, HHunnh."

Tajil approached the creature from its right, drawing it toward him. Then Gawain, barking furiously and snapping his jaws, darted in from the left and drew the monster back toward him. Beowulf stood guard in front of Ray while he doublechecked to make sure his energy rifle's safety was flicked off.

"Okay," Ray shouted to the two dogs distracting the beast, "get out of the way while I blast this sucker." Aiming right down the monster's gullet, he said, "Eat this, fishface!" and pressed the firing stud. A little cloud of smoke came out of the gun's barrel. "Uh-oh," said Ray.

Beowulf, maintaining his defensive posture in front of Ray, said, "Don't kid 'round, Ray. Shoot."

"I'm not kidding," said Ray, watching doom crawl toward them, grunting, "HHunnh, HHunnh, HHunnh."

"Our only chanct is in th' water," said Beowulf, "where we got no chanct."

"That almost makes sense," said Ray as he looked at the impotent energy rifle with speculation in his eyes.

As the monster just missed closing its jaws on Gawain, Ray decided. "Guys, you're gonna have just a few seconds to start tearing the living bejeezus out of this brute, so don't waste a moment or I'm going to be on his insides looking out."

"Ray, what you . . . " began Beowulf. Then the big dog gasped as Ray deliberately walked toward the creature's open jaws. The massive amphibian whipped its head back and forth in an instinctual frenzy to rip and tear. The monster's protruding teeth slashed the sleeve of Ray's shirt to ribbons as he thrust his arm toward the steel trap of its jaws. The dogs watched in horror as he guided the inert energy rifle into the great beast's maw. Blood flying from his arm, Ray bit his lip to keep from screaming.

"C'mon, you damn mutts!" he shouted, and the dogs belatedly leapt into action. With the energy rifle wedged in the monster's throat, blocking open its jaws, the dogs were free to go on the offensive. While the creature writhed and thrashed, they tore into its sides with their own rather substantial teeth. A strange gurgling, hissing sound came from the beast and Ray, backing away holding his bloody arm, said, "Where's that ole 'HHunnh, HHunnh, HHunnh,' now?"

Sensing the possibility of death, the giant amphibian flopped its way toward the water. As the edge of the land approached, all the dogs but Gawain dropped away from the monster's body. "Gawain, let go!" urged Beowulf. With Gawain still clinging to the creature's side, his jaws clamped securely in its pasty flesh, the creature rolled into the water with a tremendous splash.

"Chrissakes!" murmured Ray as the big amphibian disappeared in an explosion of bubbles. As they watched, the bubbles slowly stopped rising to the surface.

"Gawain, he . . . *dead*?" asked Robin.

Suddenly, the surface of the water was broken by Gawain's shaggy head as he sputtered and gasped for breath. Ray and the other dogs sighed in relief and helped pull him from the water. "You big chowderhead," Ray chided him. "Don't you know when to let go?"

"Sorry, Ray," Gawain said forlornly. He was still coughing up water.

"Hey, I didn't mean it that way," Ray said. "I was just relieved to see your big brown head."

"Ray," said Beowulf authoritatively, "we gotta get you to some help."

"Huh?"

"Your arm."

Ray looked down and saw torn flesh beneath the shreds of his ruined shirt. Blood streamed down his arm to drip from his fingertips. "Well, warn Ake to tell the hotel staff not to bother laundering this shirt," he said before passing out.

Shot up with drugs and antibiotics, Ray nonetheless briefly regained consciousness in the floater lifting them back to Midway Island and safety. "Auntie Em," he said, seeing Kate's anxious face staring down at him. Then he noticed the others. "I dreamed I was in this strange place. You were in my dream . . . and you and you and . . . " He lapsed back into unconsciousness.

"Was that for real?" asked Kate. "I mean, he's crazy as a Vapian loonybird, but not even Ray would wake up, see us, and consciously try to pull a giggler like that . . . would he?"

Ake glanced down at Ray's peaceful face. "I don't know, Kate. That's Ray for you."

Beowulf just grinned crookedly and told the other dogs, "Ray gonna be okay."

III

"Hey," said Ake, his face lighting up like a rescue beacon when he saw Ray sitting up in his hospital bed. "They tell me you're gonna be okay."

"Will I be able to play the piano?"

"Like Rubinstein."

"Good, I always wanted to be able to play the piano but never found time for lessons."

"Okay, enough silliness," Ake told him, pulling up a chair and sitting down near Ray's bed. "How *are* you?"

"Fine and dandy." Ray held his arm out in front of himself and flexed the fingers on his hand. "See—good as new. It takes more than a 'HHunnh, HHunnh, HHunnh' monster to get the better of me."

"That's what you call the thing that attacked you?"

"Yeah," Ray replied. "So what's its real name?"

"Murray."

That cracked Ray up and he couldn't stop giggling for a minute. "How're the dogs?" Ray was finally able to ask. "How's Kate?" He made a face when he realized how awful that juxtaposition may have sounded.

Ake, aware that equating Kate with the dogs was not a negative association in Ray's mind, simply answered, "They're fine. Everyone's doing great."

"Bet Kate can't wait to get back to Dinoland, eh?"

"I think 'when Hell freezes over' sums up her feelings."

"Can't say I blame her; we didn't exactly show her a good time," Ray conceded. "Ballsy character, though."

"Ballsy?"

Ray waved a hand at him. "Don't get on my case, Mr. District Attorney. You know what I mean."

"Yeah, I do, but I *like* getting on your case."

Ray made a pathetic, dramatic, and totally phony cough-of-death sound. "Sure, pick on a sickie."

Ake was about to lob a return over the net when a klaxon blared and an authoritative computer voice boomed, "Code Red Alert, Code Red Alert!"

"What's that?" Ray asked.

"An extreme emergency. Someone's had a cardiac arrest . . . or worse."

"What's going on?" Ake asked a multiarmed robot medical technician rolling rapidly down the hallway.

The robot stopped and swiveled its "head" toward Ake. "It is a Code Red Alert," the medibot answered, speaking in a well-modulated voice calculated to soothe.

"I know that, for Chrissakes!" Ake exclaimed. "Who's being brought in?"

"Someone said it was the owner," the medibot said, its head rotating back to the front as it sped off quickly.

"The owner . . . ?" Ake said, slowing to a halt. "Harris Webster?"

12

With the dogs ramming him and rubbing up against him in pure canine pleasure, Ray realized how glad he was to be back home again; well, back in their suite. He only wished he'd returned under different circumstances.

"We go out soon?" Beowulf queried. Like all the dogs, he was growing restive indoors.

"Yah, how 'bout a walk?" seconded Robin.

"Soon." Ray knuckled Robin's head, glancing over at Kate and Ake.

"Harris Webster is dead?" Kate said dully, her words more statement than question. She sat forlornly in a large, overstuffed chair.

Ake nodded affirmatively, and put down his cup of coffee. "Apparently his heart stopped and nothing could be done to get it started again in time."

Ray looked up from thumping Tajil's side and asked, "What do you mean in time?"

"In time to prevent irreversible brain damage." Ake shrugged, staring into his coffee. "The heart is a machine, a pump; it can be replaced. It would have been no problem to put in a temporary mechanical pump until a new heart could be grown from his cells.

But it all happened so quickly, there was no time to save him. His brain had been deprived of oxygen for too long."

"*Why* was there no time?" Ray asked, straightening up.

"What do you mean?"

"How did it happen? Why wasn't there anyone around? I thought Harris Webster was surrounded by medibots and assorted human flunkies. It is just not conceivable to me that one of the richest men in the galaxy could die of a heart attack. If he had a known heart problem, what was he doing with his old heart anyway? Why hadn't it been routinely replaced as a precautionary measure?"

Kate's eyes widened and she looked sharply at Ray. "Surely you don't mean to imply that there was anything suspicious about his death, do you?"

Ozma, distressed by the talk of death and seeking attention, came over and lay her head in Kate's lap; Kate reached out automatically and stroked Ozma's silky head. The big female dog closed her eyes and sighed.

"I sure as hell do!" Ray said. "Maybe this was all a tragic circumstance that should not have happened but somehow did. Maybe. And to that extent, yes, you bet your ass that his death was suspicious! It's suspicious whether or not there was any . . . any . . ."

"Foul play?" Ake stopped staring into his coffee and lifted his blue-green eyes until they locked onto Ray's.

Ray gnawed on his lower lip. "I don't know. All I know is that a man as rich and powerful as Harris Webster doesn't just up and die like this." He returned Ake's gaze, challenging him to provide answers that made sense.

"What's that supposed to mean? What do you expect *me* to do?"

"Well, for one, we could put aside all this speculation if we found out for sure what killed him," Ray told his physician partner. "His heart stopped? Okay, *what* made his heart stop? Why wasn't he being constantly monitored? You used to be a secret agent—blow the dust off and rev up the old machinery."

"That's right," Kate agreed. "At the very least, you should be able to get your hands on Webster's medical history—*Doctor* Ringgren."

Ake sighed and bridged his fingers. He stared at the floor for a long time; no one said anything. Lifting his eyes, he stood up, said, "Wait here," and headed toward the front door.

"Bye," said Gawain.

"That was fast," Ray told Ake when the latter returned in just under an hour with the telltale plaspaper printouts.

"Speed is my middle name. Okay, let's see what we have here," Ake said, removing the printouts from their folder and laying them on the table in front of Ray and Kate. He scanned the documents rapidly and with a practiced eye. "Hm-m-m, the first thing to notice is that this medical history is about as complete as you can get; the last notation was entered just six hours before his death."

Both Ray and Kate peered at Ake's prize intently. About halfway through his perusal, Ray glanced up at Ake, his eyebrows arching. Ake returned Ray's gaze with a look that acknowledged his partner's skepticism, but he said only, "I thought that would get your attention."

"What?" asked Kate. "What got Ray's attention?"

Ake tapped the printout with his finger. "This. Harris Webster got a new heart a year ago."

"Then how could he die of heart failure? I don't get it."

"Me either," Ray said. "With his new heart—and other replacement organs—Webster should have lived to be a hundred and twenty."

"That's right," agreed Ake.

"Then what made his heart stop?" Kate demanded.

"There's a tried and true way to find out," Ake said grimly, making a cutting motion in the air.

"An autopsy?" Ray wrinkled his nose in disgust.

"What's an awe-top-see?" wondered Gawain.

"I think that's when ya cuts somebody open," replied Mama-san.

"That's correct, Mama-san," Ake said.

Ozma made a strange snuffling sound. "Ah, can Ozma and I go outside?" asked Grendel.

"In the middle of the night?" Ray asked. Then he looked at Ozma's expression. "Sure," he said. "Just don't go far and be careful."

"Okay."

"Can I go with 'em?" asked Robin.

"Sure. And take Sinbad, too," Ray told him.

Ray opened the door for the four dogs, looked up and down the corridor, and then closed the door and locked it. "That squarenut at the end of the hall has to learn to duck back around the corner faster than that," Ray said to no one in particular.

Returning to the table, he picked up the thin plaspaper sheets to take a closer look at them. He noticed that page five, the final page of Webster's medical report, seemed thicker than the others. Peering at it closely, he saw that it was two pages, not one—pages five and six had stuck together. Using his thumbnail, Ray separated the top sheet from the second page which had become bonded to the first page's underside. "Hey, guys, there's another page here."

"Really? What's on it?"

Ray peered at his find. "Oh, not much . . . just that there's a notation here saying that they're going to cremate Webster's body at eight tomorrow morning."

"What!"

"Well, I can see what's coming," said Kate heavily. "I have only one question: Isn't it illegal to perform an unauthorized autopsy?"

"No more so than it is to commit murder," replied Ray grimly.

* * *

When Ray and Ake strolled into the dispensary at two A.M., the medibot staff was uncertain how to proceed. The admitting robot rotated its metal eyestalks between Ake and Ray and said, "This is all most irregular. The dispensary is not open at this hour except for emergencies. Is this an emergency?"

Knowing that the medibot would observe and record his human facial expression, if not be especially responsive to it, Ake smiled. "No, I must confess this is not an emergency. I do, however, need to make use of the dispensary's facilities."

The medibot considered that. "If your visit is not an emergency and you do not have authorization from Dr. Minasian, then you must return during regular hours."

"What I *must* do," Ake replied pleasantly, "is examine my friend's injury and change the bandage."

The medibot's metal eyestalks swiveled to look at Ray again. "He does not seem to be in discomfort at this time."

"Nonetheless, his bandage must be changed," Ake insisted.

Ray held up his arm. Beneath his clear spray-on bandage there was a small amount of blood. His wound was oozing blood because Ray had smashed his arm against a piece of machinery just outside the entrance to the dispensary, biting his lip against the pain. His self-flagellation had popped several of his sutures and induced a credible amount of bleeding.

Staring down at the medibot, Ake said, "You can see that Mr. Larkin's arm requires attention."

On cue, Ray moaned and said, "It hurts, Dr. Ringgren. It hurts."

<*What a performance, D'Artagnan,*> Ake beamed at Ray. To the medibot he said, "See, he *is* feeling discomfort."

There was a long silence. "I should contact Dr. Minasian," the medibot said.

"But it's so late," Ake pointed out.

With just enough volume for the recalcitrant 'bot to hear him, Ray said, "Maintenance and repair."

The robot understood Ray's implication. "You are correct, Dr. Ringgren. Dr. Minasian may not wish to be to be disturbed at this hour," the 'bot agreed. "All right. You may enter and use the facilities."

"Thank you," Ake said. He took Ray by the elbow—eliciting a loud "Ouch"—and led him past the robot guardians and down the corridor.

Once they were out of sight, Ake took Ray into an examining room and found a dissolving agent to remove his bandage. "You think that bucket of bolts suspected anything?" Ray asked.

"Who knows?" Ake replied. "But I'm changing your dressing for real. If anyone asks, I can say with a straight face that I did indeed re-dress your wounds."

"Ouch!"

Ake looked up. "Was that one for real?"

"Yeah."

"Good. Even more believable."

"Thanks."

As Ray slid off the metal examining table, he said, "You know, I just had a horrible thought."

"Yeah?"

"What if they got nervous and already cremated Webster's corpse?"

Ake thought that over for a minute before saying, "Unlikely. That would only arouse suspicion. No, they'll do everything by the book. I don't think this group is all that imaginative."

"This group . . ." Ray repeated. "I wonder who the hell we're talking about?"

"I don't think we'll have to wait long to find out. Even if Webster's death was planned, it may not have been meant to happen for a while yet. We may have accelerated the schedule."

"Little ole us?" Ray asked innocently.

"Yeah, we have a way of doing that."

"I think you're right."

"Me, too. Now then, let's find a corpse."

II

"Wow," exclaimed Sinbad. "Look at them stars!"

The other dogs stared up into the night sky. It was true: Neverland's system was located in an especially impressive cluster. Since the pristine air was free of pollution or anything that impaired night vision, the stars stood out like intense burning diamonds nestled in a jet-black cloth setting.

"Jeez, this better than Terra any day," Robin said.

At the mention of Terra, Ozma dropped her head for a second—causing Grendel a twinge of regret that the yellow-and-brown female dog she loved like a sister was still mired in unhappiness. Thinking about that for a moment, Grendel decided to try another approach.

"Ya know, Ozma," Grendel said, "Littlejohn woulda liked this sky, too. But since he can't be with us'ns no more, he woulda wanted you to enjoy it yourself."

"What you say?" asked Ozma, somewhat offended that Grendel would dare to mention Littlejohn's name.

"You hearded me. Littlejohn loved you and he loved life. I think he woulda wanted you to continue to love life like ya did when the two o' you was together. It would hurt him to see ya throw away everythin' cause he can't be with you no more."

Seeing Ozma tremble, both Sinbad and Robin stood absolutely still, not daring to say a word.

Finally, Ozma looked at Grendel with sad eyes and said, "You right, Grendel. I gots to stop actin' like its the end of the world. The best way to honor Littlejohn's memory is to live for him."

Grendel nodded gratefully. She turned her big head away for a moment so Ozma couldn't see how close she was to crying. "C'mon, then," she said thickly. "Let's get the heck away from the hotel and see what kinda trouble we can get into."

"Yah!" barked Robin joyously.

Ozma gonna be all right, Grendel thought. *Ozma gonna be herself agin.*

Sinbad crept through the tall grass on his belly, pushing himself along with his rear legs. He raised his head slightly and his nostrils flared as he sniffed the air. Now where were the others . . .

Suddenly, a shape materialized out of the night and nipped him on the rump. "Tag! You's it!" shouted Ozma gleefully.

"Ah, boop!" exclaimed Sinbad, disgusted to have been gotten so easily. "All right," he said. "Go hide." He put his head down on his paws and counted to fifty. The dogs used to count to one hundred, but Ray told them fifty was plenty, given how deliberately they counted the numbers off.

"Hey, Sinbad, look," said Robin, dropping down onto his belly beside Sinbad.

"You 'sposed to be hidin'," Sinbad told the red dog.

"Did you see 'em?" Grendel whispered loudly as she joined the two males.

"See what?" queried a confused Sinbad, opening his eyes.

"Them," Grendel said, gesturing with her nose as Ozma settled in beside her, using the tall grass as cover.

Their romping and playing had taken the four dogs several kilometers from the hotel grounds. Eventually their hide-and-seek game had found them crossing the same plastcrete roadway used by the massive floater that had carried them to Neverland's hotel.

His ears erect and rotated forward, Sinbad finally discerned what everyone else was talking about: a column of vehicles slowly making its way down the road toward the hotel.

"Golly," Sinbad said. "Lookit all them trucks." Then he looked at his companions. "Hey, why we hidin' from *them*?"

"Dunno," confessed Grendel. "Jes' seems like the thing to do."

"Howz come they doan got no headlights?" Robin wondered.

"Mebbe they usin' infer-red or sumpthin'," Grendel speculated.

"Geez, that could be," agreed Robin. "An' that answers why we's hidin'; if'n they doan wanna be seen, then it ain't smart to let 'em know we seen 'em."

"I think Robin's right," Ozma said.

"What all this mean?" Sinbad asked.

Grendel shrugged. "Who knows?" Then she added, "We can

ask Ray and Ake, they prob'ly know since they knows almost everythin'."

"Yeah," Ozma said. "They knows the answers."

"Well, there they go," Robin said as the last of the small convoy vehicles disappeared from sight down the road in the direction of the hotel.

"Hey, Robin," Sinbad said.

"What?"

Sinbad nudged Robin with his nose. "Tag, you's it."

"Ah, fudge!"

III

"Over here," said Ray, flexing his fingers. His reinjured wound was throbbing painfully.

"What is it?" Ake asked, coming over.

"A locked door."

"This should be it, then," Ake agreed. He pulled a small injection gun from his bag and pressed it against Ray's arm.

"What was that?" Ray asked suspiciously.

"What do you think? A painkiller."

"Got anything else useful in your little black bag—like maybe that handy, dandy little gadget that Thane Wyda gave you for Christmas eons ago? The thing that dices vegetables, removes fish scales, and opens locks?"

"It's right here," Ake said, taking out the small egg-shaped object and passing it over the door's locking mechanism. Deceived by the device's electromagnetic emission, the internal controls obligingly aligned themselves and the door hissed open.

"Bingo," Ray said. He slipped into the room and the motion and body-heat sensors automatically turned on the lighting. Ray made a face: The sterility of the interior was testimony to the fact that they were in the correct place.

Ake crossed the room to a wall which contained a dozen lockers and said, "Eeny, meeny, miny, moe." At moe, he stopped at one of the lockers and opened it.

When Ake grasped the opener on the heavy plastic body bag to unseal it, Ray hid his discomfort by saying, "Seals freshness in, odors out." Then, reluctantly, Ray forced himself to look. Ake had chosen a pull-out drawer containing the body of an elderly woman.

"Sorry to disturb you, ma'am," Ake said, resealing the bag and pushing the metal slab back into its vault. He closed the locker back up again.

"Christ, what would it hurt to put clothes on the bodies?" Ray asked, blinking.

"They're past caring about things like modesty," said Ake. Then he saw Ray's beet-red face and added, "Even if you're not."

Another locker slab and another stranger. Then they found what they'd come for.

"Hello, Mr. Webster," Ake said softly to the placid-featured body of their deceased benefactor.

"Is he really . . . ?" Ray began. He knew he was thinking crazy thoughts, but Webster appeared to be merely sleeping.

"Oh, he's dead all right," Ake said. "He may not look it, but take my word for it, he's the late Harris Webster."

Ray shivered. "Damn, it's cold in here. Come on, Ake. Let's get started so we can get this over with."

"Help me get him onto that table," Ake ordered him. When Ray did his part without hesitation, Ake said, "That's good."

Ake examined his surroundings. "Everything I need seems to be here." He pulled a small recording device from his bag and then looked at Ray. "Think you'll be able to hold the recorder steady while I do this?"

Ray swallowed. "Sure. Besides, I have eyelids, haven't I?"

"Good." Ake picked up a laser scalpel and, as soon as Ray gave him the go sign, said, "This is the audio and visual recording of the autopsy of Harris Webster. I will begin by making a small incision . . ."

★ ★ ★

"Gosh, am I glad to see you two," Kate told them as she closed the door behind them. "It's been so long, I was beginning to get worried."

"Yeah, us too," Beowulf told his leader.

"'Sides that, we's really hungry, Ray," said Tajil.

"Yah," piped up Frodo. "It's chow time."

"Food!" said Gawain emphatically.

"Yeah . . . food," said Ray dispiritedly.

"Uh-h-h, you doan look so good," observed Beowulf.

"Yah," agreed Frodo. "Ya look kinda green."

"I'll get you some food," Ray said. "As for me, I'm never going to eat again."

"At least not liver," chided Ake, delighted to have the opportunity to twit Ray for a change.

Ray counted noses. "The others aren't back yet, eh?"

"No," said Beowulf.

Ray looked at his watch. "Well, it's too soon to be worried about them, I guess. They're big dogs." He saw Beowulf's look and added, "Yeah, I know, Beowulf—I'm just saying that so I don't feel bad. I'm worried; hell, I'm always worrying about you guys."

"Ray . . ." said Beowulf softly, affectionately.

"I have a million questions," said Kate. She smiled at her exaggeration. "Or at least a dozen. But I suppose I can wait a little while longer for answers." She took in their grim expressions and Ray's pale complexion. For once he was almost as white as Ake. "I guess I don't have to ask if you found Webster's body and performed the autopsy, do I?" Kate added sympathetically.

"No, you don't," Ake confirmed.

"Whenever you're ready," she said, sitting down and folding her hands primly.

Ake said softly, "Thanks. We just need a little time." He watched Ray get out some of the dogs' food and remove it from the vacuum pouch. Ray recoiled when the odor hit his nostrils, but he ignored it and set the food down in front of the dogs. Without further ado, they dug in and Ray trudged back.

"Now?" said Kate as Ray plopped down into a chair.

"Almost," Ake said, pouring Ray a stiff shot of bourbon and handing him the glass.

"Thanks," Ray said, taking the glass and swallowing a generous amount of whiskey.

"C'mon, give," implored Kate.

"All right. It was what we suspected. Harris Webster was murdered."

Kate closed and opened her eyes. "How?"

"Poison."

Kate's face wrinkled in puzzlement. "Poison?" she repeated.

Ake nodded. "A very slow-acting and extremely difficult to detect poison."

"That's what took us so long," Ray said, holding onto his bourbon as if the glass was a life preserver. "Ake needed to get into one of the labs and run some tests on tissue samples."

"A slow-acting poison . . ." Kate repeated, as bewildered as if Ake had told her Webster had died from a witch doctor's curse. It seemed like something out of a cheap hol-vee show.

"What happens now?" Kate asked. "I mean, aren't they going to find out about the autopsy?"

"Maybe, maybe not," Ake told her. "Autopsies are not the massively invasive things they used to be. I was careful not to make any more incisions than were necessary to get access to the proper organs. The sound-imagery equipment available allowed me to forego much of the once-mandatory postmortem surgery."

"So you think they won't even notice that someone took a laser scalpel to him and just pop him into the furnace to reduce his body to ashes?" Kate asked.

Ray went even whiter. "That's a colorful and interesting way of putting it, Kate," he told her, hanging onto his whiskey glass for dear life.

"It's possible," Ake said, answering Kate's question. "But we can't kid ourselves. There's a chance someone will notice my handiwork. If so, what happens after that will be interesting. Very interesting."

A soft chime announced someone was at the door.

Already . . . ? wondered Kate.

Ray pressed a stud near the door and a small holographic image of the area just outside the door popped into being. Standing patiently in the hall were the dogs—accompanied by a beefy security man. Ray couldn't be sure that he was the same one he'd seen earlier trying to be inconspicuous.

Ray opened the door. "Lassie, you've come home!" he said.

"Your dogs," the security man said impassively before turning on his heel and walking away.

"Hi, Ray," said Robin. "We miss anythin'?"

13

"This way . . . I think." Ray stopped at an intersection and pointed down one of two possible routes to choose from at this point in the maze.

"Ya sure?" asked Beowulf.

"I said 'I think,'" Ray reiterated. "This Labyrinth of the Minotaur is hellishly clever."

"Beowulf or I can tell ya the way to go," Mama-san reminded him.

"I know you dogs can follow my scent the way I came in," Ray said, "but that would be cheating." He tapped the small plasmetal box attached to his belt. "Besides, if I get stuck, this thing's supposed to show me the way out."

"Ah, dogs is better than any ole box," Beowulf said.

"I agree," said Ray, stopping before a blank and almost frictionless wall. He looked right, then left. It was no use looking up for a clue from the sky—the labyrinth was covered by a dome as featureless as the walls.

"In any event," Ray continued, "I want to try to defeat this puzzle box myself." He looked down the right-turning path. "This way, I think."

"Ya sure you doan wanna go the other way?" teased Beowulf.

Ray smiled. "I'm not playing that game. If I said the other

direction was the way to go, you'd do the same thing to me. I know how your pea-picking little brains work."

"Yah," said Frodo. "An' Beowulf knows how your'n works, too."

"Now left again," Ray said. A moment later it was "Now straight." Then he nodded his head vigorously and said, "Yes, just as I thought."

"Yah, what?" Beowulf asked.

"I'm absofuckinglutely lost."

The dogs howled with glee. "Gonna use the box?" asked Mama-san.

Ray turned it on, thought about it, turned it off again, and said, "No." He knuckled Beowulf's broad head. "Okay, Yukon King, show me the way to go home—if you can."

Beowulf grinned and said, "This way."

Ray sighed and fell in behind the dogs. As he stared at the south end of north-going dogs, he thought about the events of the past several days. Frankly, he had a difficult time believing what had happened since Webster's death and their unauthorized autopsy.

Nothing.

While it wasn't completely correct to say that nothing had happened, it was close enough to being the truth. Boosra, Ku'brol, and other Neverland personnel had acknowledged Webster's death, of course, but they never deviated from the official line that he had died from heart failure.

That much is true, Ray thought ruefully. *Harris did die of heart failure when his cardiovascular system was paralyzed by the slow accumulation of poison "they" were feeding him for God knows how long.*

Then there was Kate. She continued to be a worry for Ake and himself. She vacillated between imagining herself as a part of their team, at least while on Neverland, and wanting to forget all about everything and hop aboard the first ship headed elsewhere. Ray couldn't blame her for thinking she was getting herself into something bigger and more deadly than she could ever have imagined. He couldn't blame her for thinking that because it was almost certainly the case.

And there was the matter of the mysterious night travelers Grendel and the others had told him about observing. Who had arrived at the hotel on Midland in the wee hours of the night in a convoy that eschewed using headlamps?

What the hell have we gotten ourselves into this time? he

wondered as Beowulf led him out of the labyrinth. *An unholy mess? An unwinnable situation?* Then he looked at Beowulf's cheerful canine face, staring back proudly at him as they moved out into the open air. *No. What we've gotten ourselves into is another goddamn, fly-by-the-seat-of-your-pants, mother-hugging adventure! And we wouldn't want it any other way!*

★ ★ ★

"It is all arranged, then," said Boosra to Kate and the others. "The lawyers and I will be expecting you at two. Goodbye."

"Goodbye," Kate said. "Now what was that all about?" she asked, breaking the phone connection and watching Boosra's holographic image collapse into a million specks of colored light that winked out of existence.

"I'm not sure," Ray mused. "But you heard her: it's all arranged, whatever *it* is."

"You think they want to see us about the . . . the you-know-what?" Ake wondered.

"The autopsy?" Ray questioned. Seeing the expression on Ake's face, he added, "Oh, for Pete's sake, Ake, I just swept the place for bugs again this morning. We can say any damn thing we wish to: autopsy, autopsy, autopsy."

"Then how about prison satellite, prison satellite—"

"Ake, there are precious few 'laws' governing Neverland," Ray shot back. "This is a privately held world accountable only to the broadest possible interpretation of the Galactic Covenant. I doubt there's any provision in there about illegal autopsies. Murder, yes; autopsies, no."

"Knock it off, you two," Kate said. "I have a more important point to bring up."

"Yeah?"

"Why is everyone acting so peculiar around us?" Kate asked. "And don't say the autopsy, because *everyone* is acting as if they just learned that we were made the kings and queen of the universe."

"About time," sniffed Ray. "I will rule with an iron fist, but with dignity and respect for my loyal subjects, each and every one of my inferiors."

"Sorry," chided Ake. "You have no inferiors."

"There's always Ku'brol and Lanskgaard," Ray countered.

"True," conceded Ake.

"Knock it off, you two clowns; I'm serious. Why are we suddenly being treated like royalty?"

"Maybe they want to be as nice to us as they can before they stretch our necks across the block for the ax," Ray said, making a chopping motion with his arm. "It's considered good form to give the executioner a good tip so he'll guarantee you a close, comfortable shave."

"Jesus and Mohammed!" Kate raged, throwing a glass across the sitting room. "Can't you ever be serious for a change?" She stomped out of their suite.

Dumbfounded, Ray looked sheepishly at Ake. "I *was* being serious," he told Ake. Ake just nodded solemnly.

"This is Mr. Bartorillo, Ms. Shaffelson, and Mr. Wu," Boosra said, introducing Ray and the others to the immaculately dressed and impeccably groomed trio who rose from their chairs in the luxuriously-appointed meeting room to greet them. "They are legal counselors from Siroccan."

Kate pulled on an earlobe, remembering that Harris Webster's home world was Siroccan. *There must be a connection*, she thought.

Ray searched Boosra's visage; she had the oddest expression on her face, one that seemed difficult to read. Ray thought about that for a moment. *Actually*, he told himself, *it's not that hard to read: It says, "Eat shit and die." Now why is she so pissed off at us?*

"Pleased to meet you," Ake said. Kate and Ray echoed his sentiment.

<*Legal counsel*?> transmitted Ake questioningly. <*Dammit! It is the autopsy, I just know it!*>

<*Relax,*> Ray told him. <*That doesn't mean a thing. They're probably here about all those unreturned library cubes.*>

Kate smiled the broadest smile she could muster and said, "Legal counsel? May I ask why we're meeting with lawyers?"

<*Way to go, Katie!*> Ray congratulated her.

The man Boosra had introduced as Mr. Bartorillo looked at his companions. When they nodded in response to his raised eyebrow, he told Kate, "It concerns Mr. Webster's will."

"His will?" Kate's smile slowly melted into a puzzled frown.

"Perhaps we had better all sit down," said Ms. Shaffelson. The small symbols she and her colleagues had tattooed on the backs of their hands attested to their high positions in the Siroccan legal system.

"Yeah, sure," Kate agreed matter-of-factly. Everyone sat down and the cuddle chairs warmly embraced them.

"Now then, I believe I should get right to the point," Bartorillo said. With his shock of snow-white hair, patrician nose, and handsome features, he looked every centimeter a high-powered and expensive practitioner of the law as might be seen in a hol-vee drama. He also looked vaguely waxlike, like he'd been incompetently embalmed. He leaned forward on his chair.

Unconsciously, Ray and Ake parroted his action although the chairs gently resisted their occupants' pulling away. "We are here to inform you that . . ." He seemed to think of something. "No, I think it best if you view the recording we brought with us from Siroccan." He turned around and activated a holoprojector, and a three-dimensional image blossomed in the middle of the room.

Bartorillo, Shaffelson, Wu, and several other conservatively attired individuals of both sexes were present in the image. Among them was a white-robed Truth Speaker, her face covered by a featureless white mask to insure her anonymity; the presence of the Truth Speaker was a guarantee of the probity of the proceedings.

"For the record," the Truth Speaker announced, "Counselors Shaffelson, Bartorillo, and Wu have never met each other before this day. Each knew that he or she was a piece of a puzzle, but none knew the identities of the other pieces." Her altered voice emanated from a small five-pointed star on the front of her robes.

The other members of the assembled group nodded, their eyes drawn to a shiny black cube in front of the Truth Speaker that Ake recognized as the most impregnable "bank box" in the galaxy.

"That is a Qumalii multidimensional security cube," Ake whispered to Ray. "Try to open one without the combination and you'll release enough energy to blast a good-sized chunk of the surrounding normal space-time continuum into null-space."

The image of Bartorillo looked out at them as he stood and announced, "Following the lead of the Truth Speaker, let me say on the record that I have been entrusted with the first third of the combination to the cube. If I understand what the Truth Speaker has just said, I presume that my two colleagues in attendance possess the others." Approaching the cube, he keyed in a series of numbers and letters, and then looked expectantly at Wu and Shaffelson.

Saying, "And I have the second," Shaffelson now rose and moved over to the cube and keyed in another series of numbers and letters. Then it was Wu's turn and he provided the final series. Rather undramatically, given the tense circumstances, the cube opened to reveal a handful of objects: plaspaper documents, message cubes, memory cores, and other less readily identifiable items.

The Truth Speaker withdrew the contents of the cube, putting aside most of the objects after giving each a cursory examination. After going through the sheath of plaspaper documents and the message cubes several times, she announced, "Here, recorded in several formats, is the last will and testament of Harris M. Webster."

Bartorillo fastforwarded the holoprojector recording until he found the moment he was searching for. The recorded Bartorillo now read from the will. "'As for the resort planet of Neverland, it is my wish that it become the property of Ake Ringgren and Ray Larkin. Further, more detailed, legal identification of both men can be found elsewhere in this document.'" There were sounds of surprise—and some consternation—both from the recorded holo and in the meeting room.

Counselor Bartorillo turned off the 'projector at that point and the vividly real office they were staring into disappeared. Facing a stunned Ray and Ake, he said, "Mr. Webster's will has been rigorously examined and shown to be properly drawn up and executed; while there may yet be challenges to it, there appears to be no question as to its authenticity or legality. Neverland is now your property."

Both Ray and Ake slumped back in their chairs, which again enfolded them eagerly.

"Well, kiss Beowulf's butt!" exclaimed Ray, not sure if he should believe his ears. Now he knew what had burnt Boosra's toast.

"Hmm-m-m, quite," said Bartorillo.

II

The twenty-four hours that followed the somewhat anticlimactic retinal and cellular confirmation of Ray and Ake's identities, and their signing of the official documents giving them possession of the resort world, passed in a haze of activity and meetings.

They were not comfortable hours, either. Boosra and Ku'brol were icily correct, nothing more. Yet, as much as it seemed to pain them to begin the process of turning over control of Neverland to its new owners, both Boosra and Ku'brol grudgingly provided whatever information Ray and Ake demanded. They needed to be asked, however; they volunteered little or nothing.

Ray put down his dowsing rod and collapsed into a chair. "Jeez, it was bad enough when I had to sweep just our rooms every chance I got," he said, blinking as he slowly downscaled his level of concentration. "Having to check out Webster's office every day now, too, is a bitch."

"Yeah," said Ake, looking around at the huge and magnificently appointed room they were in. "But now we can talk."

"Yes, we can," agreed Ray. "Hastings, get me a gin and tonic, please."

"As you wish, sir," the domestic 'bot replied, turning to its task.

"Bring me a white wine, too," added Ake. Then he looked at Ray, his eyes narrowing, and asked, "Hey, what about Hastings? Do you think *he* could be bugged?"

"Don't worry, he was one of the first things I checked out."

"Good."

"Want me to give Kate a buzz?" Ray asked as he put his feet up on an ottoman. "If she's speaking to us, that is."

Ake made a face at the memory of Kate's anger and annoyance of being left out of so much in the past day. Because the briefings were confidential, dealing with financial, contractual, and personnel matters, Boosra had insisted that Kate be excluded from them. While able to appreciate Boosra's position logically if not emotionally, Kate was understandably upset to be kept in the dark about current events—even though both Ray and Ake promised to share with her whatever they learned as soon as they could.

Before Ray could call Kate's suite, there was a knock on the karkka wood door of the office. Hastings put down the drinks and hurried to answer the knock. The opened door revealed Kate Golnikov.

"May I come in?" She was dressed in an electric blue jumpsuit that was both utilitarian and fashionable. She looked quite fetching indeed. Even her complexion appeared to have cleared up a bit during her stay on Neverland.

"Of course," Ray and Ake said simultaneously.

"Hiya, Kate," Beowulf greeted her. The other dogs called out to her as well.

"Hi, Beowulf, hi, Ozma, hi, everyone." She came into the

room, stopped for a moment when its grandness struck her, then found a cuddle chair and asked if she could sit down.

"Of course," Ake told her. "Hastings, fetch Kate whatever she wants to drink."

"A Jovian jumper," Kate said.

The little domestic 'bot stood still, the fingers on the hand of one of its many arms curling and uncurling. "Ah, I must confess I do not know how to make that," Hastings said finally.

"I'll tell ya," said Beowulf, trotting ahead of the 'bot toward the liquor cabinet.

"That Beowulf," Ray said, shaking his head in admiration. "He makes a mean omelette, too." Then he looked at Kate, blanched, and said, "Oops, I'm sorry, Kate. I'm being a wiseacre again and—"

Kate raised a hand. "It's all right, Ray. I'm over my emotional funk."

When Beowulf and Hastings returned with Kate's drink, she accepted it gratefully, took a sip, and then informed Ray and Ake that she wanted to help them assume control of Neverland. "What can I do?" she asked.

"You can come along with me when I go tell Lanskgaard he's fired," Ray told her.

"Can I? Damn, I'd even pay for the privilege!"

"Careful," cautioned Mama-san. "Ray might take ya up on that."

Both Dilon Lanskgaard and Aron Ku'brol were outraged at Ray's bland announcement that the pale youth's services were no longer needed. Ray noticed that Boosra, however, seemed to take his decision in stride. *Maybe she's been expecting it*, he told himself. *She's clearly smarter than either of these two duds.*

"My father and mother—" Lanskgaard began.

"Committed a crime against humanity by having you," Ray finished for him. "Look, I happen to know that their investment in the late Harris Webster's companies includes all his resort holdings save one: Neverland. So if they want to throw their weight around to secure a job for you, they can go find one on another resort world. On this one, you're history."

<I'd love to shove a quiver blade up your ass, dog boy!> Lanskgaard angrily transmitted without thinking what he was doing.

<I'm sure you would,> Kate shot back. <Shall I tell Ray that?

He might offer you the chance if you're willing to risk meeting him in a fair fight.>

Indeed I would, Ray thought. He was careful not to "transmit" that desire or to allow Lanskgaard to know he shared Kate's ability to receive the other's thoughts.

Lanskgaard seized his head with both hands. "Get out of my mind!" he screamed.

"As long as you keep out of mine," Kate said aloud, her statement puzzling Boosra and Ku'brol almost as much as Lanskgaard's outburst. "You seem to have forgotten I *am* an ESPer," she added.

"What the hell is going on here?" demanded Ku'brol while an expression of awareness crossed Boosra's face; her pursed lips and grim demeanor seemed to reveal that she knew the jig was up concerning Lanskgaard's ability to penetrate others' minds.

"Dick Hertz here"—Ray smiled at the wild-eyed youth and then at Ku'brol—"has been trying to pick our brains, Mr. Ku'brol. Because I'm a caring kind of guy, I'm prepared to accept that the attempted trespass was solely his idea. That's a major concession on my part because I'm aware that he lacks the brains of a Malbrodian sand flea. But should there be any such future attempts, I won't be so pleasant about it."

"Fuck you!" Lanskgaard shouted.

Ray put an arm on Lanskgaard's shoulder. "You know, pilgrim, someone oughta deck you. But it won't be me. No, I'm better than that; I'm not going to be the one to do it." He started to turn away, then suddenly said, "The hell I'm not!" He swung back around and nailed Lanskgaard flush on the jaw. The carrot-topped ESPer stiffened and toppled over like a 'Toon in a Roger Rabbit sinny. "Jesus, I almost broke my knuckles!" Ray moaned, grabbing his hand. He flexed his fingers and hopped from foot to foot.

Kate shook her head in disgust. "You've seen too many old sinnys, Ray," she scolded.

Boosra pressed a lighted square on her desk and two of the resort's muscular bellhops appeared. "Remove that, please," she said, gesturing at the heap on the floor that was Lanskgaard. The two bellhops picked him up by the legs and under his armpits and hustled him away.

Still closing and opening his hand, Ray asked rhetorically, "Can we talk?"

"It seems you're holding all the cards," Boosra replied.

"I don't think so," Ray said, shaking both his head and his hand. "Not by a long shot."

Kate shrugged, giving both Boosra and Ku'brol an evaluative look. "If they say we have the cards, Ray, then let's play a few of them."

"Why not?" Facing Boosra, he asked, "Who arrived here late one night this week?"

"Late at night? No one."

Acting as if he hadn't heard her, Ray mused aloud, "I don't think they were regular guests. I mean, regular guests don't arrive in the middle of the night, do they? Now cut the crap and tell me who they were!" When Boosra glanced at Kate, Ray snapped, "And forget about her, too! She's here because she's the only one on Neverland Ake and I can trust besides each other and the dogs."

Boosra looked at Ku'brol, who was stony-faced. "All right, I suppose you had to know sooner or later; you *are* the new owners. The people you saw arriving came for the conference."

"The conference? What conference?"

"The inaugural meeting of statespersons from all over the galaxy to begin laying the groundwork for a constitution-drafting and plenary session of the new Aligned Worlds Organization."

"My God!" Ray exclaimed. Then he rubbed the side of his nose with a finger, thinking. "This means that there is finally is going to be something to replace the Federation."

"An alliance," Kate said, wonder in her voice.

"An alliance," Boosra agreed.

III

Ray and Ake's walk with the dogs took them a few klicks from the hotel grounds proper. Since Midway was a small island, it wasn't long before they approached the high bluffs that overlooked the beach and the restless ocean. They halted at the edge and looked down at the breakers crashing onto the stony and narrow beach.

"Lookit all that water!" marveled Ozma.

"And not a drop to drink," Ray said.

"How's your arm doing?" Ake asked, suddenly acting the role of the solicitous physician. "Let me take a look at it."

"It's doing fine; it's almost completely healed," Ray said, reluctant to allow Ake to examine it.

K-9 CORPS: THE LAST RESORT 149

"Let me see it," Ake insisted in his best "I'm-the-doctor-here" voice.

"Yes, Dr. Praetorius."

"You're right, it is almost completely healed."

"Told you so." Now focused on his arm, Ray was aware of an infuriating itching sensation beneath the clear spray-on bandage. Futilely scratching at the protective coating, Ray cursed.

Ake, aware of what was going on, laughed. "It didn't itch until I made you think about it, did it?" he asked sympathetically.

"No, dammit."

Gawain and Robin, hunkered down alongside Ray, started to bite at the long hair covering their haunches. Ray guessed what was coming next: They both vigorously windmilled away at their flanks with the nails on their rear feet.

"The power of suggestion," Ake laughed.

"Yah," said Sinbad. "Doan no one fart, please. Frodo bin eatin' somethin' 'scusting lately and if'n he lets fly, we could all die."

"Look who's talking," Ray said. "You'll eat anything that even looks like it was alive once. Lord knows what it was that made you sick in the floater on the way to Dinoland."

Sinbad said, "Aw-w-w, that wasn't nuthin' 'scusting. That was jes' a piece of breakfast meat that I sneaked off the bed guy's tray when no one was lookin'."

"The bed guy? You mean Harris Webster?"

Sinbad's eyes opened wide when he suddenly realized he'd said too much. Aware he was in too deep now to fib his way out, Sinbad decided he'd better make a full confession. "Yah. He was done with his food. I mean, the tray wuz on the floor and he'd already eaten all he wuz gonna. I didn't make him sick; beoples only gets sick from dogs eatin' off their plates when they knows it. Like ya said—the power of die-gestion."

"That's 'suggestion,'" corrected Ake.

"Sinbad, I could plant a big wet one on you!" Ray said.

"For bein' bad?" Beowulf asked incredulously.

"No, for helping us to finally learn how they were poisoning Harris Webster."

14

Ray took four members of his nine-dog team with him when he visited the island continent that was home to Battlefield, the multithemed war simulation park. He made a point of bringing along Mama-san in addition to Beowulf, Robin, and Gawain because he felt he had been leaving the female members of the team behind too often lately because of their smaller size.

As for the other females, Grendel and Ozma were content to stay behind with Frodo and Kate. The final two members of the team, Sinbad and Tajil, got to play watchdog, remaining in the suite to guard against unwanted visitors. They had grumbled and complained about their assignment until Ray told them they could order the computer to run all the pro wrestling holos their little hearts desired.

Battlefield was divided into a half-dozen theme areas, each separated from the others by forty-meter-high walls. When the robot guide Ku'brol had provided them explained about that detail, Ray frowned and asked why a wall was needed at all.

"While many of Neverland's areas are as benign as archaic amusement parks once were, many others possess the potential to be extremely dangerous," the robot explained. "The wall guarantees that someone playing out one sort of adventure does not inadvertently find himself in the midst of another, unexpected one."

"Visiting Dinoland, it was easy to understand the threat posed by the 'real' dinosaurs," Ray said. "But what makes part or all of Battlefield dangerous?"

"The robots and androids which comprise the supposed combatants are, of course, programmed not to cause harm to humans whether through action or inaction; further, their weapons are only effective on nonliving participants. However, the simulated conflicts, whether they be Terra's American Civil War, World War Two, Second American Revolution, Napoleonic Wars, or Robot Wars, are waged with many real weapons which produce unavoidably dangerous situations. Fatal accidents can and do happen. We have had guests who have been hit by an out-of-control vehicle or aircraft, who have drowned, or who have been struck and killed by a piece of falling debris."

Ray gulped. "I guess I never considered the potentially lethal effects of trying to achieve verisimilitude in a 'war zone.'"

The robot responded to that by saying, "Human beings seek thrills and adventure, even at the risk of injury or death to themselves; this desire for danger is, perhaps, one of your most human traits." Ray nodded, wishing the robot's featureless "face" had an expression to read. Humanoid in shape only, the robot was a functional machine; it was not meant to fool a person into thinking it was a living, breathing human being. Most androids were constructed that way; Marla and the other pleasure androids were exceptions to the rule.

"We embrace the idea of danger, that is true," Ray replied. "But we want to be alive when the adventure is over." He thought more about that. "Still, I suppose that if there isn't at least a teeny, tiny chance that you might be killed, the thrill isn't the same. Your heart doesn't thump as much."

"Yah!" seconded Robin.

Ray thought of Littlejohn . . . and of Anson and Pandora. *Sure, the chance you could end up dead is great "fun." Actually getting killed isn't. Would you risk it again, guys?* Then he smiled sadly. He could hear all three saying, "You betcha, Ray. We wuz a team—your team. We loved ya and we died for ya and the others."

Ray stared at the robot's plain visage. "I'm not thrilled with calling you 'the robot,' or 'hey, you.' Don't you have a name?"

The robot replied, "Master Ku'brol said you would demand a name of me."

"Yeah, so?"

"He said I was to tell you that you could call me Ares."

When Ray laughed at that, Beowulf asked what was so funny. "Ku'brol has a sense of humor after all. Ares is a Greek name; in Latin it is rendered as Mars."

"Oh," said Beowulf, still not getting the name's mythological significance.

"We're here," the floater's pilot announced over the intercom.

"Huh?" The faint smile faded from Ray's lips.

"We are here." Ares repeated the pilot's words. "We have landed in the center of Battlefield."

"Yippee!" squealed Robin. "We's here!"

"Yeah," said Ray. "Yippee." He'd intended to sound a little dubious, a little cautionary—but he couldn't fool Beowulf.

"C'mon, Ray." The big golden dog easily saw through his feigned indifference.

"Oh, all right." He let out a loud whoop of pleasure that caused the robot to turn its head and stare at him curiously.

"That more like it," beamed Beowulf.

★ ★ ★

One of the perquisites of being the owner of a magnificent concert hall, Ake thought, was the luxury of having an opera performed for you alone. Actually, since he didn't have time to sit through an entire opera, Ake had asked the hotel's omnipresent computer to program just the first act of *La Bohème*; he'd catch the rest later.

Had anyone asked him, Ake would have said that the androids assuming the roles of Mimi, Marcello, Rudolfo, Musetta, and the other characters performed and sang them beautifully. Then he would have scratched his head and amended that to take into account that while the androids enacted and gave voice to the roles, they did not "perform" them in the same fallible, mistakes-can-and-do-happen style of human singer/actors.

There were other advantages to android performers besides perfection, however. Ake remembered one production of *La Bohème* in which the diva playing the consumptive Mimi was too clearly roly-poly for the audience to suspend its disbelief and accept the premise that she was wasting away. The libretto's many references to her tiny figure induced guffaws, not tears, from the audience. Such "miscasting" did not occur with artificials.

Ake closed his eyes and allowed himself to escape into Puccini's music, swept along by the melodic majesty of the score. When the holographic image of the curtain came down on the first act, Ake reluctantly forced himself to rise from his seat and prepare to resume his new role as lord and co-master of all he surveyed.

Ake stepped out of the semidarkened auditorium and into a brightly lighted corridor. While he was tucking his shirt back into the waistband of his trousers, a large, powerful man hurried past, giving Ake a curiously intense stare.

Ake's return glance was cursory and he smiled to himself. Had Ray been with him and seen the fellow's stare, he would have said something like, "All the guys find you attractive, Ake."

Still smiling, he turned down the hallway in the opposite direction when something began to nag at him. He stopped short and turned around to look back at the rapidly retreating figure. Ake wore the expression of someone trying to remember the name of an old acquaintance, someone not seen in years.

Suddenly, his eyes widened and he snapped his fingers. "Hey, you." The man did not turn around. Ake tried again, this time raising his voice even more. "Hey, you!"

The man glanced over his shoulder but kept walking. The proffered profile was enough for Ake to confirm what he'd suspected: The man had been a member of his Cadre postgraduate training unit on Terra.

"Stop!" shouted Ake. Instead of stopping, the accosted man began to run. Reaching the end of the corridor, he turned the corner and disappeared. Checking his sidearms, Ake asked, "Well, what am I waiting for?" Answering his own question, he thought, *I'm waiting for a dog to run him down and make him stay. Without one of the team to do that, it's up to me.* Ake sighed. *Why doesn't life get easier instead of more difficult?*

II

"Wow, we's gettin' in lots of walks now!" Grendel exclaimed gleefully to Kate.

When Ozma and Frodo concurred, Kate said, "Yeah, well, I want to give Midway a slow, thorough going-over. The powers that be have told us what's on this island, but I want to see with my own eyes."

"This a pretty small place, Kate," Frodo told her, his tongue lolling out as they crossed an open field of flowers under the watchful yellow eye of the sun. "Mebbe there not be much to see."

"That'll be fine and dandy with me," Kate said. She stopped, put down the energy rifle that Ake had insisted she bring along, and got out the sun-block lotion from the pack on Grendel's back. She applied another coating to her face and neck, carefully avoiding her eyes. The long-sleeved jumpsuit negated the necessity of using a spray on her arms or legs.

"That stuff keep ya from burnin' up?" asked Ozma.

"It's supposed to," Kate replied. "With my complexion, the last thing I need is a sunburn." She shaded her eyes from the sun's glare and added, "A little bit of solar radiation might be good for my skin. But just a little bit."

"Hey, there's the road again," Frodo said.

Kate looked and saw that Frodo was correct. Their walk had taken them further and further away from the hotel's end of the island and more in the direction of the landing field. They soon crossed the narrow neck of land that connected the two ends of the island. Each step was taking them closer and closer to where they'd touched down. *About a million years ago*, Kate thought ruefully.

"We goin' back to the spaceport?" Ozma asked.

"Looks that way," replied Kate.

"How's come they ain't none o' them phony dye-no-sores or nuthin'?" wondered Grendel, looking around for the holo displays that had greeted them on their arrival.

"They're probably only activated by a vehicle of some sort, like *Cleopatra's Barge*, the floater that picked us up."

"Oh, yah," agreed Grendel. "That make sense."

Kate stopped to drink some water and gave the dogs some, allowing them to drink from her cupped hand instead of bothering to pull a bowl from the pack. Feeling their huge, soft tongues lap the water gently from the palm of her hand, Kate felt closer to the dogs than she had before.

"Thanks, Kate," Grendel said, her pink tongue wiping the last drops of water from her muzzle.

Resealing the water bag, Kate realized that she was pushing herself to go all the way to the landing field. And why not? Once they'd hit their stride and fallen into a comfortable rhythm, it was easy to keep moving forward. If the dogs were surprised by Kate's stamina and determination, they made no mention of it.

"Geez," said Frodo. "There it is."

Kate shaded her eyes. Frodo was correct; a klick or two ahead, shimmering in the air rising from the plascrete, was the landing field.

"We've made it this far," said Kate. "It would be a shame to turn back now. Let's go all the way."

Tails wagging furiously, the dogs trotted out ahead of her. Ozma suddenly stopped, flopped down onto her back, and rolled around in ecstasy.

"Ozma, what the hell are you doing?" Kate demanded.

"I sorry, Kate," Ozma replied, still rolling around like she'd died and gone to heaven. "This smells so neat!"

"Yah!" agreed Frodo and Grendel, waiting their turn.

When Ozma gave way to Frodo, Kate saw that what was causing the dogs to lose all sense of decorum was the flattened carcass of a small deer or antelope.

"Is that *fun*?" Kate asked.

"Yah, it's real fun!" Grendel allowed.

Shifting from one leg to another while she waited out the orgy of sensory overload, Kate sighed. Notwithstanding the closeness and affection she felt for *these* particular dogs, Kate thought that when she retired from 'scraping she would choose a cat or two as an animal companion. Cats were more appropriate for women, she thought. Dogs were so . . . so damn *male*!

As they approached the perimeter of the field, the dogs scrunched up their faces slightly. "What is it?" Kate asked.

"Scratchy high-bitched sound," explained Grendel. "Kinda like a dog whistle."

Only then did Kate feel an electric tingle flow over the surface of her body. Already sensitized by the solar radiation, her skin produced a bumber crop of goosepimples.

"Feels like a very low-level force-field," Kate opined. "The setting is just high enough to make trespassers feel uncomfortable and unwelcome."

"It works," said Ozma.

"Just keep walking. We'll pass through it in a few seconds," Kate told Ozma and the other two dogs. After a moment, she said, "There, that's better."

Having penetrated the low-res force-field, the quartet hurried across the broad expanse of plascrete, the manmade surface of the landing field radiating back to the air all the heat of the sun it had collected.

"Whew," said Frodo.

"Yeah," agreed Kate. "Let's get off this as soon as possible." Walking faster now, following the sprinting dogs, Kate paid scant attention to *The Spirit of St. Louis*, which sat on its docking grid, a lattice of moly-steel cables crisscrossing the ship and enveloping it like a bird in a spider web. She did have a random thought about the strange scene, one which she promptly forgot: *Why's it tied down like that? They expecting a tornado?*

"Oops," said Grendel. "Runned out of island."

It was true; the landing field ended at a patch of grass. Just meters beyond the grass was the edge of the series of high bluffs that engirdled the island. Sloping downward at an angle somewhere between forty-five and ninety degrees was a cliff face that stood guard against the blue-green ocean lapping at the shore many meters below them.

"Boy," said Frodo, creeping up to the very edge of the precipice, "this not be a good place to play frisbee or drink *vez* until you is dizzy!"

When the other dogs laughed, Kate asked, "What's *vez*?"

"Oh, that was sumpthin' we had on Kye-ron."

"You mean Chiron?"

"That what I said—Kye-ron. Ya know: the Sen-tor blanket."

Kate shook her head. "I'm not drinking any *vez* and I'm getting dizzy."

"Better get outa the sun," Ozma cautioned seriously.

"Better yet, Frodo ought to get away from the edge of that cliff," Kate said impatiently. "Come on, Frodo. Don't scare the bejesus out of me by getting so close like that."

"Oh, I not so close," the big dog replied.

"Don't argue with me, Frodo. Now get—"

"Yikes!" Frodo's front paws skidded on some loose soil and before he knew what was happening, he slid over the lip of the precipice. His tail was the last part of him a horrified Kate saw.

III

Ray knew only that Kuram Freeman-Mawalzi, the president, and the three other members of the delegation from planet Uhura had selected the quadrant housing the Robot Wars as their choice of Battlefield adventures. Their "mission," coordinated by the resort's powerful central computer, was to enter the southern end of the war zone, maneuver their way through a series of carefully arranged ambushes and firefights, and emerge victorious at the northern end of the park. Easier said than done.

While the robot warriors they would encounter were programmed not to harm them, not deliberately, they did fire weapons which would register each "hit" they made. The human adventurers were permitted six hits per person before a "death" was recorded by the computer.

If the human contestants each registered the maximum number of hits, their team lost to their nonhuman opponents; if even a single human made it through without being hit more than five times, the team won. Getting just one player through successfully was more difficult than it seemed, however.

If what his robot babysitter Ares told him about the level of competition was true, Ray was certain that even a hardcore and dedicated Virtual Reality fanatic would find it taxing to make it from beginning to end without accumulating a half-dozen clean hits.

"Why is no one shooting at us?" Ray asked the 'bot.

"You and your animals have not been formally introduced into the game," Ares replied.

"Shucks," said Robin.

"That mean we's not gonna hafta fight our way to the beoples we's tryin' to find?" Beowulf asked.

"That is correct," Ares said, his head swiveling to observe a small, null-grav aircraft pass noiselessly overhead. The robot knew that the silent observer's sensory panels certainly noted their presence in the field and was sending that information to the coordinating computer.

When the little spy plane was out of sight, the robot said, "Of course, once we join the party we are seeking, under the rules of Battlefield we will become part of them and will be subject to attack."

"Atack?" asked Beowulf.

"Only in the role-playing sense," Ares reassured the big golden-haired dog.

"What that?" Gawain asked, his ears pricking up and rotating.

"What's what?" asked Ray.

"Energy weapons fire," Beowulf told Gawain. "It coming from just ahead."

Now even Ray heard it: the popping and hissing of powerful energy rifles or cannons. Plus the occasional concussive report of a grenade. "Grenades?" he asked the robot, his eyebrows arching questioningly.

"Remember, while the robots' weapons are nonlethal, the humans possess fully functional weapons. The humans can cause real damage to their robotic opponents—*if* their aim is true and their firepower adequate."

"Oh, yeah," Ray said. He'd forgotten that aspect of Battlefield already. Once again, it was a part of Neverland that justified the high fees charged guests—replacing complex AI antagonists blown to bits was enormously expensive. But, Ray understood, the "game" would not be the same if the humans didn't get to take out their opponents in a gory or spectacular fashion.

Ray also realized that the grenades also underscored what Ares had told him earlier. Since the humans were using live grenades, all it took for tragedy was for one of these would-be Rambos to make a simple miscalculation. The form the mistake took was unimportant, whether it was holding a primed grenade too long before throwing it, or having it bounce back and explode in close proximity. Unlike a *VR* exercise, gross stupidity could result in death—not a virtual death, a real death.

Entering what looked for all the world like an urban street in Boswash, Kim City, or Nasserville, Ray and the dogs were stepping into a page out of history: They were about to participate in the Robot Wars.

The statesmen/warriors from Uhura they were seeking had sequestered themselves behind a barricade of street-legals, old autos that actually ran on hydrogen fuel and sported polyglas tires. Ray examined the Uhuran diplomats' position through self-focusing binoculars. From the look of things, President Freeman-Mawalzi and his three ministers had recently overcome a small contingent of four-meter-tall battle androids. Ray put down the binoculars and waited for his eyes to readjust to normal vision.

"What the situashun?" asked Beowulf.

"It looks like they've successfully won a small skirmish. I think it's safe to approach them—if they know who we are first," Ray said, looking at Ares. "The rest of us aren't slugproof," Ray told the robot. "I think you should be the one to walk up to them waving the white flag to make sure they don't try burning little holes through us when we follow you in."

"As you wish." The robot picked his way through the debris, raising four of his six arms and saying loudly, "Do not shoot, please. I am the representative of another party of nonmechanicals—a human and his scout dogs."

When one of the men pointed his energy rifle at the submissively posed robot as if to fire, another knocked it away. "Did you not hear what the 'bot said?" he asked angrily. "Look at him; he is clearly not one of the battle androids we have been fighting."

"I am sorry, my president," the first man said, lowering his head in shame.

The second man, now identified as president Freeman-Mawalzi, made a "come here" gesture to Ares. Ares nodded, walked back toward Ray and the dogs, halted, and said, "I think it is safe to approach now."

"Let's go," Ray said. "But be careful," he added to Beowulf and the others.

"Gotcha."

They warily approached the diplomats from Uhura, careful not to make any sudden moves. "How do," Ray said, raising his hand in greeting.

"Hello. It is a surprise to find other players," Freeman-Mawalzi replied. "I thought we had been assured that we were the only gamers in this zone." He spoke perfect Fed-stan 'glish, albeit in a thick accent.

"I'm not a paying customer," Ray told him, keeping an eye on the dogs who were keeping an eye on the three others with the president.

"Mr. Larkin is the new co-owner of the resort," Ares explained, his expressionless head slowly rotating to survey the scene.

A series of wire-thin beams of light flashed overhead, causing Freeman-Mawalzi to warn Ray and his crew that they were still playing the game and did not wish to take any more hits.

"I understand perfectly," Ray said, finding better cover behind one of the destroyed autos. The dogs and Ares likewise hunkered down.

Freeman-Mawalzi said something to one of his companions in the language of his planet and then turned back to face Ray. "You are one of the new co-owners? Explain, please."

Ray waved a hand dismissively. "Not now, it's too damned complicated. Let me just say that Webster Harris is dead—murdered—and I'm here to ask you to return to the hotel with me until the unification conference begins. It's for your own safety. With unknown parties pursuing unknown ends, it is too dangerous for anyone attending the conference to be placing him-or herself at risk by playing these sorts of games."

Freeman-Mawalzi looked dubious. "A stranger tells me that Harris Webster has been murdered and there is some sort of a conspiracy which he must protect me from? I must say, I find all this extremely hard to believe. Perhaps, sir, you have been watching too much hol-vee."

"Perhaps," Ray allowed. "Or maybe this is all just a paranoid's fantasy. Nonetheless, I am here to convince you to return to Midway with me."

"I will return," Freeman-Mawalzi replied gravely. "But the path out lies to the north."

"To the north?" said Tajil, questioningly.

"Through the battle zone," Freeman-Mawalzi explained. He smiled. "We are almost halfway through and have accumulated only thirteen hits. Surely, there is no danger in going forward with the game."

"There is always danger in a situation like this one." Ray shrugged. "But, in the absence of more compelling evidence that your life is in danger, I will not argue with you, Mr. President." He looked at the eager canine faces turned his way. "We will do our best to keep you alive while you complete your simulated war."

"How very dramatic you are," the Uhuran leader said. "Come, let us show you our most recent victory over the battle 'bots."

Robin snorted derisively, but Freeman-Mawalzi seemed not to hear.

15

"Holy mackerel!" Gawain exclaimed upon seeing the smoking ruins of the three massive robots.

"Impressive, aren't they?" beamed the Uhuran president. A slender black man with a salt-and-pepper mustache, his easy air of competence both impressed and vaguely irritated Ray. Ray appreciated people who believed in themselves; the danger was believing you were immortal.

"Yes, they are impressive," Ray had to admit. He slowly approached one of the downed robots, a huge hole blown into its upper torso. There was a smell of charred metal and plastic, and a hot, rank odor of boiled lubricant also wafted from the remains.

One of Freeman-Mawalzi's companions nudged him and said something in Uhuran to him. Freeman-Mawalzi nodded and said to Ray, "Freeman-Amboma thinks you are much impressed by the battle androids. Do they seem too real for comfort for you?"

"You could say that," Ray allowed, continuing his examination of the destroyed 'bots. The sight was unnerving to Ray because the three fallen giants were identical to the two illegal 'bots he had vanquished on the prison ship.

Ares stepped forward to attempt to assuage Ray's fears. "These units, while conforming to the physical proportions of the originals, lack the pseudo-quantum-gravity brains of the outlawed models."

Freeman-Amboma said something in his native tongue and pointed at the fallen androids. "That is most certainly true," Ares said in response.

"What's true?" Ray demanded. "What did he say?"

"He observed that if these mechanical warriors possessed P-Q-G brains and real weaponry, none of you would have any chance at all against them or of getting out of Battlefield alive."

★ ★ ★

After searching futilely up and down the corridor, Ake came to the realization that his quarry must have found a way back into the concert hall—a doorway or other opening that was not immediately apparent. "Okay, where is it?" he asked out loud, running his fingers along the wall. His sensitive fingertips soon felt a vertical crack.

"Ah, hah!" he exclaimed triumphantly. The crack was just the width of a hair. *No wonder I didn't spot this right away*, he told himself. He found the pressure point that activated the door and it hissed open. He peered cautiously into the empty auditorium.

Nobody. That wasn't literally true; the android performers were still on stage and in the orchestra pit. "Nobody here but us chickens," Ake said softly, palming his needle gun. "To quote a certain short stuff, 'Here goes nothing.'" He stepped into the aisle running down the right side of the auditorium and immediately ducked down behind the nearest row of seats.

Now what? he wondered. He stared at the android singers standing motionless on stage. *That's odd. You'd think they'd be programmed to leave the stage—go walk into a storage compartment or something until they were needed again.* Then he thought about that. Maybe they were waiting for the opera to continue; patiently biding their time—as if the concept of time meant anything to them—until Ake returned and requested that they resume playing out the melodrama.

Ake stood up slowly and turned this way and that, looking for the man whom he had convinced himself had made his way inside the auditorium. After walking up and down the side and center aisles, looking down each row of seats and finding no one, he began to question the correctness of his assumption. Given a multitude of directions in which to go, he had apparently not chosen the right one.

With his growing conviction that his quarry was not to be found in the auditorium, Ake straightened up. Immediately, the tension he'd felt began to drain out of him and he massaged the back of his neck with his left hand. Sighing, he gave the android performers a perfunctory final glance before turning around to head up the center aisle and exit through the main doors at the rear of the hall.

Suddenly, his eyes widened for the second time in five minutes and the hair on the back of his neck stood up. Reflexively he threw himself to the floor a fraction of a second before a bolt of energy flashed through the space his body had occupied.

"Goddamn!" Ake cursed. *He was on the stage all the time!*

The pursued man had apparently climbed onto the stage, worked his way toward the back, and then stood stock still to blend in with the motionless android performers.

Ake peeked up over the back of a rocking-chair seat. Not a good idea—a sun-core-hot bolt of energy burned through the seat back. Ake raised his hand above the seats and fired a series of spaced shots at the stage and then dared a follow-up look.

No dice. The former Cadre trainee had leapt down into the orchestra pit. Several of the androids on stage were now moving in response to the unexpected human activity around them. Ake saw two of them pulling out and then puzzling over the thin ceramic slivers that had struck them in the face or the chest or the arm. Ake could almost hear their logical brains saying, "This isn't part of *La Bohème*." The disturbing variance in the set routine they followed was probably giving their self-defense circuitry fits trying to make sense of this strange turn of events.

Putting the mechanical actors out of his mind, Ake looked long and hard at the orchestra pit. Nothing. "Hey, Johannsen. You there?"

"What do you think, Ringgren?" a deep voice called back.

"Guess you would have made Colonel by now," Ake said. "Of course, that's if the Cadre and its entire command structure hadn't been dismantled."

"What makes you think it has been?"

A shiver ran down Ake's spine. "Damn!" he muttered. Then he confessed, "I was afraid you were gonna say that, Johannsen."

"Yeah? Well, I have more bad news for you—*Doctor*."

"Sorry, I'm only going to listen to happy thoughts from now on." Ake shook his head. *I've been around Ray too long.*

"Well, force yourself."

"Oh, all right, shoot. Er, go ahead."

"I was a year behind you at the institute, so you may not know that I took firsts in small-weapons training and one-on-one armed combat."

"Just my luck," Ake mused. Then, louder, he said, "Say, instead of this messy violence, want to see who knows more about twentieth-century trivia?"

"Huh?" said Johannsen. Then he angrily fired a bolt in Ake's direction and said, "Don't fuck with me!"

"It was just a thought," Ake said softly for his own benefit.

II

"Ohmygod!" Kate shrieked.

Kate, Grendel, and Ozma rushed over to the precipice's lip and peered down, afraid of what they might see. What their eyes revealed was Frodo wedged head first in a bush ten to twelve meters below. The bush was gently rocking back and forth, but he seemed safe for the moment.

"Frodo, are you all right?"

"I . . . I think so." Because of the howling of the wind off the ocean and up the wall of rock, his voice did not carry well. It also didn't help that he was facing away from Kate and the others, staring instead at the sea far below.

"Okay, good." *Yes, good, but now what?* Kate wrung her hands, looking around frantically for inspiration.

"What you gonna do?" asked Ozma, cowed by this unexpected and possibly fatal turn of events.

"I don't know," Kate confessed. "Something—*something*, dammit! But what . . . ?"

"They's a rope in Ozma's pack," Grendel told Kate. "We always carry one now 'cause of that time with Ray and the quicksand."

Kate heard only two words: rope and pack. "Here, Ozma, let me get it out."

Kate fumbled with the pressure fasteners on the pack, each of her fingers feeling the size of a sausage. Telling herself to *Center—center yourself and your emotions*, Kate took a deep breath and began again. This time, working deliberately, she undid the seal on the pack, pulled the contents out, and fished through them for the rope.

"Got it," she said triumphantly, pulling a lengthy coil of

polywoven rope out of the pile. "Got it," she repeated. "But now what?"

She glanced around the area near the cliff's edge. Nothing. No stubby trees, no bushes, no boulders half-buried in the soil; nothing to tie the rope to. No wait, that wasn't completely true. She dropped to her knees and brushed aside some loose dirt and stones, revealing a gnarled root at least eight centimeters thick that erupted out of the ground for a meter or so before diving back into the sandy soil.

Kate almost hugged herself with glee. This cablelike root would be more than strong enough to support her weight and Frodo's. Seeing what Kate was caressing, Ozma said, "You gonna tie the rope to the root?"

"That's the idea," Kate replied. "Anyone got a better one?" Neither dog had.

Kate examined the rope and decided that she would be better off if instead of one very long one, she had two shorter ropes. She paired up the two ends and then found the rope's middle.

"Whadda ya gonna do?" asked Ozma.

"Just watch," Kate replied. She burned through the rope with her energy rifle, producing two equal lengths. "There," she said. "One for Frodo and one for me."

"I jes' gots one question," said Grendel. "How we gonna get Frodo back up here by ourselves?"

"I have an idea," Kate said. "It's not much of one, but it's all I can come up with right now. After I tie both ropes securely to the root, I'll tie the end of one of the two sections around my waist. The second I'll throw down to Frodo—a little past him, actually—and then I'll rappel down my rope to him, tie the loose end of his rope around him, climb back up, and the three of us will haul him up."

"Can we do that?" wondered Ozma. "He a big guy."

"I think so," Kate replied. "And if that doesn't work, we'll at least have Frodo secured by the rope. He'll be okay until we can summon help to get him off the side of this damn cliff."

"Sound good," Grendel said. "Let's do it!"

With one end of the rope fastened securely around her middle and the other tied to the root, Kate took a deep breath and prepared to begin the descent.

Kate tried not to think of the tremendous physical exertion her effort would take. Getting down to Frodo and tying the other section of rope around his middle would be more demanding than anything she'd ever done before. And that was just the end of the first part of her solution to the problem of saving Frodo.

If somehow she was able to accomplish all that—a very big *if* indeed—she still had to climb back up her own rope, make sure that Frodo's was secure, and then, aided by Ozma and Grendel, do her damnedest to haul the one-hundred-and-thirty-kilogram Frodo up like a sack of cement.

It would be mostly Grendel and Ozma's strength doing the work, Kate assumed. She estimated that Ozma and Grendel each weighed approximately one hundred kilos. Between the three of them, they should have the strength to pull the bigger male dog up, especially if he could help by "walking" up the steep cliff face.

She knew she was relying heavily on the dogs; she also knew she had no choice: By the time she'd visited Frodo and returned, her arm and leg muscles would be aching and depleted by the effort of rappelling down and climbing back up the precipice.

"We knows you can do it, Kate," Ozma said, her tail only half erect.

"Yah," agreed Grendel. "You is gonna be all right—and so's Frodo." Unlike Ozma's, Grendel's tail was fully erect, indicating her confidence in Kate, Ozma, and herself.

"Uh-huh," Kate said. Then she saw the concerned expressions on the dogs' faces and relented. "Hey, thanks, you two. I really appreciate it."

Kate turned her back to the edge of the cliff and got down on her hands and knees. *Why the hell isn't Ray here to do this?* she asked herself. *He's got the muscles and the compact body of a gymnast.* Realizing that it was pointless to bemoan what she lacked in resources, Kate backed up slowly, feeling her way to the edge. First her feet and then her legs were projecting beyond the cliff's lip. Gingerly, she crawled farther back, finally putting her weight on the rope.

"Doan go *too* slow," advised Grendel. "It might take ya too long and ya get tireder that way."

"Right." Kate braced against the cliff face with her feet and began making her way down the rope. At first, her progress could be measured in centimeters but as she got better at what she was doing, she also got quicker.

"Hey, look, Grendel—no hands!" she teased, pretending she was actually going to take her hands from the rope for a fraction of a section.

"Don't!" shouted Grendel before she realized that Kate was pulling her leg.

"Not funny!" barked Ozma.

Ozma's right, Kate thought. *I'm giddy with fear and exhilaration. Knock it off and pay attention, Kate, or those rocks below will tenderize your body for the crabs.*

Kate risked looking down to see how much farther she had to go. Whatever else happened, she didn't want to work her way down successfully and then end up stepping on Frodo and clumsily knocking him from his precarious perch.

When she saw what lay underneath Frodo, she regretted her decision. "Oooh, that was a mistake!"

Kate could see jagged rocks and boulders far below, the ocean raging about them, throwing up a fine salt spray. And even though it made no sense at all, even though it was a product of her overactive imagination, she thought she could see salt-water crocodiles floating half-submerged in the water, their mouths agape.

As Kate half walked, half allowed gravity do the job, she encountered a narrow shelflike outcropping. As she clambered past it, slipping over the projection, she noticed that under the stone shelf was an opening in the cliff wall. She'd not seen the opening from the top; the shelf had concealed it from prying eyes.

A high-pitched shrieking suddenly erupted from within the cave.

"Jesus and Mohammed!" Kate shrieked herself.

III

It didn't take long for the appeal of Battlefield to become apparent to Ray.

The Uhurans—Freeman-Mawalzi, Freeman-Amboma, Freeman-Bahotta, and Freeman-Mekeena—were as heavily armed as Federation shock troops and, even better, got to make good use of all that firepower. Roughly every half a kilometer or so they were confronted by a new challenge. Putting their training to the test, they were forced to fight their way through the opposition like a squad of the best soldiers ever to put on uniforms.

The beauty of all this, decided Ray, was that the situations were artfully disguised to mask the fact that every advantage lay with the humans. Despite what Ares and Freeman-Mawalzi said, defeating the carefully programmed battle androids and other, more human-scaled mechanicals was laughably easy *if* you knew anything at all about tactics. And while the Uhurans really weren't very good, they had the advantage of expert experience available to them through the externals implanted in their skulls.

Ray allowed a smile to play about his lips as the Uhurans encountered squad after squad of robotic warriors and destroyed them with their superior—and fully functional—firepower. The victorious vacationers were amateurs; so much so that they weren't aware of how one-sided their "hard-won" firefights really were. They collected a few hits, of course, but they were on track to complete the exercise successfully.

So Ray joined in. It was like shooting fish in a barrel for him, but he got a sort of perverse pleasure out of blasting the toothless and declawed "battle" androids into tiny bits of plasmetal and carbon-steel.

"Geez, too much of this 'n' we might forget how ta fight for real," Robin said to Beowulf.

"Yah," Beowulf agreed, nodding his big shaggy head.

"Ray is havin' a good time," Mama-san observed. The other dogs agreed with her assessment.

"Think we could take them big robot beoples?" Gawain asked. "I mean, if'n this play-actin' was fir real?"

"Sure," Robin replied immediately.

Beowulf shot the newest dog a look. "Doan be so cocky, Robin. They be tough, real tough."

"I not sayin' they not," Robin said. "I jes' think we's good."

"We *are*," agreed Mama-san. "We also gots a secret weapon."

"Yah?" questioned Gawain.

"Sure. We gots Ray."

When Robin hooted skeptically at that, Beowulf's eyes narrowed and he said, "Mama-san's right, Robin. He's Mr. Jokes alla time, but when there's a fight—a real fight, to the death—you doan wanna mess with Ray."

"Geez, I sorry. I wuzn't—"

"Hi guys. What are—"

"Yowl!" Robin flinched at the sound of Ray's voice.

A bit taken aback, Ray asked, "What's the problem, Robin? You're acting like I'm gonna kill you."

At that, Mama-san and Beowulf burst into giggles.

"Dogs," Ray sighed, putting his hands on his hips.

★ ★ ★

The outburst had scared Kate half out of her wits and she contrived to hang onto the rope for dear life.

Whatever was producing the sound was both frightened and accusatory, and the high-pitched squawking increased in volume and frequency.

"What makin' that noise?" called a concerned Ozma.

Good question, Kate thought, feeling her heart pounding like it might leap right out of her chest. "It looks like some kind of half-bird, half-lizard hatchling," she finally replied.

Gulping air to calm herself, Kate saw that it was actually *two* of the ugliest little bird progeny she'd ever laid eyes on. The first one, the one with the lungs of a trumpet parrot, had at first obscured his or her so-far-silent sibling cowering further back in the nest.

"Uh-oh," said Frodo.

Her hands aching from clutching the rope for so long, Kate risked a look at Frodo. He was staring out over the ocean. Following his gaze, Kate was dismayed to see an enormous prehistoric-looking bird with a wingspan of four or five meters winging toward them.

Spiraling down out of the sky in tighter and tighter circles, the furious feathered reptile was making loud hissing and clacking noises. Kate blanched when she realized that the clacking was the sound of its powerful beak opening and closing.

Remembering the aviary in Luna Park, she recalled how large beaked birds effortlessly cracked hard-shell nuts with their beaks. She had no desire to see what this monstrosity was capable of doing with its beak.

Kate risked taking a longer look at the huge bird and immediately regretted it. *I didn't know birds had teeth*, she gulped. The dagger-tipped talons of the bird were another giveaway that its primary diet consisted of something more than berries and grubs.

Kate had a sudden vision of it plunging the tips of those claws deep into the muscles of her back and shoulders and that beak tearing at the tendons and blood vessels in her neck and the base of her skull.

Continuing to show its teeth by opening its mouth wide and cawing like some impossibly immense raven, the flying monstrosity swooped closer until Kate imagined she could feel the air from its wings—something that was literally impossible, given the updraft from the sea.

"Kate, doan stay there!" shouted Grendel. "Keep goin' down! If ya gets past the nest, mebbe it won't 'tack ya."

That made perfect sense to Kate. She had almost fallen into a trancelike state, frozen with fear; shaking it off, she lowered herself down hand over hand like she was an experienced mountain climber. *A little adrenaline rush can work wonders*, she told herself.

Twisting his head and looking up past his body, Frodo encouraged her by saying, "You almost here, keep comin'." In addition to Kate, he could see two concerned canine faces peering down from up above.

"I *am* almost there, aren't I?" Kate said in disbelief. She was doing it. As she approached Frodo's position, she worked her way out and away so she could go a little bit below him, the better to manipulate the rope onto him.

A quick glance at the parent bird reassured Kate that the half-reptilian, half-avian fighter-bomber looked like it might now be content to hover nearby threateningly without actually taking any action after seeing that the nest was no longer imperiled by invaders.

As for whether or not going back up past the nest would prove to be a problem, Kate decided that that was in the future and the future would take care of itself; she had the here and now to deal with first.

"Hang on, Frodo," Kate told the patiently waiting dog. "I'm almost there." Although her hands, arms, and legs ached with a dull, burning sensation, Kate was nonetheless able to crab her way over to a position directly parallel to the bushy outgrowth which had caught and held Frodo.

With more dexterity than she would have believed herself capable of, Kate looped the rope around Frodo's chest and then tied the ends into a timber knot. A Star Scout when she was a teenager, Kate knew that timber knots were originally devised back on Terra to secure logs or other heavy loads. Examining her handiwork, she was sure her old pack leader would have been proud of her results with the rope.

"You know, there somethin' funny 'bout this bush," Frodo said as conversationally as if he and Kate were strolling through Victory Plaza on Terra instead of hanging helplessly a hundred meters from certain death.

"Something funny?" Kate asked, impressed by the big dog's calm demeanor.

"Yeah, it doan seem real."

"It doan . . . uh . . . doesn't seem real?" repeated Kate, aware that she was mimicking everything Frodo said.

"No. I think it's blastic."

"That's ridiculous . . . " Kate began; then she looked more closely at the bush. Now that Frodo pointed it out, it *did* appear to be made out of some manmade substance.

Kate's foot slipped slightly and she glanced down at her shoe. "Now that's odd," she mused. The cliff face, at least the section below the nest, didn't appear to be natural either. That didn't make any sense to her. *I must be cracking up*, she thought.

She didn't have long to ponder whether or not what she saw was madness or reality: A two-meter-square section of the cliff face had suddenly gone from a natural—and expected—opacity to something that was impossible. It became transparent.

"My God!"

Several faces with unreadable expressions stared out at the two of them as if peering through the plasglas of an aquarium at a pair of immensely interesting-looking fish.

Her mind racing furiously, Kate fumbled for an explanation, fumbled for what to do or say next.

Setting her jaw, Kate decided on a course of action. "Ozma, Grendel," she shouted up to the waiting dogs. "Go. Run and hide."

"What you talkin' 'bout?" Grendel asked. "What—"

"There's something under the landing field, something I don't think we're supposed to know about," Kate told them. "Now do as I say. Run and hide so you won't be captured like Frodo and me. Report what's happened to Ray and Ake."

"But—"

"GO!!"

16

Ake patted his pants pocket; he still had the master control cube with him. That meant that the android performers were not only programmed to follow his voice commands, but also that their programming could not be overridden, at least not here, not by another human voice attempting to change his commands.

"Begin Act II," Ake commanded, and the androids dutifully took their places and began the picturesque scene in the Cafe Momus. The stage was filled by android performers dutifully singing with lustful abandon.

The android orchestra members also picked up their instruments and began to play, following the impassioned leadership of the conductor, whose appearance and gestures were modeled after the legendary twenty-first-century maestro Mako Hisatsune.

As the orchestra came to life around him, Johannsen cursed and scrambled to get out the way. He had to scurry around for a breathing space because the android musicians completely ignored his presence and poked and bumped him as they played their instruments. Mistakenly thinking he was out of harm's way, Johannsen was suddenly struck in the temple by a violinist's "elbow," and sent reeling to the floor of the orchestra pit.

"Goddamn you, Ringgren!"

"Not a music lover, I take it?"

Ake's jibe was answered by a fusillade of energy beams. "Missed."

Ake set his needle gun's power setting to its highest level and popped up from behind a seat back to fire several ceramic projectiles in quick succession in the direction of Johannsen's voice. The gas explosions that propelled the small shards at such an unusually high velocity made the gun buck in Ake's hand. Shaped vaguely like miniature arrowheads, the ceramic shards struck a trombone player under his raised arm and a flutist in the neck and passed through both of them, their speed barely diminished. The two shots bracketed Johannsen's head, smashing into an area just beneath the lip of the stage.

"Shit!" exclaimed Johannsen, this time throwing himself down and hugging the floor of the orchestra pit of his own volition.

Seizing his momentary advantage, Ake rolled out into the aisle and ran in a doubled-over position toward the orchestra pit as fast as he could move. When he was just two meters away, he ducked back into the safety provided by the seats.

Guessing what his pursuer was up to, Johannsen raised his weapon and unleashed a series of pencil-thick streams of energy in Ake's general direction, then retreated to the back of the orchestra, knocking over musicians and instruments as he went. He bounded up and onto the stage, hitting the floor and rolling until he could hide behind one of the android performers singing to a nonexistent audience.

The scene onstage was festive and gay as Rodolfo bought Mimi a pink bonnet and then introduced her to his friends. Oblivious of the life-and-death struggle going on around them, the androids smiled and raised their wine glasses on high for toast after toast.

Ignoring the hustle and bustle of the Cafe Momus, the two combatants exchanged fire and Ake managed to hurl himself into the orchestra pit. Given the angle between them now, neither man could get off a shot that had any chance of doing more than striking the edge of the stage.

Taking advantage of the law of trajectories that made it impossible for his opponent to shoot him from such an angle, Ake rushed toward the stage. Then he had second thoughts about the wisdom of that course of action. If he tried to mount the stage, his advantage would be lost; Johannsen would have him dead to rights. Making an instant decision, Ake sprinted toward the side of the orchestra pit. He skidded to a stop when he saw a small passageway that tunneled under the stage.

Yes! Ake exulted.

Ake crouched low so as not to strike his head on the top of the doorway, and plunged into the murky darkness beneath the proscenium.

After not seeing anything but android musicians in the pit, Johannsen dropped to his knees and cautiously crept toward the front of the stage, all the time holding his energy pistol in front of him and peering intently at the robot string players sawing away at their violins and violas, at first sedately and then vigorously.

Seeing a movement in the orchestra pit, Johannsen fired. The beam lanced through the head of an android musician which had bent over to put down one instrument and pick up another.

"Damn!" Johannsen watched as the android vibrated slightly, smoke pouring from the two holes in its head. Saying, "*Adagio*, maestro, *adagio*," it wandered about the pit, bumping into other musicians until it smacked into a wall, its legs churning purposefully but to no effect.

"Not *adagio*," said Johannsen. "*Addio*."

While Johannsen was staring intently into the pit, Ake was rising through the stage behind him, using one of the many trapdoors and elevators. The "noiseless" machinery had been little used lately and the commotion caused Johannsen to twist his head and look behind him.

"Surprise," said Ake, emerging from the floor between Marcello and Musetta. He grinned and pressed the firing stud on his needle gun.

Nothing.

Ake groaned in disbelief. *A misfire!*

Johannsen laughed and rolled over onto his back, firing as he went. Ake felt a beam of energy burn his face as he ejected the faulty shard and pressed the stud again. This time the tiny ceramic wedge-shaped sliver tore through Johannsen's right biceps and he screamed and dropped his energy pistol.

Having been struck square in the "face" by one of Johannsen's errant bolts of energy, a decapitated Musetta still strutted about the stage. The other androids were so enamored of her beauty and coquettishness that they could only stare in admiration at the space her head had so recently occupied. When the diva put out her arms beseechingly, Ake realized that the android performer was still singing gamely—albeit without a head.

Johannsen picked up a stage wine bottle made of real plasglas and threw it at Ake, catching him flush in the throat.

Ake gurgled in pain and fell over. His eyes watering and his throat throbbing, he got to his knees and drew a bead on Johannsen's forehead. This time a small amber dot glowed to tell him he needed to replace the gas cylinder.

"Goddamn!" Ake swore as Johannsen fumbled around for his energy pistol. Ake knew that if Johannsen could find his dropped weapon before he himself could reload he'd be singing a duet of the headless with Musetta.

The side of this face feeling like he left it on the barbecue grill for too long, Ake released a warrior's battle cry and hurled himself headlong at his wounded adversary. Ake's shoulder struck Johannsen smack in the middle of the larger man's chest. His momentum took the two of them over the edge of the stage and they tumbled down into the pit.

They landed in the first row, crashing down on the string section and knocking over both the concertmaster and the assistant concertmaster. Johannsen was more muscular than Ake and he was able to clout his old comrade upside the head with a meaty fist and send him reeling backwards into the percussion section.

When Johannsen tried to take advantage of his momentary edge by coming over to crush Ake's head with a French horn, Ake rolled out of the way of the blow and got to his feet again.

Thrown off balance by the force of his mighty swing, Johannsen stumbled drunkenly. Ake grabbed the huge brass cymbals from the senior percussionist and, bringing them together with a crash, made a sandwich of his opponent's head. Johannsen's eyes crossed and he collapsed in a heap.

"Goddamn, I did it!" Ake exulted, his knees nearly buckling. "Now all I have to do is restrain you, old buddy, and find someplace to hide you." His inflamed skin felt hot and dry. "Oh, and I have to do something about my injuries, too."

11

So many of the war games sported a Terran setting, it seemed to Ray. After he thought more about that he realized that the one thing the former colony worlds had in common was their ties to Old Earth and its history of never-ending conflict. People *wanted* to escape into the Napoleonic Wars, or the Second World War. Or else they wanted to fight Agincourt or Gettysburg over again, subtly changing things to see how the battle might come out if the expected reinforcements arrived on time, or if the cavalry had been brought into the fray instead of being sent out into the countryside on a futile scouting mission.

Men who had never been to Terra in their lives eagerly donned the scarlet uniforms of the British Army and relived the heroic holding off of several thousand Zulu warriors (it helped that in this particular incident it had been a case of pitting British repeating rifles against native spears).

If they wished, patrons of Battlefield could dress themselves in the handsome gray uniforms of the Confederacy and see if the Old South might triumph in the American Civil War. With hindsight in abundant supply, the Southern armies' modest successes could be quickly followed by immediate counterattacks on the exhausted Army of the Potomac, turning them into victorious routs instead of the missed opportunities they had been historically.

"I understand there is a massive tank battle going on in one of the other sectors," President Freeman-Mawalzi said to Ray as they walked down a deserted urban street, weapons held ready. Here and there floaters and wheeled vehicles—cars and trucks—lay abandoned and stripped. Piles of plascrete rubble lay in the street and on the stilled walkways. It looked for all the world like what it was: a war zone. Battlefield was nothing if not accurate down to the tiniest of details.

"That so? I haven't heard anything about it," Ray replied.

"Chancellor Venestrian and First Minister Boyeramin, both of Gregorin, are supposedly commanding the tank forces as Patton and Rommel."

"You mean George C. Scott and James Mason?" Ray asked, his tongue planted firmly in his cheek.

Freeman-Mawalzi didn't "get it"—not that Ray expected him to, really. "Um-m-m, no, I mean General George Patton and Field Marshal Erwin Rommel," he replied seriously.

"Ray jes' pullin' your leg," Beowulf told the Uhuran president.

Freeman-Mawalzi ran a finger along his mustache before shooting Ray an evaluative look. "You are not reluctant to spar with those in authority, are you?"

"Not hardly," agreed Ray with a laugh.

"You are a most . . . unique . . . individual."

The words were no sooner out of Freeman-Mawalzi's mouth than an abandoned car no more than ten meters ahead of them was lifted high into the air by an explosion.

"Battle androids," said Robin unenthusiastically. The big red dog was getting a little bored by their confrontations with the "killer" 'bots. Even the Uhurans were becoming pretty good at destroying them while avoiding their return fire.

Robin and the other dogs found the 'bots to be unchallenging after several victories that came too easily; the machines were both predictable and unimaginative. *Jeez,* Robin thought. *They can't really be that stupid, can they?*

"Let me take the point on this one, Kano," Freeman-Amboma pleaded.

"Go then," said Freeman-Mawalzi.

Grinning from ear to ear, the Uhuran diplomat dashed down the street. He ran from one place of shelter and concealment to another until he was within a dozen meters of the two battle androids.

"He is a child again," marveled Freeman-Mawalzi. "He has reverted to being the boy I remember growing up with in my village."

"And what about you?" asked Ray.

"Me? I am enjoying myself, but I do not have the luxury of losing myself completely in these trivial pursuits. As the leader of our world—of our newly freed and independent world," he added for emphasis, "there is too great a burden on my shoulders for me to ever quite forget that it is always there, pressing down relentlessly."

"Burden?" Ray frowned.

"Yes, I must do my part to see that the new Alliance does not simply replace one corrupt central authority with another. We have won the war; now we must win the peace."

"That is for worrying about later, Kano," Freeman-Mekeena told his friend and president. "Come, let us play out our adventure now. With Soddu in position, we must catch the robots in a crossfire and destroy them."

"Of course," Freeman-Mawalzi assented, moving to do just that, although with no great haste. Like Robin, he was beginning to find the robots to be disappointing foes.

"If we should encounter a ranger, I am seriously considering asking for either a partial refund or for a return engagement," Freeman-Mawalzi said to Ray as they checked their weapons.

"A return engagement?" Ray asked.

"Yes, this time with a degree of difficulty that is more challenging. This has all been too easy, I cannot help but think we have been taken advantage of or patronized."

Freeman-Mawalzi and Ray were just a few steps behind the

others when a powerful beam of energy suddenly flashed from one of the robots. It burned through Freeman-Mekenna and Freeman-Bahotta and fried the plascrete exterior of the building behind them.

"Get down, dogs!" Ray shouted. Then he reached out and grabbed Freeman-Mawalzi's shoulder, pushing him to the ground. As Ray fumbled with his energy rifle, he called out to the dogs. "Everyone okay?" he queried.

"Yah," they chorused.

"Good, we're all alive," Ray said with some satisfaction. "Now comes the hard part—staying that way." He smiled grimly at the Uhuran president. "Looks like you're going to get your wish for a more formidable challenge."

"I did not ask for *this*," Freeman-Mawalzi said hotly. Then, looking at the ruined bodies of his two compatriots and friends, he said, "My God!"

"They're dead," Ray said matter of factly. "Freeman-Amboma is alive, however."

"Soddu," said Freeman-Mawalzi. "Yes, I almost forgot about Soddu."

"I don't think we can assume that our murderous friends have forgotten him," Ray said. "But maybe they have; if he can just manage to keep a low profile and not draw attention to himself, he—"

Shouting something in Uhuran at the top of his lungs, Freeman-Amboma opened fire on the two battle androids with his energy rifle. He was so close that the full-power bolts from his weapon overwhelmed the defensive shields of the 'bot that had killed his friends.

A strange pattern of electrical energy seemed to dance about the armored exterior of the 'bot and it shook like someone shivering in the cold. Finally, a yellow-green ball of flame erupted from its torso and, after reaching out beseechingly, it toppled over backwards and ceased moving.

The other android raised a mechanical arm; instead of ending in a hand, its arm sported a rotary slug thrower capable of firing several thousand rounds a minute. Ray could see the ammunition cylinder begin to spin and almost immediately the gun started spewing forth a deadly hailstorm.

"Lordy!" said Ray.

The calculatedly brutal assault shredded the plasmetal hulk of the prop abandoned vehicle shielding Freeman-Amboma. With the vehicle blown away piece by piece, the unprotected Freeman-Amboma was literally pulverized by the angry lead bees that tore through him like he was nothing; in less than ten seconds, he *was* nothing. Nothing that anyone could look at without becoming sick.

"Soddu!" Freeman-Mawalzi screamed in horror.

Ray made a hand motion and all the dogs except Beowulf disappeared into the building on the left side of the street. Then Ray picked up the rocket launcher Freeman-Bahotta had dropped and made sure it was primed. "Here, take my rifle and occupy that moly-steel bastard's attention while I get closer."

"Wha . . . what?"

Ray slapped him hard across the face. "Snap out of it, Mr. President! Your friends are dead and we're alive. Now do as I say or you won't have long to wait before that hunk of junk gives you a plasma enema."

"Yes, of course." Freeman-Mawalzi had never been slapped by anyone before—not since his youth, anyway—and the extraordinary occurrence put a quick end to his moment of self-pitying indecision.

"There's a good-sized slab of hardened plascrete in front of us," Ray told him. "Old Gatling gun up there can chip away at it, but it isn't going to be blown away quite as easily as that pitiful excuse for a car. If you stay here and bounce a few beams of energy off his armored hide, I'll try to get an angle on him."

"And then?"

"Then I'll blow his fuckin' head off." Ray flashed a hard grin at Beowulf. "Excuse my French."

Beowulf didn't return Ray's grin. Instead he pointed with his nose over Ray's shoulder. Ray turned around to see Ares, nervously wringing several of his hands.

"I do not understand this," the robot said. "Something has gone terribly wrong."

"Yes, it has," Ray replied. He looked at the bodies of Freeman-Mekeena and Freeman-Bahotta, then at the weapon in his hands, and then back at Ares. Ray tightened his grip on the rocket launcher as he made up his mind what he was going to do about the potential fifth-columnist in their midst.

★ ★ ★

Ozma and Grendel ran as fast as they could across the exposed surface of the landing field. With heavy sea-level air rasping in and out of their throats and their tongues lolling out of their mouths, they made the relative safety of the grassy meadows surrounding the field. After running into the deep grass for about a hundred meters or so, they stopped to catch their breath.

"What happen back there?" Ozma wondered aloud.

"I dunno," said Grendel, gulping down air. "I think Kate was tellin' us that there's somethin' under the landing field, somethin' hidden that looks out over the ocean where we wuz."

"Somethin' hidden underground?" Ozma considered that for a moment. Then the big yellow-and-brown dog gasped. "Ya mean it could be somethin' like that 'spear-a-mental place in Boswash?" She appeared stunned by her own speculation.

"Not 'xactly," Grendel replied. "That Swow-bo-da guy's dead and he wuz one of a kind. But somethin' like that, some hidden fac'tree or somethin' else."

Ozma nodded and asked, "You think they gonna hurt Frodo and Kate?"

"No. Least not right away. Not till they knows what Frodo and Kate knows . . . and who wuz with 'em and got away."

"We ain't got away yet," cautioned Ozma. "We has to get back to Ake 'fore we can feel safe."

"Let's go, then," said Grendel, getting to her feet and heading back the way they'd come with Kate.

Ozma got to her feet and said, "No." She shook her head. "We can't go that way. They mebbe find us too easy. We gots to take long way 'round to get back."

Grendel accepted the wisdom of that plan. "Why don't ya show me the way ya wants to go?" Ozma nodded and moved off, trotting at a measured pace that would eat up kilometers but not tire either of them out quickly.

"Hey, I hears somethin'," Grendel said. "Get down." She looked around, searching for the source of the high-pitched whining.

No sooner had the two dogs secreted themselves in the grass than a tiny round floater on patrol passed over their position. It seemed to hesitate for just a second, hovering like a dragonfly, then continued on its way.

"Ya think it seen us?" Ozma asked.

"I dunno," Grendel replied.

III

Ake was proud of himself. In under five minutes he had tied up and gagged Johannsen, located a washroom and cleaned himself up as best he could, found a large plastic trash bag, stuffed Johannsen into it, and commandeered a cleaning robot to carry his prize back to the suite.

Sinbad and Tajil's warm greeting turned to cries of concern when they saw Ake's face. Ake shut the door quickly behind the dutiful 'bot carrying the bagged Johannsen, satisfied that no one had seen them. He and the 'bot had taken a service elevator few others knew about.

"What's goin' on?" Sinbad asked.

"Yah," seconded Tajil.

"I'm not sure," Ake told them. "But I intend to get some answers as soon as I can."

"How?"

"Good question, Sinbad." Ake went over to the bag containing Johannsen and undid the knot sealing it. He pulled the sides of the bag down to reveal his prisoner.

"Jeez!" exclaimed Tajil. "Who's that?"

"An old acquaintance from my younger days, Taddy," Ake said.

"What happen to his face and clothes?" wondered Sinbad.

"The same thing that happened to mine," Ake explained. "He was as glad to see me after all these years as I was to see him."

Tajil didn't understand. "Ake, I's missin' somethin'," he said.

"Oh, yeah. Well, Johannsen here—his first name is Erik, if I recall correctly—and I both attended a special training academy in our youth. I was already a physician and he was . . ." Ake's face clouded. "You know, I don't think I ever learned what his specific talents were. He may not have known mine, either, although I don't think I made a point of concealing the fact that I was a doctor." Then Ake remembered their battle royale. "Oh, he knew I was a doctor; he called me one just minutes ago."

"Speshul trainin' 'cademy?" Tajil said, repeating Ake's words.

"I guess I didn't clarify that, did I? It was a Cadre postgraduate training center for sleepers and intelligence agents. A few regulars, like Erik, were allowed in as well."

"The Cadre?" Sinbad bared his teeth. "You mean them beoples who killed Pandora and them sen-tors!" Even though he had been little more than a burly young puppy on Chiron, Tajil also bristled at the recollection.

"Take it easy, you two," Ake said. "Remember, I worked for the Cadre, too. That's how I met Johannsen."

"Yah, but you wuz really workin' for the Brogrammers, for the good guys, right?"

"Everyone thinks he or she's working for the good guys—even Johannsen here."

"Ake," said Sinbad.

"Yeah?"

"Ya better do somethin' 'bout your face real soon."

Ake put a hand up to the left side of his face and took it away with an exclamation; it was too tender to touch. "I've got some ointments and special radiation treatments I can begin," he said, daring to look at himself in the Hylof nonreversal mirror in the bathroom.

"I thought it was radiation that did that to ya," Tajil said.

"It was, Taddy." Ake continued to inspect the damage. "But there's radiation and there's radiation. The kind I intend to use will help to heal my tissues, not harm them."

After pouring himself a glass of wine, Ake took it into the bathroom with him, drank more than half of it, and then placed the leaded crystal glass on a small stand near the shower.

He activated the shower, making sure to set the water temperature no higher than lukewarm. Then he stripped off his clothes and stepped into the stream of water. Deciding he could stand a higher temperature, he increased the flow of hot water until the shower stall steamed up.

After he'd soaped and rinsed off, he turned the faucet's setting from hot toward the cold. When it was the correct temperature, he directed the water onto the left side of his face. The cooling spray felt wonderful.

As they listened to the sound of Ake's restorative shower, Sinbad and Tajil pondered what might happen next. Indicating the still unconscious Johannsen with a nod of his head, Tajil said, "Ake prob'ly gonna wanna talk to this guy 'bout what's goin' on 'round here."

"Yah," agreed Sinbad. The big brown dog got up, padded nervously around the room, and then sat back down on his haunches. "I wisht Ray was here. Ake is a pretty dang good fighter. Heck, he wuz a soldier onct! But Ray is Ray,—and he is the leader of the team. He always knows what to do."

"Wonder where Ray is?" Tajil said. "We doan even know if'n Ake knows how to get in touch with—"

Without warning, the lights in the suite went out.

17

"Hey," Ake shouted from the bathroom. "What happened to the lights?"

Sinbad stuck his big head in through the bathroom door as Ake scrambled out of the shower stall, found a towel, and began drying himself. "They went off, Ake."

"No kidding," said Ake. "I can see that for myself."

Tajil padded in with the clean clothes Ake had laid out in the huge dressing room. "Oh, thanks, Taddy," Ake said when the big dog dropped them at his feet and told him they were there.

Ake hurriedly pulled on his pants, almost losing his balance. He bumped the stand that contained the wine glass; it rocked back and forth on the edge but did not fall from its precarious position.

Regaining his balance, Ake slipped into a shirt and buttoned it. He sat on the edge of the toilet and quickly got his socks and shoes on. The more layers of clothing he put on, the less vulnerable he felt.

Ake blinked. He had very good night vision, but the blackness was almost complete. "Christ, the emergency lights haven't even come on. What the hell's going on here?"

Sinbad, whose monochrome canine vision was more efficient than Ake's color vision at very low light levels, slipped out of the bathroom and was back almost immediately. "Here," he said.

"Here what?"

"I bringed ya your gun," Sinbad explained.

"Thanks, Sinbad."

Start using your brain, Ake, he chided himself, feeling for the energy rifle and picking it up. *Sinbad had enough smarts to realize you might need this—wake up and smell the coffee substitute!*

Ake reached out and put his hand on Tajil's broad back. "Okay, Taddy or Sinbad, whoever I'm touching, you're a seeing-eye dog now—lead me into the living room."

"Sure," said Tajil, not certain what a seeing-eye dog was.

"You almost there," prompted Sinbad.

Something, a vibration, an errant stream of air—or, as Ake later said, "My guardian angel's breath"—caused the glass in the bathroom to topple from the stand. It shattered into dozens of shards when it struck the tile floor.

"What . . . ?" Ake said as he and the dogs turned their heads to look back toward the bathroom.

With a blinding flash, the door to the suite was blown in by a powerful, carefully directed explosion.

★ ★ ★

Twenty or thirty meters below Kate and Frodo, the cliff face opened and a floater with several armed men emerged and rose up beneath them. Kate didn't know whether to laugh or cry. Certainly, she and Frodo were to be rescued from the possibility they might fall to their deaths, but they could soon be facing another fate just as terminal.

"Well, what do we have here?" asked one of the men as the floater came to a gentle halt centimeters below their positions. "Trespassers? Spies?" He wore a simple maroon uniform without insignia, but he exuded a palpable air of command. He had short-cropped brown hair sprinkled with gray, but it was more than the length of his hair that marked him as a military man, a lifer; there was something regimented about him.

"Ornithologists," Kate said, smiling winningly and stepping down onto the floater. One of the armed men helped Frodo make the transition from the artificial bush to the floater. "We were examining the nesting place of that rather rare . . . uh, example of *Avis horribilis.*" She flinched when one of the men pulled out a quiver blade, but he simply used it to cut away the ropes.

The man who'd spoken to her now laughed heartily at Kate's

reaction to the knife and at her unbelievable story of being an ornithologist. "*Avis horribilis*! That's rich."

Kate made up her mind immediately that she would give anything to knock this smug jerk's teeth down his throat so that he gagged on them. Her better sense won out and she merely asked, "Then who are we, pray tell?"

"You're one of them goddamn rebels!" said one of the men contemptuously. He was the first of the others to speak, and he instantly had reason to regret this outburst when his commander shot him a hard, cold look that seemed to pierce him like a dagger made of Ice-7. The cowed man swallowed, his Adam's apple bobbing, and quickly lowered his eyes and mumbled something about being sorry.

"Sorry?" said the group's leader. He struck the cowed man across his face with the flat of his hand. The slap made a loud, smacking sound and a bright scarlet mark appeared on the unfortunate man's face. "Sorry?" he repeated, a vein in his temple pulsing unpleasantly. "You don't know the meaning of the word. Make sure I don't have to teach it to you."

He turned back to Kate. She was staring at him intently, her eyes full of wonder. He was acting so much like a crudely etched hol-vee "bad guy"; he seemed more a caricature of a villain than the real thing. Stereotypes had to come from somewhere, she decided.

"I take it you're not with the resort?" Kate asked.

The man made a shrugging motion and said, "Yes and no. In the way you mean, no, we're not with the resort."

Glancing at the unwise speaker who had brought down the wrath of his leader on his head, she cocked her head and repeated softly, ". . . the goddamn rebels . . ." She pointed at the crew-cut sadist and said, "You're a loyalist. You and these hyenas are supporters of the late, great Federation!"

"The Federation?" growled Frodo.

The man simply rubbed his crew cut and said, "Take us down, please. We have much to discuss with Ms. Golnikov and I should like to do it in more comfortable surroundings."

"Yes, sir," the man piloting the floater said.

So much for thinking I could pretend to be someone else, Kate thought glumly. As her mind continued to mull over her and Frodo's predicament, the floater dropped toward the rocks below, toward the opening in the cliff face from which it had emerged.

★ ★ ★

A shock wave of blast furnace–hot air and noxious gases blew Ake, Sinbad, and Tajil out of the room and hurled them to the floor. A second, almost as powerful, explosion followed immediately. *Grenades*, Ake thought.

Ake blinked, happy to be alive. Had the three of them been facing the door instead of the bathroom, they'd have been blinded by the blast. Although Ake's sight was returning with alacrity, he still fumbled like a blind man for his dropped energy rifle while multicolored spots jitterbugged crazily in front of his eyes. Since it seemed impossible that anyone in the sitting room could have survived the secondary explosions caused by the grenades, he assumed that Johannsen was dead. *Sorry, Erik*, he thought.

Automatic weapons fire and laser bolts filled the air above the fallen trio's heads. Ake pressed himself against the door jamb and fired several rapid bursts into the smoke-filled living room. He was rewarded by a loud shriek of agony.

Pencil-thin streams of coherent light energy burned into the wall and doorway and Ake flung himself to the floor again. "Piss and crackers!" he shouted while energy beams flashed and sizzled centimeters above his head.

Realizing they were no match for the weapons being used, the dogs crawled backwards on their bellies and slid around the corner until they were out of the line of fire.

Something small and round came bouncing through the doorway. Even before it stopped rolling, Ake realized what it was. "Grenade!" he shouted.

Sinbad leapt to his feet, took a step back, then hurled himself across the open doorway. Bolts of energy and metal slugs crisscrossed the doorway and Ake thought nothing living could pass through that space and live.

Fortunately, he was wrong.

Having successfully navigated the death-filled space, Sinbad grasped the grenade in his teeth and flung it to Ake. Ake received this precious gift and hurled it into the living room in one continuous motion.

The grenade exploded a millisecond after it disappeared into the acrid smoke and haze. The blast was followed by shrieks and curses, and the fire directed at Ake and the dogs' position intensified.

His face mashed against the carpeting, Ake managed to get out,

"Sinbad, have I told you lately that you're the greatest dog in the whole damn universe and I'd love to plant a big wet one on your face?"

"Golly," said an overwhelmed Sinbad.

"Mebbe you better wait and see if'n we gets out of this 'live, first," Tajil grimaced as the fusillade continued unabated. "We might not be so lucky if'n they 'cides to toss some more hand bombs our way."

"Yeah," agreed Ake. "They might get smart and let a few seconds tick off before throwing the next one."

Having seen as many hol-vee adventure serials as the next guy—unless the next guy happened to be Ray—Ake screamed so loudly and realistically that the dogs flinched and looked at him with shocked concern on their faces. Ake smiled and shook his head to reassure them. Now that they got it, they grinned.

Just as Ake had hoped, two of their attackers warily emerged from the acrid smoke, their weapons held ready. Ake fired twice just as they saw him, and the men fell backwards into the smoke like figures in a nightmare. Ake gulped. He had recognized them as the two muscular bellhops who had carried their luggage to their rooms.

"That's two more," Ake whispered to the dogs.

"Yah!" said Sinbad. Then his nose wrinkled and he asked, "What's burnin'?" He looked up. "Jeez!"

Above them, the walls and ceiling were on fire—an unsurprising result of the close-quarters combat that had erupted within the suite. The walls were thick and soundproof, but not impervious to hot beams of coherent energy.

"Sure wish there was another way out of this place," Ake said, continuing to pump bolt after bolt of energy at their still-unseen attackers. "The holoscenic in the hall by the bedrooms is gorgeous-looking, but you can't really jump into it and find yourself transported to the beach at Rio," he said, wistfully.

"Right," said Tajil, who never would have thought of the idea of jumping into a holoscenic in a million years. The dogs were intelligent, but canine imaginations were not prone to such flights of fancy.

"Give it up, Ringgren," called a harsh voice speaking Fed-stan 'glish with a Terran accent. "A couple more minutes and we won't have to bother coming in after you—the flames will get you and your goddamn mutts."

"Fuck you and your mother, you Cadre cocksucker!" Ake

shouted. He shook his head; he couldn't believe how vulgar he'd become. *I guess facing the specter in the black cowl with the scythe will do that to a guy.* Then he remembered starship Captain Peter Gabriel's naughty-little-boy response to suddenly being granted unabridged freedom of expression and said: "Shit-fuck-piss!"

"Boy, you is gettin' some kind o' dirty mouth on ya, Ake," said Tajil, half awed and half appalled by his human's unexpected display of coprolalia.

"So you finally put two and two together, eh, Ringgren?" the voice taunted. "Yeah, we're Cadre all right and we're gonna ream your ass from here to the Coal Sack Nebula for what you and your little buddy did to us and the Triumvirate."

So much for surrendering, Ake thought. "Well, then, come on in and get me. Or are you so chickenshit like the rest of your kind that you're willing to let the fire do your dirty work for you while you're busy pulling each other's puds?"

A heartfelt flurry of imaginative curses that put Ake's efforts to shame were followed by, "Open wide then, here we—"

Suddenly, instead of the expected volley of energy rifle fire, there was a cacophonous eruption of blood-curdling screams.

Without bothering to try to target anyone or anything, two maroon-clad soldiers stumbled out of the haze firing their weapons randomly. Puzzled but gratified by their suicidal behavior, Ake shot them dead.

After a few more seconds that seemed like minutes, the screaming outside the suite died out.

"Hey, in there—doan shoot! The bad guys out here is all dead."

Ake looked at Sinbad and Tajil, his eyes widening in surprise. "Is that you, Ozma?"

"It ain't Beter Ban."

II

The battle android was hunting for Ray.

The big killing machine had lost sight of Ray when Freeman-Mawalzi distracted it by laying down a withering cover fire. Aware that Christmas comes but once a year, Ray took advantage of the opening and joined the dogs inside the dilapidated building that overlooked the street.

Apparently more heavily armored than the 'bot that Freeman-

Amboma had destroyed with well-placed energy bolts, the android warrior was as impervious to the Uhuran president's rifle fire as Beowulf would be to a peashooter. Stopping the 'bot would take more than Freeman-Mawalzi's puny weapon; it would take something like the rocket launcher Ray carried. Ray knew this . . . and so did the battle android.

"Where is it, Beowulf?" Ray asked his leader. Beowulf crept to the ruined building's third-story window and peeked out.

"The machine man is kinda standin' in the middle of the street, lookin' 'round."

"Yeah, it's looking for us," Ray said, crawling over to the window, joining Beowulf in peering down at their foe. Ray glanced at Freeman-Mawalzi and the slightly lobotomized Ares, who was standing dumbly nearby. Ray had simply turned off the robot's higher functions. He had no proof that the servile robot was dangerous, but then no one suspected the battle androids until they killed three people outright.

"Must be lookin' for us," agreed Beowulf. "It ignorin' the president's potshots at it."

"Good," Ray said. "I can get off a clear shot at it from here."

Ray inspected the rocket launcher and saw that because the Uhurans had been expending the missiles as if they had an endless supply of them, there were only three arrows remaining in his quiver. He had to make each one count. If he aimed well and true the first time, like Robin of Sherwood at the archery contest, there'd be no need for a second shot. *Yeah, right*, Ray thought. *Errol Flynn had camera trickery and sinny magic working for him.*

"Uh-oh," said Beowulf.

Ray cringed. He was starting to hate that particular utterance. "What is it this time?" he asked resignedly.

"He's lookin' 'round. The robot guy, I mean. He's . . . he's thinkin'. Yeah, that's it—he's thinkin' he smells a rat."

If Ray hadn't been sure up to now that the battle androids possessed the outlawed pseudo-quantum-gravity brains, his doubts were erased by this new information. He was up against an opponent almost as shrewd and intuitive as a human being.

Unlike most people, Ray didn't kid himself about his own kind. Humans were the ultimate biological killing machines: emotional volcanoes whose periodic eruptions of hatred and lust were made even more dangerous by their intelligence and ability to plan and plot against their enemies.

That was why the battle androids were so dangerous. Since their P-Q-G brains were modeled on humans', the robots were very humanlike in the pleasure they took in killing. And, like humans, they had the cunning and the deviousness to be formidable foes.

"Let's end this farce right now," Ray said, approaching the window. He didn't want to give the android anymore time to evaluate the situation and then act on its information.

"Darn!" said Beowulf.

"What?" Ray asked, as he reached the window, the rocket launcher primed and ready to fire.

"He's comin' toward the building."

"Double darn," said Ray. "I can't get a clear shot at him if he gets too close."

"Think the machine man try to come in after us?" asked Mama-san.

"I don't know," Ray conceded. "He—it—is only four meters high; that's not too tall to get through the doorways if it wants to follow us inside." Imagining the metal monster grinning a coldly metallic smile of pleasure as it shredded their bodies with gunfire, Ray added, "And it *wants* to follow us inside, take my word for it."

"I can't see him no more," Beowulf moaned.

"It's too close," Ray said. He put the rocket launcher down and thought about what to do next. *Think, Ray, think,* he told himself.

If it had two good arms, Ray supposed, the android might begin to demolish the building, tearing it apart with its moly-steel hands, bringing the structure and its inhabitants—himself and the dogs—crashing down. *Nah,* he decided. *The bastard can't do that, he's got only one real arm. The other is that damned rotary slug thrower. That's a break for us . . . I think.*

"I gots an idea," said Robin, heading for the door. "When the machine man is out in the open, shoot him, Ray." With that he hurried out of the room and down the steps of the emergency stairwell.

"Robin, wait!" Ray called after him to no avail. "Christ, Robin, don't get yourself killed," he said softly.

"Then be ready, Ray," Beowulf told him.

"Huh?"

"He said when the machine man is out in the open, you is to shoot him, right? Well, then be ready to do that."

Ray hustled over to the window, peering out through the shards of polyglas that remained. Shouldering the rocket launcher, Ray said, "If we get out of this alive, Beowulf, you take my place and I'll assume your position. You oughta be leading this team."

"Doan talk silly, Ray."

"I'm not talking sil—hey, something's happening; something's up."

What was up was that Robin had gotten down on his belly and stealthily crept closer and closer to the half-open front entrance. He had stopped when he could see the battle android moving slowly back and forth in front of the building—pacing, patrolling, standing guard.

Without warning, the android turned and lumbered toward the entrance. It halted and slowly bent at its wasp-waist to peer into the interior. Robin knew that the robot's standard vision would pierce the gloom as readily as his own dog's vision, both of which were vastly superior to human sight in low-light situations. Even so, as long as Robin lay perfectly still, he was safe from the robot's motion detectors.

The robot's infrared sensors were another matter, however. With infrared, the robot could locate living creatures like humans and dogs by pinpointing their body heat.

Something on the other side of the room ran along the base of the wall, its nails clicking on the floor. The battle android's head swiveled toward the noise and it raised its terrible arm. The rotary barrel of the weapon spun, and it spewed out a torrent of metal slugs. The half-meter-long rodent, for that's what Robin saw it was, was obliterated.

Dust and paint chips flew from the decaying wall and were blown around the room like the ash from a volcanic explosion. This debris rained down on Robin until the russet dog was a nondescript gray. It was all Robin could do to keep from unleashing a hacking cough that would have instantly pinpointed his location for the robot.

"Robin, is you okay down there?" Mama-san called out from above.

This was immediately followed by a heartfelt "Shit!" from Ray.

Ya, shit for sure, Robin thought sourly. *These guys ain't dummies, Mama-san. Go ahead and let 'em know one of us is down here.*

Clued in that there could be another target in the room, the robot slowly edged closer and closer until its bulk filled the doorway. It bent over even more and its inhuman head craned this way and that as it peered inside. Robin assumed that it was using its infrared vision to sweep the room.

Robin tried not to exhale. He was smart enough to know not to open his mouth, aware that his breath could give him away. Robin was no machine, however, and as much as he hated the necessity, the immobile dog could not prevent himself from having to breathe; he did so as slowly and shallowly as possible.

Even with his precautions, he knew he was much warmer than his surroundings. So why wasn't the robot picking him up? Then more of the fine powder produced by the robot's pummeling of the wall drifted down to cover him and he realized the truth: The robot's sensors couldn't detect his body heat because he was covered by a thick coating of dust.

After seeming to scan the room for an eternity—it was probably no more than a minute or two—the battle android stepped through the entryway like the Cyclops Polyphemus coming into his cave in pursuit of Ulysses and the Trojans. Moving slowly and deliberately, the battle android walked toward the stairwell. So confident of itself was the robot—yet another human trait it shared—that it did not bother to try to muffle the noise of its entry and movements. It *wanted* its intended victims to know that doom was approaching.

As it passed by his hiding place, one of the giant's feet came down with a dull thud just centimeters from Robin's nose. Robin's eyes followed the android's passage as his mind raced.

Soon, Robin thought. *Soon, but not yet.*

Ray or one of the dogs stirred, and the robot's head lifted and stared at the ceiling as if it could see through the floor between it and the flesh-and-blood beings it planned to annihilate.

Aware that it had all the time in the world, the android put its foot on the first stair step.

Now!

Robin leapt to his feet and dashed out the door, pausing there just long enough to turn and shout, "Nah-nah-nah, ya big hunk o' junk!"

With a rapidity that belied its earlier movements, the robot drew back its foot, turned, and thundered across the space between it and the entryway.

Robin took off, his legs churning. The big dog was a gray-and-rust-colored blur as he sprinted across the wide boulevard, zigging and zagging like a prize border collie herding a flock of recalcitrant sheep. As Robin threw himself through the open door of the building across the street, the air behind him was filled with a torrent of metal slugs.

Too late! Robin chortled gleefully.

He hit the floor inside, rolled, and then bounced up and to the side. The slugs that followed him in through the open doorway arrived just a fraction of a second too late to find their target.

The android made a strange strangled sound and thundered out into the street. Frustrated, it unleashed a torrent of slugs in the direction of Freeman-Mawalzi and Ares. The robot, standing dumbly in the street, was struck innumerable times, the impact of the slugs sounding like someone pouring ball bearings into a metal bucket. Ares was gone in seconds, obliterated.

Satisfied it had accomplished something, the battle android moved toward the building Robin had taken refuge in. When it was halfway between the two buildings, it stopped and swiveled its head back in the direction it had come. It looked like someone who was suddenly remembering something he shouldn't have forgotten in the first place. A targeting triangle appeared on its chest.

"You figured it out too late, sucker," Ray said. He pressed the firing stud.

The rocket flew straight and true, impacting the chagrined android full in its torso. The hardened tip penetrated into the robot's chest cavity before exploding. The metal warrior's wedge-shaped head flew straight up in the air, looking for all the world like those ancient clips of Scott and Irwin's Apollo 15 lunar module suddenly blasting off from the surface of Terra's moon. Rather than achieving orbit, however, it simply fell down again.

"The machine man—he dead?" asked Mama-san.

"The machine man is not just merely dead, he's unequivocally, undeniably, really most sincerely dead," Ray replied.

"He dead," agreed Beowulf.

18

Kate's senses seemed heightened by her ongoing flirtation with danger; she could smell Frodo's doggy essence strongly as he trotted beside her in the broad underground expanse. She was aware of the big dog's raspy breath, the pounding of her own heart, and the squeaky noise her captors' boots produced.

The space beneath the landing field was partitioned into a series of rooms and open spaces with ceilings Kate estimated to be as high as five or six meters. For an underground facility, the secret structure was remarkably unclaustrophobic in nature. Kate made up her mind that the designers had probably done their best to provide for a feeling of spaciousness and airiness.

"May I?" she asked her captor. Without waiting for his permission, she stopped and turned around to stare back at the way they had come.

"You are looking at the viewports," he said. "They provide a remarkable vista of the ocean, do they not?"

"Yes," agreed Kate, staring out through the huge smoke-colored plasglas panels at Neverland's beautiful deep blue sea. "They are completely opaque from outside?"

"Completely—as you yourself can testify."

Kate then shot her captor a curious, sideways glance. "Since you know my name, it would be only fair if you would tell me yours.''

He looked at her, gestured to the others, armed with energy rifles, and began walking. One of the men prodded her in the middle of her back with the barrel of his rifle when she was slow to follow. "I am Major Morrow," he said finally.

"Major Morrow?" she said. After a brief pause, she asked, "Do you have a first name?"

"Yes."

So much for that line of conversation, Kate thought.

"Where are you taking me?" she queried. They were coming to a central core of lift/drop tubes and elevators.

"To seek the commander and the creator."

"Oh," Kate said. Then she laughed.

"What is so amusing that you laugh out loud?" he asked indignantly.

"I can just imagine someone announcing, 'Major Morrow to see the commander and the creator,'" she said, wondering if he would see the absurd alliterative nature of that combination of words.

He didn't. "Yes?"

"Never mind," Kate said.

When they approached a lift tube, Frodo shied away and said, "No."

"What is this nonsense?" Major Morrow demanded.

"They don't like lift/drop tubes," Kate explained. "Dogs, I mean. Frodo has no objections to an elevator, however."

"We don't give a shit what your mutt likes or don't like," the armed guard who'd prodded her in the back said. He was a tall man Kate would have found attractive but for the hatred that burned in his eyes. *Come to think of it*, Kate observed, *they all have hatred in their eyes*.

Major Morrow waved a hand. "It makes no difference whether we ride a lift tube or take an elevator." He called for an elevator and the doors hissed open almost immediately.

Following Frodo into the elevator, Kate looked at the display lights: eight levels. Level four glowed. She thought about that for a moment. That meant that there were three levels below the near-sea-level portal they'd entered and four levels above it. While she was far from convinced that it would do her any good to know that, she also realized that any tidbit of information about this place might come in handy in the future. If she had any future, that is.

"Level two, please," Major Morrow said.

"Level two," the elevator's well-modulated female voice repeated as Kate and Frodo felt an almost imperceptible gravitational tug as the elevator began its ascent.

After they exited the elevator on level two, a soldier dressed in the maroon uniform that almost everyone seemed to be sporting caught Morrow's eye and hurried over. He whispered something in the major's ear and then walked away.

"I take it the commander and the creator are waiting for us?" asked Kate.

"Yes," admitted Major Morrow. He looked at her strangely, still unsure why she seemed to get such perverse pleasure out of saying "the commander and the creator."

They approached an immense set of impressively ornate doors and Kate wondered, *Who the hell are they trying to impress with all this display of wealth and power?* She thought about that for a moment. *In this case, me and Frodo, I guess.*

One of the flunkies with the rifles rapped sharply on the two karkka wood doors. "Come in," a voice boomed from within.

"Jeez!" said Frodo. "Maybe we's gonna meet the great and powerful Wizard of Oz."

"The Wizard of Oz?" said Morrow, puzzled. "Who the hell's the Wizard of Oz?"

Ignoring Morrow, Kate said to Frodo, "Maybe it'll just be the mayor of Munchkinland." She had stayed up one night to watch the old sinny after Ray tried to explain where the witch on the road had come from.

"Please—the both of you just shut up!" Major Morrow said, putting a hand to the side of his head as if it ached.

Frodo shot him a look of pure canine hatred, a look that implied the big dog would like nothing better than to rip out his throat. It had a noticeable effect on the major; even though he was surrounded by armed men, he swallowed and unconsciously took a step back.

The guards opened the doors and then stepped aside as Major Morrow composed himself and led his captives inside.

The room was immense and airy; it was lighted by subtle sources of illumination that made the interior as bright as day without any harsh glare. In the middle of this voluminous space was a long table with three men standing stiffly at its sides, staring intently at something on its surface. A map, maybe, Kate thought.

The two men facing in their direction (the other, shorter man had his back to them) put what they were holding down on the table and made their way across the vastness that separated them. Their heels clicked on the hard surface of the flooring and the sound reverberated throughout the room.

As they approached, the commander—or so Kate assumed—looked up. She could see that he was wearing an old-style Federation uniform. She was no expert, but it looked like the uniform of a Cadre general. The second man also wore a uniform; his was the uniform of a high-ranking officer of the Soldiers of God. When they halted in front of the prisoners and their guards, Morrow smartly saluted them.

Returning Morrow's salute, the Cadre general said, "So, Major Morrow, you bring us the interloper, eh?" When Frodo made a low, rumbling noise in the back of his throat, the general chuckled and added, "Two interlopers, I should say."

"Yes, general. This is Katerina Golnikov and her dog."

"Frodo," Frodo said crossly. "And I ain't Kate's dog."

"Ah, yes, Frodo," the Cadre commander said. "Frodo of the infamous Larkin-Ringgren scout dog team."

"Golly geez," said Frodo, suddenly shy. He was thrilled to be told his team was famous. Then he frowned slightly. *In*famous? What did that mean?

"In any event, I am pleased to meet you," the commander said. "My colleague is the Reverend-General Joab Michael and I am General Tomás Salvaterra." He clicked his heels together lightly and bowed his head ever so slightly.

An officer and a gentleman of the old school, Kate thought. *He will be unfailingly polite and "correct," even as he signs my death order.*

"Forgive me if, under the circumstances, I transgress against tradition and refrain from saying that I am likewise pleased to meet the two of you," Kate said, a bitter smile playing about her lips.

While the reverend-general did not deign to hide his distaste for her, General Salvaterra suavely bowed again. "Your point is well taken, Ms. Golnikov." Then, saying, "Come, I must introduce you to our resident genius," he smiled a polite smile and he took her gently by the elbow and began leading her toward the table in the center of the room.

As they approached the table, Kate could see that the man standing with his back to them was notable for two reasons. One, he was wearing a white laboratory smock; two, he was quite short.

"Simon," the general said to the man's back. "Please forget about your work for a moment and take the time to meet our guest."

The little man said, "Eh?" and turned around, tugging at his beard. While Kate noticed his watery blue eyes, what Frodo saw was something—or someone—else altogether.

"Dr. Svoboda!" the dog growled, his lips curling up over his teeth and his fur rising in clumps.

"Yes?" the diminutive man asked, surprised to be greeted by name.

II

Armed to the teeth, Ake and the dogs made their way toward Harris Webster's suite of offices. The five of them were a remarkable sight, of that he had no doubts: The left side of his face was a shocking scarlet, he was carrying an energy rifle in his hands, wearing a second slung over his shoulder, and the dogs wore fierce expressions that warned they would brook no interference.

Sinbad and Ozma trotted five meters ahead of him while Tajil and Grendel stayed close by his sides. At one point, as if to test the dogs' vigilance, four men armed with energy pistols—regular Cadre, Ake assumed—came around a corner and all but collided with him and the dogs. Not only did the men not get off a single shot, they barely had time to shriek once or twice before the dogs had silenced them forever.

Ake disabled the dead men's weapons, opened a janitorial service room, and had the dogs drag the bodies inside. The lights, activated by their body heat and by the movement of air molecules, came on after a moment's hesitation. Ake saw the industrial-sized sink and said, "Good. Now I can wash the blood off you guys."

"What 'bout all that blood in the hall, Ake?" Ozma asked.

Ake shrugged. "There's nothing we can do about it, so there's no point in worrying."

They reached Webster's private offices without further incident. The suite was theirs now, of course, but Ake still thought of it as Webster's.

"What we do now?" Sinbad asked as Ake reprogrammed the lock on the door.

"Why do I even bother?" Ake said rhetorically as he finished doing what he could with the lock. "I mean, this'll do a heck of a lot of good if they come calling here the same way they did back at our suite." He stood staring at the door with his hands on his hips. Then he twitched slightly like a 'bot who'd frozen. "What was that you said, Sinbad?"

"I said, what we gonna do now?"

Realizing how very tired and hungry he was, Ake replied, "What I *want* to do, more than anything else, is lie down on a null-gee mattress and sleep the dreamless sleep of the dead. Of course, if I do that, I might never wake up." He thumped some sides and rubbed some ears and heads. "Let's get something to eat, examine what we know for sure about what's happening, and only *then* see what to do next."

"We better not take too long to do all that," Grendel told him. She nodded at the door. "Or like ya said, they's gonna be comin' right through that door."

"Yah," agreed Ozma. "We can't help nobody else if'n we's dead ourselves."

"Taddy, you have anything to add?" Ake asked.

"Yah, let's eat."

"I feel *much* better after that pig-out," Ake said, patting his stomach and belching.

"Yah," agreed Sinbad, always ready to chow down at a moment's notice.

"Now then," Ake said to Grendel and Ozma, "what in the sam hill happened to Kate and Frodo? You were both too jangled and excited for me to make heads or tails of what you said earlier."

Grendel looked at Ozma, who nodded. "Jeez, Ake, that's the thing—we's not really sure."

Ake frowned. "Just tell me what you *think* happened, what you saw."

"Okay." Grendel was sure Ake could sort out the strange happenings at the cliff better than she and Ozma could, so she related it all, beginning with the walk and ending with Kate telling them to run away and save themselves so they could return to the hotel and report that there was something beneath the landing field.

"And I hearded Frodo say somethin' like the bush he was hangin' on wasn't a real one," Ozma offered.

"Then the cliff opened up?" Ake prompted Grendel.

"Yah."

"The cliff opened up . . ." Ake mused thoughtfully. "And Kate asked you to tell us that there's something under there."

"Yah," seconded Tajil. "But what?"

Ake glanced at his watch. "Damn, look at the time. We don't have the luxury of sitting around on our big butts playing 'what if' and 'maybe.'" Grendel made a rude noise; since Ake was as thin as a laser beam, that left the four dogs as the only ones sitting on big butts.

Ake snapped his fingers. "Shit, I don't want to do this, but I have to try."

"Try what?" Ozma cocked her head.

"Getting in touch with Ray. He's supposed to be playing Jack the Robot Killer with some Uhuran dignitaries on Battlefield."

"Why donja wanna try?" Ozma pressed.

"Because if they're sending in the goon squads after us, they might be pulling something similar on Ray. I've got you guys; Ray's just got a bunch of politicians."

"That's not true," protested Sinbad. "He's got Beowulf, Robin, and the others."

Ake allowed that Sinbad was correct. "Maybe I'm being too paranoid. I mean, they're clearly trying to capture or kill Kate and us, but that might be because we stumbled onto the truth about what's going on around here."

"Do it," said Tajil.

"Huh?"

"Call him."

"Right." Ake went over and sat down by the communications console. Realizing that he not only looked a mess but also like a hamburger on the grill that needed to be flipped, Ake turned off the phone's holo capability. "People might think it strange that they can't see me," Ake explained, "but they won't know for certain that something's wrong."

He punched in a short series of digits—Ray's personal communications number on Neverland. The holophone beeped once and an amber light glowed on and off. He tried again. And again. Finally, he spoke to the computer.

"I am very sorry, but that number is not available at this time," the computer told him.

"Append H-L-P to the number and try again."

"There is still no response. The callee has clearly coded in a 'reject all calls' response for the present."

"Yeah, right," Ake said, breaking the connection. Then he muttered, "Damn!" and threw the phone down.

"Ake?"

"Yes, Ozma?"

"Why Ray not answerin' the phone?"

"The call is not getting through," Ake told the concerned dog. "No matter what Ray's privacy status may be, when I add H-L-P to the end of his number, the call is supposed to be automatically accepted. It's a signal to him that it's an emergency and he'd better answer the goddamn phone."

"Oh."

Ake scratched behind one of her big ears. "Don't worry, Too-short Jones can take care of himself."

"I hopes so," said Ozma, her voice growing small.

★ ★ ★

"Some things is followin' us," Beowulf said, looking out the rear of the armored car they had taken away from some surprised robots.

"Yeah, I've had my eye on them for a minute or two," Ray said, glancing down at the view of the rear hol-vee. "They're cyclebots."

"By the Prophet's beard!" exclaimed Freeman-Mawalzi.

"You bet your ass," Ray agreed. "Those guys can run rings around us and they're gonna be peppering our ass with laser fire in about thirty seconds."

Staring out the windshield, Freeman-Mawalzi shouted, "Watch out for that dip in the road, Larkin!" The four-wheeled armored car bounced and jounced its way over the cratered highway.

"Dip, schmip!" Ray retorted. "I was born with a steering wheel in my hand, Mr. Prez. The trick with something like that is to speed up, not slow down."

The armored car was doing approximately one hundred and twenty-five kilometers per hour when it reached the place in the highway where the road dropped off suddenly. Freeman-Mawalzi screamed in terror as the car shot through the air. The armored car, not meant to negotiate ups and downs at such speeds, landed heavily. Everyone was pressed down into the seat cushions as if by a giant hand, and then rebounded immediately as the vehicle bucked and bounced like a rodeo horse with a burr under its saddle.

"Now, that wasn't so bad, was it?" Ray asked, turning his head and giving the Uhuran president a big shit-eating grin.

"Keep your eyes on the road!" Freeman-Mawalzi shouted at him.

While Gawain, Robin, Mama-san, and Beowulf hunkered down even more in the back, Freeman-Mawalzi clutched the dash so hard he thought he might leave permanent finger marks in it.

"See, Ake's not the only one who can drive like a champion," Ray boasted. He smiled a secret smile, pleased that his braggadocio and his devil-may-care attitude was keeping their minds off their more serious predicament. *Better to have everyone worried that I'm a crazed driver than let them think about those damn cyclebots on our ass.* He sneaked a look at the rear hol-vee. The cyclebots were closing fast. He'd nearly lost control of the armored car with that insane business with the dip in the road; the cyclebots flew over it like it was nothing. They'd be on the armored car in seconds.

Cyclebots. The half-motorcycle, half-robot entities were as fast and maneuverable on their two wheels as killer whales were underwater—and they were just as deadly. They were certainly "well armed," Ray mused, unable to resist the pun that their multiarmed upper torsos inspired. Their four arms on the humanoid part of their construction could easily handle two energy rifles or slug throwers—bigger and more powerful ones than the average human-sized weapons most soldiers and law enforcement officers carried. For an especially versatile and deadly twist, they might be equipped with both an energy rifle and a slug thrower—or even a flamethrower.

Beowulf rested his lower jaw on the rear gate and looked out. His nose just centimeters from the low-res shields, he stared balefully at their three pursuers. "They's comin' on real fast."

The big dog pulled his head back down when the first beams of laser energy struck the rear of the armored car. The sound of the hot bolts being absorbed by the rear shields was initially terrifying, then reassuring. As long as the rear shields held, they had a chance of coming out of this alive.

Ray stared at what lay ahead: an impossibly complicated series of over- and underpasses. He marveled at the complexity and realism of the immense Robot War park. Then he giggled at that thought.

"What's so funny?" asked Freeman-Mawalzi.

"I was just complimenting Battlefield for being so 'realistic.' It doesn't get any more realistic than this, does it?"

"We be really dead for sure if'n those cycle guys gets us in their sights," Gawain opined.

"You say you've got one of Battlefield's externals loaded in your skull?" Ray asked Freeman-Mawalzi.

"Yes, of course. What do you think made me and my ministers such effective tacticians?" the Uhuran president replied.

Ray pulled something out of one of his safari jacket's pockets. "Good. Take this and shove it . . . into your internal reader, that is."

Freeman-Mawalzi looked at the small sliver of plastic Ray was holding in his hand. "What's that?"

"Don't be dense. It's an insert that will enable you to work the laser cannon up top like a pro. I found it in the glove compartment—under all the gloves." Ray was rewarded by Beowulf's appreciative chuckle.

Freeman-Mawalzi took the insert and held it in the palm of his hand. He stared mutely at it, looking for all the world like he was gazing dubiously at a piece of dung that Ray had told him was edible. "It's just an external, for Christ's sake," Ray said. "Pop out the old and pop in the new."

"Oh, right." Freeman-Mawalzi did as Ray suggested, taking care not to misplace the little sliver of enablement that he removed. Then he gingerly inserted the new external into the entry point on his skull.

"Got it?"

"Yes-s-s," Freeman-Mawalzi hissed, settling back in his seat, letting the flow of information pour into his brain.

"Here they come," said Robin from the back of the car.

While one of the three cyclebots stayed behind the armored car and continued peppering the rear shields with energy bolts, the other two flanked Ray's clumsy vehicle and began putting its side shields to the test.

Freeman-Mawalzi glanced at the instrument readouts and cringed. "We can't do this indefinitely; our power cells are losing their reserves at an alarming rate."

"Well, let's play chutes and ladders," Ray said, turning the wheel violently to the right. His action forced the cyclebot on that side off the road. More importantly, he hurled down an exit ramp, momentarily losing the cyclebot which had been hugging his left flank.

The cyclebot following directly behind them easily took the

turnoff with Ray and continued to direct a stream of energy at the armored car's rear shields.

"What are you waiting for? Get up top," Ray said, making it more order than request. The Uhuran president didn't protest. He merely irised open the hatch and climbed up to the laser cannon. He moved quickly and efficiently to ready the weapon, relying on the external's enriching flood of information. In seconds he possessed the ability to perform actions that were new to him yet seemed to be ingrained in his memory. He activated the turret controls and experimentally rotated the gun.

"Everything okay up there?" Ray asked via the small earphones both he and the Uhuran leader had inserted.

"Everything is A-1."

"Then you may fire when ready, Gridley."

Freeman-Mawalzi was apparently raring to go. He immediately opened fire at the trailing cyclebot, forcing it to drop back in the face of the intensity of the stream of energy now being directed at it.

Hurtling down the exit ramp, Ray merged with a new roadway, made a wide U-turn, and doubled back. The armored car picked up speed and headed back up the exit ramp, all manner of lights and voice warnings inside the cab urgently informing Ray he was going in the wrong direction.

"That's what you think," Ray said, steering around the exit ramp's sharp curve.

"Allah be merciful!" Freeman-Mawalzi exclaimed as the cyclebot which had dropped back to avoid the laser cannon fire roared blindly around the curve, heading toward them at a high rate of speed.

"Kiss your ass goodbye, metal boy!" Ray exulted.

The armored car's two tons smashed into the cyclebot, its momentum multiplying its weight and mass many times over. The sickening collision caused the cyclebot to disintegrate into a plethora of pieces that flew everywhere; some were crushed beneath the tires of the armored car.

As shards of metal and plastic streamed from the armored car's barely dented front, Ray fought the wheel to keep the vehicle from skidding out of control.

"Hooray!" the dogs yelled gleefully, oblivious of Ray's efforts to keep the vehicle on the exit ramp and then the highway.

Roaring toward the armored car in excess of two hundred kilometers per hour, the two remaining cyclebots shed as much speed as they could and flashed by the larger vehicle on either side, successfully avoiding its dangerous mass by centimeters. Ray looked in the rear hol-vee and saw them both brake hard and fishtail to a burning-brakes stop. Then they kicked into high gear and came after the armored car once again, mayhem and revenge on their minds.

Ray muscled the big steering wheel and again turned back the way they'd come. "We's sure gettin' a good look at this same stretch of road," Beowulf commented.

"You know me," Ray joked. "I never could read a map." Then he spoke urgently to the onboard computer.

"What are you telling the computer?" Freeman-Mawalzi asked from his gun turret.

"I'm programming it to take the next off-ramp and then stop at the bottom," Ray told him.

"Why are you doing that? Why don't you halt it manually?"

"Because I'm getting off at the next overpass."

"What!"

19

"Ah, yes," said Dr. Simon Svoboda. "I seem to recall that the Larkin-Ringgren team encountered the original Dr. Svoboda on Terra some time back."

"The *original* Dr. Svoboda?" Kate asked, not sure what was going on.

"Your dog and his team met Stanislas K. Svoboda, director of the Terran Genetic Institute. Dr. Svoboda was responsible for the creation of numerous genetically altered lifeforms, lifeforms which he sold to the highest bidder to be used as biological weapons."

"That's disgusting!" Kate exclaimed.

Svoboda waved a hand as if dismissing her outrage as the naive sputterings of someone unaware of how things worked. "Nonetheless, he was a genius at what he did, at creating remarkable new versions of Terran crocodiles, tigers, elephants, bears—"

"One o' them damn bears o' his killed Littlejohn!" Frodo growled.

"My condolences," said Svoboda, oozing insincerity. "Anyway, to continue: Many years before, aware that time respects no man, the good doctor had samples of his own genetic material taken so that he might reproduce himself, thereby saving his brilliance for all mankind. Not in the ordinary, sexual way, you understand, but in a manner which guaranteed an almost one-hundred-percent duplication."

"He cloned himself!" Kate said. Then, awareness dawning in her eyes, she looked at Svoboda and her jaw dropped. "You mean that you . . . ah . . . you are . . ."

Svoboda smiled and bowed slightly. "Yes, you could say he was my father, in a way. *I* am the reincarnation of Dr. Stanislas K. Svoboda."

"You killed Littlejohn!" snarled Frodo and then leapt straight for Svoboda's throat.

As quick as Frodo was, Salvaterra was quicker. He raised his energy pistol and the beam stopped Frodo in mid-leap.

★ ★ ★

The armored car roared down the exit ramp, passing beneath the overpass. Before it could rejoin the highway, it swerved and came to a complete stop, effectively blocking the ribbon of plascrete with its bulk. The cyclebots, in hot pursuit, braked hard and came to a skidding stop, their weapons firing into the car's shields.

Freeman-Mawalzi, manning the laser cannon like he'd been operating one his whole life, held off the two cyclebots with a constant barrage of energy bolts.

It was a complete standoff.

Then Ray popped up from his hiding place on the overpass and targeted the cyclebots with the rocket launcher. "Two cyclebots and two missiles," Ray told himself softly. "Make 'em count, Sergeant York." He wet his thumb with his tongue and touched the automatic sighting mechanism with the baptized digit. "Okay, Ole Betsy, do your stuff."

He fired.

The rocket flew straight and true and the targeted cyclebot blew apart like a cheap plastic model with a cherry bomb in it. The second 'bot spun around futilely on its wheels and tried to make a run for it. No dice. Ray's last missile deconstructed it in new and novel ways.

Ray slumped with relief, turning and pressing his back against the cool plascrete of the overpass. He kissed the barrel of the rocket launcher and put it down lovingly, aware that it had saved his bacon twice now. Weapons were evil things, he thought. But looking at the utilitarian sleekness of the blue-black launch cylinder, Ray was moved to reflect that guns had a strange attractiveness that was hard to define or understand. Then he laughed; that was such a male thing. Kate wouldn't have any idea what he was talking about. She hated guns.

★ ★ ★

Kate glanced around the small featureless room they'd been thrown into. There was precious little that could even remotely be considered transformable into a weapon. "Lord, I wish I had a gun or a knife," she said bitterly.

The semiconscious Frodo stirred and opened his eyes. "Oh-h-h, my head!" the groggy dog moaned. "It feels like it 'sploded."

"You're lucky it only feels like the top of your reckless head was blown off," Kate told him. "If General Salvaterra's energy pistol hadn't happened to be set on stun, you'd be dead meat now."

"Yah, yah," Frodo conceded crossly. "It woulda bin worth it if'n I coulda kilt that damn Swo-boda guy."

"He's not the same Svoboda," Kate told him. Then she reconsidered and added, "I suppose in a superficial way, he is the same Svoboda, sort of. He's a clone, derived from the original's genes. While it's true that he's an exact duplicate of the original Svoboda, he had to be born and grow up just like anyone else." She thought about that. "Well, maybe not like anyone else. He did tell us that Dr. Svoboda—the original Dr. Svoboda, that is— imposed strict rules on his education and upbringing, the better to produce a close replication of his adult self."

"Oh." Then Frodo asked, "What wuz ya sayin' when I woked up? Somethin' 'bout a gun?"

"Yes," Kate confessed. "I was thinking out loud. I was wishing for a gun or any weapon at all."

"Anythin'? Ya gots *somethin'*, ya know," Frodo told her.

"And what might that be?"

"Ya gots me."

Kate stared at the big dog open-mouthed for a moment, then clamped her jaw shut. Finally, she nodded and said, "That's right. You're as much a weapon as any quiver blade or lead pipe."

"We dint start out that way, though, ya know," Frodo told her, a touch of sadness in her voice.

"What do you mean, Frodo?"

"Us dogs wuz told we had a thing in our heads, from our trainin', that kept us from hurtin' folks."

"I remember hearing something to that effect, yes," Kate

agreed. "Scout dogs were supposed to be like robots: unable to cause harm to humans."

"Ray 'ventually 'fessed up 'bout that. He tole us it was all a fairy tale so's folks wouldn't be scared of us. Ray said it was to make us feel good 'bout ourselves, too." Frodo shook his big shaggy head sadly. "'Fore we knowed it, we wuz killin' beoples right and left. Oh, they mostly needed killin', they wuz bad folks or trying' to kill us, but it still a hard thing to ack-cept." Kate patted Frodo's head reassuringly.

"'Course, I think I be able to handle bitin' off the head of that Dr. Swo-boda if I gets a real chance," Frodo said, his eyes glinting.

II

"Oh-h-h, Christ . . . I'm gonna die, I'm gonna die!" Ake moaned as the spray from the ocean top was sucked into the craft's air intakes and caused their hijacked floater's engines to cough and sputter. A cheap model meant only to putter around in the planet's atmospheric envelope, the floater wasn't sealed against a vacuum such as that found in space or otherwise buttoned up tight.

"We all gonna die if'n you doan get up higher!" insisted Sinbad. "We's almost on top of the water."

"I've got to keep low to avoid detection," Ake replied, putting his hand over his mouth as if to hold back his rising gorge.

"This ain't no sub-marine," Grendel said, seconding Sinbad's contention that they were too close to the waves for comfort.

"We're almost there," insisted Ake. "Just leave the driving to me; I'll get us to the island in one piece."

A concerned Ozma glanced at Tajil. The big red dog looked like he was sleeping. "You dead or somethin', Taddy?" she asked him.

"No," replied Tajil without bothering to open his eyes or lift his head from his front paws. "I jes' figger that Ake's gonna get us there or he ain't. No sense worryin' 'bout things I can't do nuthin' 'bout."

"Good thinking, Taddy," Ake said, staring at a smudge on the horizon; with any luck it was the island continent he was looking for. Ake hadn't dared to use any of the navigational electronics for fear they'd be detected, so he had only his seat-of-the-pants flying skills and rudimentary sense of direction to get them to their destination.

"Hey," said Ozma, her sharp dog's eyes peering out the plasglas windscreen. "Is that the Battlefield place?"

"I sincerely hope so," Ake told her.

"How we gonna find Ray when we gets there?" asked Sinbad.

Ake tapped the side of his head. "Our communications implants will finally be in range," he said. "As soon as we're over the park, I can begin trying to zero in on him."

The island continent that hosted both Battlefield and Dinoland rushed at them with increasing velocity, or so it seemed. Before long, they'd made land and were flashing over numerous armed conflicts. Ake reflected that the battles being waged were certainly realistic-looking from up here. Then he thought about that. *What if they aren't only "realistic-looking," but the real thing itself?* he asked himself. He shook his head in disbelief. *Nah, couldn't be . . . could it?*

"Ake, what that?" asked Tajil, staring at the rearview hol-vee.

Ake saw what had caught Tajil's attention; it was a Terran World War One biplane. "That's an old-time airplane, Taddy," Ake explained.

"Why's it comin' toward us so fast?"

"I don't know," admitted Ake. "We're not a part of the theme park, it shouldn't be after us; we don't belong in this particular war game."

"I doan think anybody tole it that," said Ozma nervously.

A sinking feeling in his stomach gave Ake reason to agree with Ozma's assessment. "He *does* seem to mean business, doesn't he?"

The speculation about the biplane's intentions ended when it opened fire with the ancient machine gun mounted directly in front of the pilot. "It's shootin' at us!" wailed Ozma.

Ake looked around frantically, but the floater was unarmed and there didn't appear to be anything in the cabin they could use as a weapon. Ake had brought along an energy rifle and a pistol, but he had no way of using them against their attacker.

"Let's see if we can lose him," Ake said, first climbing and then putting the floater into a steep dive. He glanced at the rearview hol-vee.

"That dint work," said Grendel.

"Well, it half worked," disagreed Ake, turning an interesting shade of green. "While I didn't lose *him*, I did lose my stomach!"

The biplane latched onto them with the tenacity of an Ender's hawk on the tail of a stupid, slow-flying pigeon. "Jeez, listen to that," Grendel said as they could hear not only the biplane's machine gun chattering, but also the impact of the plastic-jacketed slugs. It sounded like a deadly rain of hail.

"We can't take much more of this since we don't have a single shield to protect our ass," Ake told the dogs. "I'd advise you to get ready for a rough landing."

From his position hugging the floor, Tajil just sighed. He wedged himself in tight against a bulkhead and the other dogs squeezed themselves into semisecure places beside him. Finally, Tajil looked over at Sinbad and said, "People spend money to do this?"

With the biplane pumping round after round of slugs into the floater's tail, they flew over the barrier separating the WWI field of conflict and the adjacent theme area. Ake didn't notice that they had strayed and assumed that the broad expanse of verdant vegetation was within Battlefield's confines. Seeing all the green, Ake wondered what it was supposed to be. The fields of France? The farmlands outside Gettysburg?

"Hang on, guys!" Ake shouted as the controls began to go dead in his hands. He dropped as much airspeed as he could before the floater's null-grav engines lost power and the craft plummeted to the ground like the proverbial stone.

As the WWI fighter corkscrewed into a victorious barrel roll and peeled off to return to its airbase, the floater angled into the ground at just under one hundred kilometers per hour. Even so, the craft's blunt nose dug a trench in the soft soil more than a hundred and sixty meters long.

The dogs were thrown forward against the bulkhead separating the rear from the control area, and Ake's own momentum thrust him against his waist and shoulder restraints. Several unsecured objects went ricocheting around the inside of the floater like pinballs, and one of them, a solid plastic navigational cube, struck Ake's forehead a glancing blow.

After the shrieking protests of metal and plastic stressed beyond its breaking point that seemed to go on forever, an eerie silence descended over the stilled craft like a blanket of fresh snow.

While Ake and the dogs lay stunned and semiconscious inside the floater, a brightly colored little bipedal dinosaur, its curiosity piqued by this unexpected visitor to its world, hopped toward the shiny object. It chittered and squeaked fearlessly, and soon other inhabitants began edging closer and closer to the object of the little dinosaur's fascination.

Suddenly, a bloodcurdling cry rent the midday air and all the smaller lifeforms that had been so curious about the intruder suddenly lost interest.

Something big, something dangerous, was on its way.

III

After they had turned back the threat posed by the cyclebots and abandoned the armored car that had served them so well, Ray and the others started to feel good about their chances of getting out of Battlefield alive. Not cocky, simply confident; a confidence born of their success in staying alive so far. Still, Ray knew that if they destroyed all the mechanical warriors they encountered save one, that one could kill them just as dead as a thousand battle androids could.

"What is going on, Larkin?" Freeman-Mawalzi asked as they cautiously worked their way through urban alleyways, moving carefully and slowly to avoid surveillance floaters or blimps.

Ray, watching Beowulf and Mama-san checking out the far end of the alley, turned toward the Uhuran president and said, "The robots are trying to kill us."

Freeman-Mawalzi closed his eyes and took a deep breath. "I *know* that, Larkin. Would you stop being a smartass long enough to give me a straight answer?"

Ray shrugged. "I thought it was obvious."

"Pretend I'm stupid," Freeman-Mawalzi said. Then he held up a warning finger.

"They've been equipped with P-Q-G brains and then reprogrammed by folks who don't want the conference to go ahead. Some people, probably someone working with Ku'brol and Boosra, and maybe the whole damn staff of the hotel, are opposed to the formation of an Alliance."

"But who?"

"Former Nazis," Ray said.

After he had registered Freeman-Mawalzi's puzzled look, Ray relented and said, "I was making a crude analogy based on my knowledge of twentieth-century history. After the Germans were defeated in Terra's Second World War, many of the leaders and followers of Adolf Hitler's Nazi party went underground and worked fervently for the restoration of Nazi rule in Germany and elsewhere. They could not accept the defeat of their twisted ideals and plotted for many years for a return to the power, for a return to the glories and successes of the Third Reich."

"The Federation . . ." said Freeman-Mawalzi slowly, the truth dawning in his eyes.

"Give that man a cigar."

"But they have no chance," Freeman-Mawalzi said. "No one wants to return to the ways of the old Federation."

Ray made a don't-kid-me face. "C'mon, Mr. President. You know that's not true. Most people, I'll concede, were tickled to death to see the Federation go the way of the dodo. *Most* people, however, is not everyone. There are lots of disgruntled ex-generals and footsoldiers, not to mention bureaucrats, minor functionaries, and military-industrial-complex millionaires who gave their lives to the Federation and were handsomely rewarded either financially or psychologically. I imagine they're not particularly thrilled to see the centerpiece of their twisted lives tossed onto the scrap heap of history with so many other failed enterprises."

"Yes, I see your point," Freeman-Mawalzi conceded. "But I still find it difficult to believe that they might succeed with this mad plan."

"Maybe they will, maybe they won't," Ray shrugged. "If we wish to insure that they don't, then we have to see that they're stopped here and now, on Neverland."

"Then I think—"

"Hey, lookit up in the sky!" Gawain exclaimed.

Ray, Freeman-Mawalzi, and the dogs watched in fascination as an old heavier-than-air flying machine hotly pursuing a modern floater flashed across the sky toward their position. Ominously, the imperiled floater was leaving a trail of black smoke in its wake.

"That floater doesn't have a chance," Ray said, shading his eyes with his hand. "That's the Red Baron's plane on their tail."

"Why is it shooting at the floater?" Freeman-Mawalzi wondered out loud.

"Golly gee, I don't know," said Ray sarcastically. "Do you think it might possibly have *anything* to with the robots trying to kill us?"

"Ah-h-h, you're right, of course," Freeman-Mawalzi said, embarrassed by his naivete. "I'm not using my—"

"Wait!" Ray interrupted, a stunned look on his face.

"What is it?" asked Beowulf.

Ray looked at the floater and the ancient biplane as they

disappeared over the horizon, straining toward them on tiptoes as if to reach out and snatch the tiny dots out of the sky. "Ake is on that floater."

"What!" Mama-san and Robin said at the same time.

"Yeah. It's the old carrot-top himself."

"Are you certain that your friend and partner is on that floater?" Freeman-Mawalzi asked dubiously. "Could you be mistaken?"

"About Ake?" Ray seemed surprised by the question. "No, never." He tapped the crown of his head. "Like you, the two of us have an external; we share a linked transmitter/receiver. We keep in touch that way—when we're within spitting distance of each other, that is."

"I see."

"And, of course, these babies help a little, too," Ray said, pointing to where the small leather bag of rubies hung from his neck. Since the pouch was out of sight beneath Ray's clothing, Freeman-Mawalzi had no idea what "babies" he was talking about.

"What we gonna do?" inquired Beowulf, already knowing the answer to his question.

"Go get Ake, of course."

"Do I have a vote in any of this?" asked the Uhuran president, fingering his salt-and-pepper mustache.

"Of course," Ray said. "We're a democracy. We're not like the old Federation."

"Uh, right," said Freeman-Mawalzi, suddenly certain he was about to have his pockets picked. Going ahead gamely, he said, "I vote that we continue on our current course, get the hell out of Battlefield, and then come back for your friend."

Ray looked at Beowulf, Robin, Mama-san, and Gawain. "Who votes for that option?" Silence. "Okay, that's one vote for your proposal, Mr. President."

Ray looked into the serious dog faces. "Now then, who votes for going after Ake?" Beowulf, Robin, Gawain, and Mama-san spoke up as one. "There you have it," Ray said. "The electorate have cast their votes. We're heading west, after the floater and the biplane."

"Why did I even bother?" Freeman-Mawalzi wondered out loud.

"Shall we start?" Ray said.

"Wait a minute." Freeman-Mawalzi pulled out a map cube and

studied it. "Unless this map is inaccurate, what lies in that direction is . . ."

"Yeah?"

"What lies that way is a forty-meter-high wall buttressed by a powerful force field."

"What's on the other side of the wall?" asked Ray, afraid that he knew the answer.

"Dinoland."

★ ★ ★

They were alive. There was just one problem: The floater lay upside down, its viewports covered by dirt and vegetation.

"Oh-h-h!" Ake groaned. "I feel like shit." He put his hand to his head and felt something warm and sticky. He looked at his fingertips and saw blood on them. "Christ, that's all I need."

"It doan look bad, Ake," reassured Tajil, crawling into the control room where Ake was still strapped securely to his pilot's seat.

"Thanks," Ake replied. He undid the fasteners and released himself, dropping toward the floor of the floater—which was really the ceiling, the craft being upside down. He put out his hands, ducked his head, and rolled onto his back. Feeling tumbled dry, Ake looked at Tajil. "And what about you, Taddy? How are you doing? How are all of you doing?"

"We's all still alive, if'n that's what you're askin'," said Grendel, joining Ake and Tajil.

Ake looked at the dogs and smiled weakly. "I told you I'd bring us in safely."

"Yah, you done that all right," conceded Ozma, standing up uncertainly and shaking loose debris off herself. The other dogs followed suit and Ake coughed dramatically.

"Gee, Ake, you gettin' as bad as Ray. He's all the time tryin' to make us feel bad for—"

The downed floater suddenly lifted a meter or so into the air before slamming back down to the ground with a solid *thwack*. The dogs were thrown off their feet and all began to talk at once.

"Quiet!" said Ake so loudly that they looked at him with a mixture of surprise and contrition. "Sorry, but I couldn't hear myself think."

"Speakin' o' hearin'," said Ozma, "D'hear that?"

"Hear what?" asked Ake.

"Yah!" said Sinbad. "What *is* that?"

Ake strained to hear with his human ears what the dogs were easily picking up with their wolf-keen canine hearing. "It sounds like someone sawing a piece of wood," Ake said finally. "I know it can't really be that, but that's what it sounds like."

It was true. The noise, a great rasping and remarkably rhythmic sound, bore a strong similarity to a saw being worked back and forth through a tree trunk.

"That's someone breathin'," Ozma said, her head cocked to one side.

"Someone breathin'?" repeated Grendel, the puzzlement in her voice slowly turning to awe. "Someone *big* breathin'," she growled.

The floater was again lifted several meters into the air, but this time they were more prepared for that action and for the bone-jarring fall that followed. "What goin' on?" wondered Ozma.

Remembering an old holo showing a grizzly bear pawing at a fallen log in which a badger had taken refuge, Ake guessed instantly what was happening. "Uh, guys, I don't know how to tell you this, but I think a Tyrannosaurus or one of the other big guys is toying with our floater. The plasteel hull is keeping him from getting at the meat inside."

"What meat?" asked Grendel.

"Us."

"Jeez," muttered Sinbad. "Think he can get at us?"

Remembering how the grizzly in the holo had finally gone berserk and ripped apart the rotting log to get at the badger, Ake carefully replied, "Maybe. But maybe not. I *hope* not."

"Well, dang, Ake, we all hopes that!" said Ozma reprovingly.

"Doan worry," said Tajil calmly. "That big guy ain't gonna get inside this ship. And even if he does, Ake gots his energy rifle."

Although gratified by Tajil's confidence, Ake said, "I'm not sure I want to use an energy rifle unless I absolutely have to, Taddy."

"Why not?"

"I don't want to piss him off."

"Oh."

20

It was serendipity that they found a way past the high barrier separating Battlefield and Dinoland. They had been following the high, force-field-protected wall for klicks looking for an opening or some way through the massive base of the plascrete and plasteel structure. As Ray noted in frustration at one point, "Whoever built this thing knew what he was doing. Godzilla on steroids couldn't get through or over this mother of all walls."

Tired and hungry, they moved forty meters or so from the wall and made a temporary camp. Ray and Freeman-Mawalzi got food and water out of their supply packs and everyone had something to eat and drink. Restless, Robin got up after he had finished eating and scouted the vicinity.

"Hey, Beowulf."

"What?"

"C'mere."

Beowulf lumbered to his feet and ambled over to where Robin lay prone, staring through some scrubby bushes. "Yah, what is it, Robin?"

"Lookit," the big red dog said. "Who is them guys?"

Beowulf almost yelped, so surprised was he by what Robin had to show him. He crawled backwards a few meters, turned, and urgently said, "Ray! C'mere right now!"

Ray hurried to join Beowulf and Robin, dropping to his hands and knees. The other dogs and Freeman-Mawalzi were not far behind. "Sonofabitch!" Ray hissed. Meters from the wall stood three uniformed Cadre regulars.

"What they doin'?" asked Gawain.

"It looks like they're smoking," Ray replied.

"Smoking?" said a puzzled Freeman-Mawalzi. "You mean tobacco?"

Ray shook his head. "No, they're probably sneaking in a couple of puffs on a happy stick." One of the men removed the small white cylinder from his mouth and passed it to another member of the trio. "Yeah, see that. They're sharing their forbidden fruit."

"Happy sticks ain't 'gainst the law, is they?" asked Gawain.

"Nothing's against the law on Neverland," Ray reminded him. "No, they're not 'illegal,' just not permitted for regulars on duty. Drugs and soldiering don't mix."

"Ah, I see it now," said Freeman-Mawalzi. "That is why they are outside. They are sneaking a smoke."

"Where they come from?" Beowulf asked.

"That's what I want to know, too," Ray replied.

"Hey, look," Robin said.

Ray looked. One of the soldiers had taken a last drag on the cigarette, thrown it to the ground, and stomped on it. Then, laughing, they walked over to a low mound protruding from the soil several meters from the barrier. One of the men did something and the top of the mound opened.

"It's a hatch," said Beowulf. Without further ado, the three men climbed down into an underground chamber, closing the circular hatch that had admitted them.

"Ah, ha!" cried Ray triumphantly. "I have you now, young Skywalker!" He turned to Freeman-Mawalzi said, "Give me your energy pistol, please, Mr. President."

"You aren't thinking of doing anything foolish, are you?"

"Just gimme the damn pistol and shut up," Ray said. He smiled to take the sting out of his words. Freeman-Mawalzi handed over his energy pistol without saying anything further. Ray checked the charge; it would have to do.

"Ray . . . " said Beowulf.

"Yeah?"

"Be careful."

"Yah," said Gawain. Picking up on Ray's old sinny comment, he added, "May La Forge be with you."

Ray doubled over with laughter. "Sorry, Gawain, I appreciate your sentiments, I really do."

"What I say?" asked a bewildered Gawain.

"That's from *Star Track*, 'nother old tee-vee show from the twenny-eff century," explained Mama-san.

"Oh."

While the dogs chuckled over Gawain and Ray's exchange, Ray unobtrusively made his way over to the entrance to the underground chamber, lifted the hatch, readied his energy pistols, and climbed in.

"Hey!" shouted Beowulf.

Almost immediately there were flashes of light, and several small explosions. A plume of dirty brown smoke poured from the open hatch as from a chimney. A slug thrower spoke once or twice but was quickly silenced.

"Ray! You all right?" Beowulf shouted down into the smoke-obscured interior. "Ray, you okay?"

"It's gonna be hard for you guys to negotiate the rungs, but I think you'll be able to make it," Ray's voice floated back up to them.

"Ray's okay!" Mama-san said gleefully.

"Yah," agreed a delighted Beowulf. Then his honest dog's face clouded and he added, "But he not gonna be when I gets through with him!"

★ ★ ★

"Computer, can I send a current through the hull?" Ake asked.

"That is possible," the computer conceded.

"Then do it."

"How much power, sir?"

"Start out at one hundred thousand volts. We can slowly ratchet it up if that's too low."

"Yes, sir. Beginning power diversion now."

When nothing seemed to happen—nothing other than the floater being raised and dropped again—Ake said, "Higher. Higher."

Finally, there was an outraged bellow and the ground underneath them shook as something big and powerful stomped away.

"I think that's done it," Ake said.

"We gonna be okay now?" asked Tajil.

"I hope so," Ake replied. "We can stay here briefly while we collect ourselves and plan what—"

"Warning, warning, warning," the computer announced. "Power levels are dangerously low-w-w-w-w . . ." The floater went completely dark except for what little light filtered in through the vegetation-obscured viewports.

"Shit on a stick!" exploded Ake angrily. "Not again! I'm getting sick and tired of the lights going off on me all the time."

"It only the second time," Sinbad said in an effort to cheer Ake up. He felt more than saw Ake's glare in his direction. "Ah, 'course it a pain in the butt. Yah, it is."

"Guess the power cells dead," Tajil said, stating the obvious.

"Now what?" wondered Ozma.

"Now we get out and try to find Ray and the others."

Ake crawled along the ceiling of the disabled and powerless craft, feeling for an emergency exit. He gave a tug. Nothing. He put his shoulder to it and tried pushing. Nothing.

"Sinbad, Taddy—get your butts over here and lean into this escape hatch with me." The two big males complied and the results were the same.

Frustrated, Ake said, "I guess the only thing to do is blow the hatch."

"Blow the hatch?" said Tajil. Then the import of Ake's words sank in and he repeated, "Blow the hatch! Get back, Sinbad! Get down, Ozma and Grendel!"

After initiating the countdown procedure, Ake crawled back along the ceiling/floor and said, "Holy Moses, guys, it's just a charge to blow the bolts off the emergency exit. It's not going to be that big a blast. Taddy, you have everyone ducking his or her head as if—"

A substantial explosion shook the ship and something struck Ake in the back of the head. He dropped to the bulkhead surface like a poleaxed steer.

"Ake . . . ?" began Ozma. "Ake, you all right?"

"Oh, no," said Tajil. "Not again!"

II

"I trust you find your accommodations satisfactory?" asked Leandra Boosra.

"I have no complaints," Kate replied. "Save for the obvious one—I am not free to go." Kate looked into the holo receiver carrying their images and words to each other. Kate could see part of Boosra's hotel office behind her.

"No," Boosra admitted. "For the time being, I am afraid you and the dog must remain there as our guests."

"Would you please tell me something?" Kate asked.

"If I am able to," said Boosra, a bit disconcerted.

"Why haven't your hairy-knuckled allies killed us yet? Why are you keeping Frodo and me alive?"

"Jeez," said Frodo. "Doan be givin' 'em no ideas."

Boosra smiled at the big dog's concern. "We are not murderers," Boosra told her. "We are not savages." When Kate shot her a dubious look, Boosra laughed a low, soft laugh and said, "Yes, I know how that must sound. To be perfectly honest with you, then, 'scrapers and scout dogs are not easy to come by. Unless you force us to, we have no plans to terminate you."

"What about Ray and Ake?"

"They are in Battlefield, as far as we know, and—"

"Oh, so your trained goons don't have everything under control yet, eh?"

Boosra shrugged. "It is only a matter of time. If our loyal troops cannot locate them, the robots will certainly dispose of them in a typically efficient manner. As the daughter of a Cadre officer forced to resign in the wake of the Chiron affair, I personally prefer their capture. A show trial would be most satisfying."

Kate chose to ignore all of Boosra's comments but one. "The robots?" she said, puzzled. "What robots are you talking about?"

"That's right, you don't know about the robots. The robots and battle androids on Battlefield have been reprogrammed by our brothers in arms, the Soldiers of God, to ignore their prohibitions against causing harm to human beings. They and the other mechanicals on Neverland are systematically decimating the delegates to the Conference."

Kate bit her lip. A dedicated reader who was aware of the origins of many words, Kate devoutly hoped that Boosra's use of the word decimate proved to be more in keeping with its original meaning than what it later came to mean.

"Whatta 'bout Swo-boda?" asked Frodo.

"Oh, you've met Neverland's resident clone, have you? It was he who supervised the genetic engineering of the alien creatures that were manipulated into emulating the dinosaurs of Old Earth. He's our pride and joy, our very own genius."

"He crazy nuts," said Frodo. "He should be killed dead."

"That's what they said about Stanislas Svoboda, isn't it?" asked Boosra. "I admit that the good doctor is unstable—almost a given when you consider his 'father.' But then, we had to take the bad with good, you see, to get his genius at genetic engineering and manipulation."

"What's the point of all this?" Kate asked the image hovering so realistically in front of her.

"I'm sure your friends Ray and Ake have deduced the outline of our plan by now."

"I'm a late bloomer," Kate said. "I'd love to figure it all out myself, too, but I'll accept hearing it from your lips."

Boosra shrugged. "There are many planets—Cromwell is one—where the discipline and order imposed by the Federation is badly missed. By eliminating the leaders of the embryonic Alliance, the way is opened to restoring the Federation to its rightful place in the galaxy."

"You're crazy!" exploded Kate, leaping forward so violently that Boosra was startled into drawing back involuntarily. "You can't get away with it; it'll never work."

"Won't it?" said Boosra. "Cut off the snake's head and the body is helpless. We are in the process of cutting off the serpent's head this very moment."

"They won't let ya get away with it," growled Frodo.

"Freeman-Mawalzi and the others? They are probably already dead."

"Not them flabby leaders," said Frodo, shaking his shaggy head.

"Who then?"

"Ray and Ake and Beowulf and the rest o' the team."

★ ★ ★

"It looks okay," Ray said, peering cautiously out of the open hatch. "I think I'll—" He was suddenly pulled back down inside. A second later, Beowulf's shaggy head emerged from the hatch.

"Yah, Ray's right: it *does* look okay out here." The big dog climbed out of the plascrete tube and down onto the ground. He was followed in short order by Robin, Mama-san, Ray, Freeman-Mawalzi, and Gawain.

Beowulf had seized Ray's trouser leg with his teeth and pulled him back down inside in order to protect his foolhardy master from needless risk. Ray had already acted recklessly by going into the underground bunker that passed underneath the barrier; Beowulf had served notice that he expected Ray to act like the dogs' master and use them for the purpose for which they were bred—to perform tasks too dangerous for him to risk.

Ray took a look at Beowulf's proud posture, his calm leader's demeanor, and swallowed the reprimand on the tip of his tongue. He realized he had been acting like the popular hol-vee character Captain Trimble. That was crazy; he was no invincible hol-vee hero.

I'm a short and unimposing scout dog leader, Ray told himself. *Incredibly handsome, to be sure, but no Captain Trimble.*

After the dogs had a quick look around, Ray said, "Okay, let's move out."

Freeman-Mawalzi shouldered his energy rifle like a weary combat veteran and shook his head. "I don't have an external for *this* park," he told Ray.

"Don't worry," Ray said. "It won't be a picnic, but the dinosaurs in this place are living, breathing creatures, not mechanicals. They haven't had their programming diddled with to make them killers."

"No, they *are* killers," Freeman-Mawalzi said.

"You've been watching too many hol-vee adventure shows," Ray chided the Uhuran president. "I used to watch old twentieth-century sinnys like *Jungle Jim* and *Bomba the Jungle Boy*. They made it real easy to think that leopards, lions, snakes, crocodiles, and rhinos lived only to attack humans. Most creatures, even nasty-tempered items like water buffalo, want no more to do with you than you do with them."

"I doubt that!"

"If we rely on the dogs acting as our eyes and ears and make lots of noise, we shouldn't have any problems," Ray insisted.

"That sounds very convincing," Freeman-Mawalzi said in a voice that revealed his doubts. "But what about predators that start to salivate when they think about prey as juicy and slow-moving as us? What then?"

"That's why God gave us energy rifles," Ray said, caressing the stock of his own weapon. Then he laughed and gave the Uhuran leader a solid whack on the back that propelled him forward a step or two. "C'mon, Mr. Prez, it'll be a snap. If we can just avoid any close encounters of the violent kind with bad-news items like a hungry T-rex, we'll be okay."

"I guess you're right," Freeman-Mawalzi conceded. "We're out of Battlefield and away from its killer robots. After that, anything should be a snap."

"There you go," Ray said heartily.

"Hey, Ray, lookit here!" exclaimed Mama-san, sniffing the ground.

"What is it?" Ray asked, but he quickly saw for himself: Footprints in the mud. "Human footprints," Ray said.

"I'm not the tracker that my grandfather was," said Freeman-Mawalzi, kneeling down for a closer look, "but these look like the bootprints of three—" He narrowed his eyes and peered piercingly at the marks in the mud. "No—make that four—good-sized or heavily armed men."

"They fresh," said Gawain. "Beoples went by not too long ago."

"And they goes that way," Beowulf said, gesturing in a direction at right angles to the way they were heading.

"What about your partner?" Freeman-Mawalzi asked. "Can you sense his presence nearby?"

"No, I can't," Ray admitted.

"Then we follow tracks?" asked Robin.

"We follow the tracks." Then Ray glanced at Freeman-Mawalzi and added smugly, "Unless the Prez here wants to vote on it."

"Don't be a wiseass," retorted Freeman-Mawalzi. "We follow the tracks."

Where the vegetation was lush and green and the ground was not muddy, it was more difficult to see the bootprints. Ray knew, however, that the dogs had the scent and didn't need to follow the actual physical impressions in the soil. Since he had delegated to the dogs the job of tracking the humans who'd passed by earlier, Ray paid scant attention to what lay at his feet. He was more interested in their surroundings, in the variety of dinosaur life that they caught fleeting glimpses of.

At one point in their trek, Mama-san and Gawain found a dried-up carcass, sniffed it eagerly, and began to roll around on it enthusiastically, quickly joined by Robin. Only Beowulf remained aloof.

"What in the name of the Prophet are they doing, Larkin?"

"Just being dogs," Ray replied, watching the repellent exercise in canine sensory overload.

Ray allowed them to go on for several minutes, then put a stop to it by saying, "All right, that's enough, guys. We have to get moving again."

"Boy, that wuz fun," Gawain said to Mama-san.

"Sure wuz," she agreed.

Beowulf, at the point, just sniffed. He was being melodramatically serious and dedicated, the better to show Ray and the others that such shenanigans were beneath his dignity. Then something caught his attention.

"Uh-oh."

Why don't I just swallow "the Black Capsule" right now and get it over with? Ray asked himself, rolling his eyes heavenward. Aloud, he asked, "What is it, now, Beowulf?"

"Lookit."

Ray looked. The bootprints they were following traversed a muddy patch of soil. But something new had been added: smallish three-toed tracks paralleling and overlaying the human prints. Ray was no expert, but they looked like Deinonychus tracks. And they were fresh.

Ray sighed. "I need a vacation from my vacation," he said to no one in particular.

"Remember your big speech about our abilities and our God-given energy rifles," said Freeman-Mawalzi sternly. "Don't *you* start getting all negative on *me* now."

"You're right," Ray said, snapping out of his brief moment of doubt and malaise. "C'mon. Let's see if we can catch up to whoever made these tracks."

Ten minutes of quick-march was all it took. They reached an outcropping of refrigerator-sized rocks where the humans they were following had taken refuge. Hissing and growling, a pack of ferocious little dinosaurs were darting in at their stationary prey, their jaws opening and closing like steel traps.

Ray raised his energy rifle and fired into the quartet of Deinos, striking one in the leg. His shot wounded but did not kill the little dinosaur. Acting as one, the Deinos whirled to see the origin of this challenge to their territorial imperative. Enraged by its wound, the injured Deino rushed pell-mell at them and Freeman-Mawalzi hastily got off several ineffective bolts.

Detached from the rest of the party by virtue of his place on the left point, Robin was targeted for attack by a pair of the Deinos moving with such lightning speed that they were a greenish-yellow blur.

"Yikes!" hollered Robin as the two Deinos, working with practiced skill, raked his sides with swipes of their sickle-shaped claws. Fortunately for Robin, they both caught only hair.

Ray whirled and fired his energy rifle in a fluid motion that matched the quickness of the attackers. The bolt burned across the back of one of Robin's tormenters and the Deino screeched and leapt away, whirling to face the source of its pain. Ray fired again and the Deino took the full impact of the bolt in its chest. Screaming an inhuman death cry, the dinosaur crumpled to the ground and thrashed for a few seconds before finally lying motionless. Its conspirator in the attempt to get at Robin used the opportunity to make good its escape.

The Deinos' charge had taken them through Ray's team, and the two men and the dogs now had their backs to the rocks. As the Deinos darted in and then withdrew, their legs a blur, Ray had little time to do more than marvel at their speed. *They're so damned fast!*

The Deinos, now seeing that these new creatures, and their humans, would not be easy pickings, ceased their probing attacks; at least for the moment.

"Dogs back," Ray ordered—unnecessarily, as it turned out. The dogs were premier close-in fighters, but they'd never encountered anything like the aggressive, man-sized Deinos before. They quickly backed into the rocks with Ray and Freeman-Mawalzi, barking furiously and displaying their own impressive teeth.

"Why aren't they following up on their attack?" wondered Freeman-Mawalzi. "Not that I'm complaining, you understand!"

"They're sharp characters, it appears," Ray said. "Maybe it's true that the really big brutes have pathetically tiny brains in relation to their size, but these little cowboys sure don't act like they've got BBs for brains."

Freeman-Mawalzi looked over his shoulder. "Let's go see who we've been following."

"Good idea."

The four men who'd been the subjects of the Deinos' attention slowly stepped out from their hiding places. *Christ!* Ray thought. *They look in worse shape than us!*

"We are pleased to see that all four of you are still alive," Freeman-Mawalzi said, smiling. Then his smile faded a bit as he added, "Of course, I would like to know why, once we came to your assistance, you did not provide a crossfire?"

A thin man with what used to be called a beer belly slowly stepped forward. Ray cringed at the sight; the man was not in very good shape. Pulling himself together, the wounded man answered, "It takes rifles to do that."

"You have no weapons?" Ray said incredulously.

"We have two energy pistols and a slug thrower. The pistols' power packs are just about drained, and the slug thrower hasn't very many slugs left to throw," said a second man. This second speaker, Ray observed, was bigger than the first man and in better physical condition. But there was defeat in his eyes.

"I see," said Ray. "And who might you be?"

"Me?" The man smiled wanly. "I am First Citizen Marius Ruder of Hollenwelt. These gentlemen are members of my cabinet." He indicated the first man. "That is Jorgen Meitz." The injured man stopped looking at his shirt, where a dark stain was slowly spreading, to nod. "And these two gentlemen are Franz Obuerst and Karl Ehrenreich."

"This is your whole party?" asked Ray.

Ruder blinked rapidly several times. "We were seven. One of the others was my wife."

"I'm very sorry," said Ray. Freeman-Mawalzi also offered his sympathy and his condolences.

"Who are *you*?" asked Meitz.

Ray introduced himself and the Uhuran president and then each of the dogs in turn.

"What now?" asked Ruder. "As you can plainly see, Jorgen needs medical attention as soon as possible."

"We keep moving," Ray said. "We're searching for my friend and partner. The good news is he's a physician. The bad news is he was in a floater that went down in Dinoland."

"Moving?" asked an incredulous Freeman-Mawalzi. "Did you say we start moving? Why, in the name of the One True God, should we leave the protection of these rocks?"

"What 'tection?" asked Beowulf pointedly.

"I'm afraid the big dog is right," Ruder told the astonished Uhuran president. "Had you not come along when you did we would all be dead now, killed by the ferocious little dinosaurs."

"But the rocks—" began Freeman-Mawalzi.

"These rocks might keep a Tyrannosaurus, Allosaurus, or other big meat-eater from getting at us," acknowledged Ray, "but they won't keep away the Deinos. And they've seen the set-up here," he added. "It won't take them long to figure out a way to better attack us. No, the best thing we can do is keep moving."

"I agree with Mr. Larkin," said Meitz. "I'd rather die on my feet than waste away here waiting for help that may never come."

"Like I said, if we can find him, my partner Ake might be able to do something about those injuries."

"Can ya hear Ake in your head?" asked Mama-san.
"No," admitted Ray, his face a picture of dejection.
"Ya worried 'bout him, huh?" asked Gawain.
"Yes."

21

"Who is responsible for this?" Major Morrow demanded of Aron Ku'brol, Neverland's head of security. "I can't imagine that many of the politicians and diplomats wandering around Battlefield are capable of taking out a five-man squad in such a brutal and efficient manner."

Ku'brol shifted the weight of his compact yet powerful body from one leg to another as he contemplated the carnage in the small duty room just off the tunnel that ran under the barrier connecting Battlefield with Dinoland. Ku'brol's intense and pitch-black eyes were narrow slits as he said, "Larkin and his damned dogs."

Major Morrow looked down at the bodies again. "No dogs. Just energy weapons." He turned his gaze to Ku'brol. "Is this Larkin capable of doing this by himself?"

"Oh, yes," Ku'brol said softly. "He is capable of much more than one might give him credit for. People are fooled into taking him lightly because of his size and demeanor. By the time they realize their mistake, they are dead." He gave Morrow a penetrating look. "Like the general. General Andrei Carras," he added, not wanting Morrow to miss his point.

"General Carras? The consul who was murdered by those who

did not have the stomach to do what was necessary to annex Chiron for the Federation?"

"Yes."

Major Morrow was shocked. "He is *that* Larkin?"

Again, Ku'brol simply said, "Yes."

"My God!" He slumped against the small duty room's plascrete wall. "Do Generals Salvaterra and Michael know who he is?"

"Certainly," Ku'brol said patiently. "That is why as soon as I report what happened here, I am going to ask permission for us to follow Larkin and his mutts into Dinoland."

"Into Dinoland?" said Morrow nervously. He was fearless when facing humans, but not dinosaurs.

"Yes, of course," Ku'brol said. "I have a score to settle with Larkin and his partner. Everything was proceeding smoothly here until they arrived and bollixed things up.

"Besides," Ku'brol continued, "whoever kills Larkin will forever have the Cadre in his debt." He looked at Major Morrow. "Think of what that will do for your career, Major: to be one of the men who killed the infamous Larkin and avenged the General's death and the humiliations of the Cadre and Federation. Just think!" His dark eyes burned with rage.

★ ★ ★

"Yes?" Kate said, activating the holophone in the small room that served as a cell for her and Frodo. The holophone was no stupid mistake on her captors' part; it could receive calls but not send them.

"Hello, again," said the image of Leandra Boosra.

"Oh, it's you," acknowledged Kate. "And why am I being honored with another call so soon after out last conversation? Are we a chat club of two?"

"Three," said Frodo, adamant about refusing to be left out.

Boosra chuckled in a patently phony manner. "I thought I should inform you that a floater carrying Doctor Ringgren and some of Larkin's obnoxious dogs was seen going down in flames over Dinoland." She waited for a reaction from Kate but got none.

Frodo, however, growled, "Damn!"

"Thank you, I'm sure," Kate said, reaching out to break the connection.

"Wait," Boosra told her. "There's more." Her smile became irritatingly genuine and heartfelt as she said, "It seems Larkin and the rest of his team survived their sojourn in Battlefield and are on their way to rescue their comrades. That is, assuming the doctor and the dogs were not killed in the crash." She shook her head sadly. "Dinoland is a very dangerous place."

"Jes' one minute alone with her. Thirty seconds, even," Frodo muttered under his breath.

Oblivious of Frodo's barely audible comments, Boosra continued. "The thing is, it's now even more dangerous for the Larkin-Ringgren team—Aron and Major Morrow are leading a small squad of crack Cadre regulars in after them. If the dinosaurs don't get them, surely Aron will. He is most annoyed at his ongoing humiliation from the likes of a little squirt like Ray Larkin. Aron seeks the restoration of the Federation as much as I do, but taking Larkin's life has, I fear, become an obsession for him."

When Kate continued to remain silent, Boosra finally asked, a bit crossly, "Have you nothing to say to my news?"

Kate stared intently into Boosra's eyes. "Whatever else I do, I am going to kill you. Whatever it takes, I will see you dead at my hand." Her lip curling, she added, "I will be no less dedicated in this than your damned security chief."

The living jewel in Boosra's cheek turned blood-red, and she sputtered, "Why, you dirty little 'scraper! How dare you speak to me like that!"

"Hey, lady," said Frodo. "Kiss my butt!"

Boosra reached out and broke the connection, her image dissolving into rainbow-hued specks.

"Guess we tole her, hah?" said Frodo.

"We sure did," said Kate emotionlessly.

Seeing the look in her eyes, Frodo asked, "Hey, ya think she wuz speakin' the truth 'bout Ray and Ake?"

Kate nodded affirmatively. "She was getting too much pleasure out of telling us to be lying. Besides, I could sense that her words were the truth."

"Yah," agreed Frodo. "You an Ebbs-ber."

"What?" asked Kate, turning to stare at Frodo.

"Ah-h-h, I jes' said that you an Ebbs-ber; ya kin read minds."

Kate knelt down and embraced Frodo, wrapping her arms around his barrel chest and resting her head against his. "Thank you, Frodo," she said.

"For what?" he asked, pulling back and staring into her eyes.

"For reminding me about something I had succeeded in blocking from myself. I *am* an ESPer, dammit."

Kate glanced at her watch. "I'd say we have an hour or so to live once Boosra starts stewing on our insults to her. In an hour, maybe less, someone's going to come through that door and kill us. Or at least me."

"Golly!" said Frodo.

"The good news is that we're not going to be here," Kate told the surprised canine.

"Where we gonna be?"

Kate shrugged. "That part I can't answer. Not here, however." She sat down, composed herself, and closed her eyes.

"Whadda ya doin'?"

"Sh-h-h, I'm going to finally make my abilities work for me." Kate cracked open one eye. "Go stand over by the door. When I give you the word, attack. And make it quick."

"'Tack who?"

Kate didn't answer. Instead, she breathed in and out deeply, her shoulders heaving. After a few minutes, she appeared to be fast asleep.

Wondering what was going on, Frodo took up his position to one side of the door. He sat on his haunches, looking first at Kate, then at the door, then back at Kate again. It wasn't especially warm in their small room, but Kate was perspiring profusely.

Without warning, the door hissed open. A maroon-clad young man, sweat streaming down his face, walked into the room like a zombie from the old horror sinny *Night of the Living Dead*. The door closed behind him.

Later, Frodo was to feel undeservedly ashamed for what he did in those first few moments: Nothing.

A vein in Kate's temple popped up and began pulsating. With an incredible act of will, she raised one finger of her right hand where it had clamped down on the arm of her chair.

Frodo finally got the message. "Oh," he said, leaping up and striking the catatonic guard in the middle of his back with his big paws. Falling to the floor seemed to revive the Cadre trooper, but it was too late as Frodo clamped down on his throat and closed the man's windpipe with the viselike power of his jaws. The man's legs kicked out twice, three times, and then he was still.

Kate returned to life again, her eyelids finally fluttering open. "Lordy, Frodo, I thought I was going to have to hold him like that forever; it seemed like years." She sighed. "He was weak-minded like so many who allow others to do their thinking for them, but he still resisted my will."

"I's sorry, Kate," an abject Frodo whimpered. "I jes' couldn't think."

"It was my fault," Kate disagreed. "I was too niggardly in my orders; I should have told you exactly what I expected of you."

"Worked out okay, though, huh?"

"Yes, it did," Kate allowed. She picked up the dead man's energy rifle. "Well, hello, handsome," she said, running her hands down its barrel as lovingly as Ray or Ake might in the same circumstances.

When she finished caressing her new weapon, she thumped Frodo's back and asked, "Ready to go for a little walk?"

"You betcha!"

II

After marveling over the size of the tracks outside the ruined floater, Ake and the dogs found a fallen log to sit on and take stock of the situation.

"Boy, Ake," Sinbad observed, "ya looks really awful—all burned up and bloody. If ya lives, ya might wanna kill yourself!"

Ake stopped applying salve to his burn long enough to laugh. It hurt, so he stopped immediately. "Yeah, I know I must look a fright. It can't be helped; this isn't a beauty pageant."

"How's your head?" Ozma asked, concerned about Ake's condition.

"We've just reached the section of the *1812 Overture* where they're firing the cannons."

"Huh?"

"It's throbbing like hell," Ake explained. "Get my bag, please." When Tajil returned with it, Ake opened it, withdrew his injector gun, loaded it with painkiller, and pressed it against his biceps. "Ah, that's better," he said almost instantly.

"Ake?"

"Yes, Sinbad?"

"When we wuz in Dinoland 'fore, you wuz tellin' Kate 'bout them ree-fugg . . . ref-fughh . . . resting places." He cocked his head quizzically and asked, "Why can't we find one o' them now?"

Ake sat dumbfounded and speechless. After a few moments had passed, Tajil said, "Ake, you okay?"

Ake pulled out a water packet and took a long sip of lukewarm water; it was wonderful. "Sinbad, that's a marvelous idea." He looked at the loyal and intelligent dog faces staring at him and said, "I wonder . . . did Ray pick you guys or did you choose him?"

"Both," said Grendel, smiling a canine smile that showed her sharp teeth.

"Hmmph," sniffed Tajil. "I hafta take your word for it since I was borned into the team."

"Nobody's perfect," allowed Grendel, continuing to smile.

"But you dogs are damned close," Ake allowed. Then he put his hand to his head and said, "I don't sense Ray. I'm not even getting a partial or broken signal."

"That mean he real far away?" asked Ozma.

"No, not necessarily. The atmosphere is kind of tricky here, and there's a lot of buried electronics. I'll keep trying, especially if we can find a refuge."

"Let's go, then," said Sinbad impatiently.

"Okay," agreed Ake, getting to his feet with a groan. "Gosh, what I wouldn't give for a hot shower, a hot cup of coffee, and a full-body massage."

"Yah—and pigs wants wings, too, Ake," Tajil pointedly told him.

"Taddy, just take the point and shut up," Ake told the red dog good-naturedly.

"What's that smoke up ahead?" wondered Grendel.

"Taddy will tell us when he gets back," said Sinbad.

"I think I founded one of them rescue places," barked Tajil, bounding back from his position a quarter of a klick ahead of the team.

"Good," said Ake.

"Uh, no—not 'xactly," Tajil responded carefully.

Ake opened his mouth to say something, then closed it again. Instead, he and the dogs silently followed Tajil to the refuge. The source of the smoke quickly became apparent; it was the refuge itself.

"Jeez, what happened here?" asked Ozma.

Supposed to be hidden from sight beneath two meters of soil, the refuge lay exposed to the elements, its force field no longer operative. An explosion of some sort had gone off inside the single domed chamber, the energy and hot gases erupting through the tightly packed ground covering it and opening it up like a sardine can. The mangled bodies two men and a woman lay nearby.

"Hey!" shouted Ozma. An orange-red and green little dinosaur was industriously picking at the dead woman's eyes. Ozma's angry feint sent the little saurian scavenger scurrying away.

"So much for that hot cup of coffee," Ake said, surveying the wreckage.

"What happened, Ake?" asked Sinbad.

Ake shook his head. "I don't know, Sinbad." He turned over some of the flame- and heat-damaged supplies with the toe of his boot. They were completely unsalvageable.

"What now?" wondered Grendel.

Massaging his forehead, Ake looked first at the ground and then at the darkening sky. "Where are you, Ray? Where are you?"

★ ★ ★

"I hears somethin' funny," Mama-san said, stopping, her ears erect and swiveling toward the keening sound.

"Yah, I hears it too," said Beowulf.

"What is it?" Ray asked.

"'Nother force field, I betcha," Beowulf said after a moment's deliberation.

"What did your dog say?" queried First Citizen Ruder.

"There's a force field around here somewhere," Ray told him. "The dogs have fantastic hearing, much better than humans'."

"Yah," Gawain told the Hollenwelt leader. "We can hear high-bitched sounds read good."

"Um . . ." began Ruder.

Freeman-Mawalzi smiled at him. "Don't worry, you'll soon find yourself not thinking twice about the dogs' manner of speaking."

Ignoring this, Ray asked Beowulf where the sound was coming from. "Straight ahead," Beowulf replied.

"Hey!" barked Robin, back from his place on the point, "there's somethin' hummin' up ahead."

"Yah, a force field," Gawain and Mama-san said in unison.

"Sheesh," complained Robin. "News sure travels fast 'round here!"

Since they were the walking wounded, especially the newest additions to the group, it took them ten minutes to reach the force field.

"Here it is," said Robin.

"Mama-san, please go back and cover our rear," Beowulf said.

"Okay."

Ray put out his hand and felt the strange, charged air. A shimmering translucent curtain, the force field made skin tingle and the hair on the back of the hands stand up.

"Why is there a force field here, in the middle of nowhere?" wondered Jorgen Meitz, wiping the sweat from his brow with his sleeve. The rust-colored stain on the front of his shirt had, for the moment, at least, ceased expanding. Meitz's face was too white to be reassuring, however.

"Why is there a force field anywhere?" said Freeman-Mawalzi. "To keep something in or to keep something out—or both," he added, answering his own question.

"I think it's to keep unwanted visitors out," Ray said, shielding his eyes against the glare of the morning sun. He was staring at something one hundred to one hundred and fifty meters beyond the force field.

Ruder and Freeman-Mawalzi followed his gaze. "What is that?" wondered Ruder. He rubbed his eyes and looked again. "Is it . . . ? It looks like a bridge."

"A bridge?" said Franz Obuerst. "A bridge in the middle of Dinoland? A bridge is not natural; it does not belong here."

"A freakin' force field ain't exactly natural, either," Ray snorted. He rubbed his chin. "The force field must be here to protect the bridge."

"A bridge . . ." said Freeman-Mawalzi. "If we can reach it, perhaps we can . . ." He faltered, then recovered. "Perhaps we can get out of this damned place."

Ray was about to say something about Ake, but decided not to. Counting himself, there were six human lives and four canine lives at stake here. Without some sign that Ake was still alive, he had to do what he could to save those who were undeniably still living.

Ruder put out a hand and felt the strange, ticklish feeling that came with contact with the force field. "How do we get from this side to the other? Can we turn it off somehow?"

Mama-san came bounding back to the group. "They's some o' them Day-nose headin' this way!"

"Shit!" said one of the Hollenwelters.

"I think we're about to learn the true meaning of the phrase 'between a rock and a hard place,'" Ray said, hefting his energy rifle.

III

"Hey, you can't—"

Kate burned a pencil-thin bolt of energy through the guard's head. "Wrong," she said. Then she went white, doubled over, and got rid of her breakfast.

"You okay?" Frodo asked.

"I think so," Kate said, shivering as if standing in an icy blast of air.

"Havin' ta kill folks gets easier," Frodo told her. "Not a lot, but it does get easier."

Kate nodded gratefully. "Where is we?" asked Frodo, looking around.

"I'm not sure."

"Where we goin'?"

"I'm not sure of that, either."

"What *is* ya sure of?"

"That we're getting out of here in one piece or taking the place down with us," Kate said grimly.

"Ya!" enthused Frodo. "Now ya is talkin' like a scout dog leader!" That comment didn't register with Kate, at least not consciously.

They found a series of lift/drop tubes being used by nondescript maintenance 'bots. Kate looked around and, seeing no humans, assumed that the tubes were for the robots' use only.

"C'mon," she said to Frodo. "One of these might take us to the second level. From there we can find a way to the surface."

"No," said Frodo, his tail between his legs.

"That's what you think, buster!"

Kate slung the energy rifle over her shoulder and then made Frodo stand on his hind legs, putting his front paws on her shoulders. "Now walk with me, dog boy," Kate said, taking a first tentative step toward the lift tube.

"What's goin' on?" demanded Frodo, walking backwards on his rear legs.

"Nothing—as long as you keep your eyes closed."

She maneuvered the big black-and-white dog into the lift tube. For just a moment there was that vertiginous weightless feeling; then they were whisked up the tube like a bank deposit cylinder inside pneumatic piping.

"Gee-e-e-zzz," moaned Frodo.

"Oh, don't be a baby," Kate admonished him.

They stopped and hung motionless in the air when they reached level two. Kate stepped backwards, her foot finding a hard surface, and she pulled Frodo with her. "There, that wasn't so bad, was it?"

"Can we do it again?" asked Frodo eagerly.

Kate was about to explode when she saw the twinkle in his eye. "You almost got me with that one."

Frodo nodded. "I know." Then he pawed the floor once, looked Kate in the eye, and said, "Thanks, Kate."

"That's one you owe me."

"Hey!" shouted several voices all at once, allowing Frodo to repay his debt to Kate almost immediately. Telling Kate to "Duck!" he leapt over her and sent the three Soldiers of God sprawling. He settled the accounts of one and Kate was able to whirl and see that the other two got a first-class ticket to Heaven.

"You're right, it does," Kate said, staring at the bodies and then at her rifle as if dubious that there could be any connection between the two.

"It does what?"

"Get easier."

★ ★ ★

"Hey," said Sinbad. "Lookit these footprints!"

"Wow!" chimed in Tajil. "Looks like Ray and some other beoples went this way."

"Yah," agreed Grendel, sniffing the ground. "The rest o' the team, too."

"My turn," said Ozma. "Looks like *everyone* went this way—including some o' them day-nose," she said, indicating the small three-toed tracks paralleling the other footprints.

"Can I have a look?" said Ake, squeezing in between Tajil and Ozma to stare at the marks in the yielding soil that had caught and held everyone's attention. "I think Ozma's right. It looks like a menagerie passed by."

"Wonder where they're goin'?" said Grendel, staring into the rain forest's lush canopy.

"The same way we're going," said Ake, straightening up. He pointed in the direction the tracks headed. "Thataway."

22

"What the hell are you doing, Larkin?" asked an exasperated Ruder as he watched Ray put out his hands and slowly press against the force field.

"Hey, lookit that!" marveled Robin as Ray's hands slowly sank into the nearly invisible force field.

"It's . . . ha, ha . . . it's what I thought," Ray said, slowly withdrawing his tingling hands. "It's a tortoise field."

Freeman-Mawalzi, Beowulf, and Obuerst all shot Ray looks of exaggerated disbelief.

"Honest," Ray insisted.

"What the hell's a 'tortoise field'?" demanded Ruder.

Ray didn't like the tone of the Hollenwelt leader's voice but ignored it. Patiently, he explained, "A tortoise field allows living and nonliving materials to pass through its barrier. But—and it's a big but, like Gawain's—"

"Hey!" said Gawain.

"But it does so only very deliberately, very slowly. I've heard it called a slow-motion force field."

"Is it dangerous?" asked Freeman-Mawalzi.

"Not usually. And not if you do it correctly—moving like molasses in January."

"They's comin'," said Mama-san urgently.

"Follow me," said Ray, stepping up to the force field and slowly moving forward. Immediately, the whole front of his body tingled and tickled, from his face to his shins. At the same time, Ray felt like he was forcing himself into a wall of rubber cement.

"Well-l-l?" Ray asked of the others as he waded deeper into the force field, his voice slightly muffled.

"Can you breathe?" asked Obuerst.

"Yes-s-s," Ray confirmed. "But only very slowly and deliberately. It's like wearing a Cousteauean oxygen exchanger underwater—that first breath is hard to take voluntarily, but once you do it you're okay."

"If this offers a chance to escape from those little dinosaurs, then I suppose we should accept it gratefully," said Freeman-Mawalzi, pressing himself against the force field's fluctuating surface.

The tickling sensation that Ray felt was absent in Freeman-Mawalzi's encounter with the force field. It felt more smothering than anything else; he could only compare the feeling to being shoved face first into partially solidified gelatin. At first, he held his breath; when that was no longer possible, he reluctantly breathed in. He was surprised to find that it was not an unpleasant experience.

The dogs and the Hollenwelters followed the Uhuran president and Ray's lead and took the plunge. No sooner had the last of them been enveloped by the suffocating tortoise field than the ravenous Deinos arrived on the scene.

Although the little dinosaurs raged and shrieked in frustration, it was to no avail. They were too late.

With an effort that caused his neck muscles to ache, Ray slowly twisted his head to look back. A broad smile spread across his face as he saw the Deinos hurling themselves at the force field, only to be rebuffed each time because of their rapid movement.

The force field proved to be three meters deep, and it took a good ten to twelve minutes to pass through. Ray's face was the first part of him to pop out into the clean, fresh air. Seconds later, as Ray was withdrawing his left leg from the morass like a person pulling his foot out of a bucket of wet cement, Freeman-Mawalzi followed him out.

"Hee, hee," Freeman-Mawalzi laughed. "That was the strangest, most disconcerting experience of my life." Released from the clinging, cloying power of the force field, he felt buoyant, almost weightless by comparison.

"Boy, that was fun," said Beowulf, straining to slowly pull his hindquarters from the grasp of the force field.

"Yah," agreed a similarly exiting Gawain.

Ray saw that they were all safely through except for one of the Hollenwelters. "What's wrong with Obuerst?" he asked Ruder.

"Huh?" Ruder turned and saw Obuerst standing with one leg out in front of him, in a sort of suspended animation. "Franz!" Ruder shouted at his friend, cupping his hands around his mouth to amplify his voice. "Franz! What is the matter?"

"He is not moving," said Meitz.

"Yes, he is," said Ray grimly.

It was true: Obuerst was slowly, almost imperceptibly, sliding toward the ground, his eyes open but unseeing.

"He . . . he appears to be dead," declared Ehrenreich.

"But what? How?"

"Perhaps his heart or . . ." Freeman-Mawalzi's voice trailed away as he saw the looks of anguish on the Hollenwelters' faces.

"I shall get him," said Ruder, stepping toward the force field.

"You can do nothing for him, Marius," Meitz said as Obuerst continued his slow-motion collapse.

"I can retrieve his body so we might cover it with stones," replied Ruder.

"*Ja*, there is that," agreed Meitz. "I should like you to do that for me." He grimaced. "Soon, I think."

"Do it," Ray said to Ruder. "Do it and then let's get out of here."

"Right," said Ruder. Then he reentered the force field.

II

Kate slowly lifted the hatch cover, uncertain what she would find when it was open. What she found was as rewarding as it was surprising.

"Hey!" exclaimed Frodo. "We's outside!"

It was true; the hatch led to the surface. Kate cautiously crawled out and glanced around. She was quickly joined by an exuberant Frodo. Kate grabbed one of the big dog's ears and said in a firm voice, "Act like a scout dog, Frodo! Let's make sure no one's around to write his initials in our hides with a slug thrower or an energy rifle."

Responding to a human voice of authority with years of

training, Frodo immediately became his old, competent self. "I doan see anyone, Kate," he said.

"I think you're right," Kate said, scanning the area. They were about fifty meters from the plascrete paving of the landing field. Kate could see *The Spirit of St. Louis* sitting all alone in its docking area.

Suddenly, Kate had an unshakable feeling that what was required of the two of them was that they reach and liberate the space yacht. There was no point in trying to reach the hotel, she reasoned. Boosra had told her that both Ray and Ake were in Dinoland. She shivered at the thought.

"How far would you say it is to *The Spirit of St. Louis*, Frodo?"

"The *Speer-it*? 'Bout a hunnert meters, I guess."

"Your legs ready for a workout?"

"You betcha!"

"Then let's see how quickly we can cover that hundred meters. Go!"

They leapt up and ran as hard as they could toward the *Spirit*. Frodo quickly outraced Kate and was a blur as he bounded onto and then crossed the plascrete landing field.

Kate was more than halfway there when a little floater, an orange ball with an energy tube sticking out of it, appeared overhead and opened fire at her. The plascrete directly ahead of her was blasted to pieces, and several fragments flew up and struck her in the head and neck.

"Argh!" She fell heavily to the surface and rolled over and over. Frodo turned, shouted "Kate!" and started back toward her.

The little floating gun platform rotated toward this new target of opportunity, and that allowed Kate to raise her energy rifle and without aiming fire a concentrated beam of energy into the ball. It exploded in a blinding flash.

"Kate!" Frodo was barking as he arrived by her side.

Kate's hand came away bloody from her face. She felt around carefully, decided that shards from the plascrete had opened up numerous superficial flesh wounds, and hauled herself to her feet.

"What are you staring at, dogface?" she said with more bravado than she felt. "Let's get to the ship."

When she saw the cables tying down the yacht, she cursed. "What is it?" asked Frodo.

"Those damn restraining cables. We can't fly the ship with them holding her down."

"Can't ya shoot 'em off?"

Kate looked at the energy rifle's charge pack. "Well, I've got about half a charge here." She checked the pistol shoved into the belt of her jump suit. "And three-quarters here, although it's only a pistol."

"That be enuff?"

"I don't know."

★ ★ ★

Halfway across the bridge over the dry, rock-strewn ravine, Ray decided to turn around and train his binoculars on the force field; he wasn't sure where the impulse came from, but the results were not satisfying.

"Shit and shit again!" he said, staring intently at the faintly shimmering tortoise field.

"What is it?" demanded Ruder.

"Here, look," Ray said, handing over the glasses.

"I don't see . . . my God!" Ruder handed the glasses to Freeman-Mawalzi and said, "Those damn little dinosaurs are entering the force field."

"But they are mindless animals," moaned Freeman-Mawalzi, using the glasses to confirm the dinosaurs' actions for himself.

Ray gestured at Beowulf and his team. "These guys are animals and they're pretty damned intelligent. I'd say those Deinos are fast learners; they watched what we did and they figured it out."

"The Prophet's cat! That is all we need."

They were almost at the far end of the bridge when a floater flew over their heads.

"What was that?" wondered Robin.

"It wasn't a sleigh full of toys for good little boys and girls," Ray said, checking his energy rifle's charge.

Watching Ray ready his weapon, Ruder asked, "Who was it, Larkin? You seem to know."

"I can't be sure," Ray began, "but that floater looked like it had the symbol for the Cadre on its side. I guess it's all out in the open now. With the brown stuff hitting the fan, they're not bothering to hide their presence."

"The Cadre?" said Freeman-Mawalzi, seeming to deflate. "We have no chance against the Cadre." He gazed at their bedraggled party. "Even if there is only a handful of them on that floater, they will defeat us easily."

"The President is right," agreed Ruder. "Assuming that we

could somehow keep them at bay, fend them off indefinitely, we now have the small dinosaurs behind us."

"Larkin," said Jorgen Meitz weakly. He gestured at Ray, directing him to join him at a spot several meters removed from the others. Meitz and Ray put their heads together and, speaking in whispers, the two of them had a fast and furious conversation. At first Ray nodded; then he vehemently shook his head no. Meitz pressed his argument more forcefully. Nodding yes, Ray appeared to have been won over.

Returning to the main group, Ray said, "Freeman-Mawalzi and I will go forward to those rocks and open fire on the Cadre soldiers when they approach. That will cause them to scatter and take refuge for a few minutes. Then, when they figure out that we have fled back this way, they will pursue us."

"What then?" asked Ruder.

"Then we will all hide underneath the bridge," Ray said.

"And after that?" demanded Ruder.

"Jorgen will open fire on them from the other side of the bridge, leading them to assume that we have crossed back over. I hope and pray that they will go after what they think is our whole party to finish us off."

"But Jorgen cannot do that—it is a suicide mission!" said Ruder angrily.

"Marius," Meitz said softly. "I am soon to join Franz and your beloved Maria no matter what happens." He took his hand away from his chest and stomach, and they could all see the blood seeping through his shirt. "I want my death to count for something. Please, Marius, let me do this last thing for you . . . and for myself."

A myriad of emotions quickly flitted across Ruder's face; the final one was acceptance. Ruder hugged his friend. "Go, then."

"Thank you, Marius."

"C'mon, Mr. President, we have to do our part if this scheme is to work," Ray said to Freeman-Mawalzi.

III

"That's done it," Kate said as the last cable fell away from *The Spirit of St. Louis*. "What's the entry code again?"

"Nebber mind, I'll say it," said Frodo. "Computer, 'Klaatu barada nikto.'"

"What language is that?" asked Kate as the ship obligingly lowered a ramp for them.

"I reckon that's jes' Ray language," Frodo said with a big grin.

"Jeez, lookit that," marveled Sinbad to Ake and the other dogs as they spotted the last of the Deinos disappearing into the force field.

Ake scratched his head. "A tortoise field . . ." he said, wonderingly.

"I dint know them day-nose could do stuff like that," said Tajil.

"Me either," said Ake.

"I wonder where they's goin'?" said Grendel.

When both Ake and Tajil pointed to the human prints leading toward the force field, Grendel said, "Oh."

★ ★ ★

It was agonizing for Ray and the others to wait patiently beneath the bridge for something to happen. Finally, they heard the explosive retort of Meitz's slug thrower from the far side of the span. Then he launched a few energy bolts in the direction of the pursuing Cadre troops, quickly draining his weapons' energy cells in a valiant attempt to make it appear he was more than one person.

"He musta bin convincin'," whispered Beowulf as the Cadre returned Meitz's fire.

"Yeah, so far, so good," Ray said, returning Beowulf's whisper. They could hear the wheels of the armored car and the boots of the Cadre footsoldiers on the bridge.

"Do you have any sense of how many troops they have?" asked Ruder.

"It's too hard to tell," Ray said, shaking his head. "But that wasn't an especially big floater. They brought along the armored car, so I can't imagine there's more than ten or fifteen of them."

"Ten or fifteen!" groaned Ehrenreich.

"Control yourself, Karl," said Ruder.

"Forgive me, First Citizen," said a chastised Ehrenreich.

"I think they're across," Ray said, putting his hand on one of the bridge's supports. "I can't feel any vibrations."

"Could your *hund* take a look?" asked Ruder, indicating Beowulf.

"I don't see why not," Ray replied. "*Hund*, go stick your head up top and see what you can see."

"Okay, Ray." The big dog emerged from under the bridge and scrambled up the short but steep incline to the roadway. "They's on the other side, Ray," he called back down.

"C'mon," Ray said. "Let's get up there and find some cover. With two of us on each side of the roadway, we can keep them from retreating back across the bridge."

"As long as our energy cells hold out," said Freeman-Mawalzi glumly.

"They only have to last until the Deinos arrive."

"Let's go," said Robin impatiently.

Once up top, Ray and Freeman-Mawalzi found cover behind several good-sized rocks and Ehrenreich and Ruder did the same on the other side of the bridge. Resting their energy rifles on top of the rocks, they heard a final fusillade from the far end of the bridge and beyond. There was a terrible silence punctuated by cheers from the soldiers. "They finally got him," Ray said.

"Our brave new friend is gone," said Freeman-Mawalzi.

"Yeah," agreed Ray, taking out the binoculars. "About now they must be realizing that he was alone and trying to figure out what happened to the rest of us." He peered through the binoculars. "Yep. They're gesturing wildly. At least one of them is. He's a big, dark-haired—" He stopped and looked again to be sure. "Well, hello, Ku'brol!"

"Ku'brol?" said Freeman-Mawalzi. "He is Neverland's head of security, is he not?"

"He certainly is," Ray replied. "I know that I always feel much more secure knowing that he's around."

"I wonder why he *is* here," said Freeman-Mawalzi as Ray watched the small column of troops heading back for the bridge.

"I think he hate us dogs," said Beowulf, who'd been listening to the two humans talk.

"How long can ya fight?" Mama-san asked Ray.

"Ten, maybe fifteen minutes," Ray said. "Then we're out of juice." He looked at his watch. "But right about now . . ."

"Yah, them little day-nose is 'tackin'," said Robin as a sudden flurry of shouting and shooting erupted from the Cadre's end of the bridge. The soldiers beat a hasty retreat, dashing across the narrow bridge.

"Now!" shouted Ray, and the four of them opened up on the troops, trapped in the middle of the bridge. Some of the soldiers went down immediately, torn asunder by the deadly crossfire of coherent energy. The others, including a number of troops protected by moly-weave vests, took refuge behind the armored car. The car, its laser cannon pumping bolt after bolt of white-hot energy their way, was the biggest threat to the ability of Ray's small band to keep the soldiers pinned down.

They had help, however.

"Christ, did you see that!" shouted Ehrenreich as a Deino, its sickle-shaped claws flashing, ran a gauntlet of soldiers to leap on the back of the armored car. It tore and slashed at the trooper manning the cannon in a killing frenzy. Aware that death was in their midst, the other soldiers now concentrated their firepower on the rampaging Deino and blew it to bits.

A voice shouted, "No!" That cry of anguish was quickly followed by the concussive report of a grenade. The explosion hurled two Cadre regulars and a Deino from the bridge, and they landed on the jagged rocks below.

"Jesus!" said Ray. "The Deinos usually work in groups of four. There's still six of them there, so they must have teamed up with another group."

"They're getting so close," said Freeman-Mawalzi, meaning the Cadre troops. Ray saw that the Uhuran president was correct. Aware that staying on the bridge was intolerable, Ku'brol and the others were now following the armored car toward their human tormentors.

"Make 'em count," Ray shouted across to Ruder and Ehrenreich. In response, Ruder blew the head off a man wearing a moly-weave vest, and Ehrenreich followed suit. "Damn good shooting," Ray said.

"Lookit!" said Gawain as the Deinos overwhelmed the armored car just twenty meters from their position. One of the man-sized killers had forced its way inside the cab and savaged the driver, shredding him with powerful swipes of its claws.

"Give 'em everything you've got!" shouted Ray, firing a continuous stream of energy into the maelstrom of Cadre and dinosaur bodies.

One of the Deinos rushed from the bridge and toward Ruder and Ehrenreich's position. Leaping over the rocks shielding them, the Deino came down on the two men like a demon from Hell. Both Hollenwelters were sent sprawling and their rifles skidding away.

"Beowulf, Robin!" shouted Ray.

The two big dogs dashed across the roadway and toward the Deino, which had chosen Ehrenreich as its prey. Hissing and shrieking in a hideous, high-pitched reptilian voice, the Deino swiped at Ehrenreich with its claws, disemboweling him in an instant.

Both dogs struck the Deino at once, and the trio tumbled to the ground. Before the Deino could regain its feet and lash out with the deadly tips of its toes, Beowulf had seized its neck from behind and was biting down as hard as he could. Robin, carefully avoiding the hissing Deino's powerful hind legs, was able to seize one and thus immobilize the creature while Beowulf's powerful jaws slowly closed like a vise with teeth and crushed the life out of it.

"See that, Sinbad?" asked Mama-san. "That's how ya does it."

"Yah," agreed Sinbad. He was ready, willing, and able to put to the test the killing lesson they'd observed.

He quickly got in close as a Deino rushed the two of them at the same time that a grenade landed in front of the rocks shielding Ray and Freeman-Mawalzi, stunning both humans and throwing them to the ground.

While Mama-san drew the Deino's attention, Sinbad leapt up and closed his jaws on the back of its neck in a good approximation of Beowulf's earlier move. The dinosaur thrashed and kicked and Mama-san was careful not to get too close too soon.

Flat on his back, Ray glanced over to see that Freeman-Mawalzi was dazed and disoriented. He didn't exactly feel like a million bucks himself.

"There you are, you little bastard!" screamed Ku'brol, his left arm hanging uselessly, a huge bush knife clutched in his right hand.

"Uh-oh," said Ray.

Ku'brol rushed at Ray, bringing the bush knife down in a vicious arc. Rolling over and away, Ray got out of harm's way and pulled his energy pistol from his belt. "This isn't fair, I suppose," Ray admitted, "but in love and war . . ." When he pressed the firing stud, nothing happened. The pistol's energy cell was depleted.

"I been waiting a long time for this, Larkin!" Ku'brol growled through clenched teeth.

"That makes one of us," said Ray. Even though Ku'brol was reduced to one good arm, Ray knew that the heavy-worlder was probably twice as strong as he was.

Ray's only advantage was that Ku'brol was slow and methodical. That didn't seem like much of an advantage as Ku'brol slowly and methodically forced him back until he was pressing against the grill of the armored car.

Ku'brol's arm came down inexorably and Ray tried to hold him off with his two good arms; it was no contest. Ku'brol forced the knife down and down, until . . .

"Argh!" Ray grunted in pain as Ku'brol drove the knife into his shoulder. It slid in, centimeter by centimeter.

Mesmerized, Ray waited for Ku'brol to initiate the final, fatal downward plunge to the knife's hilt. Ku'brol was savoring the moment too much to be rushed, but finally he said, "This is for the Federation and for the General, you little—"

A tight, hot beam burned a hole the size of a quarter-credit coin through Ku'brol's forehead. His mouth slackly open, Neverland's former security chief toppled over backwards.

"Move away from the armored car, Ray," a familiar, yet mechanical voice ordered him. As if drunk or sleepwalking, still shocked to be alive, Ray stumbled away. Finally, he turned and looked up.

The Spirit of St. Louis was floating motionlessly in the air over the deep ravine, its nose cannon now picking out targets of opportunity.

"Hi, Kate," Ray said, waving weakly.

23

"Boy, a week sure makes a diff'rence," marveled Beowulf, staring at Ake's quickly healing face. The other dogs, lounging about comfortably, nodded their assent.

Gently touching the area of his own still-tender upper chest wound, Ray had to agree. He picked up his gin and tonic and leaned back in his cuddle chair. It wiggled warmly and molded itself even more completely to his body.

"Now this is a vacation," he said appreciatively.

"For you, maybe," noted Freeman-Mawalzi, unsuccessfully resisting the blandishments of his own cuddle chair. "For some of us, the real work is just beginning."

"The Conference is still going to continue?" Kate inquired.

Ake glanced at her, surprised that she had to ask such a question. Then he remembered that she and the dogs had been spending a lot of time together, sweeping the surface of Midway Island for anything or anyone who might have escaped the efficiently tight sweeps by the Galactic Militia, called in by the pro tem Galactic Council.

"Yes," replied Freeman-Mawalzi. "It is more urgent than ever that we begin the building of an Alliance which will bind together the free planets of the galaxy and restore the 'Pax Federation.'"

"Without the 'Tyranny Federation,'" Ray offered.

"Yes, of course," the Uhuran president replied. Then he turned to Ray and Ake. "What about you, my friends?"

Ake glanced at Ray and vice versa. It was Ake who responded. "We still have to finish consolidating our possession and control of dear, sweet Neverland. There are a lot of Cromwellian-altered battle androids wandering around yet, using all the power in their illegal P-Q-G brains to resist capture or destruction; the parks must be cleaned up, repaired, and searched for booby traps; and Svoboda's work has to be evaluated and categorized."

Ray shook his head. "Svoboda! When Kate and Frodo told me about him, I just about popped my cork. Imagine hearing that someone you saw die a horrible, though deserved, death is alive."

"Well, not really," Kate said.

"Yeah, yeah," Ray said, waving a hand. "I know it's not the same Svoboda, not exactly. It's still a pisser."

"They find him yet?" queried Beowulf.

Ray shook his head. "That's an even bigger pisser: Both he and that Boosra broad seemed to have slipped through our fingers somehow."

When Kate saw Ake and Beowulf sneaking a peek at her, she made a face. "I guess everyone's heard about my threat to rip off Boosra's head and stuff it up her . . . well, to kill her with my bare hands, eh?"

"Frodo never could keep a see-kret," Beowulf said with a canine grin. "But doan worry, Kate—you find her some day."

Kate waved a hand. "I said that in the heat of the moment. I don't want revenge. I'm not going to spend the rest of my life tracking her down just to keep my word."

"But if you *had* found her, at the time you made the threat," persisted Ake, "would you really have . . . you know?"

Kate smiled enigmatically. "Little me—the vegetarian?"

"Heh-heh-heh," rumbled Beowulf.

Changing the subject, Freeman-Mawalzi said, "It sounds as if you all have much work ahead of you. But it will not last forever—what then?"

This time it was Ray's turn to respond to the Uhuran president. A huge grin spreading across his face, he said slyly, "Well, I always did want to see Uhura some day. Know anyone there who could put up a a scout dog team for a couple of weeks?"

Freeman-Mawalzi's grin matched Ray's. "I think someone could be found to take in even as motley a crew as yourselves."

"And after that," Ray continued, "who knows?" He glanced

across at Kate, marveling at how much her complexion had improved these last few weeks. "What about you, Kate? You say you're not concerned about Boosra. Just what *are* your plans?"

"I . . . I don't know," she said haltingly. "I'm not sure I want to continue as a 'scraper any longer, but I have no idea what else I might be qualified to do."

"You is a damn good dog person," Beowulf said, jumping into the conversation with all four feet.

"There's an idea," Ray said. "Why don't you return to Anson with us? We can introduce you to Johnny Skerchock and the trainers and other good folks there."

"You mean become a scout dog leader?" Kate asked, clearly intrigued.

"Maybe, maybe not," said Ake. "I think Ray's idea is a good one. You might find, with your psychic talents, that you are suited for working with dogs in their formative stages. You might be a teacher, a trainer. Or, as Ray has suggested, you might even consider having your own team. It's rare for a woman to lead a dog team instead of a cat team, but it's been known to happen."

"Could I really do it?" asked Kate.

"'Course ya could, Kate!" said Ozma, speaking up for the first time. "You is a great leader. You kin see things the mens can't."

"Yah!" said Frodo enthusiastically. Then his ears and tail drooped a bit and he added, "Ya could always stay with us for awhile, too, ya know."

Ray nodded. "Frodo's right. We could save a lot of money if we had our own 'scraper on board." Kate caught him flush in the face with an expertly hurled pillow.

"So whadda ya think, Kate?" asked Beowulf.

"I think I have a lot of time to decide," she replied. "Cleaning up Neverland isn't going to be a one month deal."

"No, it isn't," agreed Ake.

After making certain that their stuffy 'bot Hastings had refreshed everyone's drink, Ray suggested a toast. Once they were all ready, he raised his glass and said, "To the Alliance."

"To the Alliance," the humans responded, while the dogs raised a howl in agreement.